DATE			
SEP 2 3 1986			

PROSE WRITINGS OF N. P. WILLIS.

PROSE WRITINGS

OF

NATHANIEL PARKER WILLIS

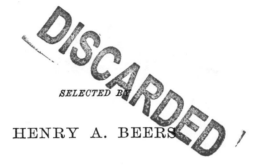

SELECTED BY

HENRY A. BEERS

AMS PRESS
NEW YORK

Reprinted from the edition of 1885, New York
First AMS EDITION published 1970
Manufactured in the United States of America

International Standard Book Number:0-404-06990-8

Library of Congress Card Catalog Number: 70-128984

AMS PRESS, INC.
NEW YORK. N.Y. 10003

CONTENTS.

INTRODUCTION.

A S long ago as 1854 Horace Greeley, in a letter to Willis, urged him to publish a selection from the best of his prose writings. "I have your big volume somewhere," he wrote, — alluding to the "Complete Works," published by Redfield in 1846, — but some venture less heavily freighted, he thought, would have a better chance of floating down to posterity. A generation has passed since then, and Willis himself has been dead nearly twenty years, yet the suggestion has never been acted upon. The swift oblivion that seems to have overtaken him may well appear unaccountable to those who remember with what·eagerness his letters from abroad were read when they first came out in the old "New-York Mirror;" or how his sparkling sketches of life and adventure, reprinted from Colburn's "New Monthly," or issued in the fresh numbers of "Graham's" and "Godey's," made him, for a time, the favorite magazinist of America. Whether he wrote any thing really lasting, whether he is to enjoy a fee-simple in fame, is still in doubt; but many will say without hesitation that his lease deserves renewing for some years to come, and in this faith the present volume is offered to the public.

Of late, while preparing a biography of Willis for the "American Men of Letters" series, I took occasion to make some inquiries among readers of my own age, and younger, and was surprised to find how completely his prose, so far as the result of these inquiries showed, had gone out of date. Most of those who had read him at all had read nothing beyond a few of his scriptural pieces. His poems, indeed, are still in circulation; but these, though smoothly written and often natural and tender in feeling, by no means exhibit his most characteristic traits, — the wit, high spirits, and knowledge of the world, the easy narrative and vivid descriptive power, which made his early sketches and stories so engaging.

Willis, in fact, outlived his own reputation. During the last ten or fifteen years of his life, contemporary readers thought of him only as the editor of the "Home Journal" and the writer of mildly interesting letters of a domestic and invalid cast from "Idlewild" or elsewhere. But his youth and early manhood had given brilliant promise. Born at Portland, Me., in 1806, and educated at Andover and Yale, he had published, on leaving college, a volume of poems, mainly on scriptural subjects, which enrolled him at once in the little band of what was then called "Columbia's bards." Then after a few years' apprenticeship to journalism and literature in Boston, where he conducted, among other things, the "American Monthly Magazine," he went to Europe in 1831 as foreign editor and correspondent of the "New-York Mirror." His "Pencillings by the Way," which he sent home to that paper during his four-years' stay abroad, were immensely popular, and were his first real hit in a wider field than that which he had occupied in his youthful verses. In England, where he spent two years, and made a decided social and literary success, he followed up the "Pencillings" with his very clever "Slingsby Papers," which were cheerful though highly improbable stories of American life and of travel in Italy and the East, — "Inklings of Adventure," in fact, as he afterwards entitled them. In the same way in which he had entertained the English public with somewhat florid representations of climes and societies foreign to it ; so, on reaching home, did he proceed to draw for the American public, pictures of high life in England, against the truth of which the critics vigorously protested, but which proved no less interesting in spite of that, and especially to the lady reader, to whose approval Willis always had an eye.

Not long after his return to America, Willis, who had brought back with him an English wife, purchased a little estate, which he named "Glenmary," on Owego Creek just above its junction with the Susquehanna. Here he lived, off and on, from 1837 to 1842 ; and hence he wrote his "Letters from Under a Bridge," charming transcripts of rural life in a wild country, where the farmer was still something of the settler, and the axe and plough were both implements of husbandry. This was the last of his books which lays any real claim to remembrance. From 1842, when he removed to New York, till his death in 1867, his life was that of a metropolitan journalist. With Gen. G. P. Morris, his old friend and associate, he edited in succession the "New Mirror," the "Evening Mirror" (a daily paper), and the

"Home Journal." During all these years his pen was never idle, and he put forth volume after volume made up from his articles and correspondence in the columns of these periodicals. A second and a third trip to Europe, visits to the South and West, to Washington, Cape Cod, Sharon Springs, and elsewhere, letters from "Idlewild," his country-seat on the Hudson, studies of city-life, and miscellaneous papers of all kinds, furnished the contents of these books. They were good enough reading at the time, but altogether ephemeral, except now and then a poem or a short sketch which showed something of original inspiration, and rose above the general mediocrity of hack-work. More than half of the titles in this volume, and a great deal more than half of the amount of matter, have been taken from his three early books, — "Pencillings by the Way," "Inklings of Adventure," and "Letters from Under a Bridge."

Bryant, Emerson, and Hawthorne were born before Willis, Longfellow and Poe only a little after him; yet the continuance of their literary influence down to the present time makes them seem really of a later generation. As compared with them, Willis belongs to a bygone period of American literature. We think of him as a contemporary of Irving and Cooper. And though himself of New-England birth and breeding, he belongs, like Irving and Cooper, by his writings to the State of New York and to the Knickerbocker group. Like theirs, his name is associated with the scenery of the Empire State, with the Hudson River, — though less profoundly so than Irving's or even Drake's, — with Trenton Falls, Niagara, the Susquehanna, and above all with Saratoga. The gay life of the Springs and the eternal movement of Broadway were his congenial element; and of both of these he has left his deeper impression in his story "The Ghost Ball at Congress Hall," and his poem "Unseen Spirits." I incline to think his title to be remembered, as one of the shaping influences of that early period in American letters, is quite as well made out as that of Irving and Cooper, though it covers, of course, a much narrower acreage. His special gift to our literature was in his instinct for *style*. Cooper had no style: his effects were produced by sheer force of invention. Irving's diction was indeed much better than Willis's, more chastened and mellowed, never running into frippery and bad taste as Willis's constantly was: yet, after all, was it as original, as American? Irving's gentle elaboration was, in fact, the last expression of the Addisonian tradition. The grace and ease, the nice artistic sense, of which Willis, at his best, was master, was a purely home product; and at a time when almost all the lighter literature of America was both feeble and dull, the bright, thin jet of his writing, interjected into the muddy stream that flows interminably through the magazines and annuals of the thirties and forties, must certainly have seemed a fountain of refreshment. It was formerly the habit to find an English analogue for every new literary genius who sprung up in this country. Cooper was the American Scott, Emerson a cis-Atlantic Carlyle, Mrs. Sigourney the Hemans of America. Willis's poetry was often compared with Barry Cornwall's, of whom he was indeed an undisguised admirer; but, taking him all in all, he certainly bore a striking resemblance to

Leigh Hunt in the cast of his mind and the tone of his writings. They were alike in their sunny philosophy, in their carelessness about money matters, and in their attention to those minor refinements and elegances which persons of sterner mould condemn as trifles. Hunt's little plea for " A Flower for Your Window," for example, might easily have been written by Willis; and the cheerful way in which he set himself to decorate the walls of his prison chamber was something quite in Willis's taste. As writers, they had the same light, airy touch and daintiness of perception. The Englishman's work is more full-flavored, and finer in grain, but lacks a certain dash which one finds in the American.

Personally, Willis was the kind of man who is described by friends as a gentleman, and by enemies as a fop. He was fastidious in his tastes and in his choice of companions. He dressed fashionably, went much into society, and could make himself very agreeable to people that he liked. His manner is variously described, as cordial and demonstrative; as marked by an aristocratic *hauteur* and reserve; as distinguished by self-complacency and affectation, — according to the standpoint of the observer. Doubtless it differed toward different persons, as that of most people does. But without question, he possessed, especially when he was young and handsome, a quite decided personal charm. He was unfixed in character; his temperament restless, sanguine, buoyant. He had the traditional impatience of a poet for business details and practical responsibilities. He was affectionate, generous, hospitable, fond of children and animals; and it is agreed by all his contemporaries, that he was entirely free from literary jealousy, and was always the first to extend a welcome, and, if need were, substantial aid, to rising talent. The last years of his life were imbittered by a lingering disease, which impaired his mind and his temper, but brought out in him a remarkable power of persistence in work. He kept his desk until a few weeks before his death.

In making my selections, it has been my aim, while choosing the best, to display also, as far as possible, the range and variety of Willis's talent. The personal element entered strongly into all his most characteristic work. He did not often project himself successfully into scenes and incidents foreign to his own experience. With the exception of " Pasquali " and " The Inlet of Peach Blossoms," all the selections in the book have this peculiarity of drawing upon their author's stock of reminiscences. His method in composing a story, as illustrated, for instance, in " Lady Ravelgold," in " The Gypsy of Sardis," and in " Edith Linsey," was not to invent, objectively, a definite situation and a number of characters dramatically conceived ; but rather to let his fancy work upon slight hints of possible adventures, latent in persons or things that he had met in his travels, and to carry out these suggestions into actual romances. The nucleus of his fictions is generally not a plot, but a recollection ; and the narrative seems to exist not so much for its own sake as for the sake of the descriptive digressions, impressions of scenery and life, outlines of character, and records of feeling, which it holds together. These stories are, in short, rather of the nature of sketches than of tales. "Edith Linsey," in particular, is so loosely constructed and overladen with episodes that I have given only passages from it, and these less as specimens of Willis's story-telling than as illustrations of the reflective and moralizing side of his mind. Indeed, in such early pieces as his three papers on "Unwritten Music," "Unwritten Poetry," and "Unwritten Philosophy," as well as in this of "Minute Philosophies," he seemed at one time to be entering upon the path of the formal essayist, as distinguished from that of the paragrapher and periodical correspondent, into which circumstances finally led him.

HENRY A. BEERS.

PROSE WRITINGS OF N. P. WILLIS.

THE LUNATIC'S SKATE.

I HAVE only, in my life, known one *lunatic*—properly so called. In the days when I carried a satchel on the banks of the Shawsheen (a river whose half-lovely, half-wild scenery is tied like a silver thread about my heart), Larry Wynn and myself were the farthest boarders from school, in a solitary farmhouse on the edge of a lake of some miles square, called by the undignified title of Pomp's Pond. An old negro, who was believed by the boys to have come over with Christopher Columbus, was the only other human being within any thing like a neighborhood of the lake (it took its name from him) ; and the only approaches to its waters, girded in as it was by an almost impenetrable forest, were the path through old Pomp's clearing, and that by our own door. Out of school, Larry and I were inseparable. He was a pale, sad-faced boy ; and in the first days of our intimacy, he had confided a secret to me which, from its uncommon nature, and the excessive caution with which he kept it from every one else, bound me to him with more than the common ties of schoolfellow attachment. We built wigwams together in the woods, had our tomahawks made of the same fashion, united our property in fox-traps, and played Indians with perfect contentment in each other's approbation.

⁎ *From " Scenes of Fear."*

1

I had found out, soon after my arrival at school, that Larry never slept on a moonlight night. With the first slender horn that dropped its silver and graceful shape behind the hills, his uneasiness commenced ; and by the time its full and perfect orb poured a flood of radiance over vale and mountain, he was like one haunted by a pursuing demon. At early twilight he closed the shutters, stuffing every crevice that could admit a ray ; and then, lighting as many candles as he could beg or steal from our thrifty landlord, he sat down with his book in moody silence, or paced the room with an uneven step, and a solemn melancholy in his fine countenance, of which, with all my familiarity with him, I was almost afraid. Violent exercise seemed the only relief ; and when the candles burnt low after midnight, and the stillness around the lone farmhouse became too absolute to endure, he would throw up the window, and, leaping desperately out into the moonlight, rush up the hill into the depths of the wild forest, and walk on with supernatural excitement till the day dawned. Faint and pale he would then creep into his bed, and, begging me to make his very common and always credited excuse of illness, sleep soundly till I returned from school. I soon became used to his way ; ceased to follow him, as I had once or twice endeavored to do, into the forest ; and never attempted to break in on the fixed and rapt silence which seemed to transform his lips to marble. And for all this Larry loved me.

Our preparatory studies were completed ; and, to our mutual despair, we were destined to different universities. Larry's father was a disciple of the great Channing, and mine a Trinitarian of uncommon zeal ; and the two institutions of Yale and Harvard were in the hands of most eminent men of either persuasion, and few are the minds that could resist a four years' ordeal in either. A student was as certain to come forth a Unitarian from one as a Calvinist

from the other; and in the New-England States these two
sects are bitterly hostile. So, to the glittering atmosphere
of Channing and Everett went poor Larry, lonely and dispirited; and I was committed to the sincere zealots of Con-
necticut, some two hundred miles off, to learn Latin and
Greek if it pleased Heaven, but the mysteries of "election
and free grace" whether or no.

Time crept, ambled, and galloped, by turns, as we were
in love or *out*, moping in term-time or revelling in vacation;
and gradually, I know not why, our correspondence had
dropped, and the four years had come to their successive
deaths, and we had never met. I grieved over it; for in
those days I believed with a schoolboy's fatuity,

"That two, or one, are almost what they seem;"

and I loved Larry Wynn, as I hope I may never love man
or woman again, — with a pain at my heart. I wrote one or
two reproachful letters in my senior year, but his answers
were overstrained, and too full of protestations by half; and,
seeing that absence had done its usual work on him, I gave
it up, and wrote an epitaph on a departed friendship. I do
not know, by the way, why I am detaining you with all this,
for it has nothing to do with my story; but let it pass as
an evidence that it is a true one. The climax of things in
real life has not the regular procession of incidents in a
tragedy.

Some two or three years after we had taken "the irrev-
ocable yoke" of life upon us (not matrimony, but money-
making), a winter occurred of uncommonly fine sleighing —
sledging, you call it in England. At such times the American
world is all abroad, either for business or pleasure. The
roads are passable at any rate of velocity of which a horse is
capable; smooth as *montagnes russes*, and hard as is good
for hoofs; and a hundred miles is diminished to ten in

facility of locomotion. The hunter brings down his venison
to the cities, the Western trader takes his family a hundred
leagues to buy calicoes and tracts, and parties of all kinds
scour the country, drinking mulled wine and "flip," and
shaking the very nests out of the fir-trees with the ringing of
their horses' bells. You would think death and sorrow were
buried in the snow with the leaves of the last autumn.

I do not know why I undertook, at this time, a journey to
the West; certainly not for scenery, for it was a world of
waste, desolate, and dazzling whiteness, for a thousand unbroken miles. The trees were weighed down with snow,
and the houses were thatched and half-buried in it, and the
mountains and valleys were like the vast waves of an illimitable sea, congealed with its yeasty foam in the wildest hour
of a tempest. The eye lost its powers in gazing on it.
The "spirit-bird" that spread his refreshing green wings
before the pained eyes of Thalaba would have been an
inestimable fellow-traveller. The worth of the eyesight lay
in the purchase of a pair of green goggles.

In the course of a week or two, after skimming over the
buried scenery of half a dozen States, each as large as Great
Britain (more or less), I found myself in a small town on
the border of one of our Western lakes. It was some twenty
years since the bears had found it thinly settled enough for
their purposes, and now it contained perhaps twenty thousand souls. The oldest inhabitant, born in the town, was a
youth in his minority. With the usual precocity of new
settlements, it had already most of the peculiarities of an old
metropolis. The burnt stumps still stood about among the
houses; but there was a fashionable circle, at the head of
which were the lawyer's wife and the member of Congress's
daughter; and people ate their peas with silver forks, and
drank their tea with scandal, and forgave men's *many* sins,
and refused to forgive woman's *one*, very much as in towns

whose history is written in black letter. I dare say there were not more than one or two offences against the moral and Levitical law, fashionable on this side the water, which had not been committed, with the authentic aggravations, in the town of —— : I would mention the name if this were not a true story.

Larry Wynn (now Lawrence Wynn, Esq.) lived here. He had, as they say in the United States, "hung out a shingle" (*Londonicé*, put up a sign) as attorney-at-law; and to all the twenty thousand innocent inhabitants of the place, he was the oracle and the squire. He was, besides, colonel of militia, church-warden, and canal commissioner; appointments which speak volumes for the prospects of "rising young men" in our flourishing Republic.

Larry was glad to see me — very. I was more glad to see *him*. I have a soft heart, and forgive a wrong generally, if it touches neither my vanity nor my purse. I forgot his neglect, and called him "Larry." By the same token, he did *not* call me "Phil." (There are very few that love me, patient reader; but those who do, thus abbreviate my pleasant name of Philip. I was called after the Indian sachem of that name, whose blood runs in this tawny hand.) Larry looked upon me as a *man*. I looked on him, with all his dignities and changes, through the sweet vista of memory, as a *boy*. His mouth had acquired the pinched corners of caution and mistrust common to those who know their fellow-men; but I never saw it unless when speculating as I am now. He was to me the pale-faced and melancholy friend of my boyhood; and I could have slept, as I used to do, with my arm around his neck, and feared to stir lest I should wake him. Had my last earthly hope lain in the palm of my hand, I could have given it to him, had he needed it, but to make him sleep; and yet he thought of me but as a stranger under his roof, and added, in his warmest moments, a "Mr."

to my name! There is but one circumstance in my life that
has wounded me more. Memory avaunt!

Why should there be no unchangeableness in the world?
why no friendship? or why am I, and you, gentle reader (for,
by your continuing to pore over these idle musings, you have
a heart too), gifted with this useless and restless organ beating in our bosoms, if its thirst for love is never to be slaked,
and its aching self-fulness never to find flow or utterance?
I would positively sell my whole stock of affections for three
farthings. Will you say "*two*"?

"You are come in good time," said Larry one morning,
with a half-smile, "and shall be groomsman to me. I am
going to be married."

"Married?"

"Married."

I repeated the word after him, for I was surprised. He
had never opened his lips about his unhappy lunacy since my
arrival; and I had felt hurt at this apparent unwillingness to
renew our ancient confidence, but had felt a repugnance to
any forcing of the topic upon him, and could only hope that
he had outgrown or overcome it. I argued, immediately on
this information of his intended marriage, that it must be so.
No man in his senses, I thought, would link an impending
madness to the fate of a confiding and lovely woman.

He took me into his sleigh, and we drove to her father's
house. She was a flower in the wilderness. Of a delicate
form, as all my countrywomen are, and lovely, as *quite* all
certainly are not, large-eyed, soft in her manners, and yet
less timid than confiding and sister-like, with a shade of melancholy in her smile, caught, perhaps, with the "trick of
sadness" from himself, and a patrician slightness of reserve,
or pride, which Nature sometimes, in very mockery of high
birth, teach s her most secluded child, — the bride elect was,
as I said before, a flower in the wilderness. She was one of

those women we sigh to look upon as they pass by, as if there went a fragment of the wreck of some blessed dream.

The day arrived for the wedding, and the sleigh-bells jingled merrily into the village. The morning was as soft and genial as June, and the light snow on the surface of the lake melted, and lay on the breast of the solid ice beneath, giving it the effect of one white silver mirror stretching to the edge of the horizon. It was exquisitely beautiful; and I was standing at the window in the afternoon, looking off upon the shining expanse, when Larry approached, and laid his hand familiarly on my shoulder.

"What glorious skating we shall have," said I, "if this smooth water freezes to-night!"

I turned the next moment to look at him; for we had not skated together since I went out, at his earnest entreaty, at midnight, to skim the little lake where we had passed our boyhood, and drive away the fever from his brain, under the light of a full moon.

He remembered it, and so did I; and I put my arm behind him, for the color fled from his face, and I thought he would have sunk to the floor.

"The moon is full to-night," said he, recovering instantly to a cold self-possession.

I took hold of his hand firmly, and, in as kind a tone as I could summon, spoke of our early friendship, and, apologizing thus for the freedom, asked if he had quite overcome his melancholy disease. His face worked with emotion, and he tried to withdraw his hand from my clasp, and evidently wished to avoid an answer.

"Tell me, dear Larry," said I.

"O God! *No!*" said he, breaking violently from me, and throwing himself with his face downward upon the sofa. The tears streamed through his fingers upon the silken cushion.

" Not cured? And does *she* know it? "

" No, no, thank God! not yet."

I remained silent a few minutes, listening to his suppressed moans (for he seemed heart-broken with the confession), and pitying while I inwardly condemned him. And then the picture of that lovely and fond woman rose up before me, and the impossibility of concealing his fearful malady from his wife, and the fixed insanity in which it must end, and the whole wreck of her hopes and his own prospects and happiness ; and my heart grew sick.

I sat down by him ; and, as it was too late to remonstrate on the injustice he was committing toward her, I asked how he came to appoint the night of a full moon for his wedding. He gave up his reserve, calmed himself, and talked of it at last as if he were relieved by the communication. Never shall I forget the doomed pallor, the straining eye, and feverish hand, of my poor friend during that half-hour.

Since he had left college, he had striven with the whole energy of his soul against it. He had plunged into business ; he had kept his bed resolutely, night after night, till his brain seemed on the verge of frenzy with the effort; he had taken opium to secure to himself an artificial sleep : but he had never dared to confide it to any one, and he had no friend to sustain him in his fearful and lonely hours ; and it grew upon him rather than diminished. He described to me with the most touching pathos how he had concealed it for years ; how he had stolen out like a thief to give vent to his insane restlessness in the silent streets of the city at midnight, and in the more silent solitudes of the forest; how he had prayed, and wrestled, and wept over it; and, finally, how he had come to believe that there was no hope for him except in the assistance and constant presence of some one who would devote life to him in love and pity. Poor Larry!

I put up a silent prayer in my heart that the desperate experiment might not end in agony and death.

The sun set, and, according to my prediction, the wind changed suddenly to the north ; and the whole surface of the lake, in a couple of hours, became of the lustre of polished steel. It was intensely cold.

The fires blazed in every room of the bride's paternal mansion, and I was there early to fulfil my office of master of ceremonies at the bridal. My heart was weighed down with a sad boding ; but I shook off at least the appearance of it, and superintended the concoction of a huge bowl of punch with a merriment which communicated itself in the shape of most joyous hilarity to a troop of juvenile relations. The house resounded with their shouts of laughter.

In the midst of our noise, in the small inner room, entered Larry. I started back, for he looked more like a demon possessed than a Christian man. He had walked to the house alone in the moonlight, not daring to trust himself in company. I turned out the turbulent troop about me, and tried to dispel his gloom ; for a face like his at that moment would have put to flight the rudest bridal party ever assembled on holy ground. He seized on the bowl of strong spirits which I had mixed for a set of hardy farmers, and, before I could tear it from his lips, had drank a quantity which, in an ordinary mood, would have intoxicated him helplessly in an hour. He then sat down with his face buried in his hands, and in a few minutes rose, his eyes sparkling with excitement, and the whole character of his face utterly changed. I thought he had gone wild.

" Now, Phil," said he, " now for my bride ! " And with an unbecoming levity he threw open the door, and went half dancing into the room where the friends were already assembled to witness the ceremony.

I followed with fear and anxiety. He took his place by

the side of the fair creature on whom he had placed his hopes
of life ; and, though sobered somewhat by the impressiveness
of the scene, the wild sparkle still danced in his eyes, and
I could see that every nerve in his frame was excited to the
last pitch of tension. If he had fallen a gibbering maniac
on the floor, I should not have been astonished.

The ceremony proceeded, and the first tone of his voice
in the response startled even the bride. If it had rung from
the depths of a cavern, it could not have been more sepul-
chral. I looked at him with a shudder. His lips were
curled with an exulting expression, mixed with an indefinable
fear ; and all the blood in his face seemed settled about his
eyes, which were so bloodshot and fiery that I have ever
since wondered he was not, at the first glance, suspected of
insanity. But oh the heavenly sweetness with which that
loveliest of creatures promised to love and cherish him, in
sickness and in health ! I never go to a bridal but it half
breaks my heart ; and as the soft voice of that beautiful
girl fell with its eloquent meaning on my ear, and I looked
at her, with lips calm and eyes moistened, vowing a love
which I knew to be stronger than death, to one who, I
feared, was to bring only pain and sorrow into her bosom,
my eyes warmed with irrepressible tears, and I wept.

The stir in the room as the clergyman closed his prayer
seemed to awake him from a trance. He looked around
with a troubled face for a moment ; and then, fixing his eyes
on his bride, he suddenly clasped his arms about her, and,
straining her violently to his bosom, broke into an hysterical
passion of tears and laughter. Then suddenly resuming his
self-command, he apologized for the over-excitement of his
feelings, and behaved with forced and gentle propriety till
the guests departed.

There was an apprehensive gloom over the spirits of the
small bridal party left in the lighted rooms ; and, as they

gathered round the fire, I approached, and endeavored to take a gay farewell. Larry was sitting with his arm about his wife; and he wrung my hand in silence as I said, " Good-night," and dropped his head upon her shoulder. I made some futile attempt to rally him ; but it jarred on the general feeling, and I left the house.

It was a glorious night. The clear, piercing air had a vitreous brilliancy which I have never seen in any other climate, the rays of the moonlight almost visibly splintering with the keenness of the frost. The moon herself was in the zenith, and there seemed nothing between her and the earth but palpable and glittering cold.

I hurried home. It was but eleven o'clock ; and, heaping up the wood in the large fireplace, I took a volume of " Ivanhoe," which had just then appeared, and endeavored to rid myself of my unpleasant thoughts. I read on till midnight ; and then, in a pause of the story, I rose to look out upon the night, hoping, for poor Larry's sake, that the moon was buried in clouds. The house was near the edge of the lake ; and, as I looked down upon the glassy waste, spreading away from the land, I saw the dark figure of a man kneeling directly in the path of the moon's rays. In another moment he rose to his feet; and the tall, slight form of my poor friend was distinctly visible, as with long and powerful strokes he sped away upon his skates along the shore.

To take my own Hollanders, put a collar of fur around my mouth, and hurry after him, was the work of but a minute. My straps were soon fastened ; and, following in the marks of the sharp irons at the top of my speed, I gained sight of him in about half an hour, and with great effort neared him sufficiently to shout his name with a hope of being heard.

" Larry ! Larry ! "

The lofty mountain-shore gave back the cry in repeated echoes ; but he redoubled his strokes, and sped on faster than before. At my utmost speed I followed on ; and when, at last, I could almost lay my hand on his shoulder, I summoned my strength to my breathless lungs, and shouted again, " Larry! Larry! "

He half looked back, and the full moon at that instant streamed full into his eyes. I have thought since that he could not have seen me for its dazzling brightness ; but I saw every line of *his* features with the distinctness of daylight, and I shall never forget them. A line of white foam ran through his half-parted lips ; his hair streamed wildly over his forehead, on which the perspiration glittered in large drops ; and every lineament of his expressive face was stamped with unutterable and awful horror. He looked back no more ; but, increasing his speed with an energy of which I did not think his slender frame capable, he began gradually to outstrip me. Trees, rocks, and hills fled back like magic. My limbs began to grow numb ; my fingers had lost all feeling. But a strong north-east wind was behind us, and the ice smoother than a mirror ; and I struck out my feet mechanically, and still sped on.

For two hours we had kept along the shore. The branches of the trees were reflected in the polished ice ; and the hills seemed hanging in the air, and floating past us with the velocity of storm-clouds. Far down the lake, however, there glimmered the just visible light of a fire ; and I was thanking God that we were probably approaching some human succor, when, to my horror, the retreating figure before me suddenly darted off to the left, and made swifter than before toward the centre of the icy waste. O God! what feelings were mine at that moment! Follow him far, I dared not; for, the sight of land once lost, as it would be almost instantly with our tremendous speed, we perished without a possibility of relief.

He was far beyond my voice, and to overtake him was the

only hope. I summoned my last nerve for the effort, and, keeping him in my eye, struck across at a sharper angle, with the advantage of the wind full in my back. I had taken note of the mountains, and knew that we were already forty miles from home, — a distance it would be impossible to retrace against the wind ; and the thought of freezing to death, even if I could overtake him, forced itself appallingly upon me.

Away I flew, despair giving new force to my limbs, and soon gained on the poor lunatic, whose efforts seemed flagging and faint. I neared him. Another struggle ! I could have dropped down where I was, and slept, if there were death in the first minute, so stiff and drowsy was every muscle in my frame.

"Larry!" I shouted. "Larry!"

He started at the sound ; and I could hear a smothered and breathless shriek, as, with supernatural strength, he straightened up his bending figure, and, leaning forward again, sped away from me like a phantom on the blast.

I could follow no longer. I stood stiff on my skates, still going on rapidly before the wind, and tried to look after him ; but the frost had stiffened my eyes, and there was a mist before them, and they felt like glass. Nothing was visible around me but moonlight and ice, and dimly and slowly I began to retrace the slight path of semicircles toward the shore. It was painful work. The wind seemed to divide the very fibres of the skin upon my face. Violent exercise no longer warmed my body ; and I felt the cold shoot sharply into my loins, and bind across my breast like a chain of ice. And, with the utmost strength of mind at my command, I could just resist the terrible inclination to lie down and sleep. I forgot poor Larry. Life — dear life — was now my only thought. So selfish are we in our extremity !

With difficulty I at last reached the shore ; and then, unbuttoning my coat, and spreading it wide for a sail, I set my feet together, and went slowly down before the wind, till the fire which I had before noticed began to blaze cheerily in the distance. It seemed an eternity in my slow progress. Tree after tree threw the shadow of its naked branches across the way; hill after hill glided slowly backward: but my knees seemed frozen together, and my joints fixed in ice. And, if my life had depended on striking out my feet, I should have died powerless. My jaws were locked, my shoulders drawn half down to my knees; and in a few minutes more, I am well convinced, the blood would have thickened in my veins, and stood still forever.

I could see the tongues of the flames; I counted the burning fagots; a form passed between me and the fire. I struck, and fell prostrate on the snow; and I remember no more.

The sun was darting a slant beam through the trees when I awoke. The genial warmth of a large bed of embers played on my cheek, a thick blanket enveloped me, and beneath my head was a soft cushion of withered leaves. On the opposite side of the fire lay four Indians wrapped in their blankets; and with her head on her knees, and her hands clasped over her ankles, sat an Indian woman, who had apparently fallen asleep upon her watch. The stir I made aroused her; and as she piled on fresh fagots, and kindled them to a bright blaze with a handful of leaves, drowsiness came over me again, and I wrapped the blanket about me more closely, and shut my eyes to sleep.

I awoke refreshed. It must have been ten o'clock, by the sun. The Indians were about, occupied in various avocations; and the woman was broiling a slice of deer's flesh on the coals. She offered it to me as I rose; and, having eaten part of it with a piece of a cake made of meal, I requested her to call in the men, and, with offers of reward, easily induced them to go with me in search of my lost friend.

We found him, as I had anticipated, frozen to death, far out on the lake. The Indians tracked him by the marks of his skate-irons; and from their appearance he had sunk quietly down, probably drowsy and exhausted, and had died, of course, without pain. His last act seemed to have been under the influence of his strange madness; for he lay on his face, turned from the quarter of the setting moon.

We carried him home to his bride. Even the Indians were affected by her uncontrollable agony. I cannot describe that scene, familiar as I am with pictures of horror.

I made inquiries with respect to the position of his bridal chamber. There were no shutters, and the moon streamed broadly into it; and, after kissing his shrinking bride with the violence of a madman, he sprang out of the room with a terrific scream, and she saw him no more till he lay dead on his bridal bed.

LOVE IN THE LIBRARY.

PART I.

FROST AND FLIRTATION.

I.

IT began to snow. The air softened; the pattering of the horses' hoofs was muffled with the impeded vibration; the sleigh glided on with a duller sound; the large, loose flakes fell soft and fast, and the low and just audible murmur, like the tread of a fairy host, melted on the ear with a drowsy influence, as if it were a descent of palpable sleep upon the earth. You may talk of falling water, of the running of a brook, of the humming song of an old crone on a sick vigil, or of the *levi susurro* of the bees of Hybla; but there is nothing like the falling of the snow for soft and soothing music. You hear it or not, as you will, but it melts into your soul unaware. If you have ever a heartache, or feel the need of "poppy or mandragora," or, like myself, grow sometimes a-weary of the stale repetitions of this unvaried world, seek me out in Massachusetts, when the wind softens and veers south, after a frost, — say in January. There shall have been a long-lying snow on the ground, well-trodden. The road shall be as smooth as the paths to our first sins, — of a seeming perpetual declivity, as it were, — and never a jolt or jar between us and the edge of the horizon, but all onward and down apparently, with an insensible ease. You sit beside me in my spring-sleigh, hung

16

with the lightness of a cobweb cradle for a fairy's child in
the trees. Our horse is, in the harness, of a swift and even
pace, and around his neck is a string of fine small bells, that
ring to his measured step in a kind of muffled music, softer
and softer as the snowflakes thicken in the air. Your seat is
of the shape of the *fauteuil* in your library, cushioned and
deep, and with a backward and gentle slope ; and you are
enveloped to the eyelids in warm furs. You settle down
with every muscle in repose, the visor of your ermine cap
just shedding the snow from your forehead ; and with a word
the groom stands back, and the horse speeds on, steady, but
beautifully fast. The bells, which you hear loudly at first,
begin to deaden ; and the low hum of the alighting flakes
steals gradually on your ear ; and soon the hoof-strokes are
as silent as if the steed were shod with wool, and away you
flee through the white air, like birds asleep upon the wing
diving through the feathery fleeces of the moon. Your eyelids fall, forgetfulness steals upon the senses, a delicious
torpor takes possession of the uneasy blood, and brain and
thought yield to an intoxicating and trance-like slumber. It
were, perhaps, too much to ask that any human bosom may
go scathless to the grave ; but in my own unworthy peti-
tions I usually supplicate that my heart may be broken about
Christmas. I know an anodyne o' that season.

Fred Fleming and I occupied one of the seven long seats
in a stage-sleigh, flying at this time twelve miles in the hour
(yet not fast enough for our impatience) westward from
the university gates. The sleighing had been perfect for a
week ; and the cold, keen air had softened for the first time
that morning, and assumed the warm and woolly complexion
that foretokened snow. Though not very cheerful in its
aspect, this is an atmosphere particularly pleasant to breathe ;
and Fred, who was making his first move after a six weeks'
fever, sat with the furs away from his mouth, nostrils ex-

panded, lips parted, and the countenance altogether of a man in a high state of physical enjoyment. I had nursed him through his illness, by the way, in my own rooms, and hence our position as fellow-travellers. A pressing invitation from his father, to come home with him to Skaneateles for the holidays, had diverted me from my usual winter journey to the North; and, for the first time in my life, I was going upon a long visit to a strange roof. My imagination had never more business upon its hands.

Fred had described to me, over and over again, every person I was to meet, brothers, sisters, aunts, cousins, and friends, — a household of thirty people, guests included; but there was one person among them of whom his descriptions, amplified as they were, were very unsatisfactory.

" Is she so *very* plain ? " I asked for the twentieth time.

" Abominably ! "

" And immense black eyes ? "

" Saucers ! "

" And large mouth ? "

" Huge ! "

" And very dark ? "

" Like a squaw ! "

" And skinny hands, did you say ? "

" Lean, long, and pokerish ! "

" And so *very* clever ? "

" Knows every thing, Phil ! "

" But a sweet voice ? "

" Um ! everybody says so ! "

" And high temper ? "

" She's the devil, Phil ! don't ask any more questions about her ! "

" You don't like her, then ? "

" She never condescends to speak to me. How should I ? "

And thereupon I put my head out of the sleigh, and

employed myself with catching the snowflakes on my nose, and thinking whether Edith Linsey would like me or no; for, through all Fred's derogatory descriptions, it was clearly evident that she was the ruling spirit of the hospitable household of the Flemings.

As we got farther on, the new snow became deeper, and we found that the last storm had been heavier here than in the country from which we had come. The occasional farmhouses were almost wholly buried, the black chimney alone appearing above the ridgy drifts; while the tops of the doors and windows lay below the level of the trodden road, from which a descending passage was cut to the threshold, like the entrance to a cave in the earth. The fences were quite invisible. The fruit-trees looked diminished to shrubberies of snow-flowers, their trunks buried under the visible surface, and their branches loaded with the still falling flakes till they bent beneath the burden. Nothing was abroad, for nothing could stir out of the road without danger of being lost; and we dreaded to meet even a single sleigh, lest, in turning out, the horses should "slump" beyond their depth in the untrodden drifts. The poor animals began to labor severely, and sunk at every step over their knees in the clogging and wool-like substance; and the long and cumbrous sleigh rose and fell in the deep pits like a boat in a heavy sea. It seemed impossible to get on. Twice we brought up with a terrible plunge, and stood suddenly still, for the runners had struck in too deep for the strength of the horses; and with the snow-shovels, which formed a part of the furniture of the vehicle, we dug them from their concrete beds. Our progress at last was reduced to scarce a mile in the hour, and we began to have apprehensions that our team would give out between the post-houses. Fortunately it was still warm, for the numbness of cold would have paralyzed our already flagging exertions.

We had reached the summit of a long hill with the greatest difficulty. The poor beasts stood panting, and reeking with sweat; the runners of the sleigh were clogged with hard cakes of snow, and the air was close and dispiriting. We came to a standstill, with the vehicle lying over almost on its side ; and I stepped out to speak to the driver, and look forward. It was a discouraging prospect : a long deep valley lay before us, closed at the distance of a couple of miles by another steep hill, through a cleft in the top of which lay our way. We could not even distinguish the line of the road between. Our disheartened animals stood at this moment buried to their breasts, and to get forward without rearing at every step seemed impossible. The driver sat on his box, looking uneasily down into the valley. It was one undulating ocean of snow, not a sign of a human habitation to be seen, and even the trees indistinguishable from the general mass by their whitened and overladen branches. The storm had ceased; but the usual sharp cold that succeeds a warm fall of snow had not yet lightened the clamminess of the new-fallen flakes, and they clung around the foot like clay, rendering every step a toil.

" Your leaders are quite blown," I said to the driver, as he slid off his uncomfortable seat.

" Pretty nearly, sir."

" And your wheelers are not much better."

" Sca'cely."

" And what do you think of the weather? "

" It'll be darnation cold in an hour." As he spoke he looked up to the sky, which was already peeling off its clouds in long stripes, like the skin of an orange, and looked as hard and cold as marble between the widening rifts. A sudden gust of a more chilling temperature followed immediately upon his prediction ; and the long cloth curtains of the sleigh flew clear of their slight pillars, and shook off their fringes of icicles.

"Could you shovel a little, mister?" said the driver, handing me one of the broad wooden utensils from his foot-board, and commencing himself, after having thrown off his box-coat, by heaving up a solid cake of the moist snow at the side of the road.

"It's just to make a place to rub down them creturs," said he, as I looked at him, quite puzzled to know what he was going to do.

Fred was too weak to assist us, and having righted the vehicle a little, and tied down the flapping curtains, he wrapped himself in his cloak; and I set heartily to work with my shovel. In a few minutes, taking advantage of the hollow of a drift, we had cleared a small area of frozen ground; and, releasing the tired animals from their harness, we rubbed them well down with the straw from the bottom of the sleigh. The persevering driver then cleared the runners of their iced and clinging masses; and, a half-hour having elapsed, he produced two bottles of rum from his box, and, giving each of the horses a dose, put them again to their traces.

We heaved out of the pit into which the sleigh had settled; and for the first mile it was down-hill, and we got on with comparative ease. The sky was by this time almost bare, a dark, slaty mass of clouds alone settling on the horizon in the quarter of the wind, while the sun, as powerless as moon-light, poured with dazzling splendor on the snow, and the gusts came keen and bitter across the sparkling waste, rimming the nostrils as if with bands of steel, and penetrating to the innermost nerve with their pungent iciness. No protection seemed of any avail. The whole surface of the body ached as if it were laid against a slab of ice. The throat closed instinctively, and contracted its unpleasant respiration; the body and limbs drew irresistibly together, to economize, like a hedgehog, the exposed surface; the hands and feet felt transmuted to lead; and across the forehead, below the pressure of the cap, there was a binding and oppressive ache, as if a bar of frosty iron had been let into the skull. The mind, meantime, seemed freezing up, — unwillingness to stir, and inability to think of any thing but the cold, becoming every instant more decided.

From the bend of the valley, our difficulties became more serious. The drifts often lay across the road like a wall, some feet above the heads of the horses ; and we had dug through one or two, and had been once upset, and often near it, before we came to the steepest part of the ascent. The horses had by this time begun to feel the excitement of the rum, and bounded on through the snow with continual leaps, jerking the sleigh after them with a violence that threatened momently to break the traces. The steam from their bodies froze instantly, and covered them with a coat like hoar-frost ; and spite of their heat, and the unnatural and violent exertions they were making, it was evident by the pricking of their ears and the sudden crouch of the body when a stronger blast swept over, that the cold struck through even their hot and intoxicated blood.

We toiled up, leap after leap ; and it seemed miraculous to me that the now infuriated animals did not burst a blood-vessel or crack a sinew with every one of those terrible springs. The sleigh plunged on after them, stopping dead and short at every other moment, and reeling over the heavy drifts like a boat in a surging sea. A finer crystallization had meantime taken place upon the surface of the moist snow, and the powdered particles flew almost insensibly on the blasts of wind, filling the eyes and hair, and cutting the skin with a sensation like the touch of needle-points. The driver and his maddened but almost exhausted team were blinded by the glittering and whirling eddies ; the cold grew intenser every moment, the forward motion gradually less and less ; and when, with the very last effort apparently, we reached a spot on the summit of the hill, which, from its exposed situation, had been kept bare by the wind, the patient and persevering whip brought his horses to a stand, and despaired, for the first time, of his prospects of getting on. I crept out of the sleigh, the iron-bound runners of which now grated on the bare ground, but found it impossible to stand upright.

"If you can use your hands," said the driver, turning his back to the wind, which stung the face like the lash of a whip, "I'll trouble you to untackle them horses."

I set about it, while he buried his hands and face in the snow, to relieve them for a moment from the agony of cold. The poor animals staggered stiffly, as I pushed them aside, and every vein stood out from their bodies like ropes under the skin.

"What are you going to do?" I asked, as he joined me again, and, taking off the harness of one of the leaders, flung it into the snow.

"Ride for life!" was his ominous answer.

"Good God! and what is to become of my sick friend?"

"The Almighty knows — if he can't ride to the tavern!"

I sprang instantly to poor Fred, who was lying in the bottom of the sleigh, almost frozen to death; informed him of the driver's decision, and asked him if he thought he could ride one of the horses. He was beginning to grow drowsy, (the first symptom of death by cold), and could with difficulty be roused. With the driver's assistance, however, I lifted him out of the sleigh, shook him soundly, and, making stirrups of the traces, set him upon one of the horses, and started him off before us. The poor beasts seemed to have a presentiment of the necessity of exertion, and, though stiff and sluggish, entered willingly upon the deep drift which blocked up the way, and toiled exhaustedly on. The cold, in our exposed position, was agonizing. Every small fibre in the skin of my own face felt splitting and cracked, and my eyelids seemed made of ice. Our limbs soon lost all sensation. I could only press with my knees to the horse's side, and the whole collected energy of my frame seemed expended in the exertion. Fred held on wonderfully. The driver had still the use of his arm, and rode behind, flogging the poor animals on, whose every step seemed to be the last summons of energy. The sun set, and it was rather a relief, for the glitter upon the snow was exceedingly painful to the sight, and there was no warmth in its beams. I could see my poor friend drooping gradually to the neck of his horse ; but, until he should drop off, it was impossible to assist him, and his faithful animal still waded on. I felt my own strength fast ebbing away. If I had been alone, I should certainly have lain down, with the almost irresistible inclination to sleep : but the thought of my friend, and the shouting of the energetic driver, nerved me from time to time ; and with hands hanging helplessly down, and elbows fastened convulsively to my side, we plunged and struggled painfully forward. I but remember being taken afterward to a fire, and shrinking from it with a shriek, the suffering of reviving consciousness was so intolerable. We had reached the tavern, literally frozen upon our horses.

II.

I was balancing my spoon on the edge of a cup at the breakfast-table, the morning after our arrival, when Fred stopped in the middle of an eulogium on my virtues as a nurse, and, a lady entering at the same moment, he said simply in parenthesis, " My cousin Edith, Mr. Slingsby," and went on with his story. I rose and bowed, and, as Fred had the *parole*, I had time to collect my courage, and take a look at the enemy's camp ; for, of that considerable household, I felt my star to be in conjunction or opposition with hers only, who was at that moment my *vis-à-vis* across a dish of stewed oysters.

In about five minutes of rapid mental portrait-painting, I had taken a likeness of Edith Linsey, which I see at this moment (I have carried it about the world for ten years) as distinctly as the incipient lines of age in this thin-wearing hand. My feelings changed in that time from dread, or admiration, or something between these, to pity; she was so unscrupulously and hopelessly plain, so wretchedly ill and suffering in her aspect, so spiritless and unhappy in every motion and look. "I'll win her heart," thought I, "by being kind to her. Poor thing! it will be something new to her, I dare say." O Philip Slingsby! what a doomed donkey thou wert for that silly soliloquy!

And yet, even as she sat there leaning over her untasted breakfast, listless, ill, and melancholy, — with her large mouth, her protruding eyes, her dead and sallow complexion, and not one redeeming feature, — there was something in her face which produced a phantom of beauty in my mind; a glimpse, a shadowing of a countenance that Beatrice Cenci might have worn at her last innocent orison; a loveliness moulded and exalted by superhuman and overpowering mind, instinct, through all its sweetness, with energy and fire. So strong was this phantom portrait, that in all my thoughts of her as an angel in heaven (for I supposed her dying, for many a month, and a future existence was her own most frequent theme), she always rose to my fancy with a face half Niobe, half Psyche, radiantly lovely. And this, too, with a face of her own, a *bona-fide* physiognomy, that must have made a mirror an unpleasant article of furniture in her chamber.

I have no suspicion in my own mind whether Time was drunk or sober during the succeeding week of those Christmas holidays. The second Saturday had come round, and I

just remember that Fred was very much out of humor with
me for having appeared to his friends to be every thing he
had said I was *not*, and nothing he had said I *was*. He had
described me as the most uproarious, noisy, good-humored,
and agreeable dog in the world. And I was not that at all,
— particularly the last. The old judge told him he had not
improved in his penetration at the university.

A week! and what a life had been clasped within its brief
calendar, for me! Edith Linsey was two years older than I,
and I was considered a boy. She was thought to be dying
slowly, but irretrievably, of consumption; and it was little
matter whom she loved, or how. They would only have
been pleased, if, by a new affection, she could beguile the
preying melancholy of illness; for by that gentle name they
called, in their kindness, a caprice and a bitterness of character that, had she been less a sufferer, would not have been
endured for a day. But she was not capricious or bitter
to *me!* Oh, no! And from the very extreme of her impatience with others, — from her rudeness, her violence, her
sarcasm, — she came to me with a heart softer than a child's,
and wept upon my hands, and weighed every word that
might give me offence, and watched to anticipate my lightest wish; and was humble, and generous, and passionately
loving, and dependent. Her heart sprang to me with a
rebound. She gave herself up to me with an utter and
desperate abandonment that owed something to her peculiar
character, but more to her own solemn conviction that she
was dying, that her best hope of life was not worth a week's
purchase.

We had begun with books, and upon them her past enthusiasm had hitherto been released. She loved her favorite
authors with a passion. They had relieved her heart; and
there was nothing of poetry or philosophy that was deep or
beautiful, in which she had not steeped her very soul. How

well I remember her repeating to me from Shelley those
glorious lines to the soaring swan! —

> "Thou hast a home,
> Beautiful bird! Thou voyagest to thy home,
> Where thy sweet mate will twine her downy neck
> With thine, and welcome thy return with eyes
> Bright with the lustre of their own fond joy!
> And what am I, that I should linger here,
> With voice far sweeter than thy dying notes,
> Spirit more vast than thine, frame more attuned
> To beauty, wasting these surpassing powers
> To the deaf air, to the blind earth, and heaven
> That echoes not my thoughts!"

There was a long room in the southern wing of the house,
fitted up as a library. It was a heavily curtained, dim old
place, with deep-embayed windows, and so many nooks, and
so much furniture, that there was that hushed air, that absence of echo within it, which is the great charm of a haunt
for study or thought. It was Edith's kingdom. She might
lock the door if she pleased, or shut or open the windows:
in short, when she was there, no one thought of disturbing
her, and she was like a "spirit in its cell," invisible and
inviolate. And here I drank into my very life and soul the
outpourings of a bosom that had been locked till (as we both
thought) the last hour of its life, a flow of mingled intellect
and passion that overran my heart like lava, sweeping every
thing into its resistless fire, and (may God forgive her!)
leaving it scorched and desolate when its mocking brightness
had gone out.

I remember that "Elia" — Charles Lamb's "Elia" —
was the favorite of favorites among her books; and partly
that the late death of this most-to-be-loved author reminded
me to look it up, and partly to have time to draw back my
indifference over a subject that it something stirs me to recall,

you shall read an imitation (or continuation, if you will) that
I did for Edith's eye, of his " Essay on Books and Reading."
I sat with her dry and fleshless hand in mine while I read it
to her, and the fingers of Psyche were never fairer to Canova
than they to me.

" It is a little singular," I began (looking into her eyes as
long as I could remember what I had written), " that, among
all the elegances of sentiment for which the age is remarkable, no one should ever have thought of writing a book upon
' Reading.' The refinements of the true epicure in books are
surely as various as those of the gastronome and the opium-
eater ; and I can conceive of no reason why a topic of such
natural occurrence should have been so long neglected, unless
it is that the taste itself, being rather a growth of indolence,
has never numbered among its votaries one of the busy craft
of writers.

" The great proportion of men read, as they eat, for hunger. I do not consider them readers. The true secret of
the thing is no more adapted to their comprehension, than
the sublimations of Louis Eustache Ude for the taste of a
day-laborer. The refined reading-taste, like the palate of
gourmanderie, must have got beyond appetite, — gross appetite. It shall be that of a man who, having fed through
childhood and youth on simple knowledge, values now only,
as it were, the apotheosis of learning, — the spiritual *nare*.
There are, it is true, instances of a keen natural relish : a
boy, as you will sometimes find one, of a premature thought-
fulness, will carry a favorite author in his bosom, and feast
greedily on it in his stolen hours. Elia tells the exquisite
story : —

> ' I saw a boy, with eager eye,
> Open a book upon a stall,
> And read as he'd devour it all;
> Which, when the stall-man did espy,
> Soon to the boy I heard him call, —

" You sir, you never buy a book,
Therefore in one you shall not look!"
The boy passed slowly on, and, with a sigh,
He wished he had never been taught to read —
Then of the old churl's books he should have had no need.'

" The pleasure as well as the profit of reading depends as much upon time and manner, as upon the book. The mind is an opal, changing its color with every shifting shade. Ease of position is especially necessary. A muscle strained, a nerve unpoised, an admitted sunbeam caught upon a mirror, are slight circumstances ; but a feather may tickle the dreamer from paradise to earth. ' Many a froward axiom,' says a refined writer, ' many an inhumane thought, hath arisen from sitting uncomfortably, or from a want of symmetry in your chamber.' Who has not felt, at times, an unaccountable disrelish for a favorite author? Who has not, by a sudden noise in the street, been startled from a reading dream, and found, afterward, that the broken spell was not to be rewound? An ill-tied cravat may unlink the rich harmonies of Taylor. You would not think Barry Cornwall the delicious heart he is, reading him in a tottering chair.

" There is much in the mood with which you come to a book. If you have been vexed out of doors, the good humor of an author seems unnatural. I think I should scarce relish the ' gentle spiriting ' of Ariel with a pulse of ninety in the minute. Or, if I had been touched by the unkindness of a friend, Jack Falstaff would not move me to laughter as easily as he is wont. There are tones of the mind, however, to which a book will vibrate with a harmony than which there is nothing more exquisite in nature. To go abroad at sunrise in June, and admit all the holy influences of the hour — stillness, and purity, and balm — to a mind subdued and dignified, as the mind will be by the sacred tranquillity of sleep, and then to come in with bathed and refreshed senses, and

a temper of as clear joyfulness as the soaring lark's, and sit
down to Milton or Spenser, or, almost loftier still, the divine
' Prometheus ' of Shelley, has seemed to me a harmony of
delight almost too heavenly to be human.   The great secret
of such pleasure is sympathy.   You must climb to the eagle
poet's eyry.   You must have senses, like his, for the music
that is only audible to the fine ear of thought, and the beauty
that is visible only to the spirit-eye of a clear and for the
time unpolluted fancy.   The stamp and pressure of the
magician's own time and season must be upon you.   You
would not read Ossian, for example, in a bath, or sitting
under a tree in a sultry noon ; but after rushing into the eye
of the wind with a fleet horse, with all his gallant pride and
glorious strength and fire obedient to your rein, and so
mingling, as it will, with his rider's consciousness, that
you feel as if you were gifted in your own body with the
swiftness and energy of an angel — after this, to sit down
to Ossian, is to read him with a magnificence of delusion, to
my mind, scarce less than reality.   I never envied Napoleon till I heard it was his habit, after a battle, to read
Ossian.

"You cannot often read to music.   But I love, when the
voluntary is pealing in church, — every breath in the congregation suppressed, and the deep-volumed notes pouring
through the arches of the roof with the sublime and almost
articulate praise of the organ, — to read, from the pew Bible,
the Book of Ecclesiastes.   The solemn stateliness of its
periods is fitted to music like a hymn.   It is to me a spring
of the most thrilling devotion — though I shame to confess
that the richness of its Eastern imagery, and, above all, the
inimitable beauty of its philosophy, stand out somewhat
definitely in the reminiscences of the hour.

"A taste for reading comes comparatively late.   ' Robin-
son Crusoe ' will turn a boy's head at ten.   The ' Arabian

Nights' are taken to bed with us at twelve. At fourteen, a forward boy will read the ' Lady of the Lake,' ' Tom Jones,' and ' Peregrine Pickle ; ' and at seventeen (not before) he is ready for Shakspeare, and, if he is of a thoughtful turn, Milton. Most men do not read these last with a true relish till after this period. The hidden beauties of standard authors break upon the mind by surprise. It is like discovering a secret spring in an old jewel. You take up the book in an idle moment, as you have done a thousand times before, perhaps wondering, as you turn over the leaves, what the world finds in it to admire ; when suddenly, as you read, your fingers press close upon the covers, your frame thrills, and the passage you have chanced upon chains you like a spell, it is so vividly true and beautiful. Milton's ' Comus ' flashed upon me in this way. I never could read the ' Rape of the Lock ' till a friend quoted some passages from it during a walk. I know no more exquisite sensation than this warming of the heart to an old author ; and it seems to me that the most delicious portion of intellectual existence is the brief period in which, one by one, the great minds of old are admitted with all their time-mellowed worth to the affections. With what delight I read for the first time the ' kind-hearted plays ' of Beaumont and Fletcher ! How I doted on Burton ! What treasures to me were the ' Fairy Queen ' and the Lyrics of Milton !

" I used to think, when studying the Greek and Latin poets in my boyhood, that to be made a school-author was a fair offset against immortality. I would as lief, it seemed to me, have my verses handed down by the town-crier. But latterly, after an interval of a few years, I have taken up my classics (the identical school copies, with the hard places all thumbed and pencilled), and have read them with no little pleasure. It is not to be believed with what a satisfaction the riper eye glides smoothly over the once difficult line, find-

ing the golden cadence of poetry beneath what once seemed
only a tangled chaos of inversion.   The associations of hard
study, instead of reviving the old distaste, added wonderfully to the interest of a re-perusal.   I could see now what
brightened the sunken eye of the pale and sickly master, as
he took up the hesitating passage, and read on, forgetful of
the delinquent, to the end.   I could enjoy now, what was a
dead letter to me then, the heightened fulness of Herodotus,
and the strong-woven style of Thucydides, and the magnificent invention of Æschylus.   I took an aversion to Homer
from hearing a classmate in the next room scan it perpetually
through his nose.   There is no music for me in the Iliad.
But, spite of the recollections scored alike upon my palm and
the margin, I own to an Augustan relish for the smooth
melody of Virgil, and freely forgive the sometime troublesome ferule — enjoying by its aid the raciness of Horace and
Juvenal, and the lofty philosophy of Lucretius.   It will be
a dear friend to whom I put down in my will that shelf of
defaced classics.

"There are some books that bear reading pleasantly once
a year. 'Tristram Shandy' is an annual with me: I read
him regularly about Christmas.   Jeremy Taylor (not to mingle things holy and profane) is a good table-book, to be used
when you would collect your thoughts and be serious a while.
A man of taste need never want for Sunday reading while he
can find the sermons of Taylor, and South, and Fuller, —
writers of good theological repute, — though, between ourselves, I think one likelier to be delighted with the poetry
and quaint fancifulness of their style, than edified by the
piety it covers.   I like to have a quarto edition of Sir Thomas
Brown on a near shelf, or Milton's prose works, or Bacon.
These are healthful moods of the mind when lighter nutri-
ment is distasteful.

"I am growing fastidious in poetry, and confine myself

more and more to the old writers. Castaly of late runs shallow. Shelley's (peace to his passionate heart!) was a deep
draught, and Wordsworth and Wilson sit near the well, and
Keats and Barry Cornwall have been to the fountain's lip,
feeding their imaginations (the latter his *heart* as well), but
they have brought back little for the world. The 'small
silver stream' will, I fear, soon cease to flow down to us;
and, as it dries back to its source, we shall close nearer and
nearer upon the 'pure English undefiled.' The dabblers in
muddy waters (tributaries to Lethe) will have Parnassus to
themselves.

"The finest pleasures of reading come unbidden. You
cannot, with your choicest appliances for the body, always
command the many-toned mind. In the twilight alcove of
a library, with a time-mellowed chair yielding luxuriously to
your pressure, a June wind laden with idleness and balm
floating in at the window, and in your hand some Russia-
bound rambling old author, as Izaak Walton, good-humored
and quaint, one would think the spirit could scarce fail to be
conjured. Yet often, after spending a morning hour rest-
lessly thus, I have risen with my mind unhinged, and strolled
off with a book in my pocket to the woods; and, as I live,
the mood has descended upon me under some chance tree,
with a crooked root under my head, and I have lain there,
reading and sleeping by turns, till the letters were blurred in
the dimness of twilight. It is the evil of refinement, that it
breeds caprice. You will sometimes stand unfatigued for
hours on the steps of a library; or, in a shop the eye will be
arrested, and all the jostling of customers and the looks
of the jealous shopman will not divert you till you have read
out the chapter.

"I do not often indulge in the supernatural; for I am an
unwilling believer in ghosts, and the topic excites me. But,
for its connection with the subject upon which I am writing,

I must conclude these rambling observations with a late mysterious visitation of my own.

" I had, during the last year, given up the early summer tea-parties common in the town in which the university stands ; and having, of course, three or four more hours than usual on my hands, I took to an afternoon habit of imaginative reading.   Shakspeare came first, naturally ; and I feasted for the hundredth time upon what I think his (and the world's) most delicate creation, — the ' Tempest.'   The twilight of the first day overtook me at the third act, where the banquet is brought in with solemn music by the fairy troop of Prospero, and set before the shipwrecked king and his followers.   I closed the book, and, leaning back in my chair, abandoned myself to the crowd of images which throng always upon the traces of Shakspeare.   The *fancy* music was still in my mind, when an apparently *real* strain of the most solemn melody came to my ear, dying, it seemed to me as it reached it, the tones were so expiringly faint and low. I was not startled, but lay quietly, holding my breath, and more fearing when the strain would be broken, than curious whence it came.   The twilight deepened till it was dark, and it still played on, changing the tune at intervals, but always of the same melancholy sweetness ; till by and by I lost all curiosity, and, giving in to the charm, the scenes I had been reading began to form again in my mind, and Ariel, with his delicate ministers, and Prospero, and Miranda, and Caliban, came moving before me to the measure, as bright and vivid as the reality.   I was disturbed in the midst of it by Alfonse, who came in at the usual hour with my tea ; and, on starting to my feet, I listened in vain for the continuance of the music.   I sat thinking of it a while, but dismissed it at last, and went out to enjoy, in a solitary walk, the loveliness of the summer night.   The next day I resumed my book, with a smile at my previous credulity, and had read through the

last scenes of the 'Tempest,' when the light failed me. I
again closed the book; and presently again, as if the sympathy was instantaneous, the strain broke in, playing the
same low and solemn melodies, and falling with the same
dying cadence upon the ear. I listened to it, as before, with
breathless attention; abandoned myself once more to its
irresistible spell; and half-waking, half-sleeping, fell again
into a vivid dream, brilliant as fairy-land, and creating itself
to the measures of the still audible music. I could not now
shake off my belief in its reality; but I was so rapt with its
strange sweetness, and the beauty of my dream, that I cared
not whether it came from earth or air. My indifference,
singularly enough, continued for several days; and, regularly at twilight, I threw aside my book, and listened with
dreamy wakefulness for the music. It never failed me, and
its results were as constant as its coming. Whatever I had
read, — sometimes a canto of Spenser, sometimes an act of
a play, or a chapter of romance, — the scene rose before me
with the stately reality of a pageant. At last I began to
think of it more seriously; and it was a relief to me one
evening when Alfonse came in earlier than usual with a message. I told him to stand perfectly still; and after a minute's pause, during which I heard distinctly an entire passage
of a funeral hymn, I asked him if he heard any music?
He said he did not. My blood chilled at his positive reply,
and I bade him listen once more. Still he heard nothing.
I could endure it no longer. It was to me as distinct and
audible as my own voice; and I rushed from my room as
he left me, shuddering to be left alone.

"The next day I thought of nothing but death. Warn-
ings by knells in the air, by apparitions, by mysterious
voices, were things I had believed in speculatively for years;
and now their truth came upon me like conviction. I felt
a dull, leaden presentiment about my heart, growing heavier

and heavier with every passing hour. Evening came at last; and with it, like a summons from the grave, a ' dead march ' swelled clearly on the air. I felt faint and sick at heart. This could not be fancy; and why was it, as I thought I had proved, audible to my ear alone? I threw open the window, and the first rush of the cool north wind refreshed me; but, as if to mock my attempts at relief, the dirge-like sounds rose, at the instant, with treble distinctness. I seized my hat, and rushed into the street; but, to my dismay, every step seemed to bring me nearer to the knell. Still I hurried on, the dismal sounds growing distractingly louder; till, on turning a corner that leads to the lovely burying-ground of New Haven, I came suddenly upon — a bell-foundery! In the rear had lately been hung, for trial, the chiming-bells just completed for the new Trinity Church; and the master of the establishment informed me that one of his journeymen was a fine player, and every day after his work he was in the habit of amusing himself with the ' Dead March in Saul,' the ' Marseilles Hymn,' and other melancholy and easy tunes, muffling the hammers that he might not disturb the neighbors.''

I have had my reward for these speculations, dear reader, — a smile that is lying at this instant, *perdu*, in the innermost recess of memory, — and I care not much (without offence) whether you like it or no. *She* thanked me; *she* thought it well done; *she* laid her head on my bosom while I read it in the old library of the Flemings : and every word has been " paid for in fairy gold.''

I have taken up a thread that lengthens as I unravel it, and I cannot well see how I shall come to the end without trespassing on your patience. We will cut it here, if you like, and resume it after a pause; but before I close I must give you a little instance of how love makes the dullest earth poetical. Edith had given me a *portefeuille* crammed with

all kinds of embossed and curious note-paper, all quite too
pretty for use ; and what I would show you are my verses
on the occasion. For a hand unpractised, then, in aught save
the " Gradus ad Parnassum," I must own I have fished
them out of that same old *portefeuille* (faded now from its
glory, and worn with travel, but oh, how cherished !) with a
pleasant feeling of paternity.

Thanks for thy gift! But heardst thou ever
  A story of a wandering fay,
Who, tired of playing sylph forever,
  Came romping to the earth one day;
And, flirting like a little Love
  With every thing that flew and flirted,
Made captive of a sober dove,
  Whose pinions (so the tale asserted),
Though neither very fresh nor fair,
Were well enough for common wear.

The dove, though plain, was gentle bred,
  And cooed agreeably, though low;
But still the fairy shook her head,
  And, patting with her foot, said "*No!*"
'Twas true that he was rather fat,
  But that was living in an abbey;
And solemn — but it was not that.
" What then? " — " *Why, sir, your wings are shabby.*"

The dove was dumb: he drooped, and sidled
  In shame along the abbey-wall;
And then the haughty fay unbridled,
  And blew her snail-shell trumpet-call;
And summoning her waiting-sprite,
  Who bore her wardrobe on his back,
She took the wings she wore at night,
  (Silvery stars on plumes of black),
And, smiling, begged that he would take
And wear them for his lady's sake.

He took them, but he could not fly!
   A fay-wing was too fine for him;
And when she pouted by and by,
   And left him for some other whim,
He laid them softly in his nest,
   And did his flying with his own;
And they were soft upon his breast,
   When many a night he slept alone;
And many a thought those wings would stir,
And many a dream of love and her.

PART II.

LOVE AND SPECULATION.

I.

EDITH LINSEY was religious. There are many *intensifiers*
(a new word, that I can't get on without: I submit it for
admission into the language), — there are many intensifiers,
I say, to the passion of love ; such as pride, jealousy, poetry
(money, sometimes, *Dio mio!*), and idleness :[1] but, if the
experience of one who first studied the art of love in an
"evangelical" country is worth a *para*, there is nothing
within the bend of the rainbow that deepens the tender passion like religion. I speak it not irreverently. The human
being that loves us throws the value of its existence into
the crucible, and it can do no more. Love's best alchemy
can only turn into affection what is in the heart. The vain,
the proud, the poetical, the selfish, the weak, can and do
fling their vanity, pride, poetry, selfishness, and weakness
into a first passion ; but these are earthly elements, and there
is an antagonism in their natures that is forever striving to

---

[1] "La paresse dans les femmes est le présage de l'amour." — LA BRUYÈRE.

resolve them back to their original earth. But religion is
of the soul as well as the heart, — the mind as well as the
affections, — and when it mingles in love, it is the infusion
of an immortal essence into an unworthy and else perishable
mixture.

Edith's religion was equally without cant, and without
hesitation or disguise. She had arrived at it by elevation of
mind, aided by the habit of never counting on her tenure
of life beyond the setting of the next sun ; and with her it
was rather an intellectual exaltation than a humility of heart.
She thought of God because the subject was illimitable, and
her powerful imagination found in it the scope for which she
pined. She talked of goodness, and purity, and disinterestedness, because she found them easy virtues with a frame
worn down with disease, and she was removed by the sheltered position of an invalid from the collision which tries so
shrewdly in common life the ring of our metal. She prayed,
because the fulness of her heart was loosed by her eloquence
when on her knees, and she found that an indistinct and
mystic unburthening of her bosom, even to the Deity, was
a hush and a relief. The heart does not always require
rhyme and reason of language and tears.

There are many persons of religious feeling, who, from a
fear of ridicule or misconception, conduct themselves as if
to express a devout sentiment was a want of taste or good
breeding. Edith was not of these. Religion was to her a
powerful enthusiasm, applied without exception to every pursuit and affection. She used it as a painter ventures on a
daring color, or a musician a new string in his instrument.
She felt that she aggrandized botany, or history, or friendship, or love, or what you will, by making it a stepping-stone
to heaven ; and she made as little mystery of it as she
did of breathing and sleep, and talked of subjects which the
serious usually enter upon with a suppressed breath, as she

would comment upon a poem or define a new philosophy. It was surprising what an impressiveness this threw over her in every thing; how elevated she seemed above the best of those about her; and with what a worshipping and half-reverent admiration she inspired all whom she did not utterly neglect or despise. For myself, my soul was drank up in hers as the lark is taken into the sky, and I forgot there was a world beneath me in my intoxication. I thought her an angel unrecognized on earth. I believed her as pure from worldliness, and as spotless from sin, as a cherub with his breast upon his lute; and I knelt by her when she prayed, and held her upon my bosom in her fits of faintness and exhaustion, and sat at her feet with my face in her hands listening to her wild speculations (often till the morning brightened behind the curtains), with an utter and irresistible abandonment of my existence to hers, which seems to me *now* like are collection of another life, — it were, with this conscious body and mind, a self-relinquishment so impossible!

Our life was a singular one. Living in the midst of a numerous household, with kind and cultivated people about us, we were as separated from them as if the ring of Gyges encircled us from their sight. Fred wished me joy of my *giraffe*, as he offensively called his cousin; and his sisters, who were quite too pretty to have been left out of my story so long, were more indulgent, I thought, to the indigenous beaux of Skaneateles than those aboriginal specimens had a right to expect; but I had no eyes, ears, sense, or civility for any thing but Edith. The library became a forbidden spot to all feet but ours; we met at noon after our late vigils, and breakfasted together; a light sleigh was set apart for our *tête-à-tête* drives over the frozen lake; and the world seemed to me to revolve on its axle with a special reference to Philip Slingsby's happiness. I wonder whether an angel out of heaven would have made me believe that I should

ever write the story of those passionate hours with a smile
and a sneer! I tell thee, Edith (for thou wilt read every
line that I have written, and feel it as far as thou *canst* feel
any thing), that I have read "Faust" since, and thought
thee Mephistopheles! I have looked on thee since, with thy
cheek rosy dark, thy lip filled with the blood of health, and
curled with thy contempt of the world and thy yet wild ambition to be its master-spirit and idol; and struck my breast
with instinctive self-questioning if thou hadst given back my
soul that was thine own! I fear thee, Edith. Thou hast
grown beautiful that wert so hideous, — the wonder-wrought
miracle of health and intellect, filling thy veins, and breathing almost a newer shape over form and feature; but it is
not thy beauty, no, nor thy enthronement in the admiration
of thy woman's world. These are little to me; for I saw
thy loveliness from the first, and I worshipped thee more in
the duration of a thought than a hecatomb of these world-
lings in their lifetime. I fear thy mysterious and unaccountable power over the human soul! I can scorn thee here, in
another land, with an ocean weltering between us, and anato-
mize the character that I alone have read truly and too well,
for the instruction of the world (its amusement, too, proud
woman! thou wilt writhe at that); but I confess to a
natural and irresistible obedience to the mastery of thy spirit
over mine. I would not willingly again touch the radius of
thy sphere. I would come out of paradise to walk alone
with the Devil as soon.

How little even the most instructed women know the secret
of this power! They make the mistake of cultivating only
their own minds. They think that by *self*-elevation they will
climb up to the intellects of men, and win them by seeming
their equals. Shallow philosophers! You never remember,
that, to subdue a human being to your will, it is more necessary to know *his* mind than your own; that, in conquering

a heart, vanity is the first outpost; that, while you are employing your wits in thinking how most effectually to dazzle *him*, you should be sounding his character for its undeveloped powers to assist him to dazzle *you;* that love is a reflected light, and to be pleased with others we must be first pleased with ourselves.

Edith (it has occurred to me in my speculations since) seemed to me always an echo of myself. She expressed my thought as it sprang into my brain. I thought that in her I had met my double and counterpart, with the reservation that I was a little the stronger spirit, and that in *my* mind lay the material of the eloquence that flowed from her lips — as the almond that you endeavor to split equally leaves the kernel in the deeper cavity of its shell. Whatever the topic, she seemed using *my* thoughts, anticipating *my* reflections, and, with an unobtrusive but thrilling flattery, referring me to myself for the truth of what I must know was but a suggestion of my own. O Lucrezia Borgia! if Machiavelli had but practised that subtle cunning upon thee, thou wouldst have had little space in thy delirious heart for the passion that, in the history of crime, has made thee the marvel and the monster.

The charm of Edith to most people was that she was no *sublimation*. Her mind seemed of any or no stature. She was as natural, and earnest, and as satisfied to converse, on the meanest subject as on the highest. She overpowered nobody. She (apparently) eclipsed nobody. Her passionate and powerful eloquence was only lavished on the passionate and powerful. She *never misapplied herself;* and what a secret of influence and superiority is contained in that single phrase! We so hate him who out-measures us, as we stand side by side before the world!

I have in my portfolio several numbers of a manuscript "Gazette," with which the Flemings amused themselves during the deep snows of the winter in which I visited them. It was contributed to by everybody in the house, and read aloud at the breakfast-table on the day of its weekly appearance ; and, quite *apropos* to these remarks upon the universality of Edith's mind, there is in one of them an essay of hers on what she calls *minute philosophies*. It is curious as showing how, with all her loftiness of speculation, she descended sometimes to the examination of the smallest machinery of enjoyment.

"The principal sources of every-day happiness" (I am copying out a part of the essay, dear reader) "are too obvious to need a place in a chapter of breakfast-table philosophy. Occupation and a clear conscience, the very truant in the fields will tell you, are craving necessities. But when these are secured, there are lighter matters, which, to the sensitive and educated at least, are to happiness what foliage is to the tree. They are refinements which add to the beauty of life without diminishing its strength ; and, as they spring only from a better use of our common gifts, they are neither costly nor rare. I have learned secrets under the roof of a poor man, which would add to the luxury of the rich. The blessings of a cheerful fancy and a quick eye come from nature, and the trailing of a vine may develop them as well as the curtaining of a king's chamber.

"Riding and driving are such stimulating pleasures, that to talk of any management in their indulgence seems superfluous. Yet we are, in motion or at rest, equally liable to the caprices of feeling ; and perhaps, the gayer the mood, the deeper the shade cast on it by untoward circumstances. The time of riding should never be regular. It then becomes a habit ; and habits, though sometimes comfortable, never amount to positive pleasure. I would ride when nature prompted, — when the shower was past, or the air balmy, or the sky beautiful ; whenever and wherever the significant finger of desire pointed. Oh! to leap into the saddle when the west wind blows freshly, and gallop off into its very eye, with an undrawn rein, careless how far or whither; or, to spring up from a book when the sun breaks through after a storm, and drive away under the white clouds, through light and shadow, while the trees are wet and the earth damp and spicy; or, in the clear sunny afternoons of autumn, with a pleasant companion on the seat beside you, and the glorious splendor of the decaying foliage flushing in the sunshine, to loiter up the valley dreaming over the thousand airy castles that are stirred by such shifting beauty, — these are pleasures indeed, and such as he who rides regularly after his dinner knows as little of as the dray-horse of the exultation of the courser.

" There is a great deal in the choice of a companion. If he is an indifferent acquaintance, or an indiscriminate talker, or has a coarse eye for beauty, or is insensible to the delicacies of sensation or thought, — if he is sensual, or stupid, or practical constitutionally, — he will never do. He must be a man who can detect a rare color in a leaf, or appreciate a peculiar passage in scenery, or admire a grand outline in a cloud; he must have accurate and fine senses, and a heart noble at least by nature, and subject still to her direct influences; he must be a lover of the beautiful, in whatever shape it comes; and, above all, he must have read and thought like a scholar, if not like a poet. He will then ride by your side without crossing your humor: if talkative, he will talk well; and if silent, you are content, for you know that the same grandeur or beauty which has wrought the silence in your own thoughts has given a color to his.

" There is much in the manner of driving. I like a capricious rein, — now fast through a hollow, and now loiteringly on the edge of a road or by the bank of a river. There is a singular delight in quickening your speed in the animation of a climax, and in coming down gently to a walk with a disgression of feeling or a sudden sadness.

" An important item in household matters is the management of light. A small room well lighted is much more imposing than a large one lighted ill. Cross-lights are painful to the eye, and they destroy besides the cool and picturesque shadows of the furniture and figures. I would have a room always partially darkened : there is a repose in the twilight dimness of a drawing-room which affects one with the proper gentleness of the place ; the out-of-door humor of men is too rude, and the secluded light subdues them fitly as they enter. I like curtains, heavy and of the richest material. There is a magnificence in large crimson folds which nothing else equals ; and the color gives every thing a beautiful tint as the light streams through them. Plants tastefully arranged are pretty ; flowers are always beautiful. I would have my own room like a painter's,— one curtain partly drawn : a double shadow has a nervous look. The effect of a proper disposal of light upon the feelings is, by most people, surprisingly neglected. I have no doubt, that, as an habitual thing, it materially affects the character : the disposition for study and thought is certainly dependent on it in no slight degree. What is more contemplative than the twilight of a deep alcove in a library? What more awakens thought than the dim interior of an old church, with its massive and shadowy pillars?

" There may be the most exquisite luxury in furniture. A crowded room has a look of comfort, and suspended lamps throw a mellow depth into the features. Descending light is always the most becoming : it deepens the eye, and distributes the shadows in the face judiciously. Chairs should be of different and curious fashions, made to humor every possible weariness. A spice-lamp should burn in the corner ; and the pictures should be colored of a pleasant tone, and the subjects should be subdued and dreamy. It should be a place you would live in for a century without an uncomfortable thought. I hate a neat room. A dozen of the finest old authors should lie about, and a new novel, and the last new prints. I rather like the French fashion of a *bonbonnière*, though that, perhaps, is an extravagance.

"There is a management of one's own familiar intercourse which is more neglected, and at the same time more important to happiness, than every other. It is particularly a pity that this is not oftener understood by newly married people. As far as my own observation goes, I have rarely failed to detect, far too early, signs of ill-disguised and disappointed weariness. It was not the re-action of excitement, not the return to the quiet ways of home, but a new manner, — a forgetful indifference, believing itself concealed, and yet betraying itself continually by unconscious and irrepressible symptoms. I believe it resulted oftenest from the same causes : partly that they saw each other too much, and partly that when the *form* of etiquette was removed, they forgot to retain its invaluable *essence*, — an assiduous and minute disinterestedness. It seems nonsense to lovers, but absence is the secret of respect, and, therefore, of affection. Love is divine, but its flame is too delicate for a perpetual household lamp : it should be burned only for incense, and even then trimmed skilfully. It is wonderful how a slight neglect, or a glimpse of a weakness, or a chance defect of knowledge, dims its new glory. Lovers, married or single, should have separate pursuits ; they should meet to respect each other for new and distinct acquisitions. It is the weakness of human affections, that they are founded on pride, and waste with over-much familiarity. And oh the delight to meet after hours of absence, — to sit down by the evening lamp, and, with a mind unexhausted by the intercourse of the day, to yield to the fascinating freedom of conversation, and

clothe the rising thoughts of affection in fresh and unhack-
neyed language! How richly the treasures of the mind are
colored, — not doled out counter by counter, as the visible
machinery of thought coins them, but heaped upon the mutual
altar in lavish and unhesitating profusion! And how a bold
fancy assumes beauty and power, — not traced up through
all its petty springs till its dignity is lost by association, but
flashing full-grown and suddenly on the sense. The gifts of
no one mind are equal to the constant draught of a lifetime ;
and, even if they were, there is no one taste which could
always relish them. It is a humiliating thought, that immortal mind must be husbanded like material treasure.

"There is a remark of Godwin, which, in rather too strong
language, contains a valuable truth : ' A judicious and limited
voluptuousness,' he says, ' is necessary to the cultivation of
the mind, to the polishing of the manners, to the refinement
of the sentiment, and to the development of the understand-
ing ; and a woman deficient in this respect may be of use in
the government of our families, but cannot add to the enjoyment, nor fix the partiality, of a man of taste.' Since the
days when ' St. Leon ' was written, the word by which the
author expressed his meaning is grown perhaps into dis-
repute ; but the remark is still one of keen and observant
discrimination. It refers (at least, so I take it) to that susceptibility to delicate attentions, that fine sense of the name-
less and exquisite tenderness of manner and thought, which
constitutes in the minds of its possessors the deepest under-
current of life, — the felt and treasured, but unseen and
inexpressible richness of affection. It is rarely found in the
characters of men : but it outweighs, when it is, all grosser
qualities ; for its possession implies a generous nature, purity, fine affections, and a heart open to all the sunshine and
meaning of the universe. It belongs more to the nature of
woman ; but, indispensable as it is to her character, it is

oftener than any thing else wanting. And without it, what is she? What is love to a being of such dull sense that she hears only its common and audible language, and sees nothing but what it brings to her feet to be eaten and worn and looked upon? What is woman, if the impassioned language of the eye, or the deepened fulness of the tone, or the tenderness of a slight attention, are things unnoticed and of no value? — one who answers you when you speak, smiles when you tell her she is grave, assents barely to the expression of your enthusiasm, but has no dream beyond, no suspicion that she has not felt and reciprocated your feelings as fully as you could expect or desire. It is a matter too little looked to. Sensitive and ardent men too often marry with a blindfold admiration of mere goodness or loveliness. The *abandon* of matrimony soon dissipates the gay dream ; and they find themselves suddenly unsphered, linked indissolubly with affections strangely different from their own, and lavishing their only treasure on those who can neither appreciate nor return it. The after-life of such men is a stifling solitude of feeling. Their avenues of enjoyment are their maniform sympathies ; and when these are shut up or neglected, the heart is dark, and they have nothing to do thenceforward but to forget.

" There are many, who, possessed of the capacity for the more elevated affections, waste and lose it by a careless and often unconscious neglect. It is not a plant to grow untended. The breath of indifference, or a rude touch, may destroy forever its delicate texture. To drop the figure, there is a daily attention to the slight courtesies of life, and an artifice in detecting the passing shadows of feeling, which alone can preserve, through life, the first freshness of passion. The easy surprises of pleasure, and earnest cheerfulness of assent to slight wishes, the habitual respect to opinions, the polite abstinence from personal topics in the

company of others, the assiduous and unwavering attention to
her comfort at home and abroad, and, above all, the absolute
preservation in private of those proprieties of conversation
and manner which are sacred before the world, are some of
the thousand secrets of that rare happiness which age and
habit alike fail to impair or diminish.''

II.

Vacation was over, but Fred and myself were still lingering at Fleming Farm. The roads were impassable with a
premature THAW. Perhaps there is nothing so peculiar in
American meteorology as the phenomenon which I alone
probably, of all the imprisoned inhabitants of Skaneateles,
attributed to a kind and ``special Providence.'' Summer
had come back, like Napoleon from Elba, and astonished
usurping Winter in the plenitude of apparent possession and
security. No cloud foreboded the change, as no alarm preceded the apparition of `` the child of destiny.'' We awoke
on a February morning, with the snow lying chin-deep on the
earth, and it was June! The air was soft and warm ; the
sky was clear, and of the milky cerulean of chrysoprase ;
the south wind (the same, save his unperfumed wings, who
had crept off like a satiated lover in October) stole back suddenly from the tropics, and found his flowery mistress asleep
and insensible to his kisses beneath her snowy mantle. The
sunset warmed back from its wintry purple to the golden
tints of heat ; the stars burned with a less vitreous sparkle ;
the meteors slid once more lambently down the sky ; and the
house-dove sat on the eaves, washing her breast in the snow-
water, and thinking (like a neglected wife at a capricious
return of her truant's tenderness) that the sunshine would
last forever.

The air was now full of music. The water trickled away
under the snow ; and as you looked around, and saw no

change or motion in the white carpet of the earth, it seemed as if a myriad of small bells were ringing under ground, — fairies, perhaps, startled in mid-revel with the false alarm of summer, and hurrying about with their silver anklets to wake up the slumbering flowers. The mountain-torrents were loosed, and rushed down upon the valleys like the children of the mist; and the hoarse war-cry, swelling and falling upon the wind, maintained its perpetual undertone like an accompaniment of bassoons; and occasionally, in a sudden lull of the breeze, you would hear the click of the under-mined snow-drifts dropping upon the earth, as if the chorister of spring were beating time to the reviving anthem of nature.

The snow sunk perhaps a foot in a day; but it was only perceptible to the eye where you could measure its wet mark against a tree from which it had fallen away, or by the rock, from which the dissolving bank shrunk and separated, as if rocks and snow were as heartless as ourselves, and threw off *their* friends, too, in their extremity! The low-lying lake, meantime, surrounded by melting mountains, received the abandoned waters upon its frozen bosom, and, spreading them into a placid and shallow lagoon, separate by a crystal plane from its own lower depths, gave them the repose denied in the more elevated sphere in which lay their birthright. And thus (oh, how full is nature of these gentle moralities!), — and thus sometimes do the lowly, whose bosom, like the frozen lake, is at first cold and unsympathetic to the rich and noble, still receive them in adversity; and when neigh-borhood and dependance have convinced them that they are made of the same common element, as the lake melts its dividing and icy plane, and mingles the strange waters with its own, do *they* dissolve the unnatural barrier of prejudice, and take the humbled wanderer to their bosom!

The face of the snow lost its dazzling whiteness as the thaw went on — as disease steals away the beauty of those we love,

— but it was only in the distance, where the sun threw a shadow into the irregular pits of the dissolving surface. Near to the eye (as the dying one pressed to the bosom), it was still of its original beauty, unchanged and spotless. And now you are tired of my loitering speculations, gentle reader, and we will return (please Heaven, only on paper!) to Edith Linsey.

The roads were at last reduced to what is expressively called, in New England, *slosh* (in New York, *posh*, but equally descriptive) ; and Fred received a hint from the judge that the mail had arrived in the usual time, and his *beaux jours* were at an end.

A slighter thing than my departure would have been sufficient to stagger the tottering spirits of Edith. We were sitting at table when the letters came in, and the dates were announced that proved the opening of the roads ; and I scarce dared to turn my eyes upon the pale face that I could just see had dropped upon her bosom. The next instant there was a general confusion, and she was carried lifeless to her chamber.

A note, scarce legible, was put into my hand in the course of the evening, requesting me to sit up for her in the library. She would come to me, she said, if she had strength.

It was a night of extraordinary beauty. The full moon was high in the heavens at midnight ; and there had been a slight shower soon after sunset, which, with the clearing-up wind, had frozen thinly into a most fragile rime, and glazed every thing open to the sky with transparent crystal. The distant forest looked serried with metallic trees, dazzlingly and unspeakably gorgeous ; and as the night-wind stirred through them, and shook their crystal points in the moonlight, the aggregated stars of heaven springing from their Maker's hand to the spheres of their destiny, or the march of the host of the Archangel Michael with their irradiate spear-points

glittering in the air, or the diamond beds of central earth
thrust up to the sun in some throe of the universe, would
each or all have been well bodied forth by such similitude.

It was an hour after midnight when Edith was supported
in by her maid, and, choosing her own position, sunk into
the broad window-seat, and lay with her head on my bosom,
and her face turned outward to the glittering night. Her
eyes had become, I thought, unnaturally bright; and she
spoke with an exhausted faintness that gradually strengthened to a tone of the most thrilling and melodious sweetness.
I shall never get that music out of my brain!

" Philip," she said.

" I listen, dear Edith."

" I am dying."

And she looked it, and I believed her; and my heart sunk
to its deepest abyss of wretchedness with the conviction.

She went on to talk of death. It was the subject that
pressed most upon her mind, and she could scarce fail to be
eloquent on any subject. She was very eloquent on this.
I was so impressed with the manner in which she seemed
almost to rhapsodize between the periods of her faintness, as
she lay in my arms that night, that every word she uttered
is still fresh in my memory. She seemed to forget my presence, and to commune with her own thoughts aloud.

" I recollect," she said, " when I was strong and well
(years ago, dear Philip), I left my books on a morning
in May, and, looking up to find the course of the wind,
started off alone for a walk into its very eye. A moist,
steady breeze came from the south-west, driving before it
fragments of the dispersed clouds. The air was elastic and
clear; a freshness that entered freely at every pore was
coming up, mingled with the profuse perfume of grass and
flowers; the colors of the new, tender foliage were particularly soothing to an eye pained with close attention; and

the just perceptible murmur of the drops shaken from the trees, and the peculiarly soft rustle of the wet leaves, made as much music as an ear accustomed to the silence of solitude could well relish. Altogether, it was one of those rarely tempered days when every sense is satisfied, and the mind is content to lie still with its common thoughts, and simply enjoy.

" I had proceeded perhaps a mile, — my forehead held up to the wind, my hair blowing back, and the blood glowing in my cheeks with the most vivid flush of exercise and health, — when I saw coming toward me a man apparently in middle life, but wasted by illness to the extremest emaciation. His lip was colorless, his skin dry and white, and his sunken eyes had that expression of inquiring earnestness which comes always with impatient sickness. He raised his head, and looked steadily at me as I came on. My lips were open, and my whole air must have been that of a person in the most exulting enjoyment of health. I was just against him, gliding past with an elastic step, when, with his eye still fixed on me, he half turned, and in a voice of inexpressible meaning exclaimed, ' Merciful Heaven! *how well she is!*' I passed on, with his voice still ringing in my ear. It haunted me like a tone in the air. It was repeated in the echo of my tread, in the panting of my heart. I felt it in the beating of the strong pulse in my temples. As if it was strange that I should be so well! I had never before realized that it could be otherwise. It seemed impossible to me that my strong limbs should fail me, or the pure blood I felt bounding so bravely through my veins could be reached and tainted by disease. How should it come? If I ate, would it not nourish me? If I slept, would it not refresh me? If I came out in the cool free air, would not my lungs heave, and my muscles spring, and my face feel its grateful freshness? I held out my arm, for the first time in my life, with a doubt of its strength. I closed my hand unconsciously, with a fear it would not obey. I drew a deep breath, to feel if it was difficult to breathe ; and even my bounding step, that was as elastic then as a fawn's, seemed to my excited imagination already to have become decrepit and feeble.

" I walked on, and thought of death. I had never before done so definitely : it was like a terrible shape that had always pursued me dimly, but which I had never before turned and looked steadily on. Strange ! that we can live so constantly with that threatening hand hung over us, and not think of it always ! Strange ! that we can use a limb, or enter with interest into any pursuit of time, when we know that our continued life is almost a daily miracle !

" How difficult it is to realize death ! How difficult it is to believe that the hand with whose every vein you are familiar will ever lose its motion and its warmth ; that the quick eye, which is so restless now, will settle and grow dull ; that the refined lip, which now shrinks so sensitively from defilement, will not feel the earth lying upon it, and the tooth of the feeding worm ; that the free breath will be choked, and the forehead be pressed heavily on by the decaying coffin, and the light and air of heaven be shut quite out ; and this very body, warm and breathing and active as it is now, will not feel uneasiness or pain ! I could not help looking at my frame as these thoughts crowded on me ; and I confess I almost doubted my own convictions, there was so much strength and quickness in it, my hand opened so freely, and my nostrils expanded with such a satisfied thirst to the moist air. Ah ! it is hard to believe at first that we must die ; harder still to believe and realize the repulsive circumstances that follow that terrible change. It is a bitter thought, at the lightest. There is little comfort in knowing that the *soul* will not be there, — that the sense and the mind that feel and measure suffering will be gone. The separation is too great a mystery to satisfy fear. It is the body that we *know*. It is this material frame in which the affections have grown up. The spirit is a mere thought, — a presence that we are told of, but do not see. Philosophize as we will, the idea of existence is connected indissolubly with the visible body, and its pleasant and familiar senses. We talk of, and believe, the soul's ascent to its Maker; but it is not ourselves, it is not our own conscious breathing identity, that we send up in imagination through the invisible air. It is some phantom that is to issue forth mysteriously, and leave us gazing on it in wonder. We do not understand, · we cannot realize it.

"At the time I speak of, my health had been always unbroken. Since then I have known disease in many forms, and have had, of course, more time and occasion for the contemplation of death. I have never, till late, known resignation. With my utmost energy I was merely able, in other days, to look upon it with quiet despair, as a terrible, unavoidable evil. I remember once, after severe suffering for weeks, I overheard the physician telling my mother that I must die; and from that moment the thought never left me. A thin line of light came in between the shutters of the south window; and with this one thought fastened on my mind, like the vulture of Prometheus, I lay and watched it, day after day, as it passed with its imperceptible progress over the folds of my curtains. The last faint gleam of sunset never faded from its damask edge, without an inexpressible sinking of my heart, and a belief that I should see its pleasant light no more. I turned from the window when even imagination could find the daylight no longer there, and felt my pulse, and lifted my head, to try my remaining strength. And then every object, yes, even the meanest, grew unutterably dear to me; my pillow, and the cup with which my lips were moistened, and the cooling amber which

I had held in my hand and pressed to my burning lips when
the fever was on me, — every thing that was connected with
life, and that would remain among the living when I was
gone.

"It is strange, but with all this clinging to the world my
affection for the living decreased sensibly. I grew selfish in
my weakness. I could not bear that they should go from
my chamber into the fresh air, and have no fear of sickness
and no pain. It seemed unfeeling that they did not stay and
breathe the close atmosphere of my room, — at least, till I
was dead. How could they walk round so carelessly, and
look on a fellow-creature dying helplessly and unwillingly,
and never shed a tear! And then the passing courtesies
exchanged with the family at the door, and the quickened
step on the sidewalk, and the wandering looks about my
room, even while I was answering with my difficult breath
their cold inquiries! There was an inhuman carelessness in
all this that stung me to the soul.

"I craved sympathy as I did life, and yet I doubted it
all. There was not a word spoken by the friends who were
admitted to see me, that I did not ponder over when they
were gone, and always with an impatient dissatisfaction.
The tone, and the manner, and the expression of face, all
seemed forced; and often, in my earlier sickness, when I
had pondered for hours on the expressed sympathy of some
one I had loved, the sense of utter helplessness which
crowded on me with my conviction of their insincerity quite
overcame me. I have lain night after night, and looked at
my indifferent watchers; and oh, how I hated them for their
careless ease, and their snatched moments of repose! I
could scarce keep from dashing aside the cup they came to
give me so sluggishly.

"It is singular, that, with all our experience of sickness,
we do not attend more to these slight circumstances. It can

scarce be conceived how an ill-managed light, or a suppressed whispering, or a careless change of attitude, in the presence of one whose senses are so sharpened and whose mind is so sensitive as a sick person's, irritate and annoy. And, perhaps, more than these to bear, is the affectedly subdued tone of condolence. I remember nothing which I endured so impatiently.

"Annoyances like these, however, scarcely diverted for a moment the one great thought of death. It became at last familiar, but, if possible, more dreadfully horrible from that very fact. It was giving it a new character. I realized it more. The minute circumstances became nearer and more real. I tried the position in which I should lie in my coffin; I lay with my arms to my side, and my feet together, and, with the cold sweat standing in large drops on my lip, composed my features into a forced expression of tranquillity.

"I awoke on the second morning after the hope of my recovery had been abandoned. There was a narrow sunbeam lying in a clear crimson line across the curtain; and I lay and watched the specks of lint sailing through it, like silver-winged insects, and the thin dust quivering and disappearing on its definite limit, in a dream of wonder. I had thought not to see another sun, and my mind was still fresh with the expectation of an immediate change; I could not believe that I was alive. The dizzy throb in my temples was done; my limbs felt cool and refreshed; my mind had that feeling of transparency which is common after healthful and sweet sleep; and an indefinite sensation of pleasure trembled in every nerve. I thought that this might be death, and that, with this exquisite feeling of repose, I was to linger thus consciously with the body till the last day; and I dwelt on it pleasantly with my delicious freedom from pain. I felt no regret for life, none for a friend even: I was willing, quite willing, to lie thus for ages. Presently the physi-

cian entered; he came and laid his fingers on my pulse, and
his face brightened. 'You will get well,' he said, and I
heard it almost without emotion. Gradually, however, the
love of life returned; and as I realized it fully, and all the
thousand chords which bound me to it vibrated once more,
the tears came thickly to my eyes, and a crowd of delightful
thoughts pressed cheerfully and glowingly on me. No language can do justice to the pleasure of convalescence from
extreme sickness. The first step upon the living grass, the
first breath of free air, the first unsuppressed salutation of a
friend, — my fainting heart, dear Philip, rallies and quickens
even now with the recollection.''

I have thrown into a continuous strain what was murmured
to me between pauses of faintness, and with difficulty of
breath that seemed overpowered only by the mastery of the
eloquent spirit apparently trembling on its departure. I
believed Edith Linsey would die that night; I believed myself listening to words spoken almost from heaven; and if
I have wearied you, dear reader, with what must be more
interesting to me than to you, it is because every syllable
was burnt like enamel into my soul, in my boundless rever-
ence and love.

It was two o'clock, and she still lay breathing painfully in
my arms. I had thrown up the window, and the soft south
wind, stirring gently among the tinkling icicles of the trees,
came in, warm and genial; and she leaned over to inhale it,
as if it came from the source of life. The stars burned
gloriously in the heavens; and, in a respite of her pain, she
lay back her head, and gazed up at them with an inarticulate
motion of her lips, and eyes so unnaturally kindled, that I
thought reason had abandoned her.

"How beautiful are the stars to-night, Edith!" I said,
with half a fear that she would answer me in madness.

"Yes," she said, putting my hand (that pressed her

closer, involuntarily, to my bosom) first to her lips, — " yes ;
and, beautiful as they are, they are all accurately numbered
and governed ; and just as they burn now have they burned
since the creation, never ' faint in their watches,' and never
absent from their place. How glorious they are ! How
thrilling it is to see them stand with such a constant silence
in the sky, unsteadied and unsupported, obeying the great
law of their Maker ! What pure and silvery light it is !
How steadily it pours from those small fountains, giving every
spot of earth its due portion ! The hovel and the palace are
shone upon equally, and the shepherd gets as broad a beam
as the king ; and these few rays that are now streaming into
my feverish eyes were meant and lavished only for me ! I
have often thought — has it never occurred to you, dear
Philip ? — how ungrateful we are to call ourselves poor, when
there is so much that no poverty can take away ! Clusters
of silver rays from every star in these heavens are *mine*.
Every breeze that breaks on my forehead was sent for *my*
refreshment. Every tinkle and ray from those stirring and
glistening icicles, and the invigorating freshness of this un-
seasonable and delicious wind, and moonlight, and sunshine,
and the glory of the planets, are all gifts that poverty could
not take away. It is not often that I forget these treasures ;
for I have loved nature, and the skies of night and day, in
all their changes, from my childhood, and they have been
unspeakably dear to me ; for in them I see the evidence of
an almighty Maker, and in the excessive beauty of the stars
and the unfading and equal splendor of their steadfast fires,
I see glimpses of an immortal life, and find an answer to the
eternal questioning within me.

" Three ! The village clock reaches us to-night. Nay,
the wind cannot harm me now. Turn me more to the window, for I would look nearer upon the stars : it is the last
time, — I am sure of it, — the very last ! Yet to-morrow

night those stars will all be there ; not one missing from the
sky, nor shining one ray the less because I am dead! It is
strange that this thought should be so bitter ; strange that
the companionship should be so close between our earthly
affections and those spiritual worlds ; and stranger yet, that,
satisfied as we must be that we shall know them nearer and
better when released from our flesh, we still cling so fondly
to our earthly and imperfect vision. I feel, Philip, that
I shall traverse hereafter every star in those bright heavens.
If the course of that career of knowledge, which I believe
in my soul it will be the reward of the blessed to run, be
determined in any degree by the strong desires that yearn so
sickeningly within us, I see the thousand gates of my future
heaven shining at this instant above me. There they are!
the clustering Pleiades, with ' their sweet influences ; ' and
the morning star, melting into the east with its transcendent
lambency and whiteness ; and the broad galaxy, with its
myriads of bright spheres, dissolving into each other's light
and belting the heavens like a girdle. I shall see them all!
I shall know them and their inhabitants as the angels of God
know them ; the mystery of their order, and the secret of
their wonderful harmony, and the duration of their appointed
courses, — all will be made clear! "

I have trespassed again, most indulgent reader, on the
limits of these Procrustean papers. I must defer the
" change " that " came o'er the spirit of my dream " till
another mood and time. Meanwhile, you may consider
Edith, if you like, the true heart she thought herself (and
I thought her) during her nine deaths in the library ; and
you will have leisure to imagine the three years over which
we shall skip with this *finale*, during which I made a journey
to the North, and danced out a winter in your own territories
at Quebec, — a circumstance I allude to, no less to record the

hospitalities of the garrison at that time (this was in '27 — were you there?) than to pluck forth from Time's hindermost wallet a modest copy of verses I addressed thence to Edith. She sent them back to me considerably mended; but I give you the original draught, scorning her finger in my poesies.

TO EDITH, FROM THE NORTH.

As, gazing on the Pleiades,
  We count each fair and starry one,
Yet wander from the light of these
  To muse upon the "Pleiad gone;"
As, bending o'er fresh-gathered flowers,
  The rose's most enchanting hue
Reminds us but of other hours,
  Whose roses were all lovely too, —
So, dearest, when I rove among
  The bright ones of this Northern sky,
And mark the smile, and list the song,
  And watch the dancers gliding by, —
The fairer still they seem to be,
The more it stirs a thought of thee.

The sad, sweet bells of twilight chime,
  Of many hearts may touch but one,
And so this seeming careless rhyme
  Will whisper to thy heart alone.
I give it to the winds. The bird,
  Let loose, to his far nest will flee;
And love, though breathed but on a word,
  Will find thee over land and sea.
Though clouds across the sky have driven,
  We trust the star at last will shine;
And like the very light of heaven,
  I trust thy love — *trust thou in mine!*

TRENTON FALLS.

TEN or fifteen years ago, the existence of Trenton Falls was not known. It was discovered, like Pæstum, by a wandering artist, when there was a town of ten thousand inhabitants, a canal, a theatre, a liberty-pole, and forty churches, within fourteen miles of it. It may be mentioned to the credit of the Americans, that, in the " hardness " of character of which travellers complain, there is the soft trait of a passion for scenery; and before the fact of its discovery had got well into the " Cahawba Democrat " and " Go-the-whole-hog Courier," there was a splendid wooden hotel on the edge of the precipice, with a French cook, soda-water, and olives, and a law was passed by the Kentucky Travellers' Club, requiring a hanging-bird's nest from the trees " frowning down the awful abysm " (so expressed in the regulation) as a qualification for membership. Thenceforward to the present time it has been a place of fashionable resort during the summer solstice; and, the pine woods in which the hotel stands being impervious to the sun, it is prescribed by oculists for gentlemen and ladies with weak eyes. If the luxury of corn-cutters had penetrated to the United States, it might be prescribed for tender feet as well; the soft floor of pine-tassels spread under the grassless woods being considered an improvement upon Turkey carpets and greensward.

Trenton Falls is rather a misnomer. I scarcely know what you would call it; but the wonder of nature which bears

*** *From "Edith Linsey."*

the name is a tremendous torrent, whose bed, for several miles, is sunk fathoms deep into the earth, — a roaring and dashing stream, so far below the surface of the forest in which it is lost, that you would think, as you come suddenly upon the edge of its long precipice, that it was a river in some inner world (coiled within ours, as we in the outer circle of the firmament), and laid open by some Titanic throe that had cracked clear asunder the crust of this " shallow earth." The idea is rather assisted if you happen to see below you, on its abysmal shore, a party of adventurous travellers ; for at that vast depth, and in contrast with the gigantic trees and rocks, the same number of well-shaped pismires, dressed in the last fashions, and philandering upon your parlor floor, would be about of their apparent size and distinctness.

They showed me at Eleusis the well by which Proserpine ascends to the regions of day on her annual visit to the plains of Thessaly ; but with the *genius loci* at my elbow in the shape of a Greek girl as lovely as Phryné, my memory reverted to the bared axle of the earth in the bed of this American river, and I was persuaded (looking the while at the *feronière* of gold sequins on the Phidian forehead of my Katinka), that, supposing Hades in the centre of the earth, you are nearer to it by some fathoms at Trenton. I confess I have had, since my first descent into those depths, an uncomfortable doubt of the solidity of the globe — how the deuce it can hold together with such a crack in its bottom !

It was a night to play Endymion, or do any tomfoolery that could be laid to the charge of the moon ; for a more omnipresent and radiant atmosphere of moonlight never sprinkled the wilderness with silver. It was a night in which to wish it might never be day again ; a night to be enamoured of the stars, and bid God bless them, like human creatures, on their bright journey ; a night to love in, to dis-

solve in, to do every thing but what night is made for, —
sleep. Oh, heaven! when I think how precious is life in such
moments, how the aroma, the celestial bloom and flower of
the soul, the yearning and fast-perishing enthusiasm of youth,
waste themselves in the solitude of such nights on the senseless and unanswering air; when I wander alone, unloving
and unloved, beneath influences that could inspire me with
the elevation of a seraph, were I at the ear of a human
creature that could summon forth and measure my limitless
capacity of devotion, — when I think this and feel this, and
so waste my existence in vain yearnings, I could extinguish
the divine spark within me, like a lamp on an unvisited
shrine, and thank Heaven for an assimilation to the animals
I walk among. And that is the substance of a speech I
made to Job as a *sequitur* of a well-meant remark of his own,
that " it was a pity Edith Linsey was not there." He took
the clause about the " animals " to himself, and I made an
apology for the same a year after. We sometimes give our
friends, quite innocently, such terrible knocks in our rhap-
sodies!

Most people talk of the *sublimity* of Trenton, but I have
haunted it by the week together for its mere loveliness. The
river, in the heart of that fearful chasm, is the most varied
and beautiful assemblage of the thousand forms and shapes
of running water that I know in the world. The soil and
the deep-striking roots of the forest terminate far above you,
looking like a black rim on the enclosing precipices; the bed
of the river and its sky-sustaining walls are of solid rock,
and, with the tremendous descent of the stream, forming for
miles one continuous succession of falls and rapids, the
channel is worn into curves and cavities, which throw the
clear waters into forms of inconceivable brilliancy and variety.
It is a sort of half-twilight below, with here and there a long
beam of sunshine reaching down to kiss the lip of an eddy,

or form a rainbow over a fall; and the reverberating and changing echoes, —

"Like a ring of bells whose sound the wind still alters," —

maintain a constant and most soothing music, varying at every step with the varying phase of the current. Cascades of from twenty to thirty feet, over which the river flies with a single and hurrying leap (not a drop missing from the glassy and bending sheet), occur frequently as you ascend; and it is from these that the place takes its name. But the falls, though beautiful, are only peculiar from the dazzling and unequalled rapidity with which the waters come to the leap. If it were not for the leaf which drops wavering down into the abysm from trees apparently painted on the sky, and which is caught away by the flashing current as if the lightning had suddenly crossed it, you would think the vault of the steadfast heavens a flying element as soon. The spot in that long gulf of beauty that I best remember is a smooth descent of some hundred yards, where the river, in full and undivided volume, skims over a plane as polished as a table of scagliola, looking, in its invisible speed, like one mirror of gleaming but motionless crystal. Just above there is a sudden turn in the glen, which sends the water, like a catapult, against the opposite angle of the rock; and in the action of years it has worn out a cavern of unknown depth, into which the whole mass of the river plunges with the abandonment of a flying fiend into hell, and, re-appearing like the angel that has pursued him, glides swiftly, but with divine serenity, on its way. (I am indebted for that last figure to Job, who travelled with a Milton in his pocket, and had a natural redolence of " Paradise Lost " in his conversation.)

Much as I detest water in small quantities (to drink), I have a hydromania in the way of lakes, rivers, and waterfalls. It is, by much, the belle in the family of the elements. *Earth* is never tolerable unless disguised in green; *Air* is so thin as only to be visible when she borrows drapery of water; and *Fire* is so staringly bright as to be unpleasant to the eyesight. But Water! soft, pure, graceful Water! there is no shape into which you can throw her that she does not seem lovelier than before. She can borrow nothing of her sisters. Earth has no jewels in her lap so brilliant as her own spray pearls and emeralds; Fire has no rubies like what she steals from the sunset; Air has no robes like the grace of her fine-woven and ever-changing drapery of silver. A health (in wine) to WATER!

Who is there that did not love some stream in his youth? Who is there in whose vision of the past there does not sparkle up, from every picture of childhood, a spring or a rivulet woven through the darkened and torn woof of first affections, like a thread of unchanged silver? How do you interpret the instinctive yearning with which you search for the river-side or the fountain in every scene of nature, — the clinging unaware to the river's course, when a truant in the fields in June; the dull void you find in every landscape of which it is not the ornament and the centre? For myself, I hold with the Greek: "Water is the first principle of all things: we were made from it, and we shall be resolved into it."[1]

---

[1] The Ionic philosophy, supported by Thales.

TOM FANE AND I.

" Common as light is love,
And its familiar voice wearies not ever."—SHELLEY.

TOM FANE'S four Canadian ponies were whizzing his
light phaeton through the sand at a rate that would
have put spirits into any thing but a lover absent from his
mistress. The " heaven-kissing " pines towered on every
side like the thousand and one columns of the Palæologi at
Constantinople; their flat and spreading tops shutting out
the light of heaven almost as effectually as the world of
Mussulmans, mosques, kiosks, bazaars, and Giaours, sustained on those innumerable capitals, darkens the subterranean
wonder of Stamboul. An American pine-forest is as like a
temple, and a sublime one, as any dream that ever entered
into the architectural brain of the slumbering Martin. The
Yankee Methodists, in their camp-meetings, have but followed an irresistible instinct to worship God in the religious
dimness of these interminable aisles of the wilderness.

Tom Fane and I had stoned the storks together in the
palace of Crœsus at Sardis. We had read Anastasius on a
mufti's tomb in the *Nekropolis* of Scutari. We had burned
with fig-fevers in the same caravansary at Smyrna. We had
cooled our hot foreheads, and cursed the Greeks in emulous
Romaic, in the dim tomb of Agamemnon at Argos. We had
been grave at Paris, and merry at Rome, and we had pic-
nicked with the beauties of the Fanar in the Valley of Sweet
Waters in pleasant Roumelia; and when, after parting in
France, he had returned to England and his regiment, and I

to New England and law, whom should I meet in a summer's
trip to the St. Lawrence but Capt. Tom Fane of the ——th,
quartered at the cliff-perched and doughty garrison of Quebec, and ready for any "lark" that would vary the monotony
of duty!

Having eaten seven mess-dinners, driven to the Falls of
Montmorenci, and paid my respects to Lord Dalhousie, the
hospitable and able governor of the Canadas, Quebec had no
longer a temptation; and obeying a magnet, of which more
anon, I announced to Fane that my traps were packed, and
my heart sent on, à l'avant-courier, to Saratoga.

"Is she pretty?" said Tom.

"As the starry-eyed Circassian we gazed at through the
grill in the slave-market at Constantinople!" (Heaven and my
mistress forgive me for the comparison! but it conveyed more
to Tom Fane than a folio of more respectful similitudes.)

"Have you any objection to be drawn to your lady-love by
four cattle that would buy the soul of Osbaldiston?"

"'Objection!' quotha?"

The next morning, four double-jointed and well-groomed
ponies were munching their corn in the bow of a steamer
upon the St. Lawrence, wondering, possibly, what in the
name of Bucephalus had set the hills and churches flying at
such a rate down the river. The hills and churches came to a
standstill with the steamer opposite Montreal; and the ponies
were landed, and put to their mettle for some twenty miles,
where they were destined to be astonished by a similar flying
phenomenon in the mountains girding the lengthening waters
of Lake Champlain. Landed at Ticonderoga, a few miles'
trot brought them to Lake George and a third steamer; and,
with a winding passage among green islands and overhanging
precipices loaded like a harvest-wagon with vegetation, we
made our last landing on the edge of the pine-forest, where
our story opens.

" Well, I must object," says Tom, setting his whip in the socket, and edging round upon his driving-box, — " I must object to this republican gravity of yours. I should take it for melancholy, did I not know it was the ' complexion ' of your never-smiling countrymen."

" Spare me, Tom ! ' I see a hand you cannot see.' Talk to your ponies, and let me be miserable, if you love me."

" For what, in the name of common-sense ? Are you not within five hours of your mistress ? Is not this cursed sand your natal soil ? Do not

> ' The pine-boughs sing
> Old songs with new gladness ' ?

and in the years that we have dangled about, ' here-and-there-ians ' together, were you ever before grave, sad, or sulky ? and will you without a precedent, and you a lawyer, inflict your stupidity upon me for the first time in this waste and being-less solitude ? Half an hour more of the dread silence of this forest, and it will not need the horn of Astolpho to set me irremediably mad ! "

" If employment will save your wits, you may invent a scheme for marrying the son of a poor gentleman to the ward of a rich trader in rice and molasses."

" The programme of our approaching campaign, I presume ? "

" Simply."

" Is the lady willing ? "

" I would fain believe so."

" Is Mr. Popkins unwilling ? "

" As the most romantic lover could desire."

" And the state of the campaign ? "

" Why, thus : Mr. George Washington Jefferson Frump, whom you have irreverently called Mr. Popkins, is sole guardian to the daughter of a dead West-Indian planter, of

whom he was once the agent. I fell in love with Kate Lorimer from description, when she was at school with my sister,
saw her by favor of a garden-wall, and after the usual
vows " —

" Too romantic for a Yankee, by half ! "

— " Proposed by letter to Mr. Frump."

" Oh, bathos ! "

" He refused me."

" Because " —

" *Imprimis*, I was not myself in the ' sugar line ; ' and *in
secundis*, my father wore gloves, and ' did nothing for a living,' — two blots in the eyes of Mr. Frump, which all the
waters of Niagara would never wash from my escutcheon."

" And what the devil hindered you from running off with
her ? "

" Fifty shares in the Manhattan Insurance Company, a
gold-mine in Florida, Heaven knows how many hogsheads of
treacle, and a million of acres on the banks of the Missouri."

" ' Pluto's flame-colored daughter ' defend us ! what a
living El Dorado ! "

" All of which she forfeits if she marries without old
Frump's consent."

" I see, I see ! And this Io and her Argus are now drinking the waters at Saratoga ? "

" Even so."

" I'll bet you my four-in-hand to a sonnet, that I get her
for you before the season is over."

" Money and all ? "

" Mines, molasses, and Missouri acres ! "

" And if you do, Tom, I'll give you a team of Virginian
bloods that would astonish Ascot, and throw you into the
bargain a forgiveness for riding over me with your camel on
the banks of the Hermus."

" Santa Maria ! do you remember that spongy foot stepping

over your frontispiece? I had already cast my eyes up to
Mont Sipylus to choose a clean niche for you out of the rock-
hewn tombs of the kings of Lydia. I thought you would
sleep with Alyattis, Phil!"

We dashed on through dark forest and open clearing,
through glens of tangled cedar and wild vine, over log
bridges, corduroy marshes, and sand-hills, till, toward evening, a scattering shanty or two, and an occasional sound of a
woodman's axe, betokened our vicinity to Saratoga. A turn
around a clump of tall pines brought us immediately into the
broad street of the village ; and the flaunting shops, the over-
grown, unsightly hotels, riddled with windows like honey-
combs, the fashionable idlers out for their evening lounge to
the waters, the indolent smokers on the colonnades, and the
dusty and loaded coaches driving from door to door in search
of lodgings, formed the usual evening picture of the Bath of
America.

As it was necessary to Tom's plan that my arrival at
Saratoga should not be known, he pulled up at a small tavern
at the entrance of the street, and, dropping me and my baggage, drove on to Congress Hall, with my best prayers, and
a letter of introduction to my sister, whom I had left on
her way to the Springs with a party at my departure for
Montreal. Unwilling to remain in such a tantalizing vicinity,
I hired a chaise the next morning, and, despatching a note to
Tom, drove to seek a retreat at Barhydt's, — a spot that
cannot well be described in the tail of a paragraph.

Herr Barhydt is an old Dutch settler, who, till the mineral-
springs of Saratoga were discovered some five miles from
his door, was buried in the depth of a forest solitude, unknown to all but the prowling Indian. The sky is supported
above him (or looks to be) by a wilderness of straight, col-
umnar pine shafts, gigantic in girth, and with no foliage
except at the top, where they branch out like round tables

spread for a banquet in the clouds. A small, ear-shaped lake, sunk as deep into the earth as the firs shoot above it, black as Erebus in the dim shadow of its hilly shore, and the obstructed light of the trees that nearly meet over it, and clear and unbroken as a mirror, save the pearl-spots of the thousand lotuses holding up their cups to the blue eye of heaven that peers through the leafy vault, sleeps beneath his window; and around him in the forest lies, still unbroken, the elastic and brown carpet of the faded pine-tassels, deposited in yearly layers since the continent rose from the flood, and rotted a foot beneath the surface to a rich mould that would fatten the Symplegades to a flower-garden. With his black tarn well stocked with trout, his bit of a farm in the clearing near by, and an old Dutch Bible, Herr Barhydt lived a life of Dutch musing, talked Dutch to his geese and chickens, sung Dutch psalms to the echoes of the mighty forest, and, except on his far-between visits to Albany, which grew rarer and rarer as the old Dutch inhabitants dropped faster away, saw never a white human face from one maple-blossoming to another.

A roving mineralogist tasted the waters of Saratoga; and, like the work of a lath-and-plaster Aladdin, up sprung a thriving village around the fountain's lip, and hotels, tin tumblers, and apothecaries multiplied in the usual proportion to each other, but out of all precedent with every thing else for rapidity. Libraries, newspapers, churches, livery-stables, and lawyers followed in their train; and it was soon established, from the Plains of Abraham to the savannas of Alabama, that no person of fashionable taste or broken constitution could exist through the months of July and August without a visit to the chalybeate springs and populous village of Saratoga. It contained seven thousand inhabitants before Herr Barhydt, living in his wooded seclusion only five miles off, became aware of its existence. A pair of lovers, philandering about the forest on horseback, popped in upon him one June morning ; and thenceforth there was no rest for the soul of the Dutchman. Everybody rode down to eat his trout, and make love in the dark shades of his mirrored lagoon ; and at last, in self-defence, he added a room or two to his shanty, enclosed his cabbage-garden, and put a price upon his trout-dinners. The traveller nowadays, who has not dined at Barhydt's, with his own champagne cold from the tarn, and the white-headed old settler " gargling " Dutch about the house, in his manifold vocation of cook, hostler, and waiter, may as well not have seen Niagara.

Installed in the back chamber of the old man's last addition to his house, with Barry Cornwall and Elia (old fellow-travellers of mine), a rude chair, a ruder but clean bed, and a troop of thoughts so perpetually from home that it mattered very little what was the complexion of any thing about me, I waited Tom's operations with a lover's usual patience. Barhydt's visitors seldom arrived before two or three o'clock ; and the long, soft mornings, quiet as a shadowy Elysium on the rim of that ebon lake, were as solitary as a melancholy man could desire. Didst thou but know, O gentle Barry Cornwall ! how gratefully thou hast been read and mused upon in those dim and whispering aisles of the forest, three thousand and more miles from thy smoky whereabout, methinks it would warm up the flush of pleasure around thine eyelids, though the "golden-tressed Adelaide " were waiting her good-night kisses at thy knee !

I could stand it no longer. On the second evening of my seclusion, I made bold to borrow old Barhydt's superannuated roadster, and, getting up the steam with infinite difficulty in his rickety engine, higgled away, with a pace to which I could not venture to affix a name, to the gay scenes of Saratoga.

It was ten o'clock when I dismounted at the stable in Congress Hall, and giving *Der Teufel,* as the old man ambitiously styled his steed, to the hands of the hostler, stole round through the garden to the eastern colonnade.

I feel called upon to describe "Congress Hall." Some fourteen or fifteen millions of white gentlemen and ladies consider that wooden and windowed Babylon as the proper palace of Delight, — a sojourn to be sighed for, and sacrificed for, and economized for; the birthplace of Love, the haunt of Hymen, the arena of Fashion; a place without which a new lease of life were valueless, for which, if the conjuring cap of King Erricus itself could not furnish a season-ticket, it might lie on a lady's toilet as unnoticed as a bride's nightcap a twelvemonth after marriage. I say to myself sometimes, as I pass the window at White's, and see a world-sick worldling with the curl of satiety and disgust on his lip, wondering how the next hour will come to its death, "If you but knew, my friend, what a campaign of pleasure you are losing in America, — what belles than the bluebells slighter and fairer, what hearts than the dewdrops fresher and clearer, are living their pretty hour, like gems undived for in the ocean; what loads of foliage, what Titans of trees, what glorious wildernesses of rocks and waters, are lavishing their splendors on the clouds that sail over them; and all within the magic circle of which Congress Hall is the centre, and which a circling dove would measure to get an appetite for his breakfast, —if you but knew this, my lord, as I know it, you would not be gazing so vacantly on the steps of Crockford's, nor consider 'the graybeard' such a laggard in his hours."

Congress Hall is a wooden building, of which the size and capacity could never be definitely ascertained. It is built on a slight elevation, just above the strongly impregnated spring whose name it bears; with little attempt at architecture, save a spacious and vine-covered colonnade, serving as a promenade, on either side, and two wings, the extremities of which

are lost in the distance. A relic or two of the still-astonished
forest towers above the chimneys, in the shape of a melancholy group of firs; and, five minutes' walk from the door,
the dim old wilderness stands looking down on the village in
its primeval grandeur, like the spirits of the wronged Indians
whose tracks are scarce vanished from the sand. In the
strength of the summer solstice, from five hundred to a
thousand people dine together at Congress Hall; and, after
absorbing as many bottles of the best wines of the world, a
sunset promenade plays the valve to the sentiment thus gen-
erated, and, with a cup of tea, the crowd separates to dress
for the nightly ball. There are several other hotels in the
village, equally crowded and equally spacious; and the ball
is given alternately at each. Congress Hall is the " crack "
place, however; and I expect that Mr. Westcott, the obliging
proprietor, will give me the preference of rooms, on my next
annual visit, for this just and honorable mention.

The dinner-tables were piled into an orchestra, and draped
with green baize and green wreaths; the floor of the immense
hall was chalked with American flags and the initials of all
the heroes of the Revolution; and the band were playing a
waltz in a style that made the candles quiver, and the pines
tremble audibly in their tassels. The ballroom was on the
ground floor; and the colonnade upon the garden side was
crowded with spectators, a row of grinning black fellows
edging the cluster of heads at every window, and keeping
time with their hands and feet in the irresistible sympathy of
their music-loving natures. Drawing my hat over my eyes,
I stood at the least-thronged window, and, concealing my face
in the curtain, waited impatiently for the appearance of the
dancers.

The bevy in the drawing-room was sufficiently strong at
last; and the lady patronesses, handed in by a State governor
or two, and here and there a member of Congress, achieved

the *entrée* with their usual intrepidity. Followed beaux, and followed belles. *Such* belles ! Slight, delicate, fragile-looking creatures, elegant as Retzsch's angels, warm-eyed as Mohammedan houries, yet timid as the antelope whose hazel orbs they eclipse, limbed like nothing earthly except an American woman — I would rather not go on. When I speak of the beauty of my countrywomen, my heart swells. I do believe the New World has a newer mould for its mothers and daughters. I *think* I am not prejudiced. I have been years away. I have sighed in France ; I have loved in Italy ; I have bargained for Circassians in an Eastern bezestein ; and I have lounged at Howell and James's on a sunny day in the season ; and my eye is trained, and my perceptions quickened : but I *do* think (honor bright! and Heath's "Book of Beauty" forgiving me) that there is no such beautiful work of God under the arch of the sky as an American girl in her bellehood.

Enter Tom Fane in a Stultz coat and Sparding tights, looking as a man who had been the mirror of Bond Street might be supposed to look, a thousand leagues from his club-house. *She* leaned on his arm. I had never seen her half so lovely. Fresh and calm from the seclusion of her chamber, her transparent cheek was just tinged with the first mounting blood from the excitement of lights and music. Her lips were slightly parted, her fine-lined eyebrows were arched with a girlish surprise, and her ungloved arm lay carelessly and confidingly within his, as white, round, and slender as if Canova had wrought it in Parian for his Psyche. If you have never seen a beauty of Northern blood nurtured in a Southern clime, the cold fairness of her race warmed up as if it had been steeped in some golden sunset, and her deep blue eye darkened and filled with a fire as unnaturally resplendent as the fusion of chrysoprase into a diamond ; and if you have never known the corresponding contrast in the charac-

ter, — the intelligence and constancy of the North kindling
with the enthusiasm and impulse, the passionateness, and the
abandon of a more burning latitude, — you have seen nothing,
let me insinuate, though you " have been i' the Indies twice,"
that could give you an idea of Kate Lorimer.

She waltzed, and then Tom danced with my sister; and
then, resigning her to another partner, he offered his arm
again to Miss Lorimer, and left the ballroom with several
other couples for a turn in the fresh air of the colonnade. I
was not jealous, but I felt unpleasantly at his returning to
her so immediately. He was the handsomest man, out of all
comparison, in the room; and he had dimmed my star too
often in our rambles in Europe and Asia not to suggest a
thought,' at least, that the same pleasant eclipse might occur
in our American astronomy. I stepped off the colonnade,
and took a turn in the garden.

Those " children of eternity," as Walter Savage Landor
poetically calls the breezes, performed their soothing ministry upon my temples; and I replaced Tom in my confidence
with an heroic effort, and turned back. A swing hung between two gigantic pines, just under the balustrade; and,
flinging myself into the cushioned seat, I abandoned myself
to the musings natural to a person " in my situation." The
sentimentalizing promenaders lounged backward and forward
above me; and, not hearing Tom's drawl among them, I
presumed he had returned to the ballroom. A lady and gentleman, walking in silence, stopped presently, and leaned
upon the railing opposite the swing. They stood a moment,
looking into the dim shadow of the pine-grove; and then a
voice, that I knew better than my own, remarked in a low
and silvery tone upon the beauty of the night.

She was not answered; and after a moment's pause, as if
resuming a conversation that had been interrupted, she turned
very earnestly to her companion, and asked, " Are you sure,

quite *sure*, that you could venture to marry without a fortune?"

" Quite, dear Miss Lorimer."

I started from the swing; but, before the words of execration that rushed choking from my heart could struggle to my
lips, they had mingled with the crowd, and vanished.

I strode down the garden-walk in a frenzy of passion.
Should I call him immediately to account? Should I rush
into the ballroom, and accuse him of his treachery to her
face? Should I drown myself in old Barhydt's tarn, or join
an Indian tribe, and make war upon the whites? Or should
I, *could* I, be magnanimous, and write him a note immediately, offering to be his groomsman at the wedding?

I stepped into the punch-room, asked for pen, ink, and
paper, and indited the following note : —

DEAR TOM, — If your approaching nuptials are to be sufficiently
public to admit of a groomsman, you will make me the happiest of
friends by selecting me for that office.

Yours ever truly,

PHIL.

Having despatched it to his room, I flew to the stable,
roused *Der Teufel*, who had gathered up his legs in the straw
for the night, flogged him furiously out of the village, and,
giving him the rein as he entered the forest, enjoyed the
scenery in the humor of mad old Hieronymo in the Spanish
tragedy, — "the moon dark, the stars extinct, the winds
blowing, the owls shrieking, the toads croaking, the minutes
jarring, and the clock striking twelve."

Early the next day Tom's "tiger" dismounted at Barhydt's
door, with an answer to my note as follows : —

DEAR PHIL, — The Devil must have informed you of a secret I
supposed safe from all the world. Be assured I should have chosen
no one but yourself to support me, on the occasion; and however you

have discovered my design upon your treasure, a thousand thanks for
your generous consent. I expected no less from your noble nature.

Yours devotedly,

Tom.

P.S. I shall endeavor to be at Barhydt's, with materials for the
fifth act of our comedy, to-morrow morning.

" 'Comedy!' call you this, Mr. Fane?" I felt my heart
turn black as I threw down the letter. After a thousand
plans of revenge formed and abandoned, borrowing old Barhydt's rifles, loading them deliberately, and discharging them
again into the air, I flung myself exhausted on the bed, and
reasoned myself back to my magnanimity. I *would* be his
groomsman !

It was a .morning like the burst of a millennium on the
world. I felt as if I should never forgive the birds for their
mocking enjoyment of it. The wild heron swung up from
the reeds, the lotuses shook out their dew into the lake as the
breeze stirred them, and the senseless old Dutchman sat
fishing in his canoe, singing one of his unintelligible psalms
to a quick measure that half-maddened me. I threw myself
upon the yielding floor of pine-tassels on the edge of the lake,
and, with the wretched school philosophy, " *Si gravis est,
brevis est*," endeavored to put down the tempest of my
feelings.

A carriage rattled over the little bridge, mounted the ascent rapidly, and brought up at Barhydt's door.

" Phil! " shouted Tom, " Phil! "

I gulped down a choking sensation in my throat, and rushed
up the bank to him. A stranger was dismounting from his
horse.

" Quick! " said Tom, shaking my hand hurriedly, " there
is no time to lose. Out with your inkhorn, Mr. Poppletree,
and have your papers signed while I tie up my ponies."

" What is this, sir? " said I, starting back as the stranger deliberately presented me with a paper, in which my own name was written in conspicuous letters.

The magistrate gazed at me with a look of astonishment. "A contract of marriage, I think, between Mr. Philip Slingsby and Miss Katherine Lorimer, spinster. Are you the gentleman named in that instrument, sir?"

At this moment my sister, leading the blushing girl by the hand, came and threw her arms about my neck, and, drawing her within my reach, ran off and left us together.

There are some pure moments in this life that description would only profane.

We were married by the village magistrate, in that magnificent sanctuary of the forest, old Barhydt and his lotuses the only indifferent witnesses of vows as passionate as ever trembled upon human lips.

I had scarce pressed her to my heart and dashed the tears from my eyes, when Fane, who had looked more at my sister than at the bride during the ceremony, left her suddenly, and, thrusting a roll of parchment into my pocket, ran off to bring up his ponies. I was on the way to Saratoga, a married man, and my bride on the seat beside me, before I had recovered from my astonishment.

"Pray," said Tom, "if it be not an impertinent question, and you can find breath in your ecstasies, how did you find out that your sister had done me the honor to accept the offer of my hand?"

The resounding woods rung with his unmerciful laughter at the explanation.

"And pray," said I, in my turn, "if it is not an impertinent question, and you can find a spare breath in *your* ecstasies, by what magic did you persuade old Frump to trust his ward and her title-deeds in your treacherous keeping?"

"It is a long story, my dear Phil, and I will give you the particulars when you pay me the 'Virginia bloods' you wot of. Suffice it for the present, that Mr. Frump believes Mr. Tom Fane (*alias* Jacob Phipps, Esq., sleeping partner of a banking-house at Liverpool) to be the accepted of his fair ward. In his extreme delight at seeing her in so fair a way to marry into a bank, he generously made her a present of her own fortune, signed over his right to control it by a document in your possession, and will undergo as agreeable a surprise in about five minutes as the greatest lover of excitement could desire."

The ponies dashed on. The sandy ascent by the Pavilion Spring was surmounted, and in another minute we were at the door of Congress Hall. The last stragglers from the breakfast-table were lounging down the colonnade, and old Frump sat reading the newspaper under the portico.

"Aha! Mr. Phipps," said he, as Tom drove up, "back so soon, eh? Why, I thought you and Kitty would be billing it till dinner-time!"

"Sir!" said Tom very gravely, "you have the honor of addressing Capt. Thomas Fane, of His Majesty's ——th Fusileers ; and whenever you have a moment's leisure, I shall be happy to submit to your perusal a certificate of the marriage of Miss Katherine Lorimer to the gentleman I have the pleasure to present to you. — Mr. Frump, Mr. Slingsby!"

At the mention of my name, the blood in Mr. Frump's ruddy complexion turned suddenly to the color of the Tiber. Poetry alone can express the feeling pictured in his countenance : —

> "If every atom of a dead man's flesh
> Should creep, each one with a particular life,
> Yet all as cold as ever, — 'twas just so;
> Or had it drizzled needle-points of frost
> Upon a feverish head made suddenly bald."

George Washington Jefferson Frump, Esq., left Congress Hall the same evening, and has since ungraciously refused an invitation to Captain Fane's wedding — possibly from his having neglected to invite him on a similar occasion at Saratoga. This last, however, I am free to say, is a gratuitous supposition of my own.

F. SMITH.

"Nature had made for him some other planet,
And pressed his soul into a human shape
By accident or malice."   COLERIDGE.

"I'll have you chronicled, and chronicled, and cut-and-chronicled, and sung in all-to-be-praised sonnets, and graved in new brave ballads, that all tongues shall troule you." — PHILASTER.

I.

IF you can imagine a buried Titan lying along the length of a continent, with one arm stretched out into the midst of the sea, the place to which I would transport you, reader mine, would lie, as it were, in the palm of the giant's hand. The small promontory to which I refer, which becomes an island in certain states of the tide, is at the end of one of the long capes of Massachusetts, and is still called by its Indian name, *Nahant*. Not to make you uncomfortable, I beg to introduce you at once to a pretentious hotel, "squat like a toad" upon the unsheltered and highest point of this citadel in mid-sea, and a very great resort for the metropolitan New-Englanders. Nahant is perhaps, liberally measured, a square half-mile; and it is distant from what may fairly be called mainland, perhaps a league.

Road to Nahant there is none. The *oi polloi* go there by steam; but when the tide is down you may drive there with a thousand chariots over the bottom of the sea. As I suppose there is not such another place in the known world, my tale will wait while I describe it more fully. If the Bible had been a fiction (not to speak profanely), I should have thought the idea of the destruction of Pharaoh and his host had its origin in some such wonder of nature.

83

Nahant is so far out into the ocean that what is called the "ground-swell" — the majestic heave of its great bosom going on forever like respiration, though its face may be like a mirror beneath the sun, and a wind may not have crisped its surface for days and weeks — is as broad and powerful within a rood of the shore as it is a thousand miles at sea.

The promontory itself is never wholly left by the ebb; but from its western extremity there runs a narrow ridge, scarce broad enough for a horse-path, impassable for the rocks and seaweed of which it is matted, and extending, at just high-water mark, from Nahant to the mainland. Seaward from this ridge, which is the only connection of the promontory with the continent, descends an expanse of sand, left bare six hours out of the twelve by the retreating sea, as smooth and hard as marble, and as broad and apparently as level as the plain of the Hermus. For three miles it stretches away without shell or stone, a surface of white, fine-grained sand, beaten so hard by the eternal hammer of the surf, that the hoof of a horse scarce marks it, and the heaviest wheel leaves it as printless as a floor of granite. This will be easily understood when you remember the tremendous rise and fall of the ocean swell, from the very bosom of which, in all its breadth and strength, roll in the waves of the flowing tide, breaking down on the beach, every one, with the thunder of a host precipitated from the battlements of a castle. Nothing could be more solemn and anthem-like than the succession of these plunging surges. And when the "tenth wave" gathers far out at sea, and rolls onward to the shore, first with a glassy and heaving swell as if some mighty monster were lurching inland beneath the water, and then bursting up into foam, with a front like an endless and sparry crystal wall, advances and overwhelms every thing in its progress, till it breaks with a centupled thunder on the beach, — it has seemed to me, standing there, as if thus might have beaten the first surge on the shore after the fiat which "divided sea and land." I am no Cameronian, but the sea (myself on shore) always drives me to Scripture for an illustration of my feelings.

The promontory of Nahant must be based on the earth's axle, else I cannot imagine how it should have lasted so long. In the mildest weather, the ground-swell of the sea gives it a fillip at every heave that would lay the "castled crag of Drachenfels" as low as Memphis. The wine trembles in your beaker of claret as you sit after dinner at the hotel; and if you look out at the eastern balcony (for it is a wooden pagoda, with balconies, verandas, and colonnades *ad libitum*), you will see the grass breathless in the sunshine upon the lawn, and the ocean as polished and calm as *Miladi's* brow beyond, and yet the spray and foam dashing fifty feet into the air between, and enveloping the " Devil's Pulpit " (a tall rock split off from the promontory's front) in a perpetual kaleidoscope of mist and rainbows. Take the trouble to transport yourself there. I will do the remaining honors on the spot. A cavern as cool (not as silent) as those of Trophonius lies just under the brow of yonder precipice, and the waiter shall come after us with our wine. You have dined with the Borromeo in the grotto of Isola Bella, I doubt not, and know the perfection of *art:* I will show you that of *nature.* (I should like to transport you, for a similar contrast, from Terni to Niagara, or from San Giovanni Laterano to an aisle in a forest of Michigan; but the Dædalian mystery, alas! is unsolved. We "fly not yet.")

Here we are, then, in the " Swallow's Cave." The floor descends by a gentle declivity to the sea; and from the long dark cleft stretching outward you look forth upon the broad Atlantic, the shore of Ireland the first *terra firma* in the path of your eye. Here is a dark pool left by the retreating tide for a refrigerator; and with the champagne in the midst, we will recline about it like the soft Asiatics of whom we learned pleasure in the East, and drink to the small-featured and purple-lipped " Mignons " of Syria, those fine-limbed and fiery slaves, adorable as Peris, and by turns languishing and stormy, whom you buy for a pinch of piastres (say 5*l.* 5*s.*) in sunny Damascus. Your drowsy Circassian, faint and dreamy, or your crockery Georgian, fit dolls for the sensual Turk, is, to him who would buy *soul,* dear at a *para* the hecatomb.

We recline, as it were, in an ebon pyramid, with a hundred feet of floor and sixty of wall, and the fourth side open to the sky. The light comes in mellow and dim, and the sharp edges of the rocky portal seem let into the pearly arch of heaven. The tide is at half-ebb, and the advancing and retreating waves, which at first just lifted the fringe of crimson dulse at the lip of the cavern, now dash their spray-pearls on the rock below, the " tenth " surge alone rallying as if in scorn of its retreating fellows, and, like the chieftain of Culloden Moor, rushing back singly to the contest. And now that the waters reach the entrance no more, come forward and look on the sea. The swell lifts: would you not think the bases of the earth rising beneath it? It falls: would you not think the foundation of the deep had given way? A plain broad enough for the navies of the world to ride at large heaves up evenly and steadily, as if it would lie against the sky, rests a moment spell-bound in its place, and falls again as far; the respiration of a sleeping child not more regular and full of slumber. It is only on the shore that it chafes. Blessed emblem! it is at peace with itself. The rocks war with a nature so unlike their own, and the hoarse din of their border onsets resounds through the caverns they have rent open; but beyond, in the calm bosom of the ocean, what heavenly dignity! what godlike unconsciousness of alarm! I did not think we should stumble on such a moral in the cave.

By the deeper bass of its hoarse organ, the sea is now playing upon its lowest stops, and the tide is down. Hear! how it rushes in beneath the rocks, broken and stilled in its tortuous way, till it ends with a washing and dull hiss among the seaweed ; and, like a myriad of small tinkling bells, the dripping from the cràgs is audible. There is fine music in the sea.

And now the beach is bare. The cave begins to cool and darken, and the first gold tint of sunset is stealing into the sky ; and the sea looks of a changing opal, green, purple, and white, as if its floor were paved with pearl, and the changing light struck up through the waters. And there heaves a ship into the horizon, like a white-winged bird lying with dark breast on the waves, abandoned of the sea-breeze within sight of port, and repelled even by the spicy breath that comes with a welcome off the shore. She comes from "merry England." She is freighted with more than merchandise. The homesick exile will gaze on her snowy sail as she sets in with the morning breeze, and bless it; for the wind that first filled it on its way swept through the green valley of his home. What links of human affection brings she over the sea? How much comes in her that is not in her "bill of lading," yet worth, to the heart that is waiting for it, a thousand times the purchase of her whole venture!

Mais montons nous! I hear the small hoofs of Thalaba ; my stanhope waits : we will leave this half-bottle of champagne, that "remainder biscuit," and the echoes of our philosophy, to the naiads who have lent us their drawing-room. Undine, or Egeria! Lurly, or Arethusa! whatever thou art called, nymph of this shadowy cave, adieu!

Slowly, Thalaba! Tread gingerly down this rocky descent! So! Here we are on the floor of the vasty deep! What a glorious race-course! The polished and printless sand spreads away before you as far as the eye can see; the surf comes in below breast-high ere it breaks, and the white fringe of the sliding wave shoots up the beach, but leaves room for the marching of a Persian phalanx on the sands it has deserted. Oh, how noiselessly runs the wheel, and how dreamily we glide along, feeling our motion but in the resistance of the wind, and by the trout-like pull of the ribbons by the excited animal before us. Mark the color of the sand, white at high-water mark, and thence deepening to a silvery gray as the water has evaporated less; a slab of Egyptian granite in the obelisk of St. Peter's not more polished and unimpressible. Shell or rock, weed or quicksand, there is none; and, mar or deface its bright surface as you will, it is ever beaten down anew, and washed even of the dust of the foot of man, by the returning sea. You may write upon its fine-grained face with a crow-quill: you may course over its dazzling expanse with a troop of chariots.

Most wondrous and beautiful of all, within twenty yards of the surf, or for an hour after the tide has left the sand, it holds the water without losing its firmness, and is like a gray mirror, bright as the bosom of the sea. (By your leave, Thalaba.) And now lean over the dasher, and see those small fetlocks striking up from beneath, the flying mane, the thoroughbred action, the small and expressive head, as perfect in the reflection as in the reality: like Wordsworth's swan, he

> "*Trots* double, *horse* and shadow."

You would swear you were skimming the surface of the sea; and the delusion is more complete as the white foam of the "tenth wave" skims in beneath wheel and hoof, and you urge on with the treacherous element gliding away visibly beneath you.

We seem not to have driven fast : yet three miles fairly measured are left behind, and Thalaba's blood is up. Fine creature ! I would not give him

"For the best horse the Sun has in his stable."

We have won champagne ere now, Thalaba and I, trotting on this silvery beach ; and if ever old age comes on me, — and I intend it never shall on aught save my mortal coil (my spirit vowed to perpetual youth), — I think these vital breezes and a trot on these exhilarating sands would sooner renew my prime than a rock in St. Hilary's cradle, or a dip in the well of Kanathos. May we try the experiment together, gentle reader !

I am not settled in my own mind whether this description of one of my favorite haunts in America was written most to introduce the story that is to follow, or the story to introduce the description. Possibly the latter ; for, having consumed my callow youth in wandering " to and fro in the earth " like Sathanas of old, and looking on my country now with an eye from which all the minor and temporary features have gradually faded, I find my pride in it (after its glory as a republic) settling principally on the superior handiwork of nature in its land and water. When I talk of it now, it is looking through another's eyes, — his who listens. I do not describe it after my own memory of what it *was once to me*, but according to my idea of what it will *seem now to a stranger*. Hence I speak not of the friends I made, rambling by lake or river. The lake and the river are there, but the friends are changed — to themselves and me. I speak not of the lovely and loving ones that stood by me, looking on glen or waterfall. The glen and the waterfall are romantic still, but the form and the heart that breathed through it are no longer lovely or loving. I should renew my joys by the old mountain and river ; for, all they ever were I should

find them still, and never seem to myself grown old, or can-
kered of the world, or changed in form or spirit, while they
reminded me but of my youth, with their familiar sunshine
and beauty.   But the friends that I knew — *as* I knew them
— are dead.   They look no longer the same : they have
another heart in them ; the kindness of the eye, the smiling-
ness of the lip, are no more there.   Philosophy tells me the
material and living body changes and renews, particle by
particle, with time ; and Experience — cold-blooded and stony
monitor — tells me, in his frozen monotone, that heart and
spirit change with it and renew.   But the name remains,
mockery that it is ! and the memory sometimes ; and so these
apparitions of the past — that we almost fear to question
when they encounter us, lest the change they have undergone
should freeze our blood — stare coldly on us, yet call us by
name, and answer, though coldly, to their own, and have
that terrible similitude to what they were, mingled with their
unsympathizing and hollow mummery, that we wish the grave
of the past, with all that it contained of kind or lovely, had
been sealed forever.   The heart we have lain near before
our birth (so read I the book of human life) is the only one
that cannot forget that it has loved us.   Saith well and affec-
tionately an American poet, in some birthday-verses to his
mother, —

> "Mother! dear mother! the feelings nurst
> As I hung at thy bosom, *clung round thee first ;*
> 'Twas the earliest link in love's warm chain,
> 'Tis the only one that will long remain;
> And as year by year, and day by day,
> Some friend, still trusted, drops away,
> Mother! dear mother! *oh, dost thou see*
> *How the shortened chain brings me nearer thee !*"

II.

I have observed, that, of all the friends one has in the course of his life, the truest and most attached is exactly the one who, from his dissimilarity to yourself, the world finds it very odd you should fancy. We hear sometimes of lovers who " are made for each other," but rarely of the same natural match in friendship. It is no great marvel. In a world like this, where we pluck so desperately at the fruit of pleasure, we prefer for company those who are not formed with precisely the same palate as ourselves. You will seldom go wrong, dear reader, if you refer any human question about which you are in doubt to that icy oracle — selfishness.

My shadow for many years was a gentle monster, whom I have before mentioned, baptized by the name of *Forbearance Smith*. He was a Vermontese, a descendant of one of the Puritan Pilgrims, and the first of his family who had left the Green Mountains since the flight of the regicides to America. We assimilate to what we live among ; and Forbearance was very *green*, and very like a *mountain*. He had a general resemblance to one of Thorwaldsen's unfinished apostles, — larger than life, and just hewn into outline. My acquaintance with him commenced during my first year at the university. He stalked into my room one morning with a hair-trunk on his back, and handed me the following note from the tutor : —

SIR, — The faculty have decided to impose upon you the fine of ten dollars and damages, for painting the president's horse on sabbath night while grazing on the college green. They, moreover, have removed Freshman Wilding from your rooms, and appoint as your future chum the studious and exemplary bearer, Forbearance Smith, to whom you are desired to show a becoming respect.

Your obedient servant,

ERASMUS SNUFFLEGREEK.

TO FRESHMAN SLINGSBY.

Rather relieved by my lenient sentence (for, till the next shedding of his well-saturated coat, the sky-blue body and red mane and tail of the president's once gray mare would interfere with that esteemed animal's usefulness), I received Mr. Smith with more politeness than he expected. He deposited his hair-trunk in the vacant bedroom, remarked with a good-humored smile that it was a cold morning, and, seating himself in my easiest chair, opened his Euclid, and went to work upon a problem, as perfectly at home as if he had furnished the room himself, and lived in it from his matriculation. I had expected some preparatory apology at least, and was a little annoyed; but being upon my good behavior, I bit my lips, and resumed the "Art of Love," upon which I was just then practising my nascent Latinity, instead of calculating logarithms for recitation. In about an hour, my new chum suddenly vociferated "*Eureka!*" shut up his book, and having stretched himself (a very unnecessary operation), coolly walked to my dressing-table, selected my best hair-brush, redolent of Macassar, and used it with the greatest apparent satisfaction.

"Have you done with that hair-brush?" I asked, as he laid it in its place again.

"Oh, yes!"

"Then perhaps you will do me the favor to throw it out of the window."

He did it without the slightest hesitation. He then resumed his seat by the fire, and I went on with my book in silence. Twenty minutes had elapsed, perhaps, when he rose very deliberately, and, without a word of preparation, gave me a cuff that sent me flying into the wood-basket in the corner behind me. As soon as I could pick myself out, I flew upon him; but I might as well have grappled with a boa-constrictor. He held me off at arm's length till I was quite exhausted with rage; and at last, when I could struggle no more, I found breath to ask him what the devil he meant.

" To resent what seemed to me, on reflection, to be an insult," he answered in the calmest tone, " and now to ask your pardon for a fault of ignorance. The first was due to myself, the second to you."

Thenceforth, to the surprise of everybody, and Bob Wilding and the tutor, we were inseparable. I took Bruin (by a double elision *Forbearance* became " *bear*," and by paraphrase *Bruin*, and he answered to the name), I took him, I say, to the omnium shop, and presented him with a dressing-case, and other appliances for his *outer* man ; and, as my *inner* man was relatively as much in need of his assistance, we mutually improved. I instructed him in poetry and politeness, and he returned the lesson in problems and politics. My star was never in more fortunate conjunction.

Four years had woven their threads of memory about us, and there was never woof more free from blemish. Our friendship was proverbial. All that much care and Macassar could do for Bruin had been done ; but there was no abating his seven feet of stature, nor reducing the size of his feet proper, nor making the muscles of his face answer to their natural wires. At his most placid smile, a strange waiter would run for a hot towel and the doctor (colic was not more like itself than that like colic) ; and for his motions — oh, Lord ! a skeleton, with each individual bone appended to its neighbor with a string, would execute a *pas seul* with the same expression. His mind, however, had none of the awkwardness of his body. A simplicity and truth amounting to the greatest *naïveté*, and a fatuitous unconsciousness of the effect on beholders of his outer man, were its only approaches to fault or foible. With the finest sense of the beautiful, the most unerring judgment in literary taste, the purest romance, a fervid enthusiasm, constancy, courage, and good temper, he walked about the world in a mask, — an admirable creature, in the guise and seeming of a ludicrous monster.

Bruin was sensitive on but one point. He never could forgive his father and mother for the wrong they had entailed on him at his baptism. " *Forbearance* Smith ! " he would say to himself sometimes, in unconscious soliloquy : " they should have given me the virtue as well as the name." And then he would sit with a pen, and scrawl " F. Smith " on a sheet of paper by the hour together. To insist upon knowing his Christian name, was the one impertinence he never forgave.

III.

My party at Nahant consisted of Thalaba, Forbearance, and myself. The place was crowded ; but I passed my time very much between my horse and my friend, and was as certain to be found on the beach when the tide was down, as the sea to have left the sands. Job (a synonyme for Forbearance, which became at this time his common *sobriquet*) was, of course, in love. Not the least to the prejudice, however, of his last faithful passion ; for he was as fond of the memory of an old love, as he was tender in the presence of the new. I intended to have had him dissected after his death, to see whether his organization was not peculiar. I strongly incline to the opinion that we should have found a mirror in the place of his heart. Strange how the same man who is so fickle in love will be so constant in friendship ! But is it fickleness ? Is it not rather a *superflu* of tenderness in the nature, which overflows to all who approach the fountain ? I have ever observed that the most susceptible men are the most remarkable for the finer qualities of character. They are more generous, more delicate, and of a more chivalrous complexion altogether, than other men. It was surprising how reasonably Bruin would argue upon this point. "Because I was happy at Niagara," he was saying one day, as we sat upon the rocks, "shall I take no pleasure in the Falls of Montmorenci? Because the sunset was glorious yesterday, shall I find no beauty in that of to-day? Is my fancy to be used but once, and the key turned upon it forever? Is the heart like a *bonbon*, to be eaten up by the first favorite, and thought of no more? Are our eyes blind, save to one shape of beauty? Are our ears insensible to the music save of one voice?"

"But do you not weaken the heart, and become incapable of a lasting attachment, by this habit of inconstancy?"

"How long, my dear Phil, will you persist in talking as if the heart was material, and held so much love, as a cup so much water, and had legs to be weary, or organs to grow dull? How is my sensibility lessened, how my capacity enfeebled? What would I have done for my first love, that I would not do for my last? I would have sacrificed my life to secure the happiness of one you wot of in days gone by: I would jump into the sea, if it would make Blanche Carroll happier to-morrow."

"*Sautez-donc!*" said a thrilling voice behind; and, as if the utterance of her name had conjured her out of the ground, the object of all Job's admiration, and a little of my own, stood before us. She had a work-basket in her hand, a gypsy-hat tossed carelessly on her head, and had preceded a whole troop of belles and matrons who were coming out to while away the morning, and breathe the invigorating sea-air on the rocks.

Blanche Carroll was what the women would call "a little love," but that phrase of endearment would not at all express the feeling with which she inspired the men. She was small, and her face and figure might have been framed in fairy-land for bewitching beauty; but with the manner of a spoiled child, and apparently the most thoughtless playfulness of mind, she was as veritable a little devil as ever took the shape of woman. Scarce seventeen at this time, she had a knowledge of character that was like an instinct, and was an accomplished actress in any part it was necessary for her purpose to play. No grave Machiavel ever managed his cards with more finesse than that little *intriguante* the limited world of which she was the star. She was a natural master-spirit and plotter; and the talent that would have employed itself in the deeper game of politics, had she been born a woman of rank in Europe, displayed itself, in the simple society of a republic, in subduing to her power every thing in the shape of a single man that ventured to her net. I have nothing to tell of her at all commensurate with the character I have drawn, for the disposal of her own heart (if she has one) must of course be the most important event of her life; but I merely pencil the outline of the portrait in passing, as a specimen of the material that exists — even in the simplest society — for the *dramatis personæ* of a court.

We followed the light-footed beauty to the shelter of one of the caves opening on the sea, and seated ourselves about her upon the rocks. Some one proposed that Job or myself should read.

"O Mr. Smith," interrupted the belle, "where is my bracelet? and where are my verses?"

At the ball the night before, she had dropped a bracelet in the waltz; and Job had been permitted to take care of the fragments, on condition of restoring them, with a sonnet, the next morning. She had just thought of it.

"Read them out! read them out!" she cried, as Job, blushing a deep blue, extracted a tri-cornered pink document from his pocket, and tried to give it to her unobserved with the packet of jewelry. Job looked at her imploringly; and she took the verses from his hand, and ran her eye through them.

" Pretty well ! " she said ; " but the last line might be improved. Give me a pencil, some one ! " And bending over it till her luxuriant hair concealed her fairy fingers in their employment, she wrote a moment upon her knee, and, tossing the paper to me, bade me read it out with the emendation. Bruin had, meantime, modestly disappeared, and I read with the more freedom : —

> "'Twas broken in the gliding dance,
>   When thou wert in the dream of power;
> When shape and motion, tone and glance,
>   Were glorious all, — the woman's hour!
> The light lay soft upon thy brow,
>   The music melted in thine ear,
> And one perhaps forgotten now
>   With 'wildered thoughts stood listening near,
> Marvelling not that links of gold
> A pulse like thine had not controlled.

> "'Tis midnight now.   The dance is done,
>   And thou, in thy soft dreams, asleep;
> And I, awake, am gazing on
>   The fragments given me to keep.
> I think of every glowing vein
>   That ran beneath these links of gold,
> And wonder if a thrill of pain
>   Made those bright channels ever cold!
> With gifts like thine, I cannot think
> Grief ever chilled this broken link.

> " Good-night!   'Tis little now to thee
>   That in my ear thy words were spoken,
> And thou wilt think of them and me
>   As long as of the bracelet broken.
> For thus is riven many a chain
>   That thou hast fastened but to break,
> And thus thou'lt sink to sleep again,
>   As careless that another wake:
> The only thought thy heart can rend
> Is — *what the fellow'll charge to mend!*"

Job's conclusion was more pathetic, but probably less true. He appeared after the applause had ceased, and resumed his place at the lady's feet, with a look in his countenance of having deserved an abatement of persecution. The beauty spread out the fragments of the broken bracelet on the rock beside her.

"Mr. Smith," said she, in her most conciliating tone.

Job leaned toward her with a look of devoted inquiry.

"Has the tide turned?"

"Certainly. Two hours since."

"The beach is passable, then?"

"Hardly, I fear."

"No matter. How many hours' drive is it to Salem?"

"Mr. Slingsby drives it in two."

"Then you'll get Mr. Slingsby to lend you his stanhope, drive to Salem, have this bracelet mended, and bring it back in time for the ball. *I have spoken*, as the Grand Turk says. *Allez!*"

"But, my dear Miss Carroll" —

She laid her hand on his mouth as he began to remonstrate; and, while I made signs to him to refuse, she said something to him which I lost in a sudden dash of the waters. He looked at me for my consent.

"Oh, you can have Mr. Slingsby's horse," said the beauty, as I hesitated whether my refusal would not check her tyranny, "and I'll drive him out this evening for his reward. *N'est-ce pas?* you cross man!"

So, with the sun hot enough to fry the brains in his skull, and a quivering reflection on the sands that would burn his face to a blister, exit Job, with the broken bracelet in his bosom.

"Stop, Mr. Slingsby," said the imperious little belle, as I was making up a mouth, after his departure, to express my disapprobation of her measures, "no lecture, if you please.

Give me that book of plays, and I'll read you a precedent. Because you are virtuous, shall we have no more cakes and ale? *Ecoutez!*" And, with an emphasis and expression that would have been perfect on the stage, she read the following passage from "The Careless Husband:" —

"*Lady Betty.* — The men of sense, my dear, make the best fools in the world: their sincerity and good breeding throw them so entirely into one's power, and give one such an agreeable thirst of using them ill, to show that power, 'tis impossible not to quench it.

"*Lady Easy.* — But my Lord Morelove —

"*Lady B.* — Pooh! my Lord Morelove's a mere Indian damask: one can't wear him out; o' my conscience, I must give him to my woman at last. I begin to be known by him; had I not best leave him off, my dear?

"*Lady E.* — Why did you ever encourage him?

"*Lady B.* — Why, what would you have one do? For my part, I could no more choose a man by my eye than a shoe: one must draw them on a little, to see if they are right to one's foot.

"*Lady E.* — But I'd no more fool on with a man I could not like, than wear a shoe that pinched me.

"*Lady B.* — Ay; but then a poor wretch tells one he'll widen 'em, or do any thing, and is so civil and silly, that one does not know how to turn such a trifle as a pair of shoes, or a heart, upon a fellow's hands again.

"*Lady E.* — And there's my Lord Foppington.

"*Lady B.* — My dear! fine fruit will have flies about it; but, poor things! they do it no harm; for, if you observe, people are generally most apt to choose that the flies have been busy with. Ha, ha!

"*Lady E.* — Thou art a strange, giddy creature!

"*Lady B.* — That may be from too much circulation of thought, my dear."

" Pray, Miss Carroll," said I, as she threw aside the book with a theatrical air, " have you any precedent for broiling a man's brains, as well as breaking his heart? For, by this time, my friend Forbearance has a *coup de soleil*, and is hissing over the beach like a steam-engine."

" How tiresome you are ! Do you really think it will kill him ? "

" It might injure him seriously, let alone the danger of driving a spirited horse over the beach, with the tide quarter-down."

" What shall I do to be 'taken out of the corner,' Mr. Slingsby ? "

" Order your horses an hour sooner, and drive to Lynn to meet him half way on his return. I will resume my stanhope, and give him the happiness of driving back with you."

" And I shall be gentle Blanche Carroll, and no ogre, if I do?"

" Yes ; Mr. Smith surviving."

" Take the trouble to give my orders, then ; and come back immediately, and read to me till it is time to go. Meantime, I shall look at myself in this black mirror." And the spoilt but most lovely girl bent over a dark pool in the corner of the cave, forming a picture on its shadowy background that drew a murmur of admiration even from the neglected group who had been the silent and disapproving witnesses of her caprice.

IV.

A thunder-cloud strode into the sky with the rapidity which marks that common phenomenon of a breathless summer afternoon in America ; darkened the air for a few minutes, so that the birds betook themselves to their nests ; and then poured out its refreshing waters with the most terrific flashes of lightning, and crashes of thunder, which for a moment seemed to still even the eternal bass of the sea. With the same fearful rapidity, the black roof of the sky tore apart, and fell back, in rolling and changing masses, upon the horizon ; the sun darted with intense brilliancy through the clarified and transparent air ; the light-stirring breeze came freighted with delicious coolness; and the heavy sea-birds, who had lain brooding on the waves while the tumult of the elements went on, rose on their cimeter-like wings, and fled away, with incomprehensible instinct, from the beautiful and freshened land. The whole face of earth and sky had been changed in an hour.

Oh, of what fulness of delight are even the senses capable! What a nerve there is sometimes in every pore! What love for all living and all inanimate things may be born of a summer shower! How stirs the fancy, and brightens hope, and warms the heart, and sings the spirit within us, at the mere animal joy with which the lark flees into heaven! And yet, of this exquisite capacity for pleasure we take so little care! We refine our taste, we elaborate and finish our mental perception, we study the beautiful that we may know it when it appears: yet the senses by which these faculties are approached, the stops by which this fine instrument is played, are trifled with and neglected. We forget that a single excess blurs and confuses the music written on our minds; we forget that an untimely vigil weakens and bewilders the delicate minister to our inner temple; we know not, or act as if we knew not, that the fine and easily jarred harmony of health is the only interpreter of nature to our souls: in short, we drink too much claret, and eat too much *pâté foie gras.* Do you understand me, *gourmand et gourmet?*

Blanche Carroll was a beautiful whip, and the two bay ponies in her phaeton were quite aware of it. La Bruyère says, with his usual wisdom, "Une belle femme qui a les qualités d'un honnête homme est ce qu'il y a au monde d'un commerce plus délicieux;" and, to a certain degree, masculine accomplishments too are very winning in a woman — if pretty: if plain, she is expected not only to be quite feminine, but quite perfect. Foibles are as hateful in a woman who does *not* possess beauty, as they are engaging in a woman who *does*.   Clouds are only lovely when the heavens are bright.

She looked loveliest while driving, did Blanche Carroll, for she was born to rule, and the expression native to her lip was energy and nerve ; and as she sat with her little foot pressed against the dasher, and reined in those spirited horses, the finely pencilled mouth, usually playful or pettish, was pressed together in a curve as warlike as Minerva's, and twice as captivating.   She drove, too, as capriciously as she acted.   At one moment her fleet ponies fled over the sand at the top of their speed, and at the next they were brought down to a walk, with a suddenness which threatened to bring them upon their haunches ; now far up on the dry sand, cutting a zigzag to lengthen the way, and again below at the tide edge, with the waves breaking over her seaward wheel ; all her powers at one instant engrossed in pushing them to their fastest trot, and in another the reins lying loose on their backs while she discussed some sudden flight of philosophy.   " Be his fairy, his page, his every thing that love and poetry have invented," said Roger Ascham to Lady Jane Grey, just before her marriage ; but Blanche Carroll was almost the only woman I ever saw capable of the *beau idéal* of fascinating characters.

Between Miss Carroll and myself, there was a safe and cordial friendship.   Besides loving another better, she was neither earnest nor true nor affectionate enough to come at all within the range of my possible attachments, and, though I admired her, she felt that the necessary sympathy was wanting for love ; and, the idea of fooling me with the rest once abandoned, we were the greatest of allies.   She told me all her triumphs, and I listened and laughed without thinking it worth while to burden her with my confidence in return ; and you may as well make a memorandum, gentle reader, that *that* is a very good basis for a friendship.   Nothing bores women or worldly persons so much as to return their secrets with your own.

As we drew near the extremity of the beach, a boy rode up on horseback, and presented Miss Carroll with a note. I observed that it was written on a very dirty slip of paper, and was waiting to be enlightened as to its contents, when she slipped it into her belt, took the whip from the box, and, flogging her ponies through the heavy sand of the outer beach, went off, at a pace which seemed to engross all her attention, on her road to Lynn. We reached the hotel, and she had not spoken a syllable ; and, as I made a point of never inquiring into any thing that seemed odd in her conduct, I merely stole a glance at her face, which wore the expression of mischievous satisfaction which I liked the least of its common expressions ; and descended from the phaeton with the simple remark, that Job could not have arrived, as I saw nothing of my stanhope in the yard.

" Mr. Slingsby." It was the usual preface to asking some particular favor.

" Miss Carroll."

" Will you be so kind as to walk to the library, and select me a book to your own taste, and ask no questions as to what I do with myself meantime? "

" But, my dear Miss Carroll — your father " —

" Will feel quite satisfied when he hears that Cato was with me. — Leave the ponies to the groom, Cato, and follow me." I looked after her as she walked down the village street with the old black behind her, not at all certain of the propriety of my acquiescence, but feeling that there was no help for it.

I lounged away a half-hour at the library, and found Miss Carroll waiting for me on my return. There were no signs of Bruin ; and, as she seemed impatient to be off, I jumped into the phaeton, and away we flew to the beach as fast as her ponies could be driven under the whip. As we descended upon the sands, she spoke for the first time : —

"It is *so* civil of you to ask no questions, Mr. Slingsby! but you are *not* offended with me?"

"If you have got into no scrape while under my charge, I shall certainly be too happy to shake hands upon it to-morrow."

"Are you *quite* sure?" she asked archly.

"Quite sure."

"So am *not* I," she said with a merry laugh; and in her excessive amusement she drove down to the sea, till the surf broke over the nearest pony's back, and filled the bottom of the phaeton with water. Our wet feet were now a fair apology for haste; and, taking the reins from her, I drove rapidly home, while she wrapped herself in her shawl, and sat apparently absorbed in the coming of the twilight over the sea.

I slept late after the ball, though I had gone to bed exceedingly anxious about Bruin, who had not yet made his appearance. The tide would prevent his crossing the beach after ten in the morning, however; and I made myself tolerably easy till the sands were passable with the evening ebb. The high-water mark was scarcely deserted by the waves, when the same boy who had delivered the note to Miss Carroll the day before rode up from the beach on a panting horse, and delivered me the following note: —

DEAR PHILIP, — You will be surprised to hear that I am in the Lynn jail on a charge of theft and utterance of counterfeit money. I do not wait to tell you the particulars. Please come and identify

Yours truly,

F. SMITH.

I got upon the boy's horse, and hurried over the beach with whip and spur. I stopped at the justice's office, and that worthy seemed uncommonly pleased to see me.

"We have got him, sir," said he.

"Got whom?" I asked rather shortly.

"Why, the fellow that stole your stanhope and Miss Car-

roll's bracelet, and passed a twenty-dollar counterfeit bill.
Ha'n't you hear*n* on't?''

The justice's incredulity, when I told him it was probably
the most intimate friend I had in the world, would have
amused me at any other time.

"Will you allow me to see the prisoner?" I asked.

"Be sure I will. I let Miss Carroll have a peep at him
yesterday, and what do you think? O Lord! he wanted to
make her believe she knew him. Good, wasn't it? Ha,
ha! And *such* an ill-looking fellow! Why, I'd know him
for a thief anywhere. *Your* intimate friend, Mr. Slingsby!
O Lord! when you come to see him! Ha, ha!''

We were at the prison-door. The grating bolts turned
slowly, the door swung rustily on its hinges as if it was not
often used; and in the next minute I was enfolded in Job's
arms, who sobbed and laughed, and was quite hysterical with
his delight. I scarce wondered at the justice's prepossessions
when I looked at the figure he made. His hat knocked in,
his coat muddy, his hair full of the dust of straw, — the natural hideousness of poor Job had every possible aggravation.

We were in the stanhope, and fairly on the beach, before
he had sufficiently recovered to tell me the story. He had
arrived quite overheated at Lynn; but, in a hurry to execute
Miss Carroll's commission, he merely took a glass of soda-
water, had Thalaba's mouth washed, and drove on. A mile
on his way, he was overtaken by a couple of hostlers on
horseback, who very roughly ordered him back to the inn.
He refused; and a fight ensued, which ended in his being tied
into the stanhope, and driven back as a prisoner. The large
note which he had given for his soda-water, it appeared,
was a counterfeit; and placards offering a reward for the
detection of a villain, described in the usual manner as an
ill-looking fellow, had been sticking up for some days in the
village. He was taken before the justice, who declared at

first sight that he answered the description in the advertisement. His stubborn refusal to give the whole of his name (he would rather have died, I suppose), his possession of my stanhope, which was immediately recognized, and, lastly, the bracelet found in his pocket, of which he refused indignantly to give any account, were circumstances enough to leave no doubt on the mind of the worthy justice. He made out his *mittimus* forthwith, granting Job's request that he might be allowed to write a noté to Miss Carroll (who, he knew, would drive over the beach toward evening), as a very great favor. She arrived as he expected.

"And what in heaven's name did she say?" said I, interested beyond my patience at this part of the story.

"Expressed the greatest astonishment when the justice showed her the bracelet, and declared she *never saw me before in her life!*"

That Job forgave Blanche Carroll in two days, and gave her a pair of gloves with some verses on the third, will surprise only those who have not seen that lady. It would seem incredible; but here are the verses, as large as life: —

"Slave of the snow-white hand! I fold
　My spirit in thy fabric fair;
And when that dainty hand is cold,
　And rudely comes the wintry air,
Press in thy light and straining form
Those slender fingers soft and warm;
　And, as the fine-traced veins within
Quicken their bright and rosy flow,
　And gratefully the dewy skin
Clings to the form that warms it so,
　Tell her my heart is hiding there,
Trembling to be so closely prest,
　Yet feels how brief its moments are,
And saddens even to be blest, —
Fated to serve her for a day,
And then, like thee, *be flung away.*"

THE FEMALE WARD.

MOST men have two or more souls; and Jem Thalimer was a doublet, with sets of manners corresponding. Indeed, one identity could never have served the pair of him. When sad, — that is to say, when in disgrace or out of money, he had the air of a good man with a broken heart. When gay, flush in pocket, and happy in his little ambitions, you would have thought him a dangerous companion for his grandmother. The last impression did him more injustice than the first, for he was really very amiably disposed when depressed, and not always wicked when gay; but he made friends in both characters. People seldom forgive us for compelling them to correct their first impressions of us; and as this was uniformly the case with Jem, whether he had begun as saint or sinner, he was commonly reckoned a deepwater fish; and, where there were young ladies in the case, early warned off the premises. The remarkable exception to this rule, in the incident I am about to relate, arose, as may naturally be supposed, from his appearing, during a certain period, in one character only.

To begin my story fairly, I must go back for a moment to our junior year in college, showing, by a little passage in our adventures, how Thalimer and I became acquainted with the confiding gentleman to be referred to.

A college suspension, very agreeably timed in June, left my friend Jem and myself masters of our travels for an uncertain period; and as our purse was always in common, like our shirts, love-letters, and disgraces, our several borrowings were thrust into a wallet, which was sometimes in his pocket, sometimes in mine, as each took the turn to be paymaster. With the (intercepted) letters in our pockets, informing the governors of our degraded position, we travelled very prosperously on, bound to Niagara, but very ready to fall into any obliquity by the way. We arrived at Albany, Thalimer chancing to be purser; and as this function tacitly conferred on the holder all other responsibilities, I made myself comfortable at the hotel for the second day and the third, up to the seventh, rather wondering at Jem's depressed spirits and the sudden falling-off of his enthusiasm for Niagara, but content to stay if he liked, and amusing myself in the side-hill city passably well. It was during my rambles without him in this week that he made the acquaintance of a bilious-looking person, lodging at the same hotel, — a Louisianian on a tour of health. This gentleman, whom he introduced to me by the name of Dauchy, seemed to have formed a sudden attachment to my friend; and as Jem had a " secret sorrow" unusual to him, and the other an unusual secretion of bile, there was; of course, between them that " secret sympathy" which is the basis of many tender friendships. I rather liked Mr. Dauchy. He seemed one of those chivalric, polysyllabic Southerners, incapable of a short word or a mean action; and, interested that Jem should retain his friendship, I was not sorry to find our departure follow close on the recovery of his spirits.

We went on toward Niagara, and in the irresistible confidence of canal-travelling I made out the secret of my *fidus achates*. He had attempted to alleviate the hardship of a deck passage for a bright-eyed girl on board the steamer, and, on going below to his berth, left her his greatcoat for a pillow. The stuffed wallet, which somewhat distended the breast-pocket, was probably in the way of her downy cheek, and Jem supposed that she simply forgot to return the

" removed deposit ; " but he did not miss his money till twelve hours after, and then, between lack of means to pursue her, and shame at the sentiment he had wasted, he kept the disaster to himself, and passed a melancholy week in devising means for replenishing. Through this *penseroso* vein, however, lay his way out of the difficulty ; for he thus touched the soul and funds of Mr. Dauchy. The correspondence (commenced by the repayment of the loan) was kept up stragglingly for several years, bolstered somewhat by barrels of marmalade, boxes of sugar, hominy, etc., till, finally, it ended in the unlooked-for consignment which forms the subject of my story.

Jem and myself had been a year out of college, and were passing through that " tight place " in life commonly understood in New England as " the going-in at the little end of the horn." Expected by our parents to take to money-making like ducks to swimming, deprived at once of college allowance, called on to be men because our education was paid for, and frowned upon at every manifestation of a lingering taste for pleasure, it was not surprising that we sometimes gave tokens of feeling " crowded," and obtained somewhat the reputation of " bad subjects " (using this expressive phrase quite literally). Jem's share of this odor of wickedness was much the greater, his unlucky deviltry of countenance doing him its usual disservice ; but, like the gentleman to whom he was attributed as a favorite *protégé*, he was " not so black as he was painted."

We had been so fortunate as to find one believer in the future culmination of our clouded stars, — Gallagher, " mine host ; " and for value *to be* received when our brains should fructify, his white soup and " red-string Madeira," his game, turtle, and all the forthcomings of the best restaurant of our epoch, were served lovingly and charged moderately. Peace be with the ashes of William Gallagher ! " The brains " *have* fructified, and "the value" *has been* received; but his name and memory are not "filed away" with the receipt; and, though years have gone over his grave, his modest welcome, and generous dispensation of entertainment and service, are, by one at least of those who enjoyed them, gratefully and freshly remembered.

We were to dine as usual at Gallagher's at six, one May day which I well remember. I was just addressing myself to my day's work, when Jem broke into my room with a letter in his hand, and an expression on his face of mingled embarrassment and fear.

"What the deuce to do with her?" said he, handing me the letter.

"A new scrape, Jem?" I asked, as I looked for an instant at the Dauchy coat-of-arms on a seal as big as a dollar.

"Scrape? yes, it *is* a scrape! for I shall never get out of it reputably. What a dunce old Dauchy must be, to send me a girl to educate! *I* a young lady's guardian! Why, I shall be the laugh of the town! What say? Isn't it a good one?"

I had been carefully perusing the letter while Thalimer walked soliloquizing about the room. It was from his old friend of marmalades and sugars; and in the most confiding and grave terms, as if Jem and he had been a couple of contemporaneous old bachelors, it consigned to his guardianship and friendly counsel Miss Adelmine Lasacque, the only daughter of a neighboring planter! Mr. Lasacque, having no friends at the North, had applied to Mr. Dauchy for his guidance in the selection of a proper person to superintend her education; and as Thalimer was the only correspondent with whom Mr. Dauchy had relations of friendship, and was, moreover, "fitted admirably for the trust by his impressive and dignified address" (?), he had "taken the liberty," etc., etc.

"Have you seen her?" I asked, after a long laugh, in which Jim joined but partially.

"No, indeed! She arrived last night in the New Orleans packet; and the captain brought me this letter at daylight, with the young lady's compliments. The old sea-dog looked a little astounded when I announced myself. Well he might, faith! I don't look like a young lady's guardian, do I?"

"Well, you are to go on board and fetch her: is that it?"

"Fetch her! Where shall I fetch her? Who is to take a young lady of my fetching? I can't find a female academy that I can approve" —

I burst into a roar of laughter; for Jem was in earnest with his scruples, and looked the picture of unhappiness.

"I say I can't find one in a minute, — don't laugh, you blackguard! — and where to lodge her meantime? What should I say to the hotel-keepers? They all know *me!* It looks devilish odd, let me tell you, to bring a young girl, without matron or other acquaintances than myself, and lodge her at a public house."

"Your mother must take your charge off your hands."

"Of course that was the first thing I thought of. You know my mother! She don't half believe the story, in the first place. *If there is* such a man as Mr. Dauchy, she says, and *if this is* a 'Miss Lasacque,' all the way from Louisiana, there is but one thing to do, — send her back in the packet she came in! She'll have nothing to do with it. There's more in it than I am willing to explain. I never mentioned this Mr. Dauchy before. Mischief will come of it! Abduction's a dreadful thing! If I will make myself notorious, I need not think to involve my mother and sisters! That's the way she talks about it."

"But couldn't we mollify your mother? for, after all, her countenance in the matter will be expected."

"Not a chance of it!"

" The money part of it is all right? "

" Turn the letter over.   Credit for a large amount on the Robinsons, payable to my order only. "

" Faith, it's a very hard case if a nice girl with plenty of money can't be permitted to land in Boston !   You didn't ask the captain if she was pretty? "

" No, indeed !   But, pretty or plain, I must get her ashore, and be civil to her.   I must ask her to dine.   I must do something besides hand her over to a boarding-school.   Will you come down to the ship with me? "

My curiosity was quite aroused, and I dressed immediately. On our way down we stopped at Gallagher's to request a little embellishment to our ordinary dinner.   It was quite clear, for a variety of reasons, that she must dine with her guardian there, or nowhere.   Gallagher looked surprised, to say the least, at our proposition to bring a young lady to dine with us, but he made no comment beyond a respectful remark that " No. 2 was very private. "

We had gone but a few steps from Devonshire Street when Jem stopped in the middle of the sidewalk.

" We have not decided yet what we are to do with Miss Lasacque all day, nor where we shall send her baggage, nor where she is to lodge to-night.   For heaven's sake, suggest something ! " added Jem, quite out of temper.

" Why, as you say, it would be heavy work to walk her about the streets from now till dinner-time, — eight hours or more !   Gallagher's is only an eating-house, unluckily, and you are so well known at all the hotels, that to take her to one of them without a chaperon, would, to say the least, give occasion for remark.   But here, around the corner, is one of the best boarding-houses in town, kept by the two old Misses Smith.   You might offer to put her under their protection.   Let's try. "

The Misses Smith were a couple of reduced gentlewomen,

who charged a very good price for board and lodging, and piqued themselves on entertaining only very good company. Begging Jem to assume the confident tone which the virtuous character of his errand required, I rang at the door ; and, in answer to our inquiry for the ladies of the house, we were shown into the basement parlor, where the eldest Miss Smith sat with her spectacles on, adding new vinegar to some pots of pickles. Our business was very briefly stated. Miss Smith had plenty of spare room. Would we wait a moment till she tied on the covers to her pickle-jars?

The cordiality of the venerable demoiselle evidently put Thalimer in spirits. He gave me a glance which said very plainly, '' You see we needn't have troubled our heads about this ! '' But the sequel was to come.

Miss Smith led the way to the second story, where were two very comfortable unoccupied bedrooms.

'' A single lady ? '' she asked.

'' Yes,'' said Jem, '' a Miss Lasacque of Louisiana.''

'' Young, did you say ? ''

'' Seventeen or thereabout, I fancy.'' (This was a guess, but Jem chose to appear to know all about her.)

'' And — ehem ! — and — quite alone ? ''

'' Quite alone ; she is come here to go to school.''

'' Oh, to go to school ! Pray, will she pass her vacations with your mother ? ''

'' No,'' said Jem, coughing, and looking rather embarrassed.

'' Indeed ! She is with Mrs. Thalimer at present, I presume.''

'' No ; she is still on shipboard. Why, my dear madam, she only arrived from New Orleans this morning.''

'' And your mother has not had time to see her ? I understand. Mrs. Thalimer will accompany her here, of course.''

Jem began to see the end of the old maid's catechism, and

thought it best to volunteer the remainder of the information.

"My mother is not acquainted with this young lady's friends," he said; "and, in fact, she comes introduced only to myself."

"She has a guardian, surely?" said Miss Smith, drawing back into her Elizabethan ruff with more dignity than she had hitherto worn.

"I am her guardian," replied Jem, looking as red and guilty as if he had really abducted the young lady, and was ashamed of his errand.

The spinster bit her lips, and looked out of the window.

"Will you walk down stairs for a moment, gentlemen," she resumed, "and let me speak to my sister. I should have told you that the rooms *might* possibly be engaged. I am not quite sure, — indeed — ehem — pray walk down, and be seated a moment."

Very much to the vexation of my discomfited friend, I burst into a laugh as we closed the door of the basement parlor behind us.

"You don't realize my confoundedly awkward position," said he. "I am responsible for every step I take, to the girl's father in the first place, and then to my friend Dauchy, one of the most chivalric old cocks in the world, who, at the same time, could never understand why there was any difficulty in the matter. And it *does* seem strange, that, in a city with eighty thousand inhabitants, it should be next to impossible to find lodging for a virtuous lady, a stranger!"

I was contriving how to tell Thalimer that "there was no objection to the camel but for the dead cat hung upon its neck," when a maid-servant opened the door with a message: "Miss Smith's compliments, and she was very sorry she had no room to spare."

"Pleasant!" said Jem, "very pleasant! I suppose every

other keeper of a respectable house will be equally sorry. Meantime, it's getting on toward noon, and that poor girl is moping on shipboard, wondering whether she is ever to be taken ashore. Do you think she might sleep at Gallagher's?"

"Certainly not. He has probably no accommodations for a lady; and to lodge in a restaurant, after dining with you there, would be an indiscreet first step in a strange city, to say the least. But let us make our visit to your fair ward, my dear Jem. Perhaps she has a face innocent enough to tell its own story, like the lady who walked through Erin ' with the snow-white wand.' "

The vessel had lain in the stream all night, and was just hauling up to the wharf with the moving tide. A crowd of spectators stood at the end of her mooring-cable; and, as she warped in, universal attention seemed to be given to a single object. Upon a heap of cotton-bales, the highest point of the confused lumber of the deck, sat a lady under a sky-blue parasol. Her gown was of pink silk; and, by the volume of this showy material which was presented to the eye, the wearer, when standing, promised to turn out of rather conspicuous stature. White gloves, a pair of superb amethyst bracelets, a string of gold beads on her neck, and shoulders quite naked enough for a ball, were all the disclosures made for a while by the envious parasol, if we except a little object in blue, which seemed the extremity of something she was sitting on, held in her left hand, and which turned out to be her right foot in a blue satin slipper.

I turned to Thalimer. He was literally pale with consternation.

" Hadn't you better send for a carriage to take your ward away? " I suggested.

" You don't believe that to be Miss Lasacque, surely! " exclaimed Jem, turning upon me with an imploring look.

"Such is my foreboding," I replied; "but wait a moment. Her face may be pretty; and you, of course, in your guardian capacity, may suggest a simplification of her toilet. Consider, the poor girl was never before off the plantation: at least, so says old Dauchy's letter."

The sailors now began to pull upon the sternline; and, as the ship came round, the face of the unconscious object of curiosity stole into view. Most of the spectators, after a single glance, turned their attention elsewhere with a smile; and Jem, putting his hands into his two coat-pockets behind him, walked off toward the end of the pier, whistling to himself very energetically. She was an exaggeration of the peculiar physiognomy of the South, lean rather than slight, sallow rather than pale. Yet I thought her eyes fine.

Thalimer joined me as the ship touched the dock, and we stepped on board together. The cabin-boy confirmed our expectations as to the lady's identity; and, putting on the very insinuating manner which was part of his objectionable exterior, Jem advanced, and begged to know if he had the honor of addressing Miss Lasacque.

Without loosing her hold upon her right foot, the lady nodded.

"Then, madam," said Jem, "permit me to introduce to you your guardian, Mr. Thalimer."

"What, that old gentleman coming this way?" asked Miss Lasacque, fixing her eyes on a custom-house officer who was walking the deck.

Jem handed the lady his card.

"That is my name," said he, "and I should be happy to know how I can begin the duties of my office."

"Dear me!" said the astonished damsel, dropping her foot to take his hand, "isn't there an older Mr. James Thalimer? Mr. Dauchy said it was a gentleman near his own age."

"I grow older, as you know me longer," Jem replied apologetically; but his ward was too well satisfied with his appearance, to need even this remarkable fact to console her. She came down with a slide from her cotton-bag elevation, called to the cook to bring the bandbox with the bonnet in it, and meantime gave us a brief history of the inconveniences she had suffered in consequence of the loss of her slave Dinah, who had died of sea-sickness three days out. This, to me, was bad news; for I had trusted to a "lady's maid" for the preservation of appearances, and the scandal threatening Jem's guardianship looked, in consequence, very imminent.

"I am dying to get my feet on land again," said Miss Lasacque, putting her arm in her guardian's, and turning toward the gangway, her bonnet not tied, nor her neck covered, and thin blue satin slippers — though her feet *were* small — showing forth in contrast with her pink silk gown with frightful conspicuousness. Jem resisted the shoreward pull, and stood motionless and aghast.

"Your baggage," he stammered at last.

"Here, cook!" cried the lady, "tell the captain, when he comes aboard, to send my trunks to Mr. Thalimer's. —They are down in the hold, and he told me he couldn't get at 'em till to-morrow," she added, by way of explanation to Thalimer.

I felt constrained to come to the rescue.

"Pardon me, madam," said I: "there is a little peculiarity in our climate, of which you probably are not advised. An east wind commonly sets in about noon, which makes a shawl very necessary. In consequence, too, of the bronchitis which this sudden change is apt to give people of tender constitutions, the ladies of Boston are obliged to sacrifice what is becoming, and wear their dresses very high in the throat."

"La!" said the astonished damsel, putting her hand upon

her bare neck, "is it sore throat that you mean? I'm very subject to it, indeed!—Cook, bring me that fur-tippet out of the cabin. I'm so sorry my dresses are all made so low, and I haven't a shawl unpacked either! Dear, dear!"

Jem and I exchanged a look of hopeless resignation, as the cook appeared with the chinchilla tippet. A bold man might have hesitated to share the conspicuousness of such a figure in a noon promenade; but we each gave her an arm when she had tied the soiled ribbon around her throat, and silently set forward.

It was a bright and very warm day, and there seemed a conspiracy among our acquaintances to cross our path. Once in the street, it was not remarkable that they looked at us, for the towering height at which the lady carried her very showy bonnet, the flashy material of her dress, the jewels, and the chinchilla tippet formed an *ensemble* which caught the eye like a rainbow; and truly people did gaze, and the boys, spite of the unconscious look which we attempted, did give rather disagreeable evidence of being amused. I had various misgivings, myself, as to the necessity for my own share in the performance, and, at every corner, felt sorely tempted to bid guardian and ward good-morning; but friendship and pity prevailed. By streets and lanes not calculated to give Miss Lasacque a very favorable first impression of Boston, we reached Washington Street, and made an intrepid dash across it, to the Marlborough Hotel.

Of this public house, Thalimer had asked my opinion during our walk, by way of introducing an apology to Miss Lasacque for not taking her to his own home. She had made it quite clear that she expected this; and Jem had nothing for it but to draw such a picture of the decrepitude of Mr. Thalimer senior, and the bedridden condition of his mother (as stout a couple as ever plodded to church), as would satisfy the lady for his shortcomings in hospitality.

This had passed off very smoothly; and Miss Lasacque entered the Marlborough, quite prepared to lodge there, but very little aware (poor girl!) of the objections to receiving her as a lodger.

Mr. ——, the proprietor, had stood in the archway as we entered. Seeing no baggage in the lady's train, however, he had not followed us in, supposing, probably, that we were callers on some of his guests. Jem left us in the drawing-room, and went upon his errand to the proprietor; but, after half an hour's absence, came back, looking very angry, and informed us that no rooms were to be had. Instead of taking the rooms without explanation, he had been unwise enough to " make a clean breast" to Mr. ——; and the story of the lady's being his " ward," and come from Louisiana to go to school, rather staggered that discreet person's credulity.

Jem beckoned me out, and we held a little council of war in the entry. Alas! I had nothing to suggest. I knew the Puritan metropolis very well; I knew its *phobia* was " the *appearance* of evil." In Jem's care-for-nothing face lay the leprosy which closed all doors against us. Even if we had succeeded, by a *coup-de-main*, in lodging Miss Lasacque at the Marlborough, her guardian's daily visits would have procured for her, in the first week, some intimation that she could no longer be accommodated.

" We had best go and dine upon it," said I. " Worst come to the worst, we can find some sort of dormitory for her at Gallagher's; and to-morrow she must be put to school, out of the reach of your ' pleasant but wrong society.' "

" I hope to heaven she'll ' stay put,' " said Jem, with a long sigh.

We got Miss Lasacque again under way, and, avoiding the now crowded *pavé* of Washington Street, made a short cut by Theatre Alley to Devonshire Street and Gallagher's. Safely landed in " No. 2," we drew a long breath of relief. Jem rang the bell.

"Dinner, waiter, as soon as possible."

"The same that was ordered at six, sir?"

"Yes, only more champagne, and bring it immediately. — Excuse me, Miss Lasacque," added Jem, with a grave bow, "but the non-appearance of that east wind my friend spoke of has given me an unnatural thirst. Will you join me in some champagne after your hot walk?"

"No, thank you," said the lady, untying her tippet, "but, if you please, I will go to my room before dinner."

Here was trouble again! It had never occurred to either of us, that ladies must go to their rooms before bedtime.

"Stop!" cried Jem, as she laid her hand on the bell to ring for the chambermaid. "Excuse me — I must first speak to the landlord. The room — the room is not ready, probably!"

He seized his hat, and made his exit, probably wishing all confiding friends, with their neighbors' daughters, in a better world! He had to do with a man of sense, however. Gallagher had but one bedroom in the house which was not a servant's room, and that was his own. In ten minutes it was ready, and at the lady's service. A black scullion was promoted for the nonce to the post of chambermaid; and, fortunately, the plantation-bred girl had not been long enough from home to be particular. She came to dinner as radiant as a summer-squash.

With the door shut, and the soup before us, Thalimer's spirits and mine flung off their burthens together. Jem was the pleasantest table-companion in the world; and he chatted and made the amiable to his ward, as if he owed her some amends for the awkward position of which she was so blessedly unconscious. Your "dangerous man" (such as he was voted) inspires, of course, no distrust in those to whom he chooses to be agreeable. Miss Lasacque grew, every minute, more delighted with him. She, too, improved on ac-

quaintance. Come to look at her closely, nature meant her
for a fine, showy creature ; and she was " out of condition,"
as the jockeys say, that was all. Her features were good,
though gamboged by a Southern climate ; and the fever and
ague had flattened what should be round and ripe lips, and
reduced to the mere frame what should be the bust and neck
of a Di Vernon. I am not sure I saw all this at the time.
Her subsequent chrysalis, and emergence into a beautiful
woman, naturally color my description now. But I did see
then that her eyes were large and lustrous, and that naturally she had high spirit, good abilities, and was a thorough
woman in sentiment ; though deplorably neglected, for, at
the age of twenty, she could hardly read and write. It was
not surprising that she was pleased with *us!* She was the
only lady present, and we were the first coxcombs she had
ever seen, and the day was summery, and the dinner in Gallagher's best style. We treated her like a princess ; and the
more agreeable man of the two being her guardian, and
responsible for the propriety of the whole affair, there was
no chance for a failure. We lingered over our coffee, and
we lingered over our *chassecafé*, and we lingered over our
tea ; and, when the Old South struck twelve, we were still at
the table in " No. 2," quite too much delighted with each
other to have thought of separating. It was the venerated
guardian who made the first move ; and after ringing up the
waiter, to discover that the scullion had six hours before
made her nightly disappearance, the lady was respectfully
dismissed with only a candle for her chambermaid, and
Mr. Gallagher's room for her destination — wherever that
might be !

We dined together every successive day for a week, and
during this time the plot rapidly thickened. Thalimer, of
course, vexed soul and body to obtain for Miss Lasacque a
less objectionable lodging ; urged scarcely more by his sense

of propriety than by a feeling for her good-natured host, who, meantime, slept on a sofa. But the unlucky first step of dining and lodging a young lady at a restaurant, inevitable as it was, gave a fatal assurance to the predisposed scandal of the affair; and every day's events heightened its glaring complexion. Miss Lasacque had ideas of her own, and very independent ones, as to the amusement of her leisure hours. She had never been before where there were shops; and she spent her first two or three mornings in perambulating Washington Street, dressed in a style perfectly amazing to beholders, and purchasing every description of gay trumpery; the parcels, of course, sent to Gallagher's, and the bills to James Thalimer, Esq. To keep her out of the street, Jem took her, on the third day, to the riding-school, leaving her (safely enough, he thought) in charge of the authoritative Mr. Roulstone, while he besieged some schoolmistress or other to undertake her ciphering and geography. She was all but born on horseback, however, and soon tired of riding round the ring. The street-door was set open for a moment, leaving exposed a tempting tangent to the circle; and out flew Miss Lasacque, saving her "Leghorn flat" by a bend to the saddle-bow that would have done credit to a dragoon; and no more was seen, for hours, of the "bonnie black mare" and her rider.

The deepening of Miss Lasacque's passion for Jem would not interest the reader. She loved like other women, timidly and pensively. Young as the passion was, however, it came too late to affect her manners before public opinion had pronounced on them. There was neither boarding-house nor "private female academy" within ten miles, into which "Mr. Thalimer's young lady" would have been permitted to set her foot, small as was the foot, and innocent as was the pulse to which it stepped.

Uncomfortable as was this state of suspense, and anxious

as we were to fall into the track marked "virtuous," if virtue would only permit, public opinion seemed to think we were enjoying ourselves quite too prosperously. On the morning of the seventh day of our guardianship, I had two calls after breakfast, — one from poor Gallagher, who reported that he had been threatened with a prosecution of his establishment as a nuisance; and another from poorer Jem, whose father had threatened to take the lady out of his hands, and lodge her in the insane-asylum.

"Not that I don't wish she was there," added Jem, "for it is a very fine place, with a nice garden, and luxuries enough for those who can pay for them. And faith, I believe it's the only lodging-house I've not applied to."

I must shorten my story. Jem anticipated his father, by riding over, and showing his papers constituting him the guardian of Miss Lasacque, in which capacity he was, of course, authorized to put his ward under the charge of keepers. Everybody who knows Massachusetts knows that its insane-asylums are sometimes brought to bear on irregular morals, as well as on diseased intellects; and, as the presiding officer of the institution was quite well assured that Miss Lasacque was well qualified to become a patient, Jem had no course left but to profit by the error. The poor girl was invited, that afternoon, to take a drive in the country; and we came back and dined without her, in abominable spirits, I must say.

Provided with the best instruction, the best of care taken of her health, and the most exemplary of matrons interesting herself in her patient's improvement, Miss Lasacque rapidly improved; more rapidly, no doubt, than she ever could have done by control less rigid and inevitable. Her father, by the advice of the matron, was not informed of her location for a year; and at the end of that time he came on, accompanied by his friend Mr. Dauchy. He found his daughter sufficiently improved in health, manners, and beauty, to be quite satisfied with Jem's discharge of his trust; and we all dined very pleasantly in " No. 2," Miss Lasacque declining, with a blush, my invitation to her to make one of the party.

PASQUALI, THE TAILOR OF VENICE.

CHAPTER I.

GIANNINO PASQUALI was a smart tailor, some five years ago, occupying a cool shop on one of the smaller canals of Venice. Four pairs of suspenders, a print of the fashions, and a motley row of the gay-colored trousers worn by the gondoliers, ornamented the window looking on the dark alley in the rear; and, attached to the post of the water-gate on the canal side, floated a small black gondola, the possession of which afforded the same proof of prosperity of the Venetian tailor which is expressed by a horse and buggy at the door of a snip in London. The place-seeking traveller, who, *nez en l'air*, threaded the tangled labyrinth of alleys and bridges between the Rialto and St. Mark's, would scarce have observed the humble shop-window of Pasquali; yet he had a consequence on the Piazza, and the lagoon had seen his triumphs as an amateur gondolier. Giannino was some thirty years of age; and his wife Fiametta, whom he had married for her *zecchini*, was on the shady side of fifty.

If the truth must be told, Pasquali had discovered, that, even with a bag of sequins for eye-water, Fiametta was not always the most lovely woman in Venice. Just across the canal lived old Donna Bentoccata the nurse, whose daughter Turturilla was like the blonde in Titian's picture of the Marys; and to the charms of Turturilla, even seen through the leaden light of poverty, the unhappy Pasquali was far from insensible.

The festa of San Antonio arrived after a damp week of November; and, though you would suppose the atmosphere of Venice not liable to any very sensible increase of moisture, Fiametta, like people who live on land, and who have the rheumatism as a punishment for their age and ugliness, was usually confined to her *brazero* of hot coals till it was dry enough on the Lido for the peacocks to walk abroad. On this festa, however, San Antonio being, as every one knows, the patron saint of Padua, the Padovese were to come down the Brenta, as was their custom, and cross over the sea to Venice to assist in the celebration; and Fiametta once more thought Pasquali loved her for herself alone when he swore by his rosary, that, unless she accompanied him to the festa in her wedding-dress, he would not turn an oar in the race, nor unfasten his gondola from the door-post. Alas! Fiametta was married in the summer solstice, and her dress was permeable to the wind as a cobweb or gossamer. Is it possible you could have remembered that, O wicked Pasquali?

It was a day to puzzle a barometer, — now bright, now rainy; now gusty as a corridor in a novel, and now calm as a lady after a fit of tears. Pasquali was up early, and waked Fiametta with a kiss; and by way of unusual tenderness, or by way of insuring the wedding-dress, he chose to play dressing-maid, and arranged with his own hands her *jupon* and *fezzoletta*. She emerged from her chamber looking like a slice of orange-peel in a flower-bed, but smiling and nodding, and vowing the day warm as April, and the sky without a cloud. The widening circles of an occasional drop of rain in the canal were nothing but the bubbles bursting after a passing oar, or perhaps the last flies of summer. Pasquali swore it was weather to win down a Peri.

As Fiametta stepped into the gondola, she glanced her eyes over the way, and saw Turturilla, with a face as sorrowful as

the first day in Lent, seated at her window. Her lap was full
of work, and it was quite evident that she had not thought of
being at the festa. Fiametta's heart was already warm, and
it melted quite at the view of the poor girl's loneliness.

"*Pasquali mio,*" she said in a deprecating tone, as if she
were uncertain how the proposition would be received, "I
think we could make room for poor Turturilla."

A gleam of pleasure, unobserved by the confiding *sposa*,
tinted faintly the smooth olive cheek of Pasquali.

"Eh! *diavolo!*" he replied, so loud that the sorrowful
seamstress heard, and hung down her head still lower.
"Must you take pity on every cheese-paring of a *regezza*
who happens to have no lover? Have reason! have reason!
The gondola is narrower than your brave heart, my fine
Fiametta." And away he pushed from the water-steps.

Turturilla rose from her work, and stepped out upon the
rusty gratings of the balcony to see them depart. Pasquali
stopped to grease the notch of his oar; and, between that and
some other embarrassments, the gondola was suffered to float
directly under her window. The compliment to the generous
nature of Fiametta was, meantime, working; and, as she
was compelled to exchange a word or two with Turturilla
while her husband was getting his oar into the socket, it
resulted (as he thought it very probable it would) in the
good wife's renewing her proposition, and making a point of
sending the deserted girl for her holiday bonnet. Pasquali
swore through all the saints and angels by the time she had
made herself ready, though she was but five minutes gone
from the window; and, telling Fiametta in her ear that she
must consider it as the purest obligation, he backed up to the
steps of old Donna Bentoccata, helped in her daughter with
a better grace than could have been expected, and, with one
or two short and deep strokes, put forth into the Grand Canal
with the velocity of a lance-fly.

A gleam of sunshine lay along the bosom of the broad silver sheet; and it was beautiful to see the gondolas with their gay-colored freights all hastening in one direction and with swift track to the festa. Far up and down they rippled the smooth water, here gliding out from below a palace-arch, there from a narrow and unseen canal, the steel beaks curved and flashing, the water glancing on the oar-blades, the curtains moving, and the fair women of Venice leaning out and touching hands as they neared neighbor or acquaintance in the close-pressing gondolas. It was a beautiful sight, indeed. And three of the happiest hearts in that swift-gliding company were in Pasquali's gondola; though the bliss of Fiametta, I am compelled to say, was entirely owing to the bandage with which Love is so significantly painted. Ah, poor Fiametta!

From the Lido, from Fusina, from under the Bridge of Sighs, from all quarters of the lagoon, and from all points of the floating city of Venice, streamed the flying gondolas to the Giudecca. The narrow walk along the edge of the long and close-built island was thronged with booths and promenaders; and the black barks by hundreds bumped their steel noses against the pier, as the agitated water rose and fell beneath them. The gondolas intended for the race pulled slowly up and down, close to the shore, exhibiting their fairy-like forms and their sinewy and gayly-dressed gondoliers to the crowds on land and water; the bands of music, attached to different parties, played here and there a strain; the criers of holy pictures and gingerbread made the air vocal with their lisping and soft Venetian; and all over the scene, as if it was the light of the sky or some other light as blessed but less common, shone glowing black eyes, black as night, and sparkling as the stars on night's darkest bosom. He who thinks lightly of Italian beauty should have seen the women of Venice on St. Antonio's Day, '32, or on any day, or at any hour when their pulses are beating high and their eyes alight, for they are neither one nor the other always. The women of that fair clime, to borrow the simile of Moore, are like lava-streams, only bright when the volcano kindles. Their long lashes cover lustreless eyes, and their blood shows dully through the cheek in common and listless hours. The calm, the passive tranquillity in which the delicate graces of colder climes find their element, are to them a torpor of the heart, when the blood scarce seems to flow. They are wakeful only to the energetic, the passionate, the joyous movements of the soul.

Pasquali stood erect in the prow of his gondola, and stole furtive glances at Turturilla, while he pointed away with his finger to call off the sharp eyes of Fiametta. But Fiametta was happy and unsuspicious. Only when now and then the wind came up chilly from the Adriatic, the poor wife shivered, and sat closer to Turturilla, who, in her plainer but thicker dress, to say nothing of younger blood, sat more comfortably on the black cushion, and thought less about the weather. An occasional drop of rain fell on the nose of poor Fiametta; but, if she did not believe it was the spray from Pasquali's oar, she at least did her best to believe so. And the perfidious tailor swore by St. Anthony that the clouds were as dry as her eyelashes. I never was very certain that Turturilla was not in the secret of this day's treacheries.

The broad centre of the Giudecca was cleared, and the boats took their places for the race. Pasquali ranged his gondola with those of the other spectators; and, telling Fiametta in her ear that he should sit on the other side of Turturilla as a punishment for their *malapropos* invitation, he placed himself on the small remainder of the deep cushion, on the farthest side from his now penitent spouse; and, while he complained almost rudely of the narrowness of his seat, he made free to hold on by Turturilla's waist, which, no doubt, made the poor girl's mind more easy on the subject of her intrusion.

Who won and who lost the race, what was the device of each flag, and what bets and bright eyes changed owners by the result, no personage of this tale knew or cared save Fiametta. She looked on eagerly. Pasquali and Turturilla, as the French say, *trouvaient autres chats à frotter*.

After the decision of the grand race, St. Antonio being the protector more particularly of the humble (" patron of pigs " in the saints' calendar), the *seignoria* and the grand people generally pulled away for St. Mark's, leaving the crowded Giudecca to the people. Pasquali, as was said before, had some renown as a gondolier. Something that would be called in other countries a scrub-race, followed the departure of the winning boat; and several gondolas, holding each one person only, took their places for the start. The tailor laid his hand on his bosom, and, with the smile that had first stirred the heart and the sequins of Fiametta, begged her to gratify his love by acting as his make-weight while he turned an oar for the pig of St. Antonio. The prize, roasted to an appetizing crisp, stood high on a platter in front of one of the booths on shore; and Fiametta smacked her lips, overcame her tears with an effort, and told him, in accents as little as possible like the creak of a dry oar in the socket, that he might set Turturilla on shore.

A word in her ear, as he handed her over the gunwale, reconciled Donna Bentoccata's fair daughter to this conjugal partiality; and, stripping his manly figure of its upper disguises, Pasquali straightened out his fine limbs, and drove his bark to the line in a style that drew applause from even his competitors. As a mark of their approbation they offered him an outside place, where his fair dame would be less likely to be spattered with the contending oars; but he was too generous to take advantage of this considerate offer, and crying out, as he took the middle, " *ben pronto, signori !* " gave Fiametta a confident look, and stood like a hound in the leash.

Off they went, at the tap of the drum ; poor Fiametta holding her breath, and clinging to the sides of the gondola, and Pasquali developing skill and muscle — not for Fiametta's eyes only. It was a short, sharp race, without jockeying or management ; all fair play and main strength ; and the tailor shot past the end of the Giudecca a boat's-length ahead. Much more applauded than a king at a coronation, or a lord-mayor taking water at London stairs, he slowly made his way back to Turturilla ; and it was only when that demure damsel rather shrunk from sitting down in two inches of water, that he discovered how the disturbed element had quite filled up the hollow of the leather cushion, and made a peninsula of the uncomplaining Fiametta. She was as well watered as a favorite plant in a flower-garden.

" *Pasquali mio !* " she said in an imploring tone, holding up the skirt of her dress with the tips of her thumb and finger, " could you just take me home while I change my dress ? "

" One moment, *Fiametta cara !* they are bringing the pig."

The crisp and succulent trophy was solemnly placed in the prow of the victor's gondola, and preparation was made to convoy him home with a triumphant procession. A half-hour before it was in order to move, an hour in first making the circuit of the Grand Canal, and an hour more in drinking a glass and exchanging good wishes at the stairs of the Rialto, and Donna Fiametta had sat too long by two hours and a half with scarce a dry thread on her body. What afterward befell will be seen in the more melancholy sequel.

CHAPTER II.

THE hospital of St. Girolamo is attached to the convent of that name, standing on one of the canals which put forth on the seaward side of Venice. It is a long building, with its low windows and latticed doors opening almost on the level of the sea; and the wards for the sick are large and well aired, but, except when the breeze is stirring, impregnated with a saline dampness from the canal, which, as Pasquali remarked, was *good* for the rheumatism. It was not so good for the patient.

The loving wife, Fiametta, grew worse and worse after the fatal festa; and the fit of rheumatism brought on by the slightness of her dress, and the spattering he had given her in the race, had increased by the end of the week to a rheumatic fever. Fiametta was old and tough, however, and struggled manfully (woman as she was) with the disease; but being one night a little out of her head, her loving husband took occasion to shudder at the responsibility of taking care of her, and, jumping into his gondola, he pulled across to St. Girolamo, and bespoke a dry bed and a sister of charity, and brought back the pious father Gasparo and a comfortable litter. Fiametta was dozing when they arrived; and the kind-hearted tailor, willing to spare her the pain of knowing that she was on her way to the hospital for the poor, set out some meat and wine for the monk, and, sending over for Turturilla and the nurse to mix the salad, they sat and ate away the hours till the poor dame's brain should be wandering again.

Toward night the monk and Dame Bentoccata were comfortably dozing with each other's support (having fallen asleep at table), and Pasquali, with a kiss from Turturilla, stole softly up stairs. Fiametta was muttering unquietly, and working her fingers in the palms of her hands, and on feeling her pulse he found the fever was at its height. She took him, besides, for the prize pig of the festa, for he knew her wits were fairly abroad. He crept down stairs, gave the monk a strong cup of coffee to get him well awake, and, between the four of them, they got poor Fiametta into the litter, drew the curtains tenderly around, and deposited her safely in the bottom of the gondola.

Lightly and smoothly the winner of the pig pulled away with his loving burden, and gliding around the slimy corners of the palaces, and hushing his voice as he cried out " right ! " or " left ! " to guard the coming gondoliers of his vicinity, he arrived, like a thought of love to a maid's mind in sleep, at the door of St. Girolamo. The abbess looked out and said, " *Benedicite !* " and the monk stood firm on his brown sandals to receive the precious burden from the arms of Pasquali. Believing firmly that it was equivalent to committing her to the hand of St. Peter, and of course abandoning all hope of seeing her again in this world, the soft-hearted tailor wiped his eye as she was lifted in, and receiving a promise from Father Gasparo that he would communicate faithfully the state of her soul in the last agony, he pulled, with lightened gondola and heart, back to his widower's home and Turturilla.

For many good reasons, and apparent as good, it is a rule in the hospital of St. Girolamo, that the sick under its holy charge shall receive the visit of neither friend nor relative. If they recover, they return to their abodes to earn candles for the altar of the restoring saint. If they die, their clothes are sent to their surviving friends, and this affecting memorial, besides communicating the melancholy news, affords all the particulars and all the consolation they are supposed to require upon the subject of their loss.

Waiting patiently for Father Gasparo and his bundle, Pasquali and Turturilla gave themselves up to hopes, which on the tailor's part (we fear it must be admitted), augured a quicker recovery from grief than might be credited to an elastic constitution. The fortune of poor Fiametta was sufficient to warrant Pasquali in neglecting his shop to celebrate every festa that the church acknowledged, and for ten days subsequent to the committal of his wife to the tender mercies of St. Girolamo, five days out of seven was the proportion of merry holidays with his new betrothed.

They were sitting one evening in the open piazza of St. Mark, in front of the most thronged *café* of that matchless square. The moon was resting her silver disk on the point of the Campanile, and the shadows of thousands of gay Venetians fell on the immense pavement below, clear and sharply drawn as a black cartoon. The four extending sides of the square lay half in shades half in light, with their innumerable columns and balconies and sculptured work, and, frowning down on all, in broken light and shadow, stood the arabesque structure of St. Mark's itself, dizzying the eyes with its mosaics and confused devices, and thrusting forth the heads of her four golden-collared steeds into the moon-beams, till they looked on that black relief, like the horses of Pluto issuing from the gates of Hades. In the centre of the square stood a tall woman, singing, in rich contralto, an old song of the better days of Venice; and against one of the pillars, Polichinello had backed his wooden stage, and beat about his puppets with an energy worthy of old Dandolo and his helmeted galley-men. To those who wore not the spectacles of grief or discontent, the square of St. Mark's that night was like some cozening *tableau*. *I* never saw any thing so gay.

Everybody who has " swam in a gondola," knows how the *cafés* of Venice thrust out their checkered awnings over a

portion of the square, and filled the shaded space below with
chairs and marble tables.   In a corner of the shadow thus
afforded, with ice and coffee on a small round slab between
them, and the flat pavement of the public promenade under
their feet, sat our two lovers.   With neither hoof nor wheel
to drown or interrupt their voices (as in cities whose streets
are stones, not water), they murmured their hopes and wishes
in the softest language under the sun, and with the *sotto voce*
acquired by all the inhabitants of this noiseless city.   Turturilla had taken ice to cool her and coffee to take off the
chill of her ice, and a *bicchiere del perfetto amore* to reconcile
these two antagonists in her digestion, when the slippers of a
monk glided by, and in a moment the recognized Father Gasparo made a third in the shadowy corner.   The expected
bundle was under his arm, and he was on his way to Pasquali's dwelling.   Having assured the disconsolate tailor that
she had unction and wafer as became the wife of a citizen
of Venice like himself, he took heart and grew content that
she was in heaven.   It was a better place, and Turturilla
for so little as a gold ring, would supply her place in his
bosom.

The moon was but a brief week older when Pasquali and
Turturilla stood in the Church of our Lady of Grief, and
Father Gasparo within the palings of the altar.   She was as
fair a maid as ever bloomed in the garden of beauty beloved
of Titian, and the tailor was nearer worth nine men to look
at, than the fraction of a man considered usually the expo-
nent of his profession.   Away mumbled the good father upon
the matrimonial service, thinking of the old wine and rich
pastries that were holding their sweetness under cork and
crust only till he had done his ceremony, and quicker by
some seconds than had ever been achieved before by priest
or bishop, he arrived at the putting on of the ring.   His
hand was tremulous, and (oh unlucky omen!) he dropped it

within the gilded fence of the chancel.   The choristers were
called, and Father Gasparo dropped on his knees to look for
it — but if the devil had not spirited it away, there was no
other reason why that search was in vain.   Short of an errand
to the goldsmith on the Rialto, it was at last determined the
wedding could not proceed.   Father Gasparo went to hide
his impatience within the restiary, and Turturilla knelt down
to pray against the arts of Sathanas.   Before they had settled severally to their pious occupations, Pasquali was half
way to the Rialto.

Half an hour elapsed, and then instead of the light grazing of a swift-sped gondola along the church stairs, the splash
of a sullen oar was heard, and Pasquali stepped on shore.
They hastened to the door to receive him — monk, choristers and bride — and to their surprise and bewilderment, he
waited to hand out a woman in a strange dress, who seemed
disposed, bridegroom as he was, to make him wait her leisure.
Her clothes fitted her ill, and she carried in her hand a pair
of shoes it was easy to see were never made for her.   She
rose at last, and as her face became visible, down dropped
Turturilla and the pious father, and motionless and aghast
stood the simple Pasquali.   Fiametta stepped on shore !

In broken words Pasquali explained.   He had landed at the
stairs near the fish market, and with two leaps reaching the
top, sped off past the buttress in the direction of the goldsmith, when his course was arrested by encountering at full
speed, the person of an old woman.   Hastily raising her up,
he recognized his wife, who, fully recovered, but without a
gondola, was threading the zigzag alleys on foot, on her way
to her own domicile.   After the first astonishment was over,
her dress explained the error of the good father and the
extent of his own misfortune.   The clothes had been hung
between the bed of Fiametta and that of a smaller woman
who had been long languishing of a consumption.   She died,

and Fiametta's clothes, brought to the door by mistake, were recognized by Father Gasparo and taken to Pasquali.

The holy monk, chop-fallen and sad, took his solitary way to the convent, but with the first step he felt something slide into the heel of his sandal. He sat down on the church stairs, and absolved the devil from theft — it was the lost ring, which had fallen upon his foot and saved Pasquali the tailor from the pains of bigamy.

THE GYPSY OF SARDIS.

. . . . "And thou art far,
Asia! who, when my being overflowed,
Wert like a golden chalice to bright wine,
Which else had sunk into the thirsty dust."

SHELLEY'S PROMETHEUS.

PART I.

I.

OUR tents were pitched in the vestibule of the house of Crœsus, on the natural terrace which was once the imperial site of Sardis. A humpbacked Dutch artist, who had been in the service of Lady Hester Stanhope as a draughtsman, and who had lingered about between Jerusalem and the Nile till he was as much at home in the East as a Hajji or a crocodile; an Englishman qualifying himself for "The Travellers';" a Smyrniote merchant in figs and opium; Job Smith (my inseparable shadow) and myself, composed a party at this time (August, 1834), rambling about Asia Minor in turbans and Turkish saddles, and pitching our tents, and cooking our *pilau*, wherever it pleased Heaven and the inexorable *suridji* who was our guide and caterer.

I thought at the time that I would compound to abandon all the romance of that renowned spot, for a clean shirt and something softer than a marble frustrum for a pillow; but in the distance of memory, and myself at this present in a deep morocco chair in the library at "The Travellers'," the same scene in the ruins of Sardis does not seem destitute of interest.

It was about four in the lazy summer afternoon. We had arrived at Sardis at mid-day, and after a quarrel whether we should eat immediately or wait till the fashionable hour of three, the wooden dish containing two chickens buried in a tumulus of rice, shaped (in compliment to the spirit of the spot) like the Mound of Alyattis in the plain below, was placed in the centre of a marble pedestal; and with Job and the Dutchman seated on the prostrate column dislodged for our benefit, and the remainder of the party squatted in the high grass, which grew in the royal palace as if it had no memory of the footprints of the kings of Lydia, we spooned away at the saturated rice, and pulled the smothered chickens to pieces with an independence of knives and forks that was worthy of the " certain poor man in Attica.'' Old Solon himself, who stood, we will suppose, while reproving the ostentatious monarch, at the base of that very column now ridden astride by an inhabitant of a country of which he never dreamed (at least it strikes me there is no mention of the Yankees in his philosophy) — the old graybeard of the Academy himself, I say, would have been edified at the primitive simplicity of our repast. The salt (he would have asked if it was Attic) was contained in a ragged playbill, which the Dutchman had purloined as a specimen of modern Greek, from the side of a house in Corfu; the mustard was in a cracked powder-horn, which had been slung at the breast of old Whalley the regicide, in the American Revolution, and which Job had brought from the Green Mountains, and held, till its present base uses, in religious veneration; the ham (I should have mentioned that respectable *entremet* before) was half enveloped in a copy of the "Morning Post;'' and the bread, which had been seven days out from Smyrna, and had been kept warm in the suridji's saddle-bags twelve hours in the twenty-four, lay in *disjecta membra* around the marble table, with marks of vain but persevering attacks in its nibbled edges. The luxury of our larder was comprised in a flask which had once held Harvey's sauce, and though the last drop had served as a condiment to a roasted kid some three months before, in the Acropolis at Athens, we still clung to it with affectionate remembrance, and it was offered and refused daily around the table for the melancholy pleasure of hearing the mention of its name. It was unlucky that the only thing which the place afforded of the best quality, and in sufficient quantities, was precisely the one thing in the world for which no individual of the party had any particular relish — water ! It was brought in a gourd from the bed of the " golden-sanded Pactolus," rippling away to the plain within pistol-shot of the dining-room ; but, to the shame of our simplicity I must record, that a high-shouldered jug of the rough wine of Samos, trodden out by the feet of the lovely slaves of the Ægean, and bought for a farthing the bottle, went oftener to the unclassical lips of the company. Methinks, now (the wind east in London, and the day wet and abominable), I could barter the dinner that I shall presently discuss, with its *suite* of sherries and anchovy, to kneel down by that golden river in the sunshine, and drink a draught of pure lymph under the sky of effeminate Asia. Yet, when I was there — so rarely do we recognize happiness till she is gone — I wished myself (where I had never been) in " merry England." " *Merry*," quotha? Scratch it out, and write comfortable. I have seen none " merry " in England, save those who have most cause to be sad, — the abandoned of themselves and the world !

Out of the reach of ladies and the laws of society, the most refined persons return very much to the natural instincts from which they have departed in the progress of civilization. Job rolled off the marble column when there was nothing more to eat, and went to sleep with the marks of the Samian wine turning up the corners of his mouth like the salacious grin of a satyr. The Dutchman got his hump into a hollow, and buried his head in the long grass with the same obedience to the prompting of nature, and *idem* the suridji and the fig-merchant, leaving me seated alone among the promiscuous ruins of Sardis and the dinner. The dish of philosophy I had with myself on that occasion will appear as a *réchauffe* in my novel (I intend to write one) ; but meantime I may as well give you the practical inference; that, as sleeping after dinner is evidently Nature's law, Washington Irving is highly excusable for the practice, and he would be a friend of reason who should introduce couches and coffee at that somnolent period, the digestive nap taking the place of the indigestible politics usually forced upon the company on the disappearance of the ladies. Why should the world be wedded forever to these bigoted inconveniences !

The grand track from the south and west of Asia Minor passes along the plain between the lofty Acropolis of Sardis and the tombs of her kings ; and, with the snore of travellers from five different nations in my ear, I sat and counted the camels in one of the immense caravans never out of sight in the valley of the Hermus. The long procession of those brown monsters wound slowly past on their way to Smyrna, their enormous burthens covered with colored trappings and swaying backward and forward with their disjointed gait, and their turbaned masters dozing on the backs of the small asses of the east, leading each a score by the tether at his back ; the tinkling of their hundred bells swarmed up through the hot air of the afternoon with the drowsiest of monotones ; the native oleanders, slender-leaved and tall, and just now in all their glory, with a color in their bright flowers stolen from the bleeding lips of Houris, brightened the plains of Lydia like the flush of sunset lying low on the earth ; the black goats of uncounted herds browsed along the ancient

Sarabat, with their bearded faces turned every one to the faintly coming wind : the eagles (that abound now in the mountains from which Sardis and a hundred silent cities once scared their bold progenitors) sailed slowly and fearlessly around the airy citadel that flung open its gates to the Lacedæmonian ; and, gradually, as you may have lost yourself in this tangled paragraph, dear reader, my senses became confused among the objects it enumerates, and I fell asleep with the speech of Solon in my ears, and my back to the crumbling portico of Crœsus.

The Dutchman was drawing my picture when I awoke, the sun was setting, and Job and the suridji were making tea. I am not a very picturesque object, generally speaking, but done as a wild Arab lying at the base of a column, in a white turban, with a stork's nest over my head, I am not so illlooking as you would suppose. As the Dutchman drew for *gelt*, and hoped to sell his picture to some traveller at Smyrna who would take that opportunity to affirm in his book that he had been at Sardis (as *vide* his own sketch), I do not despair of seeing myself yet in lithograph. And, talking of pictures, I would give something now if I had engaged that humpbacked draughtsman to make me a sketch of Job, squat on his hams before a fire in the wall, and making tea in a tin pot, with a " malignant and turbaned Turk " feeding the blaze with the dry thorn of Syria.[1] It would have been consolation to his respectable mother, whom he left in the Green Mountains (wondering what he could have to do with following such a scapegrace as myself through the world), to have seen him in the turban of a Hajji taking his tea quietly in ancient Lydia. The green turban, the sign of the Hajji, belonged more properly to myself ; for though it was Job

---

[1] It has the peculiarity of a *hooked* thorn alternating with the straight, and it is difficult to touch it without lacerating the hands. It is the common thorn of the East, and it is supposed that our Saviour's crown at his crucifixion was made of it.

who went bodily to Jerusalem (leaving me ill of a fig-fever
at Smyrna), the sanctity of the pilgrimage by the Mohammedan law falls on him who provides the pilgrim with scallop-
shell and sandals, aptly figured forth in this case, we will
suppose, by the sixty American dollars paid by myself for
his voyage to Jaffa and back. The suridji was a Hajji, too,
and it was amusing to see Job, who respected every man's
religious opinions, and had a little vanity besides in sharing
with the Turk[1] the dignity of a pilgrimage to the sacred city,
washing his knees and elbows at the hour of prayer, and
considerately, but very much to his own inconvenience, trans-
ferring the ham of the unclean beast from the Mussulman's
saddle-bags to his own. It was a delicate sacrifice to a
pagan's prejudices, worthy of Socrates or a Christian.

II.

In all simple states of society, sunset is the hour of better
angels. The traveller in the desert remembers his home;
the sea-tossed boy, his mother and her last words; the Turk
talks, for a wonder, and the chattering Greek is silent, for the
same; the Italian forgets his mustache, and hums *la patria;*
and the Englishman delivers himself of the society of his
companions, and "takes a walk." It is something in the
influences of the hour, and I shall take trouble, some day, to
maintain that morn, noon, and midnight have their ministry
as well, and exercise each an unobserved but salutary and
peculiar office on the feelings.

We all separated "after tea;" the suridji was off to find
a tethering place for his horses; the Englishman strolled
away by himself to a group of the "tents of Kedar" far

---

[1] The Mussulmans make pilgrimages to Jerusalem, and pray at all the places
consecrated to our Saviour and the Virgin, except only the tomb of Christ, which they
do not acknowledge. They believe that Christ did not die, but ascended alive into
heaven, leaving the likeness of his face to Judas, who was crucified for him.

down in the valley with their herds and herdsmen ; the Smyrniote merchant sat by the camel-track at the foot of the hill
waiting for the passing of a caravan ; the Green-Mountaineer
was wandering around the ruins of the apostolic church ; the
Dutchman was sketching the two Ionic shafts of the fair
temple of Cybele ; and I, with a passion for running water
which I have elsewhere alluded to, idled by the green bank
of the Pactolus, dreaming sometimes of Gyges and Alexan-
der, and sometimes of *you*, dear Mary !

I passed Job on my way, for the four walls over which the
" Angel of the Church of Sardis " kept his brooding watch
in the days of the Apocalypse stand not far from the swelling bank of the Pactolus, and nearly in a line between it
and the palace of Crœsus. I must say that my heart almost
stood still with awe as I stepped over the threshold. In the
next moment, the strong and never-wasting under-current of
early religious feeling rushed back on me, and I involuntarily
uncovered my head, and felt myself stricken with the spell
of holy ground. My friend, who was never without the
Bible that was his mother's parting gift, sat on the end of
the broken wall of the vestibule with the sacred volume open
at the Revelation in his hand.

" I think, Philip," said he, as I stood looking at him in
silence, " I think my mother will have been told by an angel
that I am here."

He spoke with a solemnity that, spite of every other feeling, seemed to me as weighty and true as prophecy.

" Listen, Philip," said he, " it will be something to tell
your mother as well as mine, that we have read the Apocalypse together in the Church of Sardis."

I listened with what I never thought to have heard in Asia
— my mother's voice loud at my heart, as I had heard it in
prayer in my childhood : —

" Thou hast a few names even in Sardis which have not

defiled their garments; and they shall walk with me in white: for they are worthy."

I strolled on. A little farther up the Pactolus stood the Temple of Cybele. The church to which "He" spoke "who hath the seven spirits of God and the seven stars," was a small and humble ruin of brick and mortar; but, of the temple of the heathen mother of the world, remained two fair columns of marble with their curiously carved capitals, and the earth around was strewn with the gigantic frusta of an edifice, stately even in the fragments of its prostration. I saw for a moment the religion of Jupiter and of Christ with the eyes of Crœsus and the philosopher from Athens; and then I turned to the living nations that I had left to wander among these dead empires, and looking still on the eloquent monuments of what these religions *were*, thought of them as they *are*, in wide-spread Christendom.

We visit Rome and Athens, and walk over the ruined temples of their gods of wood and stone, and take pride to ourselves that our imaginations awake the "spirit of the spot." But the primitive church of Christ, over which an angel of God kept watch; whose undefiled members, if there is truth in Holy Writ, are now "walking with him in white" before the face of the Almighty; a spot on which the Saviour and his apostles prayed, and for whose weal, with the other churches of Asia, the sublime revelation was made to John; this, the while, is an unvisited shrine, and the "classic" of pagan idolatry is dearer to the memories of men than the holy antiquities of a religion they profess!

III.

The Ionic capitals of the two fair columns of the fallen temple were still tinged with rosy light on the side toward the sunset, when the full moon, rising in the east, burnished the other like a shaft of silver. The two lights mingled in the sky in a twilight of opal.

" Job," said I, stooping to reach a handful of sand as we strolled up the western bank of the river, " can you resolve me why the poets have chosen to call this pretty stream the ' golden-sanded Pactolus '? Did you ever see sand of a duller gray? "

" As easy as give you a reason," answered Job, " why we found the *turbidus Hermus*, yesterday, the clearest stream we have forded ; why I am no more beautiful than before, though I have bathed like Venus in the Scamander ; why the pumice of Naxos no longer reduces the female bust to its virgin proportions ; and why Smyrna and Malta are *not* the best places for figs and oranges ! "

" And why the old king of Lydia, who possessed the invisible ring, and kept a devil in his dog's collar, lies quietly under the earth in the plain below us, and his ring and his devil were not bequeathed to his successors. What a pleasant auxiliary to sin must have been that invisible ring ! Spirit of Gyges, thrust thy finger out of the earth, and commit it once more to a mortal ! Sit down, my dear monster, and let us speculate in this bright moonshine on the enormities we would commit ! "

As Job was proceeding, in a cautious periphrasis, to rebuke my irreverent familiarity with the prince of darkness and his works, the twilight had deepened, and my eye was caught by a steady light twinkling far above us in the ascending bed of the river. The green valley wound down from the rear of the Acropolis, and the single frowning tower stood in broken and strong relief against the sky ; and from the mass of shadow below peered out, like a star from a cloud-rack, the steady blaze of a lamp.

" Allons ! Job ! " said I, making sure of an adventure, " let us see for whose pleasure a lamp is lit in the solitude of this ruined city."

" I could not answer to your honored mother," said my

scrupulous friend, "if I did not remind you that this is a spot much frequented by robbers, and that probably no honest man harbors at that inconvenient altitude."

I made a leap over a half-buried frieze that had served me as a pillow, and commenced the ascent.

"I could as ill answer to your anxious parent," said Job, following with uncommon alacrity, "if I did not partake your dangers when they are inevitable."

We scrambled up with some difficulty in the darkness, now rolling into an unseen hollow, now stumbling over a block of marble; held fast one moment by the lacerating hooked thorn of Syria, and the next brought to a stand-still by impenetrable thickets of brushwood. With a half-hour's toil, however, we stood on a clear platform of grass, panting and hot; and, as I was suggesting to Job that we had possibly got too high, he laid his hand on my arm, and, with a sign of silence, drew me down on the grass beside him.

In a small fairy amphitheatre, half encircled by a bend of the Pactolus, and lying a few feet below the small platform from which we looked, lay six low tents, disposed in a crescent opposite to that of the stream, and enclosing a circular area of bright and dewy grass, of scarce ten feet in diameter. The tents were round, and laced neatly with wicker-work, with their curtain-doors opening inward upon the circle. In the largest one, which faced nearly down the valley, hung a small iron lamp of an antique shape, with a wick alight in one of its two projecting extremities, and beneath it swung a basket-cradle suspended between two stakes, and kept in motion by a woman apparently of about forty, whose beauty, but for another more attractive object, would have rewarded us alone for our toil. The other tents were closed, and seemed unoccupied; but the curtain of the one into which our eyes were now straining with intense eagerness, was looped entirely back to give admission to the

cool night air; and, in and out, between the light of the lamp
and the full moon, stole on naked feet a girl of fifteen, whose
exquisite symmetry and unconscious but divine grace of
movement filled my sense of beauty as it had never been
filled by the divinest chisel of the Tribune. She was of the
height and mould of the younger water-nymph in Gibson's
Hylas,[1] with limbs and lips that, had I created and warmed
her to life like Pygmalion, I should have just hesitated
whether or not they wanted another half-shade of fulness.
The large shawl of the East, which was attached to her
girdle, and in more guarded hours concealed all but her eyes,
hung in loose folds from her waist to her heels, leaving her
bust and smoothly-rounded shoulders entirely bare; and, in
strong relief even upon her clear brown skin, the flakes of
her glossy and raven hair floated over her back, and swept
around her with the grace of a cloud in her indolent motions.
A short petticoat of striped Brusa silk stretched to her
knees, and below appeared the full trouser of the East, of
the same material, narrowed at the ankle, and bound with
what looked in the moonlight an anklet of silver. A profusion of rings on her fingers, and a gold sequin on her
forehead, suspended from a colored fillet, completed her
dress, and left nothing to be added by the prude or the
painter. She was at that ravishing and divinest moment of
female life, when almost the next hour would complete her
womanhood — like the lotus ere it lays back to the prying
moonlight the snowy leaf nearest its heart.

She was employed in filling a large jar which stood at the
back of the tent, with water from the Pactolus, and as she
turned with her empty pitcher, and came under the full blaze

---

[1] A group that will be immortal in the love and wonder of the world, when the
divine hand of the English Praxiteles has long passed from the earth. Two more
exquisite shapes of women than those lily-crowned nymphs never lay in the womb
— of marble or human mother. Rome is brighter for them.

of the lamp in her way outward, treading lightly lest she should disturb the slumber of the child in the cradle, and pressing her two round hands closely to the sides of the vessel, the gradual compression of my arm by the bony hand which still held it for sympathy, satisfied me that my own leaping pulse of admiration found an answering beat in the bosom of my friend. A silent nod from the woman, whose Greek profile was turned to us under the lamplight, informed the lovely water-bearer that her labors were at an end ; and with a gesture expressive of heat, she drew out the shawl from her girdle, untied the short petticoat, and threw them aside, and then tripping out into the moonlight with only the full silken trousers from her waist to her ankles, she sat down on the brink of the small stream, and with her feet in the water, dropped her head on her knees, and sat as motion- less as marble.

" Gibson should see her now," I whispered to Job, " with the glance of the moonlight on that dimpled and polished back, and her almost glittering hair veiling about her in such masses, like folds of gossamer ! "

" And those slender fingers clasped over her knees, and the air of melancholy repose which is breathed into her attitude, and which seems inseparable from those indolent Asiatics. She is probably a gypsy."

The noise of the water dashing over a small cascade a little farther up the stream had covered our approach and rendered our whispers inaudible. Job's conjecture was probably right, and we had stumbled on a small encampment of gypsies — the men possibly asleep in those closed tents, or possibly absent at Smyrna. After a little consultation, I agreed with Job that it would be impolitic to alarm the camp at night, and resolving on a visit in the morning, we quietly and unobserved withdrew from our position, and descended to our own tents in the ruins of the palace.

IV.

The suridji had given us our spiced coffee in the small china cups and filagree holders, and we sat discussing, to the great annoyance of the storks over our heads, whether we should loiter another day at Sardis, or eat melons at noon at Casabar on our way to Constantinople. To the very great surprise of the Dutchman, who wished to stay to finish his drawings, Job and myself voted for remaining — a view of the subject which was in direct contradiction to our vote of the preceding evening. The Englishman, who was always in a hurry, flew into a passion, and went off with the phlegmatic suridji to look after his horse ; and having disposed of our Smyrniote, by seeing a caravan (which was not to be seen) coming southward from Mount Tmolus, I and my monster started for the encampment of the gypsies.

As we rounded the battered wall of the Christian church, a woman stepped out from the shadow ; through a tattered dress, and under a turban of soiled cotton set far over her forehead, and throwing a deep shadow into her eyes, I recognized at once the gypsy woman whom we had seen sitting by the cradle.

" *Buon giorno, signori,*" she said, making a kind of salaam, and relieving me at once by the Italian salutation of my fears of being unintelligible.

Job gáve her the good-morning, but she looked at him with a very unsatisfactory glance, and coming close to my ear, she wished me to speak to her out of the hearing of " *il mio domestico !* "

" *Amico piu tosto !* " I added immediately with a consideration for Job's feelings, which, I must do myself the justice to say, I always manifested, except in very elegant society. I gave myself the greater credit in this case, as, in my impatience to know the nature of the gypsy's communication, I might be excused for caring little at the moment whether my friend was taken for a gentleman or a gentleman's gentleman.

The gypsy looked vexed at her mistake, and with a half-apologetic inclination to Job, she drew me into the shade of the ruin, and perused my face with great earnestness. " The same to yourself," thought I, as I gave back her glance, and searched for her meaning in two as liquid and loving eyes as ever looked out of the gates of the Prophet's paradise for the coming of a young believer. It was a face that *had been* divine, and in the hands of a lady of fashion would have still made a *bello rifacimento*.

" *Inglese?* " she said at last.

" No, *madre — Americano*."

She looked disappointed.

" And where are you going, *filio mio?* "

" To Stamboul."

" *Benissimo!* " she answered, and her face brightened. " Do you want a servant? "

" Unless it is yourself, no ! "

" It is my son."

It was on my lips to ask if he was like her daughter, but an air of uneasiness and mystery in her manner put me on the reserve, and I kept my knowledge to myself. She persevered in her suit, and at last the truth came out, that her boy was bound on an errand to Constantinople, and she wished safe conduct for him. The rest of the troop, she said, were at Smyrna, and she was left in care of the tents with the boy and an infant child. As she did not mention the girl, — who, from the resemblance, was evidently her daughter, — I thought it unwise to allude to our discovery : and promising that, if the boy was mounted, every possible care should be taken of him, I told her the hour on the following morning when we should be in the saddle, and rid myself of her with the intention of stealing a march on the camp.

I took rather a circuitous route ; but the gypsy was there
before me, and apparently alone. She had sent the boy to
the plains for a horse, and though I presumed that the loveliest creature in Asia was concealed in one or the other of
those small tents, the curtains were closely tied, and I could
find no apology for intruding either my eyes or my inquiries.
The handsome Zingara, too, began to look rather becomingly
fière; and as I had left Job behind, and was always naturally afraid of a woman, I reluctantly felt myself under the
necessity of comprehending her last injunction, and with a
promise that the boy should join us before we reached the
foot of Mount Sipylus, she fairly bowed me off the premises.
I could have forsworn my complexion and studied palmistry
for a gypsy, had the devil then tempted me !

V.

We struck our tents at sunrise, and were soon dashing on
through the oleanders upon the broad plain of the Hermus,
the dew lying upon their bright vermeil flowers like the pellucid gum on the petals of the ice-plant, and nature, and my
five companions, in their gayest humor. I was not. My
thoughts were of moonlight and the Pactolus, and two round
feet ankle-deep in running water.   Job rode up to my side.

" My dear Phil ! take notice that you are nearing Mount
Sipylus, in which the magnetic ore was first discovered."

" It acts negatively on me, my dear chum ! for I drag a
lengthening chain from the other direction."

Silence once more, and the bright red flowers still fled backward in our career.   Job rode up again.

" You must excuse my interrupting your revery, but I
thought you would like to know that the town where we sleep
to-night is the residence of the ' beys of Oglou,' mentioned
in the ' Bride of Abydos.' "

No answer, and the bright red blossoms still flew scattered

in our path as our steeds flew through the coppice, and the shovel-like blades of the Turkish stirrups cut into them right and left in the irregular gallop. Job rode again to my side.

"My dear Philip, did you know that this town of Magnesia was once the capital of the Turkish empire — the city of Timour the Tartar?"

"Well!"

"And did you know that when Themistocles was in exile, and Artaxerxes presented him with the tribute of three cities to provide the necessaries of life, Magnesia[1] found him in bread?"

"And Lampascus in wine. Don't bore me, Job."

We sped on. As we neared Casabar toward noon, and (spite of romance) I was beginning to think with complacency upon the melons, for which the town is famous, a rattling of hoofs behind put our horses upon their mettle, and in another moment a boy dashed into the midst of our troop, and, reining up with a fine display of horsemanship, put the promised token into my hand. He was mounted on a small Arabian mare, remarkable for nothing but a thin and fiery nostril, and a most lavish action, and his jacket and turban were fitted to a shape and head that could not well be disguised. The beauty of the gypsy-camp was beside me!

It was as well for my self-command, that I had sworn Job to secrecy in case of the boy's joining us, and that I had given the elder gypsy, as a token, a very voluminous and closely-written letter of my mother's. In the twenty minutes which the reading of so apparently "lengthy" a document would occupy, I had leisure to resume my self-control, and resolve on my own course of conduct toward the fair masquerader. My travelling companions were not a little aston-

---

[1] *Not* pronounced as in the apothecary's shop. It is a fine large town at the foot of Mount Sipylus.

ished to see me receive a letter by courier in the heart of
Asia, but that was for their own digestion. All the information I condescended to give, was that the boy was sent to
my charge on his road to Constantinople ; and as Job displayed no astonishment, and entered simply into my arrange-
ments, and I was the only person in the company who could
communicate with the suridji (I had picked up a little modern
Greek in the Morea), they were compelled (the Dutchman,
John Bull, and the fig-merchant) to content themselves with
such theories on the subject as Heaven might supply them
withal.

How Job and I speculated apart on what could be the
errand of this fair creature to Constantinople ; how beautifully she rode, and sustained her character as a boy ; how I
requested her, though she spoke Italian like her mother,
never to open her lips in any Christian language to my companions ; how she slept at my feet at the khans, and rode at
my side on the journey, and, at the end of seven days, arriving at Scutari, and beholding across the Bosphorus the golden
spires of Stamboul, how she looked at me with tears in her
unfathomable eyes, and spurred her fleet Arab to his speed
to conceal her emotion, and how I felt that I could bury
myself with her in the vizier's tomb we were passing at the
moment, and be fed on rice with a ghoul's bodkin, if so alone
we might not be parted, — all these are matters which would
make sundry respectable chapters in a novel, but of which
you are spared the particulars in a true story. There was a
convenience both to the dramatist and the audience in the
" *cetera intus agentur* " of the Romans.

VI.

We emerged from the pinnacled cypresses of the cemetery
overlooking Constantinople, and dismounting from my horse,
I climbed upon the gilded turban crowning the mausoleum

of a royal Ichoglan (a sultan's page, honored more in his burial than in his life), and feasted my eyes on the desecrated but princely fair birthright of the Palæologi. The *Nekropolis* — the city of the dead — on the outermost tomb of whose gloomy precincts I had profanely mounted, stands high and black over the Bosphorus on one side, while on the other, upon similar eminences, stand the gleaming minarets and latticed gardens of the matchless city of the living — as if, while Europe flung up her laughing and breathing child to the sun, expiring Asia, the bereaved empress of the world, lifted her head to the same heavens in majestic and speechless sorrow.

But oh! how fairer than Venice in her waters, than Florence and Rome in their hills and habitations, than all the cities of the world in that which is most their pride and glory, is this fairest metropolis of the Mahomets! With its two hundred mosques, each with a golden sheaf of minarets laying their pointed fingers against the stars, and encircled with the fretted galleries of the callers to prayer, like the hand of a cardinal with its costly ring; with its seraglio gardens washed on one side by the sea, and on the other by the gentle stream that glides out of the " Valley of Sweet Waters," — men-of-war on one side, flaunting their red pennants over the nightingale's nest which sings for the delight of a princess, and the swift caïque on the other gliding in protected waters, where the same imprisoned fair one might fling into it a flower (so slender is the dividing cape that shuts in the bay) ; with its Bosphorus, its radiant and unmatched Bosphorus, the most richly-gemmed river within the span of the sun, extending with its fringe of palaces and castles from sea to sea, and reflecting in its glassy eddies a pomp and sumptuousness of costume and architecture which exceeds even your boyish dreams of Bagdad and the caliphs, — Constantinople, I say, with its turbaned and bright-garmented population, its swarm-

ing sea and rivers, its columns and aqueducts, and strange
ships of the East, — its impenetrable seraglio and its close-
shuttered harems, its bezestein and its Hippodrome, — Constantinople lay before me ! If the star I had worshipped had
descended to my hand out of the sky ; if my unapproachable
and yearning dream of woman's beauty had been bodied forth
warm and real ; if the missing star in the heel of Serpentarius,
and the lost sister of the Pleiades had waltzed back together
to their places ; if poets were once more prophets, not felons,
and books were read for the good that is in them, not for the
evil ; if love and truth had been seen again, or any impossible
or improbable thing had come to pass, — I should not have
felt more thrillingly than now the emotions of surprise and
wonder !

While I stood upon the marble turban of the Ichoglan, my
companions had descended the streets of Scutari, and I was
left alone with the gypsy. She sat on her Arab with her
head bowed to his neck, and when I withdrew my eye from
the scene I have faintly described, the tear-drops were glistening in the flowing mane, and her breast was heaving under
her embroidered jacket with uncontrollable grief. I jumped
to the ground, and, taking her head between my hands,
pressed her wet cheek to my lips.

"We part here, signor," said she, winding around her
head the masses of hair that had escaped from her turban,
and raising herself in the saddle as if to go on.

"I hope not, Maimuna ! "

She bent her moist eyes on me with a look of earnest
inquiry.

"You are forbidden to intrust me with your errand to
Constantinople, and you have kept your word to your mother.
But whatever that errand may be, I hope it does not involve
your personal liberty ? "

She looked embarrassed, but did not answer.

" You are very young to be trusted so far from your mother, Maimuna ! "

" Signor, sì ! "

" But I think she can scarce have loved you so well as I do, to have suffered you to come here alone ! "

" She intrusted me to you, signor."

I was well reminded of my promise. I had given my word to the gypsy that I would leave her child at the Persian fountain of Tophana. Maimuna was evidently under a coi - trol stronger than the love I half hoped and half feared I had awakened.

" Andiamo ! " she said, dropping her head upon her bosom with the tears pouring once more over it like rain ; and driving her stirrups with abandoned energy into the sides of her Arabian, she dashed headlong down the uneven streets of Scutari, and in a few minutes we stood on the limit of Asia.

We left our horses in the " silver city," [1] crossing to the " golden " in a caïque ; and with Maimuna in my bosom, and every contending emotion at work in my heart, the scene about me still made an indelible impression on my memory. The star-shaped bay, a mile perhaps in diameter, was one swarm of boats of every most slender and graceful form, the caikjis in their silken shirts and vari-colored turbans driving them through the water with a speed and skill which put to shame the gondolier of Venice, and almost the Indian in his canoe ; the gilded lattices and belvideres of the seraglio, and the cypresses and flowering trees that mingle their gay and sad foliage above them, were already so near that I could count the roses upon the bars, and see the moving of the trees in the evening wind ; the muezzins were calling to sunset-prayer, their voices coming clear and pro-

---

[1] Galata, the suburb on the European side, was the *Chrysopolis*, and Scutari, on the Asian, the *Argentopolis* of the ancients.

longed over the water; the men-of-war in the mouth of the
Bosphorus were lowering their blood-red flags; the shore we
were approaching was thronged with veiled women, and
bearded old men, and boys with the yellow slipper and red
skull-cap of the East; and, watching our approach, stood
apart, a group of Jews and Armenians, marked by their
costume for an inferior race, but looking to my cosmopolite
eye as noble in their black robes and towering caps as the
haughty Mussulman that stood aloof from their company.

We set foot in Constantinople. It was the suburb of
Tophana; and the suridji pointed out to Maimuna, as we
landed, a fountain of inlaid marble and brass, around whose
projecting frieze were traced inscriptions in the Persian.
She sprang to my hand.

"Remember, Maimuna!" I said, "that I offer you a
mother and a home in another and a happier land. I will
not interfere with your duty, but when your errand is done
you may find me if you will. Farewell."

With a passionate kiss in the palm of my hand, and one
beaming look of love and sorrow in her large and lustrous
eyes, the gypsy turned to the fountain, and striking suddenly
to the left around the mosque of Sultan Selim, she plunged
into the narrow street running along the water-side to Galata.

VII.

We had wandered out from our semi-European, semi-
Turkish lodgings on the third morning after our arrival at
Constantinople, and picking our way listlessly over the bad
pavement of the suburb of Pera, stood at last in the small
burying-ground at the summit of the hill, disputing amicably
upon what quarter of the fair city beneath us we should
bestow our share in the bliss of that June morning.

"It is a heavenly day," said Job, sitting down unthinkingly upon a large sculptured turban that formed the head-

stone to the grave of some once-wealthy pagan, and looking off wistfully toward the green summit of Bulgurlu.

The difference between Job and myself was a mania on his part for green fields, and on mine for human faces. I knew very well that his remark was a leader to some proposition for a stroll over the wilder hills of the Bosphorus, and I was determined that he should enjoy, instead, the pleasure of sympathy in my never-tiring amusement of wandering in the crowded bazaars on the other side of the water. The only way to accomplish it was to appear to yield the point, and then rally upon his generosity. I had that delicacy for his feelings (I had brought him all the way from the Green Mountains at my own expense), never to carry my measures too ostentatiously.

Job was looking south, and my face was as resolutely turned north. We must take a caique in any case at Galata (lying just below us), but if we turned the prow south in the first instance, farewell at every stroke to the city! whereas a northern course took us straight up the Golden Horn, and I could appear to change my mind at any moment, and land immediately in a street leading to the bazaars. Luckily, while I was devising an errand to go up the channel instead of down, a small red flag appeared gliding through the forest of masts around the curve of the water-side at Tophana, and in a moment more a high-pooped vessel, with the carved railings and outlandish rigging of the ships from the far East, shot out into the middle of the bay with the strong current of the Bosphorus, and squaring her lateen sail, she rounded a vessel lying at anchor with the flag of Palestine, and steered with a fair wind up the channel of the Golden Horn. A second look at her deck disclosed to me a crowd of people, mostly women, standing amidships; and the supposition with which I was about inducing Job to take a caique and pull up the harbor after her seemed to me now almost a certainty.

"It is a slave-ship from Trebizond, ten to one, my dear Job!"

He slid off the marble turban which he had profaned so unscrupulously; and the next minute we passed the gate that divides the European from the commercial suburb, and were plunging down the steep and narrow straits of Galata with a haste that, to the slippered and shuffling Turks we met or left behind, seemed probably little short of madness. Of a hundred slender and tossing caïques lying in the disturbed waters of the bay, we selected the slenderest and best-manned; and getting Job in with the usual imminent danger of driving his long legs through the bottom of the egg-shell craft, we took in one of the obsequious Jews who swarm about the pier as interpreters, coiled our legs under us in the hollow womb of the caïque, and shot away like a nautilus after the slaver.

The deep-lying river that coils around the throbbing heart of Constantinople is a place of as delicate navigation as a Venetian lagoon on a festa, or a soirée of middling authors. The Turk, like your plain-spoken friend, rows backward; and with ten thousand egg-shells swarming about him in every direction, and his own prow rounded off in a pretty iron point, an extra piastre for speed draws down curses on the caikji and the Christian dogs who pay him for the holes he lets into his neighbors' boats, which are only equalled in bitterness and profusion by the execrations which follow what is called "speaking your mind." The Jew laughed, as Jews do since Shylock, at the misfortunes of his oppressors; and, in the exercise of his vocation, translated us the oaths as they came in right and left; most of them very gratuitous attacks on those (as Job gravely remarked) of whom they could know very little, — our respected mothers.

The slackening vessel lost her way as she got opposite the bazaar of dried fruits; and as her yards came down by

the run, she put up her helm, and ran her towering prow
between a piratical-looking Egyptian craft, and a black and
bluff English collier inscribed appropriately on the stern as
the "Snowdrop" from Newcastle. Down plumped her
anchor, and in the next moment the Jew hailed her by our
orders, and my conjecture was proved to be right. She was
from Trebizond, with slaves and spices.

"What would they do if we were to climb up her side?"
I asked the Israelite.

He stretched up his crouching neck till his twisted beard
hung clear off like a waterfall from his chin, and looked
through the carved railing very intently.

"The slaves are Georgians," he answered, after a while;
"and if there were no Turkish purchasers on board, they
might simply order you down again."

"And if there were" —

"The women would be considered damaged by a Christian
eye, and the slave-merchant might shoot you or pitch you
overboard."

"Is that all?" said Job, evolving his length very deliberately from his coil, and offering me a hand the next moment
from the deck of the slaver. Whether the precedence he
took in all dangers arose from affection for me, or from a
praiseworthy indifference to the fate of such a trumpery collection as his own body and limbs, I have never decided to
my own satisfaction.

In the confusion of port-officers and boats alongside, all
hailing and crying out together, we stood on the outer side
of the deck unobserved; and I was soon intently occupied
in watching the surprise and wonder of the pretty toys who
found themselves for the first time in the heart of a great
city. The owner of their charms, whichever of a dozen vil-
lanous Turks I saw about them it might be, had no time to pay
them very particular attention, and dropping their dirty veils

about their shoulders, they stood open-mouthed and staring, — ten or twelve rosy damsels in their teens, with eyes as deep as a well, and almost as large and liquid. Their features were all good, their skins without a flaw, hair abundant, and figures of a healthy plumpness ; looking, with the exception of their eyes, which were very oriental and magnificent, like the great, fat, pie-eating, yawning boarding-school misses one sees over a hedge at Hampstead. It was delicious to see their excessive astonishment at the splendors of the Golden Horn, — they from the desert mountains of Georgia or Circassia, and the scene about them (mosques, minarets, people, and men-of-war, all together) probably the most brilliant and striking in the world. I was busy following their eyes and trying to divine their impressions, when Job seized me by the arm. An old Turk had just entered the vessel from the land side, and was assisting a closely veiled female to mount after him. Half a glance satisfied me that it was the gypsy of Sardis, — the lovely companion of our journey to Constantinople.

"Maimuna!" I exclaimed, darting forward on the instant.

A heavy hand struck me back as I touched her ; and as I returned the blow, the swarthy crew of Arabs closed about us, and we were hurried with a most unceremonious haste to the side of the vessel. I scarce know, between my indignation and the stunning effect of the blow I had received, how I got into the caïque ; but we were pulling fast up the Golden Horn by the time I could speak, and in half an hour were set ashore on the green bank of the Barbyses, bound on a solitary ramble up the Valley of Sweet Waters.

VIII.

The art of printing was introduced into the Mohammedan empire in the reigns of Achmet III. and Louis XV. I seldom state a statistical fact, but this is one I happen to know, and

I mention it because the most fanciful and romantic abode with which I am acquainted in the world was originally built to contain the first printing-press brought from the court of Versailles by Mehemet Effendi, ambassador from the " Brother of the Sun." It is now a *maison de plaisance* for the sultan's favorite women ; and in all the dreams of perfect felicity which visit those who have once seen it, it rises as the paradise of retreats from the world.

The serai of Khyat-Khana is a building of gold and marble dropped down unfenced upon the greensward in the middle of a long emerald valley, more like some fairy vision, conjured and forgotten to be dissolved, than a house to live in, real, weather-proof, and to be seen for the value of one and sixpence. The Barbyses falls over the lip of a sea-shell (a marble cascade sculptured in that pretty device), sending up its spray and its perpetual music close under the gilded lattice of the sultana ; and, following it back with the eye, like a silver thread in a broidery of green velvet, it comes stealing down through miles of the tenderest verdure, without tree or shrub upon its borders, but shut in with the seclusion of an enchanted stream and valley by mountains which rise in abrupt precipices from the edges of its carpet of grass, and fling their irregular shadows across it at every hour save high noon — sacred in the East to the sleep of beauty and idleness.

In the loving month of May, it is death to set foot in the Khyat-Khana. The ascending caïque is stopped in the Golden Horn, and on the point of every hill is stationed a mounted eunuch with drawn sabre. The Arab steeds of the sultan are picketed on the low-lying grass of the valley ; and his hundred Circassians come from their perfumed chambers in the seraglio, and sun their untold loveliness on the velvet banks of the Barbyses. From the Golden Horn to Belgrade, twelve miles of greensward (sheltered like a vein of ore in

the bosom of the earth, and winding away after the course
of that pebbly river, unseen save by the eye of the sun and
stars) are sacred in this passion-born month from the foot
of man; and riding in their scarlet *arubas*, with the many-
colored ribbons floating back from the horns of their bul-
locks, and their own snowy veils dropped from their guarded
shoulders and deep-dyed lips, wander, from sunrise to sunset,
these caged birds of a sultan's delight, longing as wildly
(who shall doubt?) to pass that guarded barrier into the
forbidden world, as we, who sigh for them without, to fly
from falsehood and wrong, and forget that same world in
their bosoms!

How few are content! How restless are even the most
spoiled children of fortune! How inevitably the heart sighs
for that which it has not, even though its only want is a cloud
on its perpetual sunshine! We were not of those, — Job
and I, — for we were of that school of philosophers[1] who
"had little, and wanted nothing;" but we agreed, as we
sat upon the marble bridge sprung like a wind-lifted cobweb
over the Barbyses, that the envy of a human heart would
poison even the content of a beggar! He is a fool who is
sheltered from hunger and cold, and still complains of fortune; but he is only not a slave or a seraph, who, feeling on
the innermost fibre of his sensibility the icy breath of malice,
utters his eternal malison on the fiend who can neither be
grappled with nor avoided. I could make a paradise with
loveliness and sunshine, if envy could be forbidden at the
gate!

We had walked around the serai, and tried all its entrances
in vain, when Job spied, under the shelter of the southern
hill, a blood-red flag flying at the top of a small tent of the
Prophet's green, — doubtless concealing the kervas, who kept

---

[1] With a difference. "*Nihil est, nihil deest,*" was their motto.

his lonely guard over the precincts. I sent my friend with a " pinch of piastres " to tempt the trousered infidel to our will ; and he soon came shuffling in his unmilitary slippers with keys, which, the month before, were guarded like the lamp of Aladdin. We entered. We rambled over the chambers of the chosen houries of the East ; we looked through their lattices, and laid the palms of our hands on the silken cushions dimmed in oval spots by the moisture of their cheeks as they slept ; we could see by the tarnished gold, breast-high at the windows, where they had pressed to the slender lattices to look forth upon the valley ; and Job, more watchfully alive to the thrilling traces of beauty, showed me in the diamond-shaped bars the marks of their moist fingers and the stain as of lips between, betraying where they had clung, and laid their faces against the trellis in the indolent attitude of gazers from a wearisome prison. Mirrors and ottomans were the only furniture ; and never, for me, would the wand of Cornelius Agrippa have been more welcome than to wave back into those senseless mirrors the images of beauty they had lost.

I sat down on a raised corner of the divan, probably the privileged seat of the favorite of the hour. Job stood with his lips apart, brooding in speechless poeticalness on his own thoughts.

" Do you think, after all," said I, reverting to the matter-of-fact vein of my own mind, which was paramount usually to the romantic, — " do you think really, Job, that the Zuleikas and Fatimas who have by turns pressed this silken cushion with their crossed feet, were not probably inferior in attraction to the most third-rate belle of New England ? How long would you love a woman that could neither read nor write, nor think five minutes on any given theme ? The utmost exertion of intellect in the loveliest of these deep-eyed Circassians is probably the language of flowers ; and, good heavens ! think how one of your *della Cruscan* sentiments would be lost upon her ! And yet here you are, ready to go mad with romantic fancies about women that were never taught even their letters."

Job began to hum a stave of his favorite song, which was always a sign that he was vexed and disenchanted of himself.

"How little women think," said I, proceeding with my unsentimental vein, while Job looked out of the window, and the kervas smoked his pipe on the sultana's ottoman, "how little women think that the birch and the dark closet, and the thumbed and dog-eared spelling-book (or whatever else, more refined, torments their tender years in the shape of education), was, after all, the groundwork and secret of their fascination over men. What a process it is to arrive at love ! 'D-o-g, *dog* — c-a-t, *cat !*' If you had not learned *this*, bright Lady Melicent, I fear Captain Augustus Fitz-Somerset would never have sat, as I saw him last night, cutting your initials with a diamond ring on the purple claret-glass which had just poured a bumper to your beauty !"

"You are not far wrong," said Job, after a long pause, during which I had delivered myself, unheard, of the above practical apostrophe, — "you are not far wrong, *quoad* the women of New England. They would be considerable bores if they had not learned, in their days of bread-and-butter, to read, write, and reason. But, for the women of the softer South and East, I am by no means clear that education would not be inconsistent with the genius of the clime. Take yourself back to Italy, for example, where, for two mortal years, you philandered up and down between Venice and Amalfi, never out of the sunshine or away from the feet of women, and, in all that precious episode of your youth, never guilty, I will venture to presume, of either suggesting or expressing a new thought. And the reason is, not that the imagination is dull, but that nobody thinks, except upon exigency, in these

latitudes. It would be violent, and inapt to the spirit of the
hour. Indolence, voluptuous indolence of body and mind
(the latter at the same time lying broad awake in its chamber,
and alive to every pleasurable image that passes uncalled
before its windows) is the genius, the only genius, of the
night and day. What would be so discordant as an argument
by moonlight in the Coliseum? What so ill-bred and atro-
cious as the destruction by logic of the most loose-spun
theory, by the murmuring fountains of the Pamfili? *To live*
is enough in these lands of the sun. But *merely* to live, in
ours, is to be bound, Prometheus-like, to a rock, with a vulture at our vitals. Even in the most passionate intercourse
of love in your Northern clime, you read to your mistress, or
she sings to you, or you think it necessary to drive or ride ;
but I know nothing that would more have astonished your
Venetian *bionda* than, when the lamp was lit in the gondola
that you might see her beauty on the lagoon in the starless
night, to have pulled a book from your pocket, and read even
a tale of love from Boccaccio. And that is why I could be
more content to be a pipe-bearer in Asia, than a schoolmaster
in Vermont ; or, sooner than a judge's ermine in England, to
wear a scrivener's rags, and sit in the shade of a portico,
writing love-letters for the peasant-girls of Rome. Talk of
republics! your only land of equality is that in which to
breathe is the supreme happiness. The monarch throws
open his window for the air that comes to him past the brow
of a lazzaroni, and the wine on the patrician's lip intoxicates
less than the water from the fountain that is free to all,
though it gush from the marble bosom of a nymph. If I
were to make a world, I would have the climate of Greece,
and no knowledge that did not come by intuition. Men and
women should grow wise enough, as the flowers grow fair
enough, with sunshine and air ; and they should follow their
instincts like the birds, and go from sweet to sweet with as

little reason or trouble.   Exertion should be a misdemeanor,
and desire of action, if it were not too monstrous to require
legislation, should be treason to the state.''

" Long live King Job ! ''

PART II.

I.

I HAD many unhappy thoughts about Maimuna : the glance
I had snatched on board the Trebizond slaver left in my
memory a pair of dark eyes full of uneasiness and doubt,
and I knew her elastic motions so well that there was something in her single step as she came over the gangway which
assured me that she was dispirited and uncertain of her
errand.   Who was the old Turk who dragged her up the
vessel's side with so little ceremony ?   What could the child
of a gypsy be doing on the deck of a slaver from Trebizond ?

With no very definite ideas as to the disposal of this lovely
child should I succeed in my wishes, I had insensibly made
up my mind that she could never be happy without me, and
that my one object in Constantinople was to get her into
my possession.   I had a delicacy in communicating the full
extent of my design to Job ; for, aside from the grave view
he would take of the morality of the step and her probable
fate as a woman, he would have painful and just doubts of
my ability to bear this additional demand upon my means.
Though entirely dependent himself, Job had that natural
contempt for the precious metals, that he could not too freely
assist any one to their possession who happened to set a
value on the amount in his pocket ; and this, I may say, was
the one point which, between my affectionate monster and
myself, was not discussed as harmoniously as the loves of

Corydon and Alexis. The account of his expenditure, which I regularly exacted of him before he tied on his bandanna at night, was always more or less unsatisfactory; and though he would not have hesitated to bestow a whole scudo unthinkingly on the first dirty dervish he should meet, he was still sufficiently impressed with the necessity of economy to remember it in an argument of any length or importance: and for this and some other reasons I reserved my confidence upon the intended addition to my *suite.*

Not far from the Burnt Column, in the very heart of Stamboul, lived an old merchant in attar and jessamine, called Mustapha. Every one who has been at Constantinople will remember him and his Nubian slave in a small shop on the right, as you ascend to the Hippodrome. He calls himself essence-seller to the sultan, but his principal source of profit is the stranger who is brought to his divans by the interpreters in his pay; and to his credit be it said, that, for the courtesy of his dealings, and for the excellence of his extracts, the stranger could not well fall into better hands.

It had been my fortune, on my first visit to Mustapha, to conciliate his good-will. I had laid in my small stock of spice-woods and essences on that occasion, and the call which I made religiously every time I crossed the Golden Horn was purely a matter of friendship. In addition to one or two trifling presents, which (with a knowledge of human nature) I had returned in the shape of two mortal sins, — a keg of brandy and a flask of gin, bought out of the English collier lying in the bay, — in addition to his kind presents, I say, my large-trousered friend had made me many pressing offers of service. There was little probability, it was true, that I should ever find occasion to profit by them; but I nevertheless believed that his hand was laid upon his heart in earnest sincerity, and, in the course of my reflections upon the fate of Maimuna, it had occurred to me more than once that he might be of use in clearing up the mystery of her motions.

"Job!" said I, as we were dawdling along the street of confectioners with our Jew behind us one lovely morning, "I am going to call at Mustapha's."

We had started to go to the haunt of the opium-eaters, and he was rather surprised at my proposition; but, with his usual amiableness (very inconvenient and vexatious in this particular instance), he stepped over the gutter without saying a word, and made for the first turning to the right. It was the first time since we had left New England that I wished myself rid of his company.

"But, Job," said I, calling him back to the shady side of the street, and giving him a great lump of candy from the nearest stall (its Oriental name, by the way, is "peace-to-your-throat"), "I thought you were bent on eating opium to-day?"

My poor friend looked at me for a minute, as if to comprehend the drift of my remark; and, as he arrived by regular deduction at the result, I read very clearly in his hideous physiognomy the painful embarrassment it occasioned him. It was only the day before, that, in descending the Bosphorus, we had seen a party of the summary administrators of justice quietly suspending a Turkish woman and her Greek paramour from the shutters of a chamber-window, — intercourse with a Christian, in that country of liberal legislation, being punishable without trial or benefit of dervish. From certain observations on my disposition in the course of my adventures, Job had made up his mind, I well knew, that my danger was more from Delilah than the Philistines; and while these victims of love were kicking their silken trousers in the air, I saw by the look of tender anxiety he cast upon me from the bottom of the caïque, that the moral in his mind would result in an increased vigilance over my motions.

While he stood with his teeth stuck full of "peace-to-your-throat," therefore, forgetting even the instinct of mastication in his surprise and sorrow, I well understood what picture was in his mind, and what construction he put upon my sudden desire to solitude.

"My dear Philip!" he began, speaking with difficulty from the stickiness of the candy in his teeth, "your respected mother" —

At this instant a kervas, preceding a Turk of rank, jostled suddenly against him; and as the mounted Mussulman, with his train of runners and pipe-bearers, came sweeping by, I took the opportunity of Job's surprise to slip past with the rest, and, turning down an alley, quietly mounted one of the saddle-horses standing for hire at the first mosque, and pursued my way alone to the shop of the attar-merchant. To dismount, and hurry Mustapha into his inner and private apartment, with an order to the Nubian to deny me to everybody who should inquire, was the work of a minute, but it was scarcely done before I heard Job breathless at the door.

"*Ha visto il signore?*" he exclaimed, getting to the back of the shop with a single stride.

"*Effendi, no!*" said the imperturbable Turk, and he laid his hand on his heart, as he advanced, and offered him with grave courtesy the pipe from his lips.

The Jew had come puffing into the shop with his slippers in his hand, and dropping upon his hams near the door, he took off his small gray turban, and was wiping the perspiration from his high and narrow forehead, when Job darted again into the street with a sign to him to follow. The look of despair and exhaustion with which he shook out his baggy trousers, and made after the striding Yankee, was too much even for the gravity of Mustapha. He laid aside his pipe, and, as the Nubian struck in with the peculiar cackle of his race, I joined myself in their merriment with a heartiness to which many a better joke might have failed to move me.

While Mustapha was concluding his laugh between the puffs of his amber pipe, I had thrown myself along the divan, and was studying with some curiosity the inner apartment in which I had been concealed. A curtain of thick but tarnished gold cloth (as sacred from intrusion in the East as the bolted and barred doors of Europe) separated from the outer shop a small octagonal room, that, in size and furniture, resembled the Turkish boudoirs which, in the luxurious palaces of Europe, sometimes adjoin a lady's chamber. The slippered foot was almost buried in the rich carpets laid but not fitted to the floor. The divans were covered with the flowered and lustrous silk of Brusa, and piled with varicolored cushions. A perpetual spice-lamp sent up its thin wreaths of smoke to the black and carved ceiling, diffusing through the room a perfume which, while it stole to the innermost fibres of the brain with a sense of pleasure, weighed on the eyelids and relaxed the limbs; and as the eye became more accustomed to the dim light which struggled in from a window in the arched ceiling, and dissolved in the luxurious and spicy atmosphere, heaps of the rich shawls of the East became distinguishable with their sumptuous dyes, and in a corner stood a cluster of crystal *narghiles*, faintly reflecting the light in their dim globes of rose-water, while costly pipes, silver-mounted pistols, and a rich Damascus sabre in a sheath of red velvet, added gorgeousness to the apartment.

Mustapha was a bit of a philosopher in his way, and he had made his own observations on the Europeans who came to his shop. The secluded and Oriental luxuriousness of the room I have described was one of his lures to that passion for the picturesque which he saw in every traveller; and another was his gigantic Nubian, who, with bracelets and anklets of gold, a white turban, and naked legs and arms, stood always at the door of his shop, inviting the passers-by — not to buy essences and pastilles, but to come in and take sherbet with his master. You will have been an hour upon his comfortable divans, have smoked a pipe or two, and eaten a snowy sherbet or a dish of rice-paste and sugar, before Mustapha nods to his slave, and produces his gold-rimmed jars of essences, from which, with his fat forefinger, he anoints the palm of your hand, or, with a compliment to the beauty of your hair, throws a drop into the curl on your temples. Meanwhile, as you smoke, the slave lays in the bowl of your pipe a small pastille wrapped in gold-leaf, from which presently arrives to your nostrils a perfume that might delight a sultan ; and then, from the two black hands which are held to you full of cubical-edged vials with gilded stoppers, you are requested with the same bland courtesy to select such as in size or shape suite your taste and convenience — the smallest of them, when filled with attar, worth near a gold piaster.

This is not very ruinous ; and your next temptation comes in the shape of a curiously wrought censer, upon the filagree grating of which are laid strips of odorent wood which, with the heat of the coals beneath, give out a perfume like gums from Araby. This, Mustapha swears to you by his beard, has a spell in its spicy breath provocative as a philter, and is to be burnt in your lady's chamber. It is worth its weight in gold, and for a handful of black chips you are persuaded to pay a price which would freight a caïque with cinnamon. Then come bracelets and amulets and purses, all fragrant and precious ; and while you hesitate, the Nubian brings you coffee that would open the heart of Shylock, and you drink and purchase. And when you have spent all your money, you go away delighted with Mustapha, and quite persuaded that you are vastly obliged to him. And, all things considered, so you are !

When Mustapha had finished his prayers (did I say that it was noon?), he called in the Nubian to roll up the sacred carpet, and then, closing the curtain between us and the shop, listened patiently to my story of the gypsy, which I told him faithfully from the beginning. When I arrived at the incident on board the slaver, a sudden light seemed to strike upon his mind.

" Pekhe, filio mio! pekhe!" he exclaimed, running his forefinger down the middle of his beard, and pouring out a volume of smoke from his mouth and nostrils which obscured him for a moment from my sight.

(I dislike the introduction of foreign words into a story, but the Turkish dissyllable in the foregoing sentence is as constantly on an Eastern lip as the amber of the pipe.)

He clapped his hands as I finished my narration, and the Nubian appeared. Some conversation passed between them in Turkish, and the slave tightened his girdle, made a salaam, and, taking his slippers at the outer door, left the shop.

" We shall find her at the slave-market," said Mustapha.

I started. The thought had once or twice passed through my mind, but I had as often rejected it as impossible. A freeborn Zingara, and on a confidential errand from her own mother! I did not see how her freedom, if there were danger, should have been so carelessly put in peril.

" And if she is there!" said I, remembering first, that it was against the Mohammedan law for a Christian to purchase a slave; and next, that the price, if it did not ruin me at once, would certainly leave me in a situation rather to lessen than increase my expenses.

" I will buy her for you," said Mustapha.

The Nubian returned at this moment, and laid at my feet a bundle of wearing apparel. He then took from a shelf a shaving apparatus, with which he proceeded to lather my forehead and temples; and after a short argument with

Mustapha, in which I pleaded in vain for two very seducing clusters of curls, those caressed minions dropped into the black hand of the slave, and nothing was left for the *petits soins* of my thumb and forefinger in their leisure hours save a well-coaxed and rather respectable mustache. A skull-cap and turban completed the transformation of my head; and then, with some awkwardness, I got into a silk shirt, big trowsers, jacket, and slippers, and stood up to look at myself in the mirror. I was as like one of the common Turks of the street as possible, save that the European cravat and stockings had preserved an unoriental whiteness in my neck and ankles. This was soon remedied with a little brown juice; and, after a few cautions from Mustapha as to my behavior, I settled my turban, and followed him into the street.

It is a singular sensation to be walking about in a strange costume, and find that nobody looks surprised. I could not avoid a slight feeling of mortification at the rude manner with which every dirty Mussulman took the wall of me. After long travel in foreign lands, the habit of everywhere exciting notice as a stranger, and the species of consequence attached to the person and movements of a traveller, become rather pleasures than otherwise, and it is not without pain that one finds one's self once more like common people. I have not yet returned to my own land (Slingsby is an American, gentle reader), and cannot judge, therefore, how far this feeling is modified by the pleasures of a recovered home; but I was vexed not to be stared at when playing the Turk at Constantinople; and, amusing as it was to be taken for an Englishman on first arriving in England (different as it is from every land I have seen, and still more different from my own), I must confess to have experienced again a feeling of lessened consequence, when, on my first entrance into an hotel in London, I was taken for an Oxonian " come up for

a lark " in term-time. Perhaps I have stumbled in this remark upon one of those unconfessed reasons why a returned
traveller is proverbially discontented with his home.

Whether Mustapha wished to exhibit his new pipe-bearer
to his acquaintances, or whether there was fun enough in
his obese composition to enjoy my difficulties in adapting
myself to my new circumstances, I cannot precisely say ; but
I soon found that we were not going straight to the slave-
market.   I had several times forgotten my disguise so far as
to keep the narrow walk till I stood face to face with the
bearded Mussulmans, who were only so much astonished at
my audacity that they forgot to kick me over the gutter ; and
passing, in the bazaar of saddle-cloths, an English officer of
my acquaintance, who belonged to the corvette lying in the
Bosphorus, I could not resist the temptation of whispering
in his ear the name of his sweetheart (which he had confided
to me over a bottle at Smyrna), though I rather expected to
be seized by the turban the next moment, with the pleasant
consequences of a mob and an exposure.   My friend was so
thoroughly amazed, however, that I was deep in the crowd
before he had drawn breath ; and I look daily now for his
arrival in England (I have not seen him since) with a curiosity to know how he supposes a " blackguard Turk " knew
any thing of the lock of hair he carried in his waistcoat-
pocket.

The essence-seller had stopped in the book-bazaar, and was
condescendingly smoking a pipe, with his legs crossed on the
counter of a venerable Armenian, who sat buried to the chin
in his own wares, when who should come *pottering along* (as
Mrs. Butler would say) but Job with his Jew behind him !
Mustapha (probably unwilling to be seen smoking with an
Armenian) had ensconced himself behind a towering heap of
folios, and his vexed and impatient pipe-bearer had taken
his more humble position on the narrow base of one of the

checkered columns which are peculiar to the bazaar devoted to the bibliopolists. As my friend came floundering along, " all abroad " with his legs and arms, as usual, I contrived, by an adroit insertion of one of my feet between his, to spread him over the musty tomes of the Armenian in a way calculated to derange materially the well-ordered sequence of the volumes.

" Allah ! Mashallah ! " exclaimed Mustapha, whose spreading lap was filled with black-letter copies of the Koran, while the bowl of his pipe was buried in the fallen pyramid.

" Bestia Inglese ! " muttered the Armenian, as Job put one hand in the inkstand in endeavoring to rise, and with the next effort laid his blackened fingers on a heap of choice volumes bound in snowy vellum.

The officious Jew took up the topmost copy, marked like a *cinq-foil* with his spreading thumb and fingers, and quietly asked the Armenian what il signore would be expected to pay. As I knew he had no money in his pocket, I calculated safely on his new embarrassment to divert his anger from the original cause of his overthrow.

" Tre colonati," said the bookseller.

Job opened the book, and his well-known guttural of surprise and delight assured me that I might come out from behind the column and look over his shoulder. It was an illuminated copy of Hafiz, with a Latin translation, a treasure which his heart had been set upon from our first arrival in the East, and for which I well knew he would sell his coat off his back without hesitation. The desire to give it him passed through my mind, but I could see no means, under my present circumstances, either of buying the book or relieving him from his embarrassment ; and as he buried his nose deeper between the leaves, and sat down on the low counter, forgetful alike of his dilemma and his lost friend, I nodded to Mustapha to get off as quietly as possible, and, fortunately slipping past both him and the Jew unrecognized, left him to finish the loves of Gulistan and settle his account with the incensed Armenian.

II.

As we entered the gates of the slave-market, Mustapha renewed his cautions to me with regard to my conduct; reminded me that, as a Christian, I should see the white female slaves at the peril of my life; and immediately assumed, himself, a sauntering and *poco-curante* manner, equally favorable to concealment and to his interests as a purchaser. I followed close at his heels with his pipe, and as he stopped to chat with his acquaintances, I now and then gave a shove with the bowl between his jacket and girdle, rendered impatient to the last degree by the sight of the close lattices on every side of us, and the sounds of the chattering voices within.

I should have been interested, had I been a mere spectator, in the scene about me; but Mustapha's unnecessary and provoking delay while (as I thought possible, if she really were in the market) Maimuna might be bartered for at that moment within, wound my rage to a pitch at last scarcely endurable.

We had come up from a cellar to which one of Mustapha's acquaintances had taken him to see a young white lad he was about to purchase, and I was hoping that my suspense was nearly over, when a man came forward into the middle of the court, ringing a hand-bell, and followed by a black girl covered with a scant blanket. Like most of her race (she was an Abyssinian), her head was that of a brute, but never were body and limbs more exquisitely moulded. She gazed about without either surprise or shame, stepping after the crier with an elastic, leopard-like tread, her feet turned in like those of the North American Indian, her neck bent

gracefully forward, and her shoulders and hips working with
that easy play so lost in the constrained dress and motion
of civilized women. The Mercury of Giovanni di Bologna
springs not lighter from the jet of the fountain than did this
ebon Venus from the ground on which she stood.

I ventured to whisper to Mustapha that, under cover of
the sale of the Abyssinian, we might see the white slaves
more unobserved.

A bid was made for her.

"Fifteen piasters," said the attar-seller, wholly absorbed
in the sale, and not hearing a syllable I said to him. "She
would be worth twice as much to gild my pastilles!" And
handing me his pipe, he waddled into the centre of the court,
lifted the blanket from the slave's shoulders, turned her
round and round like a Venus on a pivot, looked at her
teeth and hands, and, after a conversation aside with the
crier, he resumed his pipe, and the black disappeared from
the ground.

"I have bought her!" he said with a salacious grin, as I
handed him his tobacco-bag, and muttered a round Italian
execration in his ear.

The idea that Maimuna might have become the property
of that gross and sensual monster just as easily as the pretty
negress he had bought, sent my blood boiling for an instant
to my cheek. Yet I had seen this poor savage of seventeen
sold without a thought save mental congratulation that she
would be better fed and clad. What a difference one's private feelings make in one's sympathies!

I was speculating, in a kind of tranquil despair, on the
luxurious evils of slavery, when Mustapha called to him an
Egyptian in a hooded blue cloak, whom I remembered to
have seen on board the Trebizondian. He was a small-
featured, black-lipped, willowy Asiatic, with heavy-lidded
eyes, and hands as dry and rusty as the claws of a harpy.

After a little conversation, he rose from the platform on which he had crossed his legs, and, taking my *pro-tempore* master by the sleeve, traversed the quadrangle to a closed door in the best-looking of the miserable houses that surrounded the court. I followed close upon his heels with a beating heart. It seemed to me as if every eye in the crowded market-place must penetrate my disguise. He knocked, and, answering to some one who spoke from within, the door was opened; and the next moment I found myself in the presence of a dozen veiled women, seated in various attitudes on the floor. At the command of our conductor, carpets were brought for Mustapha and himself; and, as they dropped upon their hams, every veil was removed, and a battery of staring and unwinking eyes was levied full upon us.

"Is she here?" said Mustapha to me in Italian, as I stooped over to hand him his eternal pipe.

"*Dio mio!* no!"

I felt insulted that, with half a glance at the Circassian and Georgian dolls sitting before us, he could ask me the question. Yet they were handsome. Red cheeks, white teeth, black eyes, and youth could scarce compose a plain woman; and thus much of beauty seemed equally bestowed on all.

"Has he no more?" I asked, stooping to Mustapha's ear.

I looked around while he was getting the information I wanted in his own deliberate way, and, scarce knowing what I did, applied my eye to a crack in the wall, through which had been coming for some time a strong aroma of coffee. I saw at first only a small dim room, in the midst of which stood a Turkish manghal or brazier of coals sustaining the coffee-pot, from which came the agreeable perfume I had inhaled. As my eye became accustomed to the light, I could distinguish a heap of what I took to be shawls lying in the centre of the floor; and, presuming it was the dormitory of one of the slave-owners, I was about turning my head away, when the coffee on the manghal suddenly boiled over, and at the same instant started from the heap, at which I had been gazing, the living form of Maimuna!

"Mustapha!" I cried, starting back, and clasping my hands before him.

Before I could utter another word, a grasp upon my ankle, that drew blood with every nail, restored me to my self-possession. The Circassians began to giggle; and the wary old Turk, taking no apparent notice of my agitation, ordered me, in a stern tone, to fill his pipe, and went on conversing with the Egyptian.

I leaned with an effort at carelessness against the wall, and looked once more through the crevice. She stood by the manghal, filling a cup with a small fllagree holder from the coffee-pot, and by the light of the fire I could see every feature of her face as distinctly as daylight. She was alone, and had been sitting with her head on her knees, and the shawl, which had now fallen to her shoulders, drawn over her till it concealed her feet. A narrow carpet was beneath her, and as she moved from the fire a slight noise drew my attention downward, and I saw that she was chained by the ankle to the floor. I stooped to the ear of Mustapha, told him in a whisper of my discovery, and implored him, for the love of Heaven, to get admission into her apartment.

"*Pekhe! pekhe! filio mio!*" was the unsatisfactory answer to my impatience, while the Egyptian rose and proceeded to turn around, in the light of the window, the fattest of the fair Circassians, from whom he had removed every article of dress save her slippers and trousers.

I returned to the crevice. Maimuna had drunk her coffee, and stood, with her arms folded, thoughtfully gazing on the fire. The expression in her beautiful and youthful face was one I could scarcely read to my satisfaction. The slight lips were firmly but calmly compressed, the forehead untroubled, the eye alone strained, and unnaturally fixed and lowering. I looked at her with the heart beating like a hammer in my bosom, and the impatience in my trembling limbs which it required every consideration of prudence to suppress. She moved slowly away at last, and, sinking again to her carpet, drew out the chain from beneath her, and drawing the shawl once more over her head, lay down, and sunk apparently to sleep.

Mustapha left the Circassian, whose beauties he had risen to examine more nearly, and came to my side.

"Are you sure that it is she?" he asked, in an almost inaudible whisper.

"*Si!*"

He took the pipe from my hand, and requested me, in the same suppressed voice, to return to his shop.

"And Maimuna" —

His only answer was to point to the door ; and thinking it best to obey his orders implicitly, I made the best of my way out of the slave-market, and was soon drinking a sherbet in his inner apartment, and listening to the shuffle of every passing slipper for the coming of the light step of the gypsy.

III.

The rules of good-breeding discountenance in society what is usually called "a scene." I detest it as well on paper. There is no sufficient reason, apparent to me, why my sensibilities should be drawn upon at sight. as I read, any more than when I please myself by following my own devices in company. Violent sensations are, abstractly as well as conventionally, ill-bred. They derange the serenity, fluster the manner, and irritate the complexion. It is for this reason

that I forbear to describe the meeting between Maimuna and
myself after she had been bought for forty pounds by the
wily and worthy seller of essences and pastilles.   How she
fell on my neck when she discovered that I, and not Mustapha, was her purchaser and master ; how she explained,
between her hysterical sobs, that the Turk who had sold her
to the slave-dealer was a renegade gypsy, and her mother's
brother (to whom she had been on an errand of affection) ;
and how she sobbed herself to sleep with her face in the
palms of my hands, and her masses of raven hair covering
my knees and feet like the spreading fountains of San Pietro ;
and how I pressed my lips to the starry parting of those
raven tresses on the top of her fairest head, and blessed the
relying child as she slept, — are circumstances, you will allow,
my dear madam ! that could not be told passably well without moving your amiable tenderness to tears.   You will consider this paragraph, therefore, less as an ingenious manner
of disposing of the awkward angles of my story, than as a
polite and praiseworthy consideration of your feelings and
complexion.   Flushed eyelids are so *very* unbecoming !

IV.

My confidential interviews with Job began to take rather
an unpleasant coloring.   The forty pounds I had paid for
Maimuna's liberty, with the premium to Mustapha, the suit
of European clothes necessary to disguise my new companion, and the addition of a third person in our European
lodgings at Pera, rather drove my finances to the wall.   Job
cared very little for the loss of his allowance of pocket-
money, and made no resistance to eating kibaubs at a meat-
shop, instead of his usual silver fork and French dinner at
Madame Josepino's.   He submitted with the same resignation to a one-oared caïque on the Bosphorus, and several
minor reductions in his expenses, thinking nothing a hard-

ship, in short, which I shared cheerfully with them. He
would have donned the sugar-loaf hat of a dervish, and
begged his way home by Jerusalem or Mecca, so only I was
content. But the *morality* of the thing!

"What will you do with this beautiful girl when you get
to Rome? how will you dispose of her in Paris? how will
your friends receive a female, already arrived at the age of
womanhood, who shall have travelled with you two or three
years on the Continent? how will you provide for her? how
educate her? how rid yourself of her, with any Christian
feeling of compassion, when she has become irrevocably
attached to you?"

We were pulling up to the Symplegades while my plain-
spoken Mentor thrust me these home questions, and Maimuna
sat coiled between my feet in the bottom of the caïque, gazing into my face with eyes that seemed as if they would
search my very soul for the cause of my emotion. We seldom spoke English in her presence, for the pain it gave her
when she felt excluded from the conversation amounted in
her all-expressive features to a look of anguish that made it
seem to me a cruelty. She dared not ask me, in words, why
I was vexed; but she gathered from Job's tone that there
was reproof in what he said, and flashing a glance of inquiring anger at his serious face, she gently stole her hand under
the cloak to mine, and laid the back of it softly in my palm.
There was a delicacy and a confidingness in the motion that
started a tear into my eye; and as I smiled through it, and
drew her to me, and impressed a kiss on her forehead, I inwardly resolved, that, as long as that lovely creature should
choose to eat of my bread, it should be free to her in all
honor and kindness, and, if need were, I would supply to
her, with the devotion of my life, the wrong and miscon-
struction of the world. As I turned over that leaf in my
heart, there crept through it a breath of peace, and I felt

that my good angel had taken me into favor. Job began to fumble for the lunch, and the dancing caïque shot forth merrily into the Black Sea.

" My dearest chum ! " said I, as we sat round our brown paper of kibaubs on the highest point of the Symplegades, " you see yourself here at the outermost limit of your travels."

His mouth was full, but as soon as he could conveniently swallow, he responded with the appropriate sigh.

" Six thousand miles, more or less, lie between you and your spectacled and respectable mother ; but nineteen thousand, the small remainder of the earth's circumference, extending due east from this paper of cold meat, remain to you untravelled."

Job fixed his eye on a white sea-bird apparently asleep on the wing, but diving away eastward into the sky, as if it were the heart within us sped onward with our boundless wishes.

" *Do* you not envy him ? " he asked enthusiastically.

" Yes ; for nature pays his travelling expenses, and I would our common mother were as considerate to me. How soon, think you, he will see Trebizond, posting at that courier speed ? "

" And Shiraz, and Ispahan, and the Valley of Cashmere ! To think how that stupid bird will fly over them, and spite of all that Hafiz and Saadi and Tom Moore have written on the lands that his shadow may glide through, will return, as wise as he went, to Marmora ! To compound natures with him were a nice arrangement, now ! "

" You would be better-looking, my dear Job ! "

" How very unpleasant you are, Mr. Slingsby ! But really, Philip, to cast the slough of this expensive and il-locomotive humanity, and find yourself afloat with all the necessary apparatus of life stowed snugly into breast and tail, your

legs tucked quietly away under you, and instead of coat
and unmentionables to be put off and on, and renewed at
such inconvenient expense, a self-renewing tegument of
cleanly feathers, brushed and washed in the common course
of nature by wind and rain, no valet to be paid and drilled,
no dressing-case to be supplied and left behind, no tooth-
brushes to be mislaid, no tight boots, no corns, no pass-
ports, nor post-horses! Do you know, Phil, on reflection, I
find this ' mortal coil' a very inferior and inconvenient
apparatus!"

"If you mean your own, I quite agree with you."

"I am surprised, Mr. Slingsby, that you, who value yourself on knowing what is due from one highly civilized individual to another, should indulge in these very disagreeable
reflections!"

Maimuna did not quite comprehend the argument, but she
saw that the tables were turned; and, without ill-will to Job,
she paid me the compliment of always taking my side. I
felt her slender arm around my neck, and as she got upon
her knees behind me, and put forward her little head to get a
peep at my lips, her clear bird-like laugh of enjoyment and
triumph added visibly to my friend's mortification. A com-
punctious visiting stole over me, and I began to feel that I
should scarce have revenged myself for what was, after all,
but a kind severity.

"Do you know, Job," said I (anxious to restore his self-
complacency without a direct apology for my rudeness), "do
you know there is a very deep human truth hidden in the
familiar story of ' Beauty and the Beast'? I really am of
opinion that, between the extremes of hideousness and the
highest perfection of loveliness, there is no face which, after
a month's intercourse, does not depend exclusively on its
expression (or, in other words, on the amiable qualities of
the individual) for the admiration it excites. The plainest

features become handsome unaware when associated only with kind feelings, and the loveliest face disagreeable when linked with ill-humor or caprice. People should remember this when selecting a face which they are to see every morning across the breakfast-table for the remainder of their natural lives. "

Job was appeased by the indirect compliment contained in this speech; and, gathering up our kibaubs, we descended to the caique, and pulling around the easternmost point of the Symplegades, bade adieu to the Orient, and took the first step westward with the smile of conciliation on our lips.

We were soon in the strong current of the Bosphorus, and shot swiftly down between Europe and Asia, by the light of a sunset that seemed to brighten the west for our return. It was a golden path homeward. The east looked cold behind; and the welcome of our far-away kinsmen seemed sent to us on those purpling clouds, winning us back. Beneath that kindling horizon, below that departed sun, lay the fresh and free land of our inheritance. The light of the world seemed gone over to it. These, from which the day had declined, were countries of memory; ours, of hope. The sun that was setting on these was dawning gloriously on ours.

On ordinary occasions, Job would have given me a stave of "Hail Columbia!" after such a burst of patriotism. The cloud was on his soul, however.

"We have turned to *go back*," he said, in a kind of musing bitterness, "and see what we are leaving behind! In this fairy-shaped boat you are gliding like a dream down the Bosphorus. The curving shore of Therapia yonder is fringed for miles with the pleasure-loving inhabitants of this delicious land, who think a life too short, of which the highest pleasure is to ramble on the edge of these calm waters with their kinsmen and children. Is there a picture in the world more beautiful than that palace-lined shore? Is there a city

so magnificent under the sun as that in which it terminates?
Are there softer skies, greener hills, simpler or better people
to live among, than these? O Philip! ours, with all its
freedom, is a 'working-day' land. There is no idleness
there! The sweat is ever on the brow, the 'serpent of care'
never loosened about the heart. I confess myself a wor-
shipper of leisure: I would let no moment of my golden
youth go by unrecorded with a pleasure. Toil is ungodlike,
and unworthy of the immortal spirit, that should walk un-
chained through the world. I love these idle Orientals.
Their sliding and haste-forbidding slippers, their flowing and
ungirded habiliments, are signs most expressive of their joy
in life. Look around, and see how on every hilltop stands a
maison de plaisance; how every hillside is shelved into those
green platforms,[1] so expressive of their habits of enjoyment! Rich or poor, their pleasures are the same. The
open air, freedom to roam, a caïque at the water-side, and a
sairgah on the hill, — these are their means of happiness, and
they are within the reach of all. They are nearer Utopia than
we, my dear Philip! We shall be more like Turks than
Christians in Paradise!"

"Inglorious Job!"

"Why? Because I love idleness? Are there braver
people in the world than the Turks? Are there people more
capable of the romance of heroism? Energy, though it
sound a paradox, is the child of idleness. All extremes are
natural and easy; and the most indolent in peace is likely to
be the most fiery in war. Here we are, opposite the summer
serai of Sultan Mahmoud; and who more luxurious and idle?
Yet the massacre of the Janissaries was one of the boldest

---

[1] All around Constantinople are seen what are called *sairgahs,* — small greensward platforms levelled in the side of a hill, and usually commanding some lovely
view, intended as spots on which those who are abroad for pleasure may spread
their carpets. I know nothing so expressive as this of the simple and natural lives
led by these gentle Orientals.

measures in history. There is the most perfect orientalism
in the description of the Persian beauty by Hafiz : —

'Her heart is full of passion, and her eyes are full of sleep.'

Perhaps nothing would be so contradictory as the true analy-
sis of the character of what is called an indolent man.
With all the tastes I have just professed, my strongest feeling on leaving the Symplegades, for example, was, and is
still, an unwillingness to retrace my steps. 'Onward ! onward !' is the perpetual cry of my heart. I could pass my
life in going from land to land, so only that every successive
one was new. Italy will be old to us ; France, Germany,
can scarce lure the imagination to adventure, with the knowledge we have : and England, though we have not seen it, is
so familiar to us from its universality that it will not seem,
even on a first visit, a strange country. We have satiety
before us, and the thought saddens me. I hate to go back.
I could start now, with Maimuna for a guide, and turn gypsy
in the wilds of Asia."

" Will you go with him, Maimuna? "

" *Signor, no !* "

I am the worst of story-tellers, gentle reader ; for I never
get to the end. The truth is, that in these rambling papers
I go over the incidents I describe, not as they should be
written in a romance, but as they occurred in my travels : I
write what I remember. There are, of course, long intervals
in adventure, filled up sometimes by feasting or philosophy,
sometimes with idleness or love ; and, to please myself, I
must unweave the thread as it was woven. It is strange
how, in the memory of a traveller, the most wayside and
unimportant things are the best remembered. You may
have stood in the Parthenon ; and, looking back upon it
through the distance of years, a chance word of the com-

panion who happened to be with you, or the attitude of a
Greek seen in the plain below, may come up more vividly to
the recollection than the immortal sculptures on the frieze.
There is a natural antipathy in the human mind to fulfil
expectations. We wander from the thing we are told to
admire, to dwell on something we have discovered ourselves.
The child in church occupies itself with the fly on its prayer-
book, and " the child is father of the man." If I indulge
in the same perversity in story-telling, dear reader; if, in
the most important crisis of my tale, I digress to some trifling vein of speculation; if, at the close even, the climax
seem incomplete, and the moral vain, — I plead, upon all
these counts, an adherence to truth and nature. Life — real
life — is made up of half-finished romance. The most interesting procession of events is delayed, and travestied, and
mixed with the ridiculous and the trifling, and at the end,
oftenest left imperfect. Who ever saw, off the stage, a five-
act tragedy, with its proprieties and its climax?

PART III.

I.

TEN o'clock A.M., and the weather like the Prophet's
paradise,

" Warmth without heat, and coolness without cold."

Madame Josepino stood at the door of her Turco-Italian
boarding-house in the nasty and fashionable main street of
Pera, dividing her attention between a handsome Armenian
with a red button in the top of his black lamb's-wool cap,[1]

---

[1] The Armenians at Constantinople are despised by the Turks, and tacitly submit,
like the Jews, to occupy a degraded position as a people. A few, however, are

and her three boarders, Job, Maimuna, and myself, at that critical moment about mounting our horses for a gallop to Belgrade.

We kissed our hands to the fat and fair Italian, and, with a promise to be at home for supper, kicked our shovel-shaped stirrups into the sides of our horses, and pranced away up the street, getting many a glance of curiosity, and one or two that might be more freely translated, from the dark eyes that are seen day and night at the windows of the leaden-colored houses of the Armenians.

We should have been an odd-looking cavalcade for the Boulevard or Bond Street; but, blessed privilege of the East! we were sufficiently *comme il faut* for Pera. To avoid the embarrassment of Maimuna's sex, I had dressed her, from an English "slop-shop" at Galata, in the checked shirt, jacket, and trousers of a sailor-boy; but, as she was obstinately determined that her long black hair should not be shorn, a turban was her only resource for concealment, and the dark and glossy mass was hidden in the folds of an Albanian shawl, forming altogether as inharmonious a costume as could well be imagined. With the white duck trousers tight over her hips, and the jacket, which was a little too large for her, loose over her shoulders and breast, the checked collar tied with a black silk cravat close round her throat, and the silken and gold fringe of the shawl flowing coquettishly over her left cheek and ear, she was certainly an odd figure on horseback; and but for her admirable riding and excessive grace of attitude, she might have been as much a subject for a caricature as her companion. Job rode soberly along at her side, in the green turban of a Hajji (which he had persisted in wearing ever since his pilgrimage to Jeru-

---

employed as interpreters by the embassies, and these are allowed to wear the mark of a red worsted button in the high black cap of the race, — a distinction which just serves to make them the greatest possible coxcombs.

salem) ; and as he usually put it on askew, the *gaillard* and rakish character of his head-dress, and the grave respectability of his black coat and salt-and-pepper trousers, produced a contrast which elicited a smile even from the admiring damsels at the windows.

Maimuna went caracoling along till the road entered the black shadow of the cemetery of Pera ; and then, pulling up her well-managed horse, she rode close to my side, with the air of subdued respect which was more fitting to the spirit of the scene. It was a lovely morning, as I said ; and the Turks, who are early risers, were sitting on the graves of their kindred with their veiled wives and children ; the marble turbans in that thickly-sown *nekropolis* less numerous than those of the living, who had come, not to mourn the dead who lay beneath, but to pass a day of idleness and pleasure on the spot endeared by their memories.

"I declare to you," said Job, following Maimuna's example in waiting till I came up, " that I think the Turks the most misrepresented and abused people on earth. Look at this scene ! Here are whole families seated upon graves over which the grass grows green and fresh, the children playing at their feet, and their own faces the pictures of calm cheerfulness and enjoyment. They are the byword for brutes, and there is not a gentler or more poetical race of beings between the Indus and the Arkansas ! "

It was really a scene of great beauty. The Turkish tombs are as splendid as white marble can make them, with letters and devices in red and gold, and often the most delicious sculptures ; and with the crowded closeness of the monuments, the vast extent of the burial-ground over hill and dale, and the cypresses (nowhere so magnificent) veiling all in a deep religious shadow, dim, and yet broken by spots of the clearest sunshine, a more impressive and peculiar scene could scarce be imagined. It might exist in other countries,

but it would be a desert. To the Mussulman, death is
not repulsive, and he makes it a resort when he would be
happiest. At all hours of the day you find the tombs of
Constantinople surrounded by the living. They spread their
carpets, and arrange their simple repast around the stone
which records the name and virtues of their own dead, and
talk of them as they do of the living and absent, — parted
from them to meet again, if not in life, in paradise.

"For my own part," continued Job, "I see nothing in
Scripture which contradicts the supposition that we shall
haunt, in the intermediate state between death and heaven,
the familiar places to which we have been accustomed. In
that case, how delightful are the habits of these people, and
how cheeringly vanish the horrors of the grave! Death,
with us, is appalling! The smile has scarce faded from our
lips, the light scarce dead in our eye, when we are thrust into
a noisome vault, and thought of but with a shudder and a
fear. We are connected thenceforth, in the memories of our
friends, with the pestilent air in which we lie, with the ver-
min that infest the gloom, with chillness, with darkness, with
disease; and, memento as it is of their own coming destiny,
what wonder if they chase us, and the forecast shadows of
the grave, with the same hurried disgust from their remembrance? Suppose, for an instant (what is by no means improbable), that the spirits of the dead are about us, conscious
and watchful! Suppose that they have still a feeling of
sympathy in the decaying form they have so long inhabited,
in its organs, its senses, its once-admired and long-cherished
grace and proportion; that they feel the contumely and disgust with which the features we professed to love are cast
like garbage into the earth, and the indecent haste with which
we turn away from the solitary spot, and think of it but as
the abode of festering and revolting corruption!"

At this moment we turned to the left, descending to the

Bosphorus, and Maimuna, who had ridden a little in advance
during Job's unintelligible monologue, came galloping back
to tell us that there was a corpse in the road. We quickened our pace, and the next moment our horses started aside
from the bier, left in a bend of the highway with a single
individual, the grave-digger, sitting cross-legged beside it.
Without looking up at our approach, the man mumbled something between his teeth, and held up his hand as if to arrest
us in our path.

"What does he say?" I asked of Maimuna.

"He repeats a verse of the Koran," she replied, "which
promises a reward in paradise to him who bears the dead
forty steps on its way to the grave."

Job sprang instantly from his horse, threw the bridle
over the nearest tombstone, and made a sign to the grave-
digger that he would officiate as bearer. The man nodded
assent, but looked down the road without arising from his
seat.

"You are but three," said Maimuna, "and he waits for a
fourth."

I had dismounted by this time, not to be behind my friend
in the humanities of life; and the grave-digger, seeing that
we were Europeans, smiled with a kind of pleased surprise,
and uttering the all-expressive "*Pekhe!*" resumed his look-
out for the fourth bearer.

The corpse was that of a poor old man. The coffin was
without a cover, and he lay in it, in his turban and slippers,
his hands crossed over his breast, and the folds of his girdle
stuck full of flowers. He might have been asleep, for any
look of death about him. His lips were slightly unclosed,
and his long beard was combed smoothly over his breast.
The odor of the pipe and the pastille struggled with the perfume of the flowers; and there was in his whole aspect a
lifelikeness and peace, that the shroud and the close coffin,

and the additional horrors of approaching death, perhaps, combine, in other countries, utterly to do away.

" Hitherto," said Job, as he gazed attentively on the calm old man, " I have envied the Scaligers their uplifted and airy tombs in the midst of the cheerful street of Verona, and, next to theirs, the sunny sarcophagus of Petrarch, looking away over the peaceful Campagna of Lombardy ; but here is a Turkish beggar who will be buried still more enviably. Is it not a paradise of tombs — a kind of Utopia of the dead? "

A young man with a load of vegetables for the market of Pera came toiling up the hill behind his mule. Sure of his assistance, the grave-digger arose, and, as we took our places at the poles, the marketer quietly turned his beast out of the road, and assisted us in lifting the dead on our shoulders. The grave was not far off, and having deposited the corpse on its border, we returned to our horses, and, soon getting clear of the cemetery, galloped away with light hearts toward the Valley of Sweet Waters.

II.

We were taking breath on the silken banks of the Barbyses, Maimuna prancing along the pebbly bed, up to her barb's girths in sparkling water, and Job and myself laughing at her frolics from either side, when an old woman, bent double with age, came hobbling toward us from a hovel in the hillside.

" Maimuna," said Job, fishing out some trumpery *paras* from the corner of his waistcoat pocket, " give this to that good woman, and tell her that he who gives it is happy, and would share his joy with her."

The gypsy spurred up the bank, dismounted at a short distance from the decrepit creature, and, after a little conversation, returned, leading her horse.

"She is not a beggar, and wishes to know why you give her money."

"Tell her, to buy bread for her children," said my patriarchal friend.

Maimuna went back, conversed with her again, and returned with the money.

"She says she has no need of it. *There is no human creature between her and Allah!*"

The old woman hobbled on, Job pocketed his rejected *paras*, and Maimuna rode between us in silence.

It was a gem of natural poetry that was worthy of the lips of an angel.

III.

We kept up the Valley of Sweet Waters, tracing the Barbyses through its bosom, to the hills; and then, mounting a steep ascent, struck across to the east, over a country which, though so near the capital of the Turkish empire, is as wild as the plains of the Hermus. Shrubs, forest-trees, and wild grass cover the apparently illimitable waste, and, save a half-visible horse-path which guides the traveller across, there is scarce an evidence that you are not the first adventurer in the wilderness.

What a natural delight is freedom! What a bound gives the heart at the sight of the unfenced earth, the unseparated hill-sides, the unhedged and unharvested valleys! How thrilling it is — unlike any other joy — to spur a fiery horse to the hilltop, and gaze away over dell and precipice to the horizon, and never a wall between, nor a human limit to say, "Thus far shalt thou go, and no farther"! Oh! I think we have an instinct, dulled by civilization, which is like the caged eaglet's, or the antelope's that is reared in the Arab's tent, — an instinct of nature that scorns boundary and chain; that yearns to the free desert; that would have the earth, like the sea or the sky, unappropriated and open; that rejoices in immeasurable liberty of foot and dwelling-place, and springs passionately back to its freedom even after years of subduing method and spirit-breaking confinement! I have felt it on the sea, in the forests of America, on the desolated plains of Asia and Roumelia; I should feel it till my heart burst, had I the wings of a bird!

The house once occupied by Lady Mary Wortley Montagu stands on the descent of a hill in the little village of Belgrade, some twelve or fourteen miles from Constantinople. It is a commonplace two-story affair, but the best house of the dozen that form the village, and overlooks a dell below that reminds one of the " Emerald valleys of Cashmeer." We wandered through its deserted rooms, discussed the clever woman who has described her travels so graphically, and then followed Maimuna to the narrow street in search of *kibaubs.* The butcher's shop in Turkey is as open as the *trottoir* to the street; and with only an entire sheep hanging between us and a dozen hungry beggars, attracted by the presence of strangers, we crossed our legs on the straw carpet, and, setting the wooden tripod in the centre, waited patiently the movements of our feeder, who combined in his single person the three vocations of butcher, cook, and waiter. One must have travelled east of Cape Colonna to relish a dinner so slightly disguised; but, once rid of European prejudices, there is nothing more simple than the fact that it is rather an attractive mode of feeding, — a traveller's appetite *subauditur.*

Our friend was a wholesome-looking Turk, with a snow-white turban, a black, well-conditioned beard, a mouth incapable of a smile, yet honest, and a most trenchant and *janissaresque* style of handling his cleaver. Having laid open his bed of coals with a kind of conjuror's flourish of the poker, he slapped the pendent mutton on the thigh in a fashion of encouragement, and waiting an instant for our admiration to subside, he whipped his knife from its sheath, and had out a dozen strips from the chine (as Job expressed it in Vermontese) "in no time." With the same alacrity these were cut into bits "of the size of a piece of chalk" (another favorite expression of Job's), run upon a skewer, and laid on the coals ; and in three minutes, more or less, they appeared smoking on the trencher, half lost in a fine green salad, well peppered, and of a most seducing and provocative savor. If you have performed your four ablutions A.M., like a devout Mussulman, it is not conceived in Turkey that you have occasion for the medium of a fork ; and I frankly own that I might have been seen at Belgrade, cross-legged in a *kibaub*-shop, between my friend and the gypsy, and making a most diligent use of my thumb and forefinger. I have dined since at the Rocher de Cancale and the Travellers' with less satisfaction.

Having paid something like sixpence sterling for our three dinners (rather an over-charge, Maimuna thought), we un-picketed our horses from the long grass, and bade adieu to Belgrade, on our way to the aqueducts. We were to follow down a verdant valley ; and exhilarated by a flask of Greek wine (which I forgot to mention), and the ever-thrilling circumstances of unlimited greensward, and horses that wait not for the spur, we followed the daring little Asiatic up hill and down, over bush and precipice, till Job cried us mercy. We pulled up on the edge of a sheet of calm water ; and the vast marble wall, built by the sultans in the days of their magnificence and crossing the valley from side to side, burst upon us like a scene of enchantment in the wilderness.

Those same sultans must have lived a great deal at Belgrade. Save these vast aqueducts, which are splendid monuments of architecture, there is little in the first aspect to remind you that you are not in the wilds of Missouri ; but a

further search discloses, in the recesses of the hidden wind-
ings of the valley, circular staircases of marble leading to
secluded baths, now filled with leaves and neglected, but
evidently on a scale of the most imperial sumptuousness.
From the perishable construction of Turkish dwelling-houses,
all traces even of the most costly serai may easily have disappeared in a few years, when once abandoned to ruin ; and
I pleased myself with imagining, as we slackened bridle,
and rode slowly beneath the gigantic trees of the forest, the
gilded pavilions and gay scenes of oriental pleasure that must
have existed here in the days of the warlike yet effeminate
Selims.   It is a place for the enchantments of the " Arabian
Nights " to have been realized.

I have followed the common error in giving these struc-
tures in the forest of Belgrade the name of aqueducts.   They
are rather walls built across the deep valleys, of different
altitudes, to create reservoirs for the supply of aqueducts,
but are built with all the magnificence and ornament of a
façade to a temple.

We rode on from one to the other, arriving at last at the
lowest, which divides the valley at its wildest part, forming a
giddy wall across an apparently bottomless ravine, as dark
and impracticable as the glen of the Cauterskill in America.
Our road lay on the other side ; but though with a steady eye
one might venture to cross the parapet on foot, there were
no means of getting our horses over, short of a return of
half a mile to the path we had neglected higher up the valley.
We might swim it, above the embankment, but the opposite
shore was a precipice.

" What shall we do? " I asked.

Job made no answer, but pulled round his beast, and
started off in a sober canter to return.

I stood a moment, gazing on the placid sheet of water
above, and the abyss of rock and darkness below, and then

calling to Maimuna, who had ridden farther down the bank, I turned my horse's head after him.

" Signore ! " cried the gypsy from below.

" What is it, Carissima ? "

" Maimuna never goes back ! "

" Silly child ! " I answered, " you are not going to cross the ravine ? "

" Yes," was the reply, and the voice became more indistinguishable as she galloped away. " I will be over before you."

I was vexed ; but I knew the self-will and temerity of the wild Asiatic, and, very certain that if there were danger it would be run before I could reach her, I drove the stirrups into my horse's sides, and overtook Job at the descent into the valley. We ascended again, and rode down the opposite shore to the embankment, at a sharp gallop. Maimuna was not there.

" She will have perished in the abyss," said Job.

I sprang from my horse to cross the parapet on foot in search of her, when I heard her horse's footsteps, and the next moment she dashed up the steep, having failed in her attempt, and stood once more where we had parted. The sun was setting, and we had ten miles to ride ; and, impatient of her obstinacy, I sharply ordered her to go up the ravine at speed, and cross as we had done.

I think I never shall forget, angry as I was at the moment, the appearance of that lovely creature, as she resolutely refused to obey me. Her horse, the same fiery Arabian she had ridden from Sardis (an animal that, except when she was on his back, would scarce have sold for a gold sequin) stood with head erect and panting nostrils, glancing down with his wild eyes upon the abyss into which he had been urged ; the whole group, horse and rider, completely relieved against the sky from the isolated mound they occupied, and,

at this instant, the gold flood of the setting sun pouring full
on them through a break in the masses of the forest. Her
own fierce attitude, and beautiful and frowning face, the thin
lip curled resolutely, and the brown and polished cheek deepened with a rosy glow, her full and breathing bosom swelling
beneath its jacket, and her hair, which had escaped from the
turban, flowing over her neck and shoulders, and mingling
with the loosened fringes of red and gold in rich disorder —
it was a picture which the pencil of Martin (and it would
have suited his genius) could scarce have exaggerated. The
stately half-Arabic, half-Grecian architecture of the aqueducts, and the cold and frowning tints of the abyss and the
forest around, would have left him nothing to add to it as a
composition.

I was crossing the giddy edge of the parapet, looking well
to my feet, with the intention of reasoning with the obsti-
nate being, who, vexed at my reproaches and her own failure,
was now in as pretty a rage as myself, when I heard the
trampling of horses in the forest. I stopped mid-way to
listen, and presently there sprang a horseman up the bank in
an oriental costume, with pistols and ataghan flashing in the
sun, and a cast of features that at once betrayed his origin.

"A Zingara!" I shouted back to Job.

The gypsy, who was about nineteen, and as well-made and
gallant a figure for a man as Maimuna for a woman, seemed
as much astonished as ourselves, and sat in his saddle gazing on the extraordinary figure I have described, evidently
recognizing one of his own race, but probably puzzled with
the mixture of costumes, and struck, at the same time, with
Maimuna's excessive beauty. Lovely as she always was, I
had never seen her to such advantage as now. She might
have come from fairy-land, for the radiant vision she seemed
in the gold of that burning sunset.

I gazed on them both a moment, and was about finishing

my traverse of the parapet, when a troop of mounted gypsies and baggage-horses came up the bank at a quick pace, and in another minute Maimuna was surrounded. I sprang to her bridle, and, apprehensive of I scarce knew what danger, gave her one of the two pistols I carried always in my bosom.

The gypsy chief (for such he evidently was) measured me from head to foot with a look of dislike, and, speaking for the first time, addressed Maimuna in his own language, with a remark which sent the blood to her temples with a suddenness I had never before seen.

"What does he say?" I asked.

"It is no matter, signore, but it is false!" Her black eyes were like coals of fire as she spoke.

"Leave your horse," I said to her in a low tone, "and cross the parapet. I will prevent his following you, and will join you on your own before you can reach Constantinople. Turn the horses' heads homeward!" I continued in English to Job, who was crying out to me from the other side to come back.

Maimuna laid her hand on the pommel to dismount; but the gypsy, anticipating her motion, touched his horse with the stirrup, and sprang, with a single leap, between her and the parapet. The troop had gathered into a circle behind us, and, seeing our retreat thus cut off, I presented my pistol to the young chief, and demanded, in Italian, that he should clear the way.

A blow from behind, the instant that I was pulling the trigger, sent the discharged pistol into the ravine; and, in the same instant, Maimuna dashed her horse against the unguarded gypsy, nearly overturning him into the abyss, and spurred desperately upon the parapet. One cry from the whole gypsy troop, and then all was as silent as the grave, except the click of her horse's hoofs on the marble verge, as, trembling palpably in every limb, the terrified animal crossed the giddy chasm at a half trot, and, in the next minute, bounded up the opposite bank, and disappeared with a snort of fear and delight amid the branches of the forest.

What with horror and wonder, and the shock of the blow which had nearly broken my arm, I stood motionless where Maimuna had left me, till the gypsy, recovering from his amazement, dismounted, and put his pistol to my breast.

" Call her back ! " he said to me in very good Italian, and with a tone in which rage and determination were strangely mingled, " or you die where you stand ! "

Without regarding his threat, I looked at him with a new thought stealing into my mind. He probably read the pacific change in my feelings, for he dropped his arm, and the frown on his own features moderated to a steadfast and inquisitive regard.

" Zingara ! " I said, " Maimuna is my slave ! "

A clutch of his pistol-stock, and a fiery and impatient look from his fine eyes, interrupted me for an instant. I proceeded to tell him briefly how I had obtained possession of her, while the troop gradually closed around, attracted by his excessive look of interest in the tale, though they probably did not understand the language in which I spoke, and all fixing their wild eyes earnestly on my face.

" And now, Zingara," I said, " I will bring her back on one condition, — that, when the offer is fairly made her, if she chooses still to go with me, she shall be free to do so. I have protected her, and sworn still to protect her as long as she should choose to eat of my bread. Though my slave, she is pure and guiltless as when she left the tent of her mother, and is worthy of the bosom of an emperor."

The Zingara took my hand, and put it to his lips.

" You agree to our compact, then ? " I asked.

He put his hand on his forehead, and then laid it, with a slight inclination, on his breast.

" She cannot have gone far," I said, and stepping on the mound above the parapet, I shouted her name till the woods rang again with the echo.

A moment, and Job and Maimuna came riding to the verge of the opposite hill, and, with a few words of explanation, fastened their horses to a tree, and crossed to us by the parapet.

The chief returned his pistols to his girdle, and stood aside while I spoke to Maimuna.   It was a difficult task, but I felt that it was a moment decisive of her destiny, and the responsibility weighed heavily on my breast.   Though excessively attached to her; though she had been endeared to me by sacrifices and by the ties of protection; though, in short, I loved her, not with a passion, but with an affection, — as a father more than as a lover, — I still felt it to be my duty to leave no means untried to induce her to abandon me, to return to her own people, and remain in her own land of the sun.   What her fate would be in the state of society to which I must else introduce her, had been eloquently depicted by Job, and will readily be imagined by the reader.

After the first burst of incredulity and astonishment at my proposal, she folded her arms on her bosom, and, with the tears streaming like rain over her jacket, listened in silence and with averted eyes.   I concluded with representing to her, in rather strong colors, the feelings with which she might be received by my friends, and the difficulty she would find in accommodating herself to the customs of people to whom not only she must be inferior in the accomplishments of a woman, but who might find, even in the color of that loveliest cheek, a reason to despise her.

Her lip curled for an instant, but the grief in her heart was stronger than the scorn for an imaginary wrong, and she bowed her head again, and her tears flowed on.

I was silent at last, and she looked up into my face.

"I am a burthen to you," she said.

"No, dearest Maimuna! no! but if I were to see you wretched hereafter, you would become so. Tell me: the chief will make you his wife; will you rejoin your people?"

She flung herself upon the ground, and wept as if her heart would break. I thought it best to let her feelings have way, and, walking apart with the young gypsy, I gave him more of the particulars of her history, and exacted a promise that, if she should finally be left with the troop, he would return with her to the tribe of her mother at Sardis.

Maimuna stood gazing fixedly into the ravine when we turned back; and there was an erectness in her attitude, and a *fierté* in the air of her head, that, I must acknowledge, promised more for my fears than my wishes. Her pride was roused, it was easy with half a glance to see.

With the suddenness of oriental passion, the young chief had become already enamoured of her; and with a feeling of jealousy which, even though I wished him success, I could not control, I saw him kneel at her feet, and plead with her in an inaudible tone. She had been less than woman if she had been insensible to that passionate cadence, and the imploring earnestness of the noble countenance on which she looked. It was evident that she was interested, though she began with scarce deigning to lift her eyes from the ground.

I felt a sinking of the heart which I cannot describe when he rose to his feet, and left her standing alone. The troop had withdrawn at his command, and Job, to whom the scene was too painful, had recrossed the parapet, and stood by his horse's head, waiting the result. The twilight had deepened, the forest looked black around us, and a single star sprang into the sky, while the west was still glowing in a fast-purpling gold and crimson.

"Signore," said Maimuna, walking calmly to my hand,

which I stretched instinctively to receive her, " I am breaking my heart; I know not what to do."

At this instant a faint meteor shot over the sky, and drew
its reflection across the calm mirror whose verge we were
approaching.

" Stay!" she cried; " the next shall decide the fate of
Maimuna! If it cross to the east, the will of Allah be
done! I will leave you!"

I called to the gypsy, and we stood on the verge of the
parapet in breathless expectation. The darkness deepened
around us, the abyss grew black and indistinguishable, and
the night-birds flitted past like audible shadows. I drew
Maimuna to my bosom, and, with my hands buried in her
long hair, pressed her to my heart, that beat as painfully and
as heavily as her own.

A sudden shriek! She started from my bosom, and, as
she fell upon the earth, my eye caught, on the face of the
mirror from which I had forgetfully withdrawn my gaze, the
vanishing pencil of a meteor, drawn like a beam of the sunset from west to east!

I lifted the insensible child, impressed one long kiss on
her lips, and, flinging her into the arms of the gypsy, crossed
the parapet, and rode, with a speed that tried in vain to out-
run my anguish, to Constantinople.

A LOG IN THE ARCHIPELAGO.

THE American frigate, in which I had cruised as the ward-room guest for more than six months, had sailed for winter quarters at Mahon, and my name was up at the pier of Smyrna, as a passenger in the first ship that should leave the port, whatever her destination.

The flags of all nations flew at the crowded peaks of the merchantmen lying off the Marina, and among them lay two small twin brigs loading with figs and opium for my native town in America. They were owned by an old schoolfellow of my own, one of the most distinguished and hospitable of the Smyrniote merchants; and, if nothing more adventurous turned up, he had offered to land me from one of his craft at Malta or Gibraltar.

Time wore on, and I had loitered up and down the narrow street "in melancholy idleness" by day, and smoked the *narghile* with those "merchant princes" by night, till I knew every paving-stone between the beach and the bazaar, and had learned the thrilling events of the Greek persecution with the particularity of a historian. My heart, too, unsusceptible enough when "packed for travel," began to uncoil with absence of adventure, and expose its sluggish pulses to the "Greek fire" still burning in those Asiatic eyes; and I felt sensibly, that if, Telemachus-like, I did not soon throw myself into the sea, I should yield, past praying for, to the cup of some Smyrniote Circe. Darker eyes than are seen on that Marina swim not in delight out of paradise!

I was sitting on an opium-box in the counting-house of my friend L——n (the princely and hospitable merchant spoken of above), when enter a Yankee " skipper," whom I would have clapped on the shoulder for a townsman if I had seen him on the top cf the minaret of the mosque of Sultan Bajazet. His go-ashore black coat and trousers, worn only one month in twelve, were of costly cloth, but of the fashion prevailing in the days of his promotion to be second mate of a codfisher; his hat was of the richest beaver, but getting brown with the same paucity of wear, and exposure to the corroding air of the ocean ; and on his hands were stretched (and they had well need to be elastic) a pair of Woodstock gloves that might have descended to him from Paul Jones " the pilot." A bulge just over his lowest rib gave token of the ship's chronometer; and in obedience to the new fashion of a guard, a fine chain of the softest auburn hair (doubtless his wife's, and, I would have wagered my passage-money, as pretty a woman as he would see in his v'yage), — a chain, I say, braided of silken blond ringlets, passed around his neck, and drew its glossy line over his broad-breasted white waistcoat; the dewdrop on the lion's mane not more entitled to be astonished.

A face of hard weather, but with an expression of care equal to the amount of his invoice, yet honest and fearless as the truck of his mainmast ; a round sailor's back, that looked as if he would hoist up his deck if you battered him beneath hatches against his will ; and teeth as white as his new foresail, — completed the picture of the master of the brig Metamora. Jolly old H——t ! I shall never feel the grip of an honester hand, nor return one (as far as I *can* with the fist you crippled at parting) with a more kindly pressure ! A fair wind on your quarter, my old boy, wherever you may be trading !

" What sort of accommodations have you, captain ?" I asked, as my friend introduced me.

" Why, none to speak of, sir ! There's a starboard berth

that a'n't got much in it, — a few boxes of figs, and the new
spritsail, and some of the mate's traps ; but I could stow
away a little, perhaps, sir."

" You sail to-morrow morning? "

" Off with the land-breeze, sir."

I took leave of the kindest of friends, laid in a few hasty
stores, and was on board at midnight. The next morning I
awoke with the water rippling beside me, and, creeping on
deck, I saw a line of foam stretching behind us far up the
gulf, and the ruins of the primitive church of Smyrna, mingled with the turrets of a Turkish castle, far away in the
horizon.

The morning was cool and fresh, the sky of an oriental
purity, and the small low brig sped on like a nautilus. The
captain stood by the binnacle, looking off to the westward
with a glass, a tarpaulin hat over his black locks, a pair of
sail-cloth pumps on his feet, and trousers and roundabout
of an indefinable tarriness and texture. He handed me the
glass, and obeying his direction I saw, stealing from behind
a point of land shaped like a cat's back, the well-known
topsails of the two frigates that had sailed before us.

We were off Vourla ; and the commodore had gone to
pay his respects to Sir Pulteney Malcolm, then lying with his
fleet in this little bay, and waiting, we supposed, for orders
to force the Dardanelles. The frigates soon appeared on the
bosom of the gulf, and, heading down, neared our larboard
bow, and stood for the Archipelago. The Metamora kept
her way, but the " United States," the fleetest of our ships,
soon left us behind with a strengthening breeze ; and, following her with the glass till I could no longer distinguish the
cap of the officer of the deck, I breathed a blessing after
her, and went below to breakfast. It is strange how the
lessening in the distance of a ship in which one has cruised
in these southern seas, pulls on the heartstrings !

I sat on deck most of the day, cracking pecan-nuts with the captain, and gossiping about schooldays in our native town, occasionally looking off over the hills of Asia Minor, and trying to realize (the Ixion labor of the imagination in travel) the history of which these barren lands have been the scene. I know not whether it is easy for a native of old countries to people these desolated lands from the past, but for me, accustomed to look on the face of the surrounding earth as mere vegetation, unstoried and unassociated, it is with a constant mental effort alone that I can be classic on classic ground, — find Plato in the desert wastes of the Academy, or Priam among the Turk-stridden and prostrate columns of Troy. In my recollections of Athens, the Parthenon and the Theseion and the solemn and sublime ruins by the Fount of Callirhoë stand forth prominent enough; but when I was on the spot — a biped to whom three meals a day, a washerwoman, and a banker, were urgent necessities — I shame to confess that I sat dangling my legs over the classic Pelasgicum, not "fishing for philosophers with gold and figs," but musing on the mundane and proximate matters of daily economy. I could see my six shirts hanging to dry, close by the Temple of the Winds, and I knew my dinner was cooking three doors from the crumbling capitals of the Agora.

As the sun set over Ephesus, we neared the mouth of the Gulf of Smyrna, and the captain stood looking over the leeward bow rather earnestly.

"We shall have a snorter out of the nor'east," he said, taking hold of the tiller, and sending the helmsman forward. "I never was up this sea but once afore; and it's a dirty passage through these islands in any weather, let alone a Levanter."

He followed up his soliloquy by jamming his tiller hard a-port; and in ten minutes the little brig was running her nose, as it seemed to me, right upon an inhospitable rock at the northern headland of the gulf. At the distance of a biscuit-toss from the shore, however, the rock was dropped to leeward, and a small passage appeared, opening with a sharp curve into the miniature but sheltered bay of Fourgas. We dropped anchor off a small hamlet of forty or fifty houses, and lay beyond the reach of Levanters in a circular basin that seemed shut in by a rim of granite from the sea.

The captain's judgment of the weather was correct, and, after the sun set, the wind rose gradually to a violence which sent the spray high over the barriers of our protected position. Congratulating ourselves that we were on the right side of the granite wall, we got out our jolly-boat on the following morning, and ran ashore upon the beach half a mile from town, proposing to climb first to the peak of the neighboring hill, and then forage for a dinner in the village below.

We scrambled up the rocky mountain-side, with some loss of our private stock of wind, and considerable increase from the nor'easter, and, getting under the lee of a projecting shelf, sat looking over toward Lesbos, and ruminating in silence; I, upon the old question, "*an Sappho publica fuerit*," and the captain probably on his wife at Cape Cod, and his pecan-nuts, figs, and opium in the emerald-green brig below us. I don't know why she should have been painted *green*, by the by (and I never thought to suggest that to the captain), being named after an Indian chief who was as red as her copper bottom.

The sea toward Mitylene looked as wild as an eagle's wing ruffling against the wind ; and there was that smoke in the sky as if the blast was igniting with its speed, — the look of a gale in those seas when unaccompanied with rain. The crazy-looking vessels of the Levant were scudding with mere rags of sails for the gulf ; and while we sat on the rock, eight or ten of those black and unsightly craft shot into the little bay below us, and dropped anchor, blessing, no doubt, every saint in the Greek calendar.

Having looked toward Lesbos an hour, and come to the conclusion, that, admitting the worst with regard to the private character of Sappho, it would have been very pleasant to have known her ; and the captain having washed his feet in a slender tricklet oozing from a cleft in a rock, — we descended the hill on the other side, and stole a march on the rear to the town of Fourgas. Four or five Greek women were picking up olives in a grove lying half way down the hill, and on our coming in sight they made for us with such speed that I feared the reverse of the Sabine rape — not yet having seen a man on this desolate shore ; they ran well, but they resembled Atalanta in no other possible particular. We should have taken them for the Furies, but there were five. They wanted snuff and money, — making signs easily for the first, but attempting amicably to put their hands in our pockets when we refused to comprehend the Greek for " Give us a para." The captain pulled from his pocket an American dollar-note (payable at Nantucket), and offered it to the youngest of the women, who smelt at it and returned it to him, evidently unacquainted with the Cape Cod currency. On farther search he found a few of the tinsel paras of the country, which he substituted for his " dollar-bill ; " a saving of ninety-nine cents to him, if the bank has not broke when he arrives at Massachusetts.

Fourgas is surrounded by a very old wall, very much battered. We passed under a high arch containing marks of having once been closed with a heavy gate ; and disputing our passage with cows, and men that seemed less cleanly and civilized, penetrated to the heart of the town in search of the barber's shop, café, and kibaub-shop, — three conveniences usually united in a single room, and dispensed by a single Figaro in Turkish and Greek towns of this descrip-

tion. The word café is universal, and we needed only to
pronounce it to be led by a low door into a square apartment
of a ruinous old building, around which, upon a kind of
shelf, waist-high, sat as many of the inhabitants of the town
as could cross their legs conveniently. As soon as we were
discerned through the smoke by the omnifarious proprietor
of the establishment, two of the worst-dressed customers
were turned off the shelf unceremoniously to make room for
us, the fire beneath the coffee-pot was raked open, and the
agreeable flavor of the spiced beverage of the East ascended
refreshingly to our nostrils. With his baggy trousers tucked
up to his thigh, his silk shirt to his armpits, and his smoke-
dried but clean feet wandering at large in a pair of red
morocco slippers, our Turkish Ganymede presented the small
cups in their filagree holders ; and never was beverage more
delicious or more welcome. Thirsty with our ramble, and
unaccustomed to such small quantities as seem to satisfy the
natives of the East, the captain and myself soon became
objects of no small amusement to the wondering beards
about us. A large tablespoon holds rather more than a
Turkish coffee-cup, and one or at most two of these satis-
fies the dryest clay in the Orient. To us, a dozen of them
was a bagatelle, and we soon exhausted the copper pot, and
intimated to the astonished cafidji that we should want
another. He looked at us a minute to see if we were in
earnest, and then laid his hand on his stomach, and, rolling
up his eyes, made some remark to his other customers which
provoked a general laugh. It was our last " lark " ashore
for some time, however ; and, spite of this apparent prophecy
of a colic, we smoked our *narghiles*, and kept him running
with his fairy cups for some time longer. One never gets
enough of that fragrant liquor.

The sun broke through the clouds as we sat on the high
bench, and, hastily paying our Turk, we hurried to the sea-

side.   The wind seemed to have lulled, and was blowing
lightly off shore ; and, impatient of loitering on his voyage,
the captain got up his anchor and ran across the bay, and in
half an hour was driving through a sea that left not a dry
plank on the deck of the Metamora.

The other vessels at Fourgas had not stirred, and the sky
in the north-east looked to my eye very threatening.   It was
the middle of the afternoon ; and the captain crowded sail
and sped on like a sea-bird, though I could see by his face
when he looked in the quarter of the wind, that he had acted
more from impulse than judgment in leaving his shelter.
The heavy sea kicked us on our course, however, and the
smart little brig shot buoyantly over the crests of the waves
as she outran them, and it was difficult not to feel that the
bounding and obedient fabric beneath our feet was instinct
with self-confidence, and rode the waters like their master.

I well knew that the passage of the Archipelago was a
difficult one in a storm, even to an experienced pilot, and
with the advantage of daylight ; and I could not but remember with some anxiety that we were entering upon it at
nightfall, and with a wind strengthening every moment,
while the captain confessedly had made the passage but once
before, and then in a calm sea of August.   The skipper,
however, walked his deck confidently, though he began to
manage his canvas with a more wary care ; and, before
dark, we were scudding under a single sail, and pitching
onward with the heave of the sea at a rate that, if we were
to see Malta at all, promised a speedy arrival.   As the night
closed in we passed a large frigate lying-to, which we afterward found out was the Superbe, a French eighty-gun ship
(wrecked a few hours after on the island of Andros).   The
two American frigates had run up by Mitylene, and were
still behind us ; and the fear of being run down in the night,
in our small craft, induced the captain to scud on, though he

would else have lain-to with the Frenchman, and perhaps have shared his fate.

I staid on deck an hour or two after dark, and before going below satisfied myself that we should owe it to the merest chance if we escaped striking in the night. The storm had become so furious that we ran with bare poles before it; and though it set us pretty fairly on our way, the course lay through a narrow and most intricate channel, among small and rocky islands; and we had nothing for it but to trust to a providential drift.

The captain prepared himself for a night on deck, lashed every thing that was loose, and filled the two jugs suspended in the cabin, which, as the sea had been too violent for any hope from the cook, were to sustain us through the storm. We took a biscuit and a glass of Hollands and water, holding on hard by the berths lest we should be pitched through the skylight; and as the captain tied up the dim lantern, I got a look at his face, which would have told me, if I had not known it before, that, though resolute and unmoved, he knew himself to be entering on the most imminent hazard of his life.

The waves now broke over the brig at every heave, and occasionally the descent of the solid mass of water on the quarter-deck seemed to drive her under like a cork. My own situation was the worst on board, for I was inactive. It required a seaman to keep the deck; and, as there was no standing in the cabin without great effort, I disembarrassed myself of all that would impede a swimmer, and got into my berth to await a wreck which I considered almost inevitable. Braced with both hands and feet, I lay and watched the *imbroglio* in the bottom of the cabin; my own dressing-case among other things emptied of its contents, and swimming with some of my own clothes and the captain's, and the water rushing down the companion-way with every wave that broke over us. The last voice I heard on deck was from the deep throat of the captain, calling his men aft to assist in lashing the helm, and then, in the pauses of the gale, came the awful crash upon deck, more like the descent of a falling house than a body of water, and a swash through the scuppers immediately after, seconded by the smaller sea below, in which my coat and waistcoat were undergoing a rehearsal of the tragedy outside.

At midnight the gale increased, and the seas that descended on the brig shook her to the very keel. We could feel her struck under by the shock, and reel and quiver as she recovered and rose again ; and, as if to distract my attention, the little epitome of the tempest going on in the bottom of the cabin grew more and more serious. The unoccupied berths were packed with boxes of figs and bags of nuts, which " brought away " one after another, and rolled from side to side with a violence which threatened to drive them through the side of the vessel ; my portmanteau broke its lashings, and shot heavily backward and forward with the roll of the sea ; and if I was not to be drowned like a dog in a locked cabin, I feared, at least, I should have my legs broken by the leap of a fig-box into my berth. My situation was wholly uncomfortable, yet half ludicrous.

An hour after midnight the captain came down, pale and exhausted, and with no small difficulty managed to get a tumbler of grog.

" How does she head? " I asked.

" Side to wind, drifting five knots an hour."

" Where are you? "

" God only knows. I expect her to strike every minute."

He quietly picked up the wick of the lamp as it tossed to and fro, and, watching the roll of the vessel, gained the companion-way, and mounted to the deck. The door was locked, and I was once more a prisoner and alone.

An hour elapsed; the sea, it appeared to me, strengthening in its heaves beneath us, and the wind howling and hissing in the rigging like a hundred devils. An awful surge then burst down upon the deck, racking the brig in every seam. The hurried tread of feet overhead told me that they were cutting the lashings of the helm; the seas succeeded each other quicker and quicker; and, conjecturing from the shortness of the pitch, that we were nearing a reef, I was half out of my berth when the cabin-door was wrenched open, and a deluging sea washed down the companion-way.

"On deck for your life!" screamed the hoarse voice of the captain.

I sprang up through streaming water, barefoot and bareheaded; but the pitch of the brig was so violent that I dared not leave the ropes of the companion-ladder, and, almost blinded with the spray and wind, I stood waiting for the stroke.

"Hard down!" cried the captain in a voice I shall never forget, and as the rudder creaked with the strain, the brig fell slightly off, and, rising with a tremendous surge, I saw the sky dimly relieved against the edge of a ragged precipice; and in the next moment, as if with the repulse of a catapult, we were flung back into the trough of the sea by the retreating wave, and surged heavily beyond the rock. The noise of the breakers, and the rapid commands of the captain, now drowned the hiss of the wind; and in a few minutes we were plunging once more through the uncertain darkness, the long and regular heavings of the sea alone assuring us that we were driving from the shore.

The wind was cold, and I was wet to the skin. Every third sea broke over the brig, and added to the deluge in the cabin; and from the straining of the masts I feared they would come down with every succeeding shock. I crept once more below, and regained my berth, where, wet and aching in every joint, I awaited fate or the daylight.

Morning broke, but no abatement of the storm. The captain came below, and informed me (what I had already presumed) that we had run upon the southernmost point of Negropont, and had been saved by a miracle from shipwreck. The back wave had taken us off, and with the next sea we had shot beyond it. We were now running in the same narrow channel for Cape Colonna, and were surrounded with dangers. The skipper looked beaten out; his eyes were protruding and strained, and his face seemed to me to have emaciated in the night. He swallowed his grog, and flung himself for half an hour into his berth, and then went on deck again to relieve his mate, where, tired of my wretched berth, I soon followed him.

The deck was a scene of desolation. The bulwarks were carried clean away, the jolly-boat swept off, and the long-boat the only movable thing remaining. The men were holding on to the shrouds, haggard and sleepy, clinging mechanically to their support as the sea broke down upon them; and silent at the helm stood the captain and the second mate, keeping the brig stern-on to the sea, and straining their eyes for land through the thick spray before them.

The day crept on, and another night, and we passed it like the last. The storm never slacked; and all through the long hours the same succession went on, the brig plunging and rising, struggling beneath the overwhelming and overtaking waves, and recovering herself again, till it seemed to me as if I had never known any other motion. The captain came below for his biscuit and grog, and went up again without speaking a word; the mates did the same with the same silence; and at last the bracing and holding on to prevent being flung from my berth became mechanical, and I did it while I slept. Cold, wet, hungry, and exhausted, what a blessing from Heaven were five minutes of forgetfulness!

How the third night wore on, I scarce remember. The storm continued with unabated fury; and when the dawn of the third morning broke upon us, the captain conjectured that we had drifted four hundred miles before the wind. The crew were exhausted with watching; the brig labored more and more heavily, and the storm seemed eternal.

At noon of the third day the clouds broke up a little, and the wind, though still violent, slacked somewhat in its fury. The sun struggled down upon the lashed and raging sea; and, taking our bearings, we found ourselves about two hundred miles from Malta. With great exertions, the cook contrived to get up a fire in the binnacle, and boil a little rice; and never *gourmet* sucked the brain of a woodcock with the relish which welcomed that dark mess of pottage.

It was still impossible to carry more than a hand's-breadth of sail, but we were now in open waters, and flew merrily before the driving sea. The pitching and racking motion, and the occasional shipping of a heavy wave, still forbade all thoughts or hopes of comfort; but the dread of shipwreck troubled us no more, and I passed the day in contriving how to stand long enough on my legs to get my wet traps from my floating portmanteau, and go into quarantine like a Christian.

The following day, at noon, Malta became visible from the top of an occasional mountain wave; and, still driving under a reefed topsail before the hurricane, we rapidly neared it, and I began to hope for the repose of *terra firma*. The watch-towers of the castellated rock soon became distinct through the atmosphere of spray; and at a distance of a mile, we took in sail, and waited for a pilot.

While tossing in the trough of the sea the following half-hour, the captain communicated to me some embarrassment with respect to my landing which had not occurred to me. It appeared that the agreement to land me at Malta was not mentioned in his policy of insurance, and the underwriters of course were not responsible for any accident that might happen to the brig after a variation from his original plan of passage. This he would not have minded if he could have set me ashore in a half-hour, as he had anticipated; but his small boat was lost in the storm, and it was now a question whether the pilot-boat would take ashore a passenger liable to quarantine. To run his brig into harbor would be a great expense, and positive loss of insurance; and to get out the long-boat with his broken tackle and exhausted crew was not to be thought of. I knew very well that no passenger from a plague port (such as Smyrna and Constantinople) was permitted to land on any terms at Gibraltar; and if the pilot here should refuse to take me off, the alternative was clear, — I must make a voyage against my will to America!

I was not in a very pleasant state of mind during the delay which followed; for though I had been three years absent from my country, and loved it well, I had laid my plans for still two years of travel on this side the Atlantic, and certain moneys for my "charges" lay waiting my arrival at Malta. Among lesser reasons, I had not a rag of clothes dry or clean, and was heartily out of love with salt water and the smell of figs.

As if to aggravate my unhappiness, the sun broke through a rift in the clouds, and lit up the white and turreted battlements of Malta like an isle of the blessed, — the only bright spot within the limits of the stormy horizon. The mountain waves on which we were tossing were tempestuous and black; the comfortless and battered brig with her weary crew looked more like a wreck than a seaworthy merchantman; and, no pilot appearing, the captain looked anxiously seaward, as if he grudged every minute of the strong wind rushing by on his course.

A small speck at last appeared, making toward us from

the shore, and, riding slowly over the tremendous waves, a boat manned by four men came within hailing-distance. One moment as high as our topmast, and another in the depths of the gulf a hundred feet below us, it was like conversing from two buckets in a well.

" Do you want a pilot? " screamed the Maltese in English, as the American flag blew out to the wind.

" No! " roared the captain, like a thunder-peal, through his tin trumpet.

The Maltese, without deigning another look, put up his helm with a gesture of disappointment, and bore away.

" Boat ahoy! " bellowed the captain.

" Ahoy! ahoy! " answered the pilot.

" Will you take a passenger ashore? "

" Where from? "

" Smyrna! "

" No—o—o—o! "

There was a sound of doom in the angry prolongation of that detested monosyllable, that sunk to the bottom of my heart like lead.

" Clear away the mainsail! " cried the captain, getting round once more to the wind. " I knew how it would be, sir," he continued to me, as I bit my lips in the effort to be reconciled to an involuntary voyage of four thousand miles: " it wasn't likely he'd put himself and his boat's crew into twenty days' quarantine to oblige you and me."

I could not but own that it was an unreasonable expectation.

" Never mind, sir," said the skipper consolingly: " plenty of salt fish in the locker, and I'll set you on Long Wharf in no time."

" Brig ahoy! " came a voice faintly across the waves.

The captain looked over his shoulder without losing a capful of wind from his sail, and sent back the hail impatiently.

The pilot was running rapidly down upon us, and had

come back to offer to tow me ashore in the brig's jolly-boat for a large sum of money.

"We've lost our boat, and you're a bloody shark," answered the skipper, enraged at the attempt at extortion. "Head your course!" he muttered gruffly to the man at the helm, who had let the brig fall off that the pilot might come up.

Irritated by this new and gratuitous disappointment, I stamped on the deck in an ungovernable fit of rage, and wished the brig at the Devil.

The skipper looked at me a moment, and instead of the angry answer I expected, an expression of kind commiseration stole over his rough face. The next moment he seized the helm, and put the brig away from the wind, and then, making a trumpet of his two immense hands, he once more hailed the returning pilot.

"I can't bear to see you take it so much to heart, sir," said the kind sailor, "and I'll do for you what I wouldn't do for another man on the face o' the 'arth. — All hands there!"

The men came aft; and the captain in brief words stated the case to them, and appealed to their sense of kindness for a fellow-countryman, to undertake a task, which, in the sea then running, and with their exhausted strength, was not a service he could well demand in other terms. It was to get out the long-boat, and wait off while the pilot towed me ashore and returned with her.

"Ay, ay, sir!" was the immediate response from every lip, and, from the chief mate to the black cabin-boy, every man sprang cheerily to the lashings. It was no momentary task, for the boat was as firmly set in her place as the mainmast, and stowed compactly with barrels of pork, extra rigging, and spars — in short, all the furniture and provision of the voyage. In the course of an hour, however, the tackle

was rigged on the fore and main yards, and, with a desperate
effort its immense bulk was heaved over the side, and lay
tossing on the tempestuous waters. I shook hands with the
men, who refused every remuneration beyond my thanks ;
and, following the captain over the side, was soon toiling
heavily on the surging waters, thanking Heaven for the generous sympathies of home and country implanted in the
human bosom. Those who knew the reluctance with which
a merchant captain lays-to, even to pick up a man overboard,
in a fair wind, and those who understand the meaning of a
forfeited insurance, will appreciate this instance of difficult
generosity. I shook the hard fist of the kind-hearted skipper
on the quarantine stairs, and watched his heavy boat as she
crept out of the little harbor, with the tears in my eyes. I
shall travel far before I find again a man I honor more
heartily.

A DINNER AT LADY BLESSINGTON'S.

DINED at Lady Blessington's, in company with several authors, three or four noblemen, and a clever exquisite or two. The authors were Bulwer the novelist, and his brother the statist; Procter (better known as Barry Cornwall) ; D'Israeli, the author of Vivian Grey; and Fonblanc, of the Examiner. The principal nobleman was Lord Durham ; and the principal exquisite (though the word scarce applies to the magnificent scale on which nature has made him, and on which he makes himself) was Count D'Orsay. There were plates for twelve.

I had never seen Procter, and with my passionate love for his poetry, he was the person at table of the most interest to me. He came late, and as twilight was just darkening the drawing-room, I could only see that a small man followed the announcement, with a remarkably timid manner, and a very white forehead.

D'Israeli had arrived before me, and sat in the deep window, looking out upon Hyde Park, with the last rays of daylight reflected from the gorgeous gold flowers of a splendidly embroidered waistcoat. Patent-leather pumps, a white stick, with a black cord and tassel, and a quantity of chains about his neck and pockets, served to make him, even in the dim light, rather a conspicuous object.

Bulwer was very badly dressed, as usual, and wore a flashy waistcoat of the same description as D'Israeli's. Count D'Orsay was very splendid, but very undefinable. He

∗∗∗ *From Pencillings by the Way. Letter cxviii.*

seemed showily dressed till you looked to particulars, and then it seemed only a simple thing, well fitted to a very magnificent person. Lord Albert Conyngham was a dandy of common materials ; and my Lord Durham, though he looked a young man, if he passed for a lord at all in America, would pass for a very ill-dressed one.

For Lady Blessington, she is one of the most handsome, and quite the best-dressed woman in London ; and, without farther description, I trust the readers of the Mirror will have little difficulty in imagining a scene that, taking a wild American into the account, was made up of rather various material.

The blaze of lamps on the dinner-table was very favorable to my curiosity ; and as Procter and D'Israeli sat directly opposite me, I studied their faces to advantage. Barry Cornwall's forehead and eye are all that would strike you in his features. His brows are heavy ; and his eye, deeply sunk, has a quick, restless fire, that would have struck me, I think, had I not known he was a poet. His voice has the huskiness and elevation of a man more accustomed to think than converse, and it was never heard except to give a brief and very condensed opinion, or an illustration, admirably to the point, of the subject under discussion. He evidently felt that he was only an observer in the party.

D'Israeli has one of the most remarkable faces I ever saw. He is lividly pale, and but for the energy of his action, and the strength of his lungs, would seem a victim to consumption. His eye is as black as Erebus, and has the most mocking and lying-in-wait sort of expression conceivable. His mouth is alive with a kind of working and impatient nervousness ; and when he has burst forth, as he does constantly, with a particularly successful cataract of expression, it assumes a curl of triumphant scorn that would be worthy of a Mephistopheles. His hair is as extraordinary as his

taste in waistcoats. A thick heavy mass of jet-black ringlets falls over his left cheek almost to his collarless stock,
while on the right temple it is parted and put away with the
smooth carefulness of a girl's, and shines most unctuously,

"With thy incomparable oil, Macassar!"

The anxieties of the first course, as usual, kept every
mouth occupied for a while, and then the dandies led off with
a discussion of Count D'Orsay's rifle-match (he is the best
rifle-shot in England) and various matters as uninteresting
to transatlantic readers. The new poem, Philip Van Arte-
velde, came up after a while, and was very much over-praised
(*me judice*). Bulwer said, that as the author was the principal writer for the Quarterly Review, it was a pity it was
first praised in that periodical, and praised so unqualifiedly.
Procter said nothing about it, and I respected his silence;
for, as a poet, he must have felt the poverty of the poem,
and was probably unwilling to attack a new aspirant in his
laurels.

The next book discussed was Beckford's Italy; or rather
the next author, for the *writer* of Vathek is more original
and more talked of than his books, and just now occupies
much of the attention of London. Mr. Beckford has been
all his life enormously rich, has luxuriated in every country
with the fancy of a poet, and the refined splendor of a Sybarite; was the admiration of Lord Byron, who visited him
at Cintra; was the owner of Fonthill; and, *plus fort encore*,
his is one of the oldest families in England. What could
such a man attempt that would not be considered extraordinary!

D'Israeli was the only one at table who knew him, and
the style in which he gave a sketch of his habits and manners was worthy of himself. I might as well attempt to
gather up the foam of the sea as to convey an idea of the

extraordinary language in which he clothed his description. There were at least five words in every sentence that must have been very much astonished at the use they were put to, and yet no others apparently could so well have conveyed his idea. He talked like a race-horse approaching the winning-post, every muscle in action, and the utmost energy of expression flung out in every burst. It is a great pity he is not in parliament.[1]

The particulars he gave of Beckford, though stripped of his gorgeous digressions and parentheses, may be interesting. He lives now at Bath, where he has built a house on two sides of the street, connected by a covered bridge *à la Ponte de Sospiri* at Venice. His servants live on one side, and he and his sole companion on the other. This companion is a hideous dwarf, who imagines himself, or is, a Spanish duke ; and Mr. Beckford for many years has supported him in a style befitting his rank, treats him with all the deference due to his title, and has, in general, no other society (I should not wonder, myself, if it turned out a woman). Neither of them is often seen, and when in London, Mr. Beckford is only to be approached through his man of business. If you call, he is not at home. If you would leave a card or address him a note, his servant has strict orders not to take in any thing of the kind. At Bath he has built a high tower, which is a great mystery to the inhabitants. Around the interior, to the very top, it is lined with books, approachable with a light spiral staircase ; and in the pavement below, the owner has constructed a double crypt for his own body, and that of his dwarf companion, intending, with a desire for human neighborhood which has not appeared in his life, to

---

[1] I have been told that he stood once for a London borough. A coarse fellow came up at the hustings, and said to him, "I should like to know on what ground you stand here, sir?" — "On my head, sir!" answered D'Israeli. The populace had not read Vivian Grey, however, and he lost his election.

leave the library to the city, that all who enjoy it shall pass over the bodies below.

Mr. Beckford thinks very highly of his own books, and talks of his early production (Vathek) in terms of unbounded admiration. He speaks slightingly of Byron, and of his praise, and affects to despise utterly the popular taste. It appeared altogether, from D'Israeli's account, that he is a splendid egotist, determined to free life as much as possible from its usual fetters, and to enjoy it to the highest degree of which his genius, backed by an immense fortune, is capable. He is reputed, however, to be excessively liberal, and to exercise his ingenuity to contrive secret charities in his neighborhood.

Victor Hugo and his extraordinary novels came next under discussion; and D'Israeli, who was fired with his own eloquence, started off, *àpropos des bottes*, with a long story of an impalement he had seen in Upper Egypt. It was as good, and perhaps as authentic, as the description of the chow-chow-tow in Vivian Grey. He had arrived in Cairo on the third day after the man was transfixed by two stakes from hip to shoulder, and he was still alive! The circumstantiality of the account was equally horrible and amusing. Then followed the sufferer's history, with a score of murders and barbarities, heaped together like Martin's Feast of Belshazzar, with a mixture of horror and splendor that was unparalleled in my experience of improvisation. No mystic priest of the Corybantes could have worked himself up into a finer frenzy of language.

Count D'Orsay kept up, through the whole of the conversation and narration, a running fire of witty parentheses, half French and half English; and, with champagne in all the pauses, the hours flew on very dashingly. Lady Blessington left us toward midnight, and then the conversation took a rather political turn, and something was said of

O'Connell. D'Israeli's lips were playing upon the edge of a champagne-glass which he had just drained, and off he shot again with a description of an interview he had had with the agitator the day before; ending in a story of an Irish dragoon who was killed in the Peninsula. His name was Sarsfield. His arm was shot off, and he was bleeding to death. When told that he could not live, he called for a large silver goblet, out of which he usually drank his claret. He held it to the gushing artery, and filled it to the brim with blood, looked at it a moment, turned it out slowly upon the ground, muttering to himself, "If that had been shed for old Ireland!" and expired. You can have no idea how thrillingly this little story was told. Fonblanc, however, who is a cold political satirist, could see nothing in a man's "decanting his claret," that was in the least sublime; and so Vivian Grey got into a passion, and for a while was silent.

Bulwer asked me if there was any distinguished literary American in town. I said Mr. Slidell, one of our best writers, was here.

"Because," said he, "I received a week or more ago a letter of introduction by some one from Washington Irving. It lay on the table, when a lady came in to call on my wife, who seized upon it as an autograph, and immediately left town, leaving me with neither name nor address."

There was a general laugh, and a cry of "Pelham! Pelham!" as he finished his story. Nobody chose to believe it.

"I think the name *was* Slidell," said Bulwer.

"Slidell!" said D'Israeli, "I owe him two-pence, by Jove!" and he went on in his dashing way to narrate that he had sat next Mr. Slidell at a bull-fight in Seville, that he wanted to buy a fan to keep off the flies, and having nothing but doubloons in his pocket, Mr. S. had lent him a small Spanish coin of that value, which he owed him to this day.

There was another general laugh, and it was agreed that on the whole the Americans were ' *done.*'

Apropos to this, D'Israeli gave us a description in a gorgeous, burlesque, galloping style, of a Spanish bull-fight; and when we were nearly dead with laughter at it, some one made a move, and we went up to Lady Blessington in the drawing-room. Lord Durham requested her ladyship to introduce him particularly to D'Israeli (the effect of his eloquence). I sat down in the corner with Sir Martin Shee, the president of the Royal Academy, and had a long talk about Allston and Harding and Cole, whose pictures he knew; and " somewhere in the small hours " we took our leave, and Procter left me at my door in Cavendish Street, weary, but in a better humor with the world than usual.

A BREAKFAST WITH CHARLES LAMB.

INVITED to breakfast with a gentleman in the Temple to meet Charles Lamb and his sister, — " Elia, and Bridget Elia." I never in my life had an invitation more to my taste. The essays of Elia are certainly the most charming things in the world, and it has been for the last ten years my highest compliment to the literary taste of a friend to present him with a copy. Who has not smiled over the humorous description of Mrs. Battle? Who that has read Elia would not give more to see him than all the other authors of his time put together?

Our host was rather a character. I had brought a letter of introduction to him from Walter Savage Landor, the author of Imaginary Conversations, living at Florence, with a request that he would put me in a way of seeing one or two men about whom I had a curiosity, Lamb more particularly. I could not have been recommended to a better person. Mr. R. is a gentleman who, everybody says, *should have been* an author, but who never wrote a book. He is a profound German scholar, has travelled much, is the intimate friend of Southey, Coleridge, and Lamb, has breakfasted with Goethe, travelled with Wordsworth through France and Italy, and spends part of every summer with him, and knows every thing and every body that is distinguished, — in short, is, in his bachelor's chambers in the Temple, the friendly nucleus of a great part of the talent of England.

I arrived a half-hour before Lamb, and had time to learn

*** From Pencillings by the Way. Letter cxvii.

some of his peculiarities.   He lives a little out of London, and is very much of an invalid.   Some family circumstances have tended to depress him very much of late years, and unless excited by convivial intercourse, he scarce shows a trace of what he was.   He was very much pleased with the American reprint of his Elia, though it contains several things which are not his — written so in his style, however, that it is scarce a wonder the editor should mistake them. If I remember right, they were " Valentine's Day," the " Nuns of Caverswell," and " Twelfth Night."   He is excessively given to mystifying his friends, and is never so delighted as when he has persuaded some one into the belief of one of his grave inventions.   His amusing biographical sketch of Liston was in this vein, and there was no doubt in anybody's mind that it was authentic, and written in perfectly good faith.   Liston was highly enraged with it, and Lamb was delighted in proportion.

There was a rap at the door at last, and enter a gentleman in black small-clothes and gaiters, short and very slight in his person, his head set on his shoulders with a thoughtful forward bent, his hair just sprinkled with gray, a beautiful deep-set eye, aquiline nose, and a very indescribable mouth. Whether it expressed most humor or feeling, good-nature or a kind of whimsical peevishness, or twenty other things which passed over it by turns, I cannot in the least be certain.

His sister, whose literary reputation is associated very closely with her brother's, and who, as the original of " Bridget Elia," is a kind of object for literary affection, came in after him.   She is a small, bent figure, evidently a victim to illness, and hears with difficulty.   Her face has been, I should think, a fine and handsome one, and her bright gray eye is still full of intelligence and fire.   They both seemed quite at home in our friend's chambers, and as there was to be no one else we immediately drew round the

breakfast-table.   I had set a large arm-chair for Miss Lamb.
"Don't take it, Mary," said Lamb, pulling it away from
her very gravely : "it appears as if you were going to have
a tooth drawn."

The conversation was very local.   Our host and his guest
had not met for some weeks, and they had a great deal to
say of their mutual friends.   Perhaps in this way, however,
I saw more of the author ; for his manner of speaking of
them, and the quaint humor with which he complained of one,
and spoke well of another, was so in the vein of his inimitable writings, that I could have fancied myself listening to
an audible composition of a new Elia.   Nothing could be
more delightful than the kindness and affection between the
brother and the sister, though Lamb was continually taking
advantage of her deafness to mystify her with the most
singular gravity upon every topic that was started.   "Poor
Mary!" said he, "she hears all of an epigram but the
point." — "What are you saying of me, Charles?" she
asked.   "Mr. Willis," said he, raising his voice, "admires
your Confessions of a Drunkard very much ; and I was saying that it was no merit of yours, that you understood the
subject."   We had been speaking of this admirable essay
(which is his own) half an hour before.

The conversation turned upon literature after a while ; and
our host, the Templar, could not express himself strongly
enough in admiration of Webster's speeches, which he said
were exciting the greatest attention among the politicians
and lawyers of England.   Lamb said, "I don't know much
of American authors.   Mary, there, devours Cooper's novels
with a ravenous appetite, with which I have no sympathy.
The only American book I ever read twice was the ' Journal
of Edward Woolman,' a Quaker preacher and tailor, whose
character is one of the finest I ever met with.   He tells a
story or two about negro slaves, that brought the tears into

my eyes. I can read no prose now, though Hazlitt sometimes, to be sure — but then, Hazlitt is worth all modern
prose-writers put together.''

Mr. R. spoke of buying a book of Lamb's a few days
before; and I mentioned my having bought a copy of Elia
the last day I was in America, to send as a parting gift to
one of the most lovely and talented women in our country.

'' What did you give for it? '' said Lamb.

'' About seven and sixpence.''

'' Permit me to pay you that,'' said he, and with the
utmost earnestness he counted out the money upon the
table.

'' I never yet wrote any thing that would sell,'' he continued. '' I am the publisher's ruin. My last poem won't
sell a copy. Have you seen it, Mr. Willis? ''

I had not.

'' It's only eighteen pence, and 'I'll give you sixpence
toward it; '' and he described to me where I should find it
sticking up in a shop-window in the Strand.

Lamb ate nothing, and complained in a querulous tone of
the veal-pie. There was a kind of potted fish (of which I
forget the name at this moment) which he had expected our
friend would procure for him. He inquired whether there
was not a morsel left perhaps in the bottom of the last pot.
Mr. R. was not sure.

'' Send and see,'' said Lamb; '' and if the pot has been
cleaned, bring me the cover. I think the sight of it would
do me good.''

The cover was brought, upon which there was a picture
of the fish. Lamb kissed it with a reproachful look at his
friend, and then left the table, and began to wander round the
room with a broken, uncertain step, as if he almost forgot to
put one leg before the other. His sister rose after a while,
and commenced walking up and down very much in the same

manner on the opposite side of the table ; and in the course of half an hour they took their leave.

To any one who loves the writings of Charles Lamb with but half my own enthusiasm, even these little particulars of an hour passed in his company will have an interest. To him who does not, they will seem dull and idle. Wreck as he certainly is, and must be, however, of what he was, I would rather have seen him for that single hour, than the hundred and one sights of London put together.

A WEEK AT GORDON CASTLE.

I TOOK two places in the coach at last (one for my leg), and bowled away seventy miles across the country, with the delightful speed of these admirable conveyances, for Gordon Castle. I arrived at Lochabers, a small town on the estate of the Duke of Gordon, at three in the afternoon, and immediately took a post-chaise for the castle, the gate of which was a stone's-throw from the inn.

The immense iron gate surmounted by the Gordon arms, the handsome and spacious stone lodges on either side, the canonically fat porter in white stockings and gay livery lifting his hat as he swung open the massive portal, all bespoke the entrance to a noble residence. The road within was edged with velvet sward, and rolled to the smoothness of a terrace-walk; the winding avenue lengthened away before, with trees of every variety of foliage; light carriages passed me, driven by ladies or gentlemen bound on their afternoon airing; a groom led up and down two beautiful blood-horses, prancing along with side-saddles and morocco stirrups, and keepers with hounds and terriers; gentlemen on foot idling along the walks, and servants in different liveries hurrying to and fro, betokened a scene of busy gayety before me. I had hardly noted these various circumstances before a sudden curve in the road brought the castle into view, — a vast stone pile with castellated wings; and in another moment I was at the door, where a dozen lounging and powdered menials were waiting on a party of ladies and gentlemen to

⁎ *From Pencillings by the Way. Letters cxxviii. to cxxxi.*
236

their several carriages. It was the moment for the afternoon drive.

The last phaeton dashed away, and my chaise advanced to the door. A handsome boy in a kind of page's dress immediately came to the window, addressed me by name, and informed me that his grace was out deer-shooting, but that my room was prepared, and he was ordered to wait on me. I followed him through a hall lined with statues, deer's horns, and armor, and was ushered into a large chamber looking out on a park extending with its lawns and woods to the edge of the horizon. A more lovely view never feasted human eye.

"Who is at the castle?" I asked, as the boy busied himself in unstrapping my portmanteau.

"Oh, a great many, sir!" He stopped in his occupation, and began counting on his fingers. "There's Lord Aberdeen, and Lord Claud Hamilton and Lady Harriette Hamilton (them's his lordship's two step-children, you know, sir), and the Duchess of Richmond, and Lady Sophia Lennox, and Lady Keith, and Lord Mandeville, and Lord Aboyne, and Lord Stormont and Lady Stormont, and Lord Morton and Lady Morton, and Lady Alicia, and — and — and — twenty more, sir."

"Twenty more lords and ladies?"

"No, sir! that's all the nobility."

"And you can't remember the names of the others?"

"No, sir."

He was a proper page. He could not trouble his memory with the names of commoners.

"And how many sit down to dinner?"

"Above thirty, sir, besides the duke and duchess."

"That will do." And off tripped my slender gentleman with his laced jacket, giving the fire a terrible stir-up in his way out, and turning back to inform me that the dinner hour seven precisely.

It was a mild, bright afternoon, quite warm for the end of an English September; and with a fire in the room, and a soft sunshine pouring in at the windows, a seat by the open casement was far from disagreeable. I passed the time till the sun set, looking out on the park. Hill and valley lay between my eye and the horizon; sheep fed in picturesque flocks, and small fallow deer grazed near them; the trees were planted, and the distant forest shaped, by the hand of taste; and, broad and beautiful as was the expanse taken in by the eye, it was evidently one princely possession. A mile from the castle wall, the shaven sward extended in a carpet of velvet softness, as bright as emerald, studded by clumps of shubbery like flowers wrought elegantly on tapestry; and across it bounded occasionally a hare, and the pheasants fed undisturbed near the thickets, or a lady with flowing riding-dress and flaunting feather dashed into sight upon her fleet blood-palfrey, and was lost the next moment in the woods, or a boy put his pony to its mettle up the ascent, or a gamekeeper idled into sight with his gun in the hollow of his arm, and his hounds at his heels; and all this little world of enjoyment and luxury and beauty lay in the hand of one man, and was created by his wealth in these northern wilds of Scotland, a day's journey almost from the possession of another human being. I never realized so forcibly the splendid result of wealth and primogeniture.

The sun set in a blaze of fire among the pointed firs crowning the hills, and by the occasional prance of a horse's feet on the gravel, and the roll of rapid wheels, and now and then a gay laugh and merry voices, the different parties were returning to the castle. Soon after, a loud gong sounded through the gallery, the signal to dress; and I left my musing occupation unwillingly to make my toilet for an appearance in a formidable circle of titled aristocrats, not one of whom I had ever seen, the duke himself a stranger to me except through the kind letter of invitation lying upon the table.

I was sitting by the fire imagining forms and faces for the different persons who had been named to me, when there was a knock at the door, and a tall, white-haired gentleman of noble physiognomy but singularly cordial address entered, with the broad red ribbon of a duke across his breast, and welcomed me most heartily to the castle. The gong sounded at the next moment; and in our way down, he named over his other guests, and prepared me in a measure for the introductions which followed. The drawing-room was crowded like a *soirée*. The duchess, a very tall and very handsome woman, with a smile of the most winning sweetness, received me at the door, and I was presented successively to every person present. Dinner was announced immediately, and the difficult question of precedence being sooner settled than I had ever seen it before in so large a party, we passed through files of servants to the dining-room.

It was a large and very lofty hall, supported at the ends by marble columns, within which was stationed a band of music playing delightfully. The walls were lined with full-length family pictures from old knights in armor to the modern dukes in kilt of the Gordon plaid; and on the sideboards stood services of gold plate, the most gorgeously massive and the most beautiful in workmanship I have ever seen. There were, among the vases, several large coursing-cups, won by the duke's hounds, of exquisite shape and ornament.

I fell into my place between a gentleman and a very beautiful woman, of perhaps twenty-two, neither of whose names I remembered, though I had but just been introduced. The duke probably anticipated as much, and as I took my seat he called out to me from the top of the table, that I had upon my right, Lady ——, " the most agreeable woman in Scotland." It was unnecessary to say that she was the most lovely.

I have been struck everywhere in England with the beauty of the higher classes ; and as I looked around me upon the aristocratic company at the table, I thought I never had seen "Heaven's image double-stamped as man and noble" so unequivocally clear. There were two young men and four or five young ladies of rank, and five or six people of more decided personal attractions could scarcely be found ; the style of form and face at the same time being of that cast of superiority which goes by the expressive name of "thorough-bred." There is a striking difference in this respect between England and the countries of the Continent, — the *paysans* of France and the *contadini* of Italy being physically far superior to their degenerate masters ; while the gentry and nobility of England differ from the peasantry in limb and feature as the racer differs from the drayhorse, or the greyhound from the cur. The contrast between the manners of English and French gentlemen is quite as striking. The *empressement*, the warmth, the shrug and gesture of the Parisian, and the working eyebrow, dilating or contracting eye, and conspirator-like action of the Italian in the most common conversation, are the antipodes of English high breeding. I should say a North-American Indian, in his more dignified phase, approached nearer to the manner of an English nobleman than any other person. The calm repose of person and feature, the self-possession under all circumstances, that incapability of surprise or *déréglément*, and that decision about the slightest circumstance, and the apparent certainty that he is acting absolutely *comme il faut*, is equally "gentlemanlike" and Indianlike. You cannot astonish an English gentleman. If a man goes into a fit at his side, or a servant drops a dish upon his shoulder, or he hears that the house is on fire, he sets down his wineglass with the same deliberation.

He has made up his mind what to do in all possible cases, and he does it. He is cold at a first introduction, and may bow stiffly (which he always does) in drinking wine with you, but it is his manner; and he would think an Englishman out of his senses who should bow down to his very plate and smile as a Frenchman does on a similar occasion. Rather chilled by this, you are a little astonished when the ladies have left the table, and he closes his chair up to you, to receive an invitation to pass a month with him at his country-house, and to discover that at the very moment he bowed so coldly he was thinking how he should contrive to facilitate your plans for getting to him, or seeing the country to advantage on the way.

The band ceased playing when the ladies left the table, the gentlemen closed up, conversation assumed a merrier cast, coffee and *chasse-café* were brought in when the wines began to be circulated more slowly; and at eleven there was a general move to the drawing-room. Cards, tea, and music filled up the time till twelve, and then the ladies took their departure, and the gentlemen sat down to supper. I got to bed somewhere about two o'clock; and thus ended an evening which I had anticipated as stiff and embarrassing, but which is marked in my tablets as one of the most social and kindly I have had the good fortune to record on my travels. I have described it and shall describe others minutely, and I hope there is no necessity of reminding any one that my apology for thus disclosing scenes of private life has been already made. Their interest as sketches by an American of the society that most interests Americans, and the distance at which they are published, justify them, I would hope, from any charge of indelicacy.

I arose late on the first morning after my arrival at Gordon Castle, and found the large party already assembled about the breakfast-table. I was struck on entering with the dif-

ferent air of the room. The deep windows opening out upon
the park had the effect of sombre landscapes in oaken frames ;
the troops of liveried servants, the glitter of plate, the music,
that had contributed to the splendor of the scene the night
before, were gone ; the duke sat laughing at the head of the
table, with a newspaper in his hand, dressed in a coarse
shooting-jacket and colored cravat ; the duchess was in a
plain morning-dress and cap of the simplest character ; and
the high-born women about the table, whom I had left glittering with jewels and dressed in all the attractions of fashion,
appeared with the simplest *coiffure* and a toilet of studied
plainness. The ten or twelve noblemen present were engrossed with their letters or newspapers over tea and toast ;
and in them, perhaps, the transformation was still greater.
The *soigné* man of fashion of the night before, faultless in
costume and distinguished in his appearance, in the full force
of the term, was enveloped now in a coat of fustian, with a
coarse waistcoat of plaid, a gingham cravat, and hob-nailed
shoes (for shooting), and in place of the gay hilarity of the
supper-table, wore a face of calm indifference, and ate his
breakfast and read the paper in a rarely broken silence. I
wondered as I looked about me, what would be the impression of many people in my own country, could they look in
upon that plain party, aware that it was composed of the
proudest nobility and the highest fashion of England.

Breakfast in England is a confidential and unceremonious
hour, and servants are generally dispensed with. This is to
me, I confess, an advantage it has over every other meal.
I detest eating with twenty tall fellows standing opposite,
whose business it is to watch me. The coffee and tea were
on the table, with toast, muffins, oat-cakes, marmalade,
jellies, fish, and all the paraphernalia of a Scotch breakfast ;
and on the sideboard stood cold meats for those who liked
them, and they were expected to go to it and help themselves.

Nothing could be more easy, unceremonious, and affable than the whole tone of the meal. One after another rose and fell into groups in the windows, or walked up and down the long room; and, with one or two others, I joined the duke at the head of the table, who gave us some interesting particulars of the salmon-fisheries of the Spey. The privilege of fishing the river within his lands is bought of him at the pretty sum of eight thousand pounds a year! A salmon was brought in for me to see, as of remarkable size, which was not more than half the weight of our common American salmon.

The ladies went off unaccompanied to their walks in the park and other avocations; those bound for the covers joined the gamekeepers, who were waiting with their dogs in the leash at the stables; some paired off to the billiard-room, and I was left with Lord Aberdeen in the breakfast-room alone. The Tory ex-minister made a thousand inquiries, with great apparent interest, about America. When secretary for foreign affairs in the Wellington cabinet, he had known Mr. McLane intimately. He said he seldom had been so impressed with a man's honesty and straightforwardness, and never did public business with any one with more pleasure. He admired Mr. McLane, and hoped he enjoyed his friendship. He wished he might return as our minister to England. One such honorable, uncompromising man, he said, was worth a score of practised diplomatists. He spoke of Gallatin and Rush in the same flattering manner, but recurred continually to Mr. McLane, of whom he could scarcely say enough. His politics would naturally lead him to approve of the administration of General Jackson, but he seemed to admire the president very much as a man.

Lord Aberdeen has the name of being the proudest and coldest aristocrat of England. It is amusing to see the person who bears such a character. He is of the middle height, rather clumsily made, with an address more of sober dignity than of pride or reserve. With a black coat much worn, and always too large for him, a pair of coarse check trousers very ill made, a waistcoat buttoned up to his throat, and a cravat of the most primitive *negligé*, his aristocracy is certainly not in his dress. His manners are of absolute simplicity, amounting almost to want of style. He crosses his hands behind him, and balances on his heels ; in conversation his voice is low and cold, and he seldom smiles. Yet there is a certain benignity in his countenance, and an indefinable superiority and high breeding in his simple address, that would betray his rank after a few minutes' conversation to any shrewd observer. It is only in his manner toward the ladies of the party that he would be immediately distinguishable from men of lower rank in society.

Still suffering from lameness, I declined all invitations to the shooting-parties, who started across the park with the dogs leaping about them in a frenzy of delight, and accepted the duchess's kind offer of a pony-phaeton to drive down to the kennels. The duke's breed, both of setters and hounds, is celebrated throughout the kingdom. They occupy a spacious building in the centre of a wood, a quadrangle enclosing a court, and large enough for a respectable poorhouse. The chief huntsman and his family, and perhaps a gamekeeper or two, lodge on the premises, and the dogs are divided by palings across the court. I was rather startled to be introduced into the small enclosure with a dozen gigantic bloodhounds, as high as my breast, the keeper's whip in my hand the only defence. I was not easier for the man's assertion that, without it, they would " hae the life oot o' me in a brack." They came around me very quietly, and one immense fellow, with a chest like a horse, and a head of the finest expression, stood up and laid his paws on my shoulders, with the deliberation of a friend about to favor me with some grave advice. One can scarce believe these noble creatures have not reason like ourselves. Those slender, thorough-bred heads, large speaking eyes, and beautiful limbs and graceful action, should be gifted with more than mere animal instinct. The greyhounds were the beauties of the kennel, however. I never had seen such perfect creatures. "Dinna tak' pains to caress 'em, sir," said the huntsman, "they'll only be hangit for it!" I asked for an explanation ; and the man, with an air as if I was uncommonly ignorant, told me that a hound was hung the moment he betrayed attachment to any one, or in any way showed signs of superior sagacity. In coursing the hare, for instance, if the dog abandoned the scent to cut across and intercept the poor animal, he was considered as spoiling the sport. Greyhounds are valuable only as they obey their mere natural instinct ; and if they leave the track of the hare, either in their own sagacity, or to follow their master, in intercepting it, they spoil the pack, and are hung without mercy. It is an object, of course, to preserve them what they usually are, the greatest fools as well as the handsomest of the canine species ; and on the first sign of attachment to their master, their death-warrant is signed. They are too sensible to live. The duchess told me afterward that she had the greatest difficulty in saving the life of the finest hound in the pack, who had committed the sin of showing pleasure once or twice when she appeared.

The setters were in the next division, and really they were quite lovely. The rare tan and black dog of this race, with his silky floss hair, intelligent muzzle, good-humored face and caressing fondness (lucky dog! that affection is permitted in *his* family!), quite excited my admiration. There were thirty or forty of these, old and young ; and a friend of the duke's would as soon ask him for a church living as for the present of one of them. The former would be by

much the smaller favor.   Then there were terriers of four or
five breeds, of one family of which (long-haired, long-bodied,
short-legged, and perfectly white little wretches) the keeper
seemed particularly proud.   I evidently sunk in his opinion
for not admiring them.

I passed the remainder of the morning in threading the
lovely alleys and avenues of the park, miles after miles of
gravel-walk, extending away in every direction, with every
variety of turn and shade, now a deep wood, now a sunny
opening upon a glade, here along the bank of a stream, and
there around the borders of a small lagoon ; the little ponies
flying on over the smoothly rolled paths, and tossing their
mimicking heads, as if they too enjoyed the beauty of the
princely domain.   This, I thought to myself, as I sped on
through light and shadow, is very like what is called happiness ; and this (if to be a duke were to enjoy it as I do with
this fresh feeling of novelty and delight) is a condition of
life it is not quite irrational to envy.   And giving my little
steeds the rein, I repeated to myself Scott's graphic description, which seems written for the park of Gordon Castle, and
thanked Heaven for one more day of unalloyed happiness.

> " And there soft swept in velvet green,
>   The plain with many a glade between,
>   Whose tangled alleys far invade
>   The depths of the brown forest shade;
>   And the tall fern obscured the lawn,
>   Fair shelter for the sportive fawn.
>   There, tufted close with copse-wood green,
>   Was many a swelling hillock seen,
>   And all around was verdure meet
>   For pressure of the fairies' feet.
>   The glossy valley loved the park,
>   The yew-tree lent its shadows dark,
>   And many an old oak worn and bare
>   With all its shivered boughs was there."

The aim of Scotch hospitality seems to be, to convince you that the house and all that is in it is your own, and you are at liberty to enjoy it as if you were, in the French sense of the French phrase, *chez vous.*   The routine of Gordon Castle was what each one chose to make it.   Between breakfast and lunch the ladies were generally invisible, and the gentlemen rode or shot, or played billiards, or kept their rooms. At two o'clock, a dish or two of hot game and a profusion of cold meats were set on the small tables in the dining-room, and everybody came in for a kind of lounging half-meal, which occupied perhaps an hour.   Thence all adjourned to the drawing-room, under the windows of which were drawn up carriages of all descriptions, with grooms, outriders, footmen, and saddle-horses for gentlemen and ladies.   Parties were then made up for driving or riding, and from a pony-chaise to a phaeton and four, there was no class of vehicle which was not at your disposal.   In ten minutes the carriages were usually all filled, and away they flew, some to the banks of the Spey or the seaside, some to the drives in the park, and with the delightful consciousness that, speed where you would, the horizon scarce limited the possession of your host, and you were everywhere at home.   The ornamental gates flying open at your approach, miles distant from the castle ; the herds of red deer trooping away from the sound of wheels in the silent park ; the stately pheasants feeding tamely in the immense preserves ; the h..res scarce troubling themselves to get out of the length of the whip ; the stalking game-keepers lifting their hats in the dark recesses of the forest, — there was something in this perpetual reminding of your privileges, which, as a novelty, was far from disagreeable.   I could not at the time bring myself to feel, what perhaps would be more poetical and republican, that a ride in the wild and unfenced forest of my own country would have been more to my taste.

LADY RAVELGOLD.

CHAPTER I.

"What would it pleasure me to have my throat cut
With diamonds? or to be smothered quick
With cassia, or be shot to death with pearls?"

DUCHESS OF MALFY.

"I've been i' the Indies twice, and seen strange things —
But two honest women! — *One*, I read of once!"

RULE A WIFE.

IT was what is called by people on the Continent a "London day." A thin gray mist drizzled down through the smoke which darkened the long cavern of Fleet Street; the sidewalks were slippery and clammy; the drays slid from side to side on the greasy pavement, creating a perpetual clamor among the lighter carriages with which they came in contact; the porters wondered that "gemmen" would carry their umbrellas up when there was no rain, and the gentlemen wondered that porters should be permitted on the sidewalks; there were passengers in box-coats, though it was the first of May, and beggars with bare breasts, though it was chilly as November; the boys were looking wistfully into the hosier's windows who were generally at the pastrycook's; and there were persons who wished to know the time, trying in vain to see the dial of St. Paul's through the gamboge atmosphere.

It was twelve o'clock, and a plain chariot with a simple crest on the panels slowly picked its way through the choked and disputed thoroughfare east of Temple Bar. The smart glazed hat of the coachman, the well-fitted drab greatcoat

248

and gaiters of the footman, and the sort of half-submissive, half-contemptuous look on both their faces (implying that they were bound to drive to the devil if it were miladi's orders, but that the rabble of Fleet Street was a *leetle* too vulgar for their contact), expressed very plainly that the lady within was a denizen of a more privileged quarter, but had chosen a rainy day for some compulsory visit to " the city."

At the rate of perhaps a mile an hour, the well-groomed night-horses (a pair of smart, hardy, twelve-mile cabs, all bottom, but little style, kept for night-work and forced journeys) had threaded the tortuous entrails of London, and had arrived at the arch of a dark court in Throgmorton Street. The coachman put his wheels snug against the edge of the sidewalk, to avoid being crushed by the passing drays, and settled his many-caped benjamin about him ; while the footman spread his umbrella, and, making a balustrade of his arm for his mistress's assistance, a closely-veiled lady descended, and disappeared up the wet and ill-paved avenue.

The green-baize door of Firkins & Co. opened on its silent hinges, and admitted the mysterious visitor, who, inquiring of the nearest clerk if the junior partner were in, was shown to a small inner room containing a desk, two chairs, a coal fire, and a young gentleman. The last article of furniture rose on the lady's entrance ; and as she threw off her veil he made a low bow, with the air of a gentleman, who is neither surprised nor embarrassed, and, pushing aside the door-check, they were left alone.

There was that forced complaisance in the lady's manner on her first entrance, which produced the slightest possible elevation in a very scornful lip owned by the junior partner ; but the lady was only forty-five, high-born, and very hand-some, and as she looked at the fine specimen of nature's nobility, who met her with a look as proud and yet as gentle as her own, the smoke of Fleet Street passed away from her memory, and she became natural and even gracious. The effect upon the junior partner was simply that of removing from his breast the shade of her first impression.

"I have brought you," said his visitor, drawing a card from her reticule, "an invitation to the Duchess of Haut-aigle's ball. She sent me half a dozen to fill up for what she calls ' ornamentals ; ' and I am sure I shall scarce find another who comes so decidedly under her grace's category."

The fair speaker had delivered this pretty speech in the sweetest and best-bred tone of St. James's, looking the while at the toe of the small *brodequin* which she held up to the fire, *perhaps* thinking only of drying it. As she concluded her sentence, she turned to her companion for an answer, and was surprised at the impassive politeness of his bow of acknowledgment.

"I regret that I shall not be able to avail myself of your ladyship's kindness," said the junior partner, in the same well-enunciated tone of courtesy.

"Then," replied the lady with a smile, "Lord Augustus Fitz-Moi, who looks at himself all dinner-time in a spoon, will be the Apollo of the hour. What a pity such a handsome creature should be so vain ! By the way, Mr. Firkins, you live without a looking-glass, I see."

"Your ladyship reminds me that this is merely a place of business. May I ask at once what errand has procured me the honor of a visit on so unpleasant a day?"

A slight flush brightened the cheek and forehead of the beautiful woman, as she compressed her lips, and forced herself to say with affected ease, "The want of five hundred pounds."

The junior partner paused an instant, while the lady tapped with her boot upon the fender in ill-dissembled anxiety, and then, turning to his desk, he filled up the check

without remark, presented it, and took his hat to wait on her
to her carriage. A gleam of relief and pleasure shot over
her countenance as she closed her small jewelled hand over
it, followed immediately by a look of embarrassed inquiry
into the face of the unquestioning banker.

" I am in your debt already."

" Thirty thousand pounds, madam ! "

" And for this you think the securities on the estate of
Rockland " —

" Are worth nothing, madam ! But it rains. I regret that
your ladyship's carriage cannot come to the door. In the
old-fashioned days of sedan-chairs, now, the dark courts of
Lothbury must have been more attractive. By the way,
talking of Lothbury, there is Lady Roseberry's *fête champêtre*
next week. If you should chance to have a spare card " —

" Twenty, if you like ; I am too happy — really, Mr.
Firkins " —

" It's on the fifteenth ; I shall have the honor of seeing
your ladyship there ! Good-morning. — Home, coachman ! "

" Does this man love me? " was Lady Ravelgold's first
thought, as she sank back in her returning chariot. " Yet
no ! he was even rude in his haste to be rid of me. And I
would willingly have staid too, for there is something about
him of a mark that I like. Ay, and he must have seen it :
a lighter encouragement has been interpreted more readily.
Five hundred pounds ! — really five hundred pounds ! And
thirty thousand at the back of it ! What does he mean?
Heavens ! if he should be deeper than I thought ! If he
should wish to involve me first ! "

And spite of the horror with which the thought was met
in the mind of Lady Ravelgold, the blush over her forehead
died away into a half smile and a brighter tint in her lips ;
and as the carriage wound slowly on through the confused
press of Fleet Street and the Strand, the image of the hand-

some and haughty young banker shut her eyes from all sounds without, and she was at her own door in Grosvenor Square before she had changed position or wandered half a moment from the subject of those busy dreams.

CHAPTER II.

THE morning of the fifteenth of May seemed to have been appointed by all the flowers as a jubilee of perfume and bloom. The birds had been invited, and sang in the summer with a welcome as full-throated as a prima donna singing down the tenor in a duet; the most laggard buds turned out their hearts to the sunshine, and promised leaves on the morrow; and that portion of London that had been invited to Lady Roseberry's fête thought it a very fine day. That portion which was not wondered how people would go sweltering about in such a glare for a cold dinner!

At about half-past two, a very elegant dark green cab without a crest, and with a servant in whose slight figure and plain blue livery there was not a fault, whirled out at the gate of the Regent's Park, and took its way up the well-watered road leading to Hampstead. The gentlemen whom it passed or met turned to admire the performance of the dark-gray horse, and the ladies looked after the cab as if they could see the handsome occupant once more through its leather back. Whether by conspiracy among the coach-makers, or by an aristocracy of taste, the degree of elegance in a turn-out attained by the cab just described is usually confined to the acquaintances of Lady —— ; that list being understood to enumerate all "the nice young men" of the West End, beside the guardsmen. (The *ton* of the latter, in all matters that affect the style of the regiment, is looked after by the club and the colonel.) The junior Firkins seemed an exception to this exclusive rule. No " nice man " could come from Lothbury, and he did not visit Lady —— ; but his horse was faultless, and when he turned into the gate of Rose-Eden, the policeman at the porter's lodge, though he did not know him, thought it unnecessary to ask for his name. Away he spattered up the hilly avenue, and, giving the reins to his groom at the end of a green arbor leading to the reception-lawn, he walked in and made his bow to Lady Roseberry, who remarked, " How very handsome ! Who can he be? " and the junior partner walked on and disappeared down an avenue of laburnums.

Ah ! but Rose-Eden looked a paradise that day ! Hundreds had passed across the close-shaven lawn, with a bow to the lady mistress of this fair abode. Yet the grounds were still private enough for Milton's pair, so lost were they in the green labyrinths of hill and dale. Some had descended through heavily shaded paths to a fancy dairy, built over a fountain in the bottom of a cool dell ; and here, amid her milk-pans of old and costly china, the prettiest maid in the country round pattered about upon a floor of Dutch tiles, and served her visitors with creams and ices, already, as it were, adapted to fashionable comprehension. Some had strayed to the ornamental cottages in the skirts of the flower-garden, — poetical abodes, built from a picturesque drawing, with imitation roughness ; thatch, lattice-window, and low paling, all complete ; and inhabited by superannuated dependants of Lord Roseberry, whose only duties were to look like patriarchs, and give tea and new cream-cheese to visitors on fête-days. Some had gone to see the silver and gold pheasants in their wire houses, stately aristocrats of the game tribe, who carry their finely pencilled feathers like " Marmalet Madarus," strutting in hoop and farthingale. Some had gone to the kennels, to see setters and pointers, hounds and terriers, lodged like gentlemen, each breed in its own apartment, — the puppies, as elsewhere, treated with most attention. Some were in the flower-garden, some in the greenhouses, some in the graperies, aviaries, and grottoes ; and at the side of a bright sparkling fountain, in the recesses of a fir-grove, with her foot upon its marble lip, and one hand on the shoulder of a small Cupid who archly made a drinking-cup of his wing, and caught the bright water as it fell, stood Lady Imogen Ravelgold, the loveliest girl of nineteen that prayed night and morning within the parish of May Fair, listening to very passionate language from the young banker of Lothbury.

A bugle on the lawn rang a recall. From every alley, and by every path, poured in the gay multitude ; and the smooth sward looked like a plateau of animated flowers, waked by magic from a broidery on green velvet. Ah ! the beautiful *demi-toilettes !* — so difficult to attain, yet, when attained, the dress most modest, most captivating, most worthy the divine grace of woman. Those airy hats, sheltering from the sun, yet not enviously concealing a feature or a ringlet that a painter would draw for his exhibition-picture ! Those summery and shapeless robes, covering the person more to show its outline better, and provoke more the worship, which, like all worship, is made more adoring by mystery ! Those complexions which but betray their transparency in the sun ; lips in which the blood is translucent when between you and the light ; cheeks finer-grained than alabaster, yet as cool in their virgin purity as a tint in the dark corner of a Ruysdael : the human race was at less perfection in Athens in the days of Lais, in Egypt in the days of Cleopatra, than that day on the lawn of Rose-Eden.

Cartloads of ribbons, of every gay color, had been laced through the trees in all directions ; and amid every variety of foliage, and every shade of green, the tulip-tints shone vivid and brilliant like an American forest after the first frost. From the left edge of the lawn the ground suddenly sunk into a dell, shaped like an amphitheatre, with a level platform at its bottom, and all around, above and below, thickened a shady wood. The music of a delicious band stole up from the recesses of a grove, draped as an orchestra and green-room on the lower side ; and while the audience disposed themselves in the shade of the upper grove, a company of players and dancing-girls commenced their theatricals. Imogen Ravelgold, who was separated by a pine-tree only from the junior partner, could scarce tell you, when it was finished, what was the plot of the play.

The recall-bugle sounded again, and the band wound away from the lawn, playing a gay march ; followed Lady Roseberry and her suite of gentlemen, followed dames and their daughters, followed all who wished to see the flight of my lord's falcons. By a narrow path and a wicket-gate the long, music-guided train stole out upon an open hill-side, looking down on a verdant and spreading meadow. The band played at a short distance behind the gay groups of spectators, and it was a pretty picture to look down upon the splendidly dressed falconer and his men, holding their fierce birds upon their wrists, in their hoods and jesses, — a foreground of old chivalry and romance ; while far beyond extended, like a sea over the horizon, the smoke-clad pinnacles of busy and every-day London. There are such contrasts for the eyes of the rich !

The scarlet hood was taken from the trustiest falcon, and a dove, confined at first with a string, was thrown up, and brought back, to excite his attention. As he fixed his eye upon him, the frightened victim was let loose, and the falcon flung off. Away skimmed the dove in a low flight over the meadow ; and up to the very zenith, in circles of amazing swiftness and power, sped the exulting falcon, apparently forgetful of his prey, and bound for the eye of the sun with his strong wings and his liberty. The falconer's whistle and cry were heard; the dove circled round the edge of the meadow in his wavy flight; and down, with the speed of lightning, shot the falcon, striking his prey dead to the earth before the eye could settle on his form. As the proud bird stood upon his victim, looking around with a lifted crest and fierce eye, Lady Imogen Ravelgold heard, in a voice of which her heart knew the music, "They who soar highest strike surest: the dove lies in the falcon's bosom."

CHAPTER III.

The afternoon had, meantime, been wearing on, and at six the "breakfast" was announced. The tents beneath which the tables were spread were in different parts of the grounds, and the guests had made up their own parties. Each sped to his rendezvous, and as the last loiterers disappeared from the lawn a gentleman in a claret coat and a brown study found himself stopping to let a lady pass who had obeyed the summons as tardily as himself. In a white chip hat, Hairbault's last, a few lilies of the valley laid among her raven curls beneath, a simple white robe, the *chef-d'œuvre* of Victotine in style and *tournure*, Lady Ravelgold would have been the belle of the fête, but for her daughter.

"Well emerged from Lothbury!" she said, courtesying, with a slight flush over her features, but immediately taking his arm; "I have lost my party, and meeting you is opportune. Where shall we breakfast?"

There was a small tent standing invitingly open on the opposite side of the lawn, and by the fainter rattle of soup-spoons from that quarter it promised to be less crowded than the others. The junior partner would willingly have declined the proffered honor, but he saw at a glance that there was no escape, and submitted with a grace.

" You know very few people here," said his fair creditor, taking the bread from her napkin.

" Your ladyship, and one other."

" Ah! we shall have dancing by and by, and I must introduce you to my daughter. By the way, have you no name from your mother's side? 'Firkins' sounds so very odd! Give me some prettier word to drink in this champagne."

" What do you think of Tremlet?"

" Too effeminate for your severe style of beauty — but it will do. Mr. Tremlet, your health! Will you give me a little of the *paté* before you? Pray, if it is not indiscreet, how comes that classic profile, and, more surprising still, that distinguished look of yours, to have found no gayer destiny than the signing of 'Firkins & Co.' to notes of hand? Though I thought you became your den in Lothbury, upon my honor you look more at home here."

And Lady Ravelgold fixed her superb eyes upon the beautiful features of her companion, wondering partly why he did not speak, and partly why she had not observed before that he was incomparably the handsomest creature she had ever seen.

" I can regret no vocation," he answered after a moment, " which procures me an acquaintance with your ladyship's family."

" There is an *arrière pensée* in that formal speech, Mr. Tremlet. You are insincere. I am the only one in my family whom you know, and what pleasure have you taken in my acquaintance? And, now I think of it, there is a mystery about you, which, but for the noble truth written so legibly on your features, I should be afraid to fathom. Why have you suffered me to overdraw my credit so enormously, and without a shadow of a protest?''

When Lady Ravelgold had disburdened her heart of this direct question, she turned half round, and looked her companion in the face with an intense interest, which produced upon her own features an expression of earnestness very uncommon upon their pale and impassive lines. She was one of those persons of little thought, who care nothing for causes or consequences, so that the present difficulty is removed, or the present hour provided with its wings; but the repeated relief she had received from the young banker, when total ruin would have been the consequence of his refusal, and the marked coldness in his manner to her, had stimulated the utmost curiosity of which she was capable. Her vanity, founded upon her high rank and great renown as a beauty, would have argued that he might be willing to get her into his power at that price, had he been less agreeable in his own person, or more eager in his manner. But she had wanted money sufficiently to know that thirty thousand pounds are not a bagatelle, and her brain was busy till she discovered the equivalent he sought for it. Meantime her fear that he would turn out to be a lover grew rapidly into a fear that he would not.

Lady Ravelgold had been the wife of a dissolute earl, who had died leaving his estate inextricably involved. With no male heir to the title or property, and no very near relation, the beautiful widow shut her eyes to the difficulties by which she was surrounded; and at the first decent moment after the death of her lord, she had re-entered the gay society of which she had been the bright and particular star, and never dreamed either of diminishing her establishment, or of calculating her possible income. The first heavy draft she had made upon the house of Firkins & Co., her husband's bankers, had been returned with a statement of the Ravelgold

debt and credit on their books, by which it appeared that
Lord Ravelgold had overdrawn four or five thousand pounds
before his death, and that, from some legal difficulties, nothing could be realized from the securities given on his estates.
This bad news arrived on the morning of a fête to be given
by the Russian ambassador, at which her only child, Lady
Imogen, was to make her *début* in society. With the facility
of disposition which was peculiar to her, Lady Ravelgold
thrust the papers into her drawer, and determining to visit her
banker on the following morning, threw the matter entirely
from her mind, and made preparations for the ball. With
the Russian government the house of Firkins & Co. had long
carried on very extensive fiscal transactions; and in obedience to instructions from the emperor, regular invitations
for the embassy fêtes were sent to the bankers, accepted
occasionally by the junior partner only, who was generally
supposed to be a natural son of old Firkins. Out of the
banking-house he was known as Mr. Tremlet; and it was by
this name, which was presumed to be his mother's, that he
was casually introduced to Lady Imogen on the night of the
fête, while she was separated from her mother in the dancing-
room. The consequence was a sudden, deep, ineffaceable
passion in the bosom of the young banker, checked and
silenced, but never lessened or chilled, by the recollection of
the obstacle of his birth. The impression of his subdued
manner, his worshipping yet most respectful tones, and the
bright soul that breathed through his handsome features with
his unusual excitement, was, to say the least, favorable upon
Lady Imogen; and they parted on the night of the fête,
mutually aware of each other's preference.

On the following morning Lady Ravelgold made her proposed visit to the city; and, inquiring for Mr. Firkins, was
shown in as usual to the junior partner, to whom the collo-
quial business of the concern had long been intrusted. To

her surprise she found no difficulty in obtaining the sum of money which had been refused her on the preceding day, — a result which she attributed to her powers of persuasion, or to some new turn in the affairs of the estate; and for two years these visits had been repeated at intervals of three or four months, with the same success, though not with the same delusion as to the cause. She had discovered that the estate was worse than nothing, and the junior partner cared little to prolong his *tête-à-têtes* with her; and, up to the visit with which this tale opened, she had looked to every succeeding one with increased fear and doubt.

During these two years, Tremlet had seen Lady Imogen occasionally at balls and public places, and every look they exchanged wove more strongly between them the subtle threads of love. Once or twice she had endeavored to interest her mother in conversation on the subject, with the intention of making a confidence of her feelings; but Lady Ravelgold, when not anxious, was giddy with her own success, and the unfamiliar name never rested a moment on her ear. With this explanation to render the tale intelligible, "let us," as the French say, "return to our muttons."

Of the conversation between Tremlet and her mother, Lady Imogen was an unobserved and astonished witness. The tent which they had entered was large, with a *buffet* in the centre, and a circular table waited on by servants within the ring; and just concealed by the drapery around the pole, sat Lady Imogen with a party of her friends, discussing very seriously the threatened fashion of tight sleeves. She had half risen, when her mother entered, to offer her a seat by her side; but the sight of Tremlet, who immediately followed, had checked the words upon her lip, and to her surprise they seated themselves on the side that was wholly unoccupied, and conversed in a tone inaudible to all but themselves. Not aware that her lover knew Lady Ravelgold,

she supposed that she might have been casually introduced,
till the earnestness of her mother's manner, and a certain
ease between them in the little courtesies of the table, assured her that this could not be their first interview. Tremlet's face was turned from her, and she could not judge
whether he was equally interested; but she had been so
accustomed to consider her mother as irresistible when she
chose to please, that she supposed it of course; and very
soon the heightened color of Lady Ravelgold, and the unwavering look of mingled admiration and curiosity which
she bent upon the handsome face of her companion, left no
doubt in her mind that her reserved and exclusive lover
was in the dangerous toils of a rival whose power she knew.
From the mortal pangs of a first jealousy, Heaven send thee
deliverance, fair Lady Imogen!

" We shall find our account in the advances on your ladyship's credit," said Tremlet, in reply to the direct question
that was put to him. " Meantime permit me to admire the
courage with which you look so disagreeable a subject in the
face."

" For ' disagreeable subject,' read ' Mr. Tremlet.' I
show my temerity more in that. *Apropos* of faces, yours
would become the new fashion of cravat. The men at
Crockford's slip the ends through a ring of their lady-love's,
if they chance to have one, — thus! " And untying the loose
knot of his black satin cravat, Lady Ravelgold slipped over
the ends a diamond of small value, conspicuously set in
pearls.

" The men at Crockford's," said Tremlet, hesitating to
commit the rudeness of removing the ring, " are not of my
school of manners. If I had been so fortunate as to inspire
a lady with a preference for me, I should not advertise it on
my cravat."

" But suppose the lady were proud of her preference, as

dames were of the devotion of their knights in the days of chivalry, would you not wear her favor as conspicuously as they?"

A flush of mingled embarrassment and surprise shot over the forehead of Tremlet; and he was turning the ring with his fingers, when Lady Imogen, attempting to pass out of the tent, was stopped by her mother.

"Imogen, my daughter! this is Mr. Tremlet. Lady Imogen Ravelgold, Mr. Tremlet!"

The cold and scarce perceptible bow which the wounded girl gave to her lover betrayed no previous acquaintance to the careless Lady Ravelgold. Without giving a second thought to her daughter, she held her glass for some champagne to a passing servant; and as Lady Imogen and her friends crossed the lawn to the dancing-tent, she resumed the conversation which they had interrupted, while Tremlet, with his heart brooding on the altered look he had received, listened and replied almost unconsciously, yet, from this very circumstance, in a manner which was interpreted by his companion as the embarrassment of a timid and long-repressed passion for herself.

While Lady Ravelgold and the junior partner were thus playing at cross purposes over their champagne and *bon-bons*, Grisi and Lablache were singing a duet from *I Puritani* to a full audience in the saloon; the drinking young men sat over their wine at the nearly deserted tables; Lady Imogen and her friends waltzed to Collinet's band; and the artisans were busy below the lawn erecting the machinery for the fire-works. Meantime every alley and avenue, grot and labyrinth, had been dimly illuminated with colored lamps, showing like vari-colored glow-worms amid the foliage and shells; and if the bright scenery of Rose-Eden had been lovely by day, it was fay-land and witchery by night. Fatal impulse of our nature, that these approaches to paradise in the

" delight of the eye," stir only in our bosoms the passions upon which law and holy writ have put ban and bridle!

" Shall we stroll down this alley of crimson lamps?" said Lady Ravelgold, crossing the lawn from the tent where their coffee had been brought to them, and putting her slender arm far into that of her now pale and silent companion.

A lady in a white dress stood at the entrance of that crimson avenue, as Tremlet and his passionate admirer disappeared beneath the closing lines of the long perspective; and, remaining a moment gazing through the unbroken twinkle of the confusing lamps, she pressed her hand hard upon her forehead, drew up her form as if struggling with some irrepressible feeling, and in another moment was whirling in the waltz with Lord Ernest Fitzantelope, whose mother wrote a complimentary paragraph about their performance for the next Saturday's Court Journal.

The bugle sounded, and the band played a march upon the lawn. From the breakfast-tents, from the coffee-rooms, from the dance, from the card-tables, poured all who wished to witness the marvels that lie in saltpetre. Gentlemen who stood in a tender attitude in the darkness held themselves ready to lean the other way when the rockets blazed up, and mammas who were encouraging flirtations with eligibles whispered a caution on the same subject to their less experienced daughters.

Up sped the missiles, round spun the wheels, fair burned the pagodas, swift flew the fire-doves off and back again on their wires, and softly floated down through the dewy atmosphere of that May night the lambent and many-colored stars flung burning from the exploded rockets. Device followed device, and Lady Imogen almost forgot, in her child's delight at the spectacle, that she had taken into her bosom a green serpent, whose folds were closing like suffocation about her heart.

The *finale* was to consist of a new light, invented by the pyrotechnist, promised to Lady Roseberry to be several degrees brighter than the sun — comparatively with the quantity of matter. Before this last flourish came a pause ; and while all the world were murmuring love and applause around her, Lady Imogen, with her eyes fixed on an indefinite point in the darkness, took advantage of the cessation of light to feed her serpent with thoughts of passionate and uncontrollable pain. A French *attaché*, Phillipiste to the very tips of his mustache, addressed to her ear, meantime, the compliments he had found most effective in the *Chaussée d' Antin.*

The light burst suddenly from a hundred blazing points, clear, dazzling, intense, — illuminating as by the instantaneous burst of day the farthest corner of Rose-Eden. And Monsieur Mangepoire, with a French contempt for English fireworks, took advantage of the first ray to look into Lady Imogen's eyes.

" *Mais. Miladi !* " was his immediate exclamation, after following their direction with a glance, " *ce n'est qu'un tableau vivant, cela !* Help, gentlemen ! *Elle s'évanoûit.* Some salts ! *Misericorde ! Mon Dieu ! Mon Dieu !* " And Lady Imogen Ravelgold was carried fainting to Lady Roseberry's chamber.

In a small opening at the end of a long avenue of lilacs, extended from the lawn in the direction of Lady Imogen's fixed and unconscious gaze, was presented, by the unexpected illumination, the *tableau vivant* seen by her ladyship and Monsieur Mangepoire at the same instant, — a gentleman drawn up to his fullest height, with his arms folded ; and a lady kneeling on the ground at his feet, with her arms stretched up to his bosom.

CHAPTER IV.

A LITTLE after two o'clock on the following Wednesday, Tremlet's cabriolet stopped near the *perron* of Willis's rooms in King Street; and while he sent up his card to the lady patronesses for his ticket to that night's Almack's, he busied himself in looking into the crowd of carriages about him, and reading on the faces of their fair occupants the hope and anxiety to which they were a prey, till John the footman brought them tickets or despair. Drawn up on the opposite side of the street, stood a family-carriage of the old style, covered with half the arms of the herald's office, and containing a fat dowager and three very over-dressed daughters. Watching them, to see the effect of their application, stood upon the sidewalk three or four young men from the neighboring club-house; and at the moment Tremlet was observing these circumstances, a foreign britzska, containing a beautiful woman of a reputation better understood than expressed in the conclave above stairs, flew round the corner of St. James's Street, and very nearly drove into the open mouth of the junior partner's cabriolet.

" I will bet you a Ukraine colt against this fine bay of yours," said the Russian secretary of legation, advancing from the group of dandies to Tremlet, " that miladi yonder, with all the best blood of England in her own and her daughters' red faces, gets no tickets this morning."

" I'll take a bet upon the lady who has nearly extinguished me, if you like," answered Tremlet, gazing with admiration at the calm, delicate, childlike-looking creature, who sat before him in the britzska.

" No!" said the secretary, " for Almack's is a republic of beauty, and she'll be voted in without either blood or virtue.   *Par exemple*, Lady Ravelgold's voucher is good here, though she does study *tableaux* in Lothbury — eh, Tremlet?''

Totally unaware of the unlucky discovery by the fireworks at Lady Roseberry's fête, Tremlet colored and was inclined to take the insinuation as an affront; but a laugh from the dandies drew off his companion's attention, and he observed the dowager's footman standing at her coach window with his empty hands held up in most expressive negation, while the three young ladies within sat aghast, in all the agonies of disappointed hopes.   The lumbering carriage got into motion, — its ineffective blazonry paled by the mortified blush of its occupants, — and as the junior partner drove away, philosophizing on the arbitrary opinions and unprovoked insults of polite society, the britzska shot by, showing him, as he leaned forward, a lovely woman who bent on him the most dangerous eyes in London, and an Almack's ticket lying on the unoccupied cushion beside her.

The white *relievo* upon the pale blue wall of Almack's showed every crack in its stucco flowers; and the faded chaperones who had defects of a similar description to conceal took warning of the walls, and retreated to the friendlier dimness of the tea-room.   Collinet was beginning the second set of quadrilles; and among the fairest of the surpassingly beautiful women who were moving to his heavenly music, was Lady Imogen Ravelgold, the lovelier to-night for the first heavy sadness that had ever dimmed the roses in her cheek.   Her lady-mother divided her thoughts between what this could mean, and whether Mr. Tremlet would come to the ball; and when, presently after, in the *dos-à-dos*, she forgot to look at her daughter on seeing that gentleman enter, she lost a very good opportunity for a guess at the cause of Lady Imogen's paleness.

To the pure and true eye that appreciates the divinity of

the form after which woman is made, it would have been a glorious feast to have seen the perfection of shape, color, motion, and countenance, shown that night on the bright floor of Almack's. For the young and beautiful girls whose envied destiny is to commence their woman's history in this exclusive hall, there exist aids to beauty known to no other class or nation. Perpetual vigilance over every limb from the cradle up; physical education of a perfection, discipline, and judgment, pursued only at great expense and under great responsibility; moral education of the highest kind, habitual consciousness of rank, exclusive contact with elegance and luxury, and a freedom of intellectual culture which breathes a soul through the face before passion has touched it with a line or a shade, — these are some of the circumstances which make Almack's the cynosure of the world for adorable and radiant beauty.

There were three ladies who had come to Almack's with a definite object that night, each of whom was destined to be surprised and foiled, — Lady Ravelgold, who feared she had been abrupt with the inexperienced banker, but trusted to find him softened by a day or two's reflection; Mrs. St. Leger, the lady of the britzska, who had ordered supper for two on her arrival at home from her morning's drive, and intended to have the company of the handsome creature she had nearly run over in King Street; and Lady Imogen Ravelgold, as will appear in the sequel.

Tremlet stood in the entrance from the tea-room a moment, gathering courage to walk alone into such a dazzling scene, and then, having caught a glimpse of the glossy lines of Lady Imogen's head at the farthest end of the room, he was advancing toward her, when he was addressed by a lady who leaned against one of the slender columns of the orchestra. After a sweetly phrased apology for having nearly knocked out his brains that morning with her horses' forefeet, Mrs. St. Leger took his arm, and, walking deliberately two or three times up and down the room, took possession at last of a *banquette* on the highest range, so far from any other person that it would have been a marked rudeness to have left her alone. Tremlet took his seat by her with this instinctive feeling, trusting that some of her acquaintances would soon approach, and give him a fair excuse to leave her; but he soon became amused with her piquant style of conversation, and, not aware of being observed, fell into the attitude of a pleased and earnest listener.

Lady Ravelgold's feelings during this *petit entretien* were of a very positive description. She had an instinctive knowledge, and consequently a jealous dislike, of Mrs. St. Leger's character ; and, still under the delusion that the young banker's liberality was prompted by a secret passion for herself, she saw her credit in the city and her hold upon the affections of Tremlet (for whom she had really conceived a violent affection) melting away in every smile of the dangerous woman who engrossed him. As she looked around for a friend, to whose ear she might communicate some of the suffocating poison in her own heart, Lady Imogen returned to her from a galopade ; and, like a second dagger into the heart of the pure-minded girl, went this second proof of her lover's corrupt principle and conduct. Unwilling to believe even her own eyes on the night of Lady Roseberry's fête, she had summoned resolution on the road home to ask an explanation of her mother. Embarrassed by the abrupt question, Lady Ravelgold felt obliged to make a partial confidence of the state of her pecuniary affairs ; and, to clear herself, she represented Tremlet as having taken advantage of her obligations to him to push a dishonorable suit. The scene disclosed by the sudden blaze of the fireworks being thus simply explained, Lady Imogen determined at once to give up Tremlet's acquaintance altogether, — a resolution which

his open flirtation with a woman of Mrs. St. Leger's character served to confirm. She had, however, one errand with
him, prompted by her filial feelings, and favored by an acci-
dental circumstance which will appear.

"Do you believe in animal magnetism?" asked Mrs. St.
Leger; "for, by the fixedness of Lady Ravelgold's eyes in
this quarter, something is going to happen to one of us."

The next moment the Russian secretary approached and
took his seat by Mrs. St. Leger, and with diplomatic address
contrived to convey to Tremlet's ear that Lady Ravelgold
wished to speak with him. The banker rose, but the quick
wit of his companion comprehended the manœuvre.

"Ah! I see how it is," she said, "but stay — you'll sup
with me to-night? Promise me — *parole d'honneur!*"

"*Parole!*" answered Tremlet, making his way out between the seats, half pleased and half embarrassed.

"As for you, *Monsieur le Secrétaire*," said Mrs. St.
Leger, "you have forfeited my favor, and may sup elsewhere. How dare you conspire against me?"

While the Russian was making his peace, Tremlet crossed
over to Lady Ravelgold; but, astonished at the change in
Lady Imogen, he soon broke in abruptly upon her mother's
conversation, to ask her to dance. She accepted his hand
for a quadrille; but as they walked down the room in search
of a *vis-à-vis*, she complained of heat, and asked timidly if
he would take her to the tea-room.

"Mr. Tremlet," she said, fixing her eyes upon the cup of
tea which he had given her, and which she found some difficulty in holding, "I have come here to-night to communicate
to you some important information, to ask a favor, and to
break off an acquaintance which has lasted too long."

Lady Imogen stopped, for the blood had fled from her
lips, and she was compelled to ask his arm for a support.
She drew herself up to her fullest height the next moment,

looked at Tremlet, who stood in speechless astonishment, and with a strong effort, commenced again in a low, firm tone, —

"I have been acquainted with you some time, sir, and have never inquired, nor knew more than your name, up to this day. I suffered myself to be pleased too blindly " —

" Dear Lady Imogen ! "

" Stay a moment, sir ! I will proceed directly to my business. I received this morning a letter from the senior partner of a mercantile house in the city, with which you are connected. It is written on the supposition that I have some interest in you, and informs me you are not, as you yourself suppose, the son of the gentleman who writes the letter."

" Madam ! "

" That gentleman, sir, as you know, never was married. He informs me that in the course of many financial visits to St. Petersburg, he formed a friendship with Count Manteuffel, then minister of finance to the emperor, whose tragical end, in consequence of his extensive defalcations, is well known. In brief, sir, you were his child, and were taken by this English banker, and carefully educated as his own, in happy ignorance, as he imagined, of your father's misfortunes and mournful death."

Tremlet leaned against the wall, unable to reply to this astounding intelligence, and Lady Imogen went on, —

" Your title and estates have been restored to you at the request of your kind benefactor, and you are now the heir to a princely fortune, and a count of the Russian empire. Here is the letter, sir, which is of no value to me now. Mr. Tremlet ! one word more, sir."

Lady Imogen gasped for breath.

" In return, sir, for much interest given you heretofore — in return, sir, for this information " —

" Speak, dear Lady Imogen ! "

" Spare my mother ! "

" Mrs. St. Leger's carriage stops the way," shouted a servant at that moment, at the top of the stairs ; and as if there were a spell in the sound to nerve her resolution anew, Lady Imogen Ravelgold shook the tears from her eyes, bowed coldly to Tremlet, and passed out into the dressing-room.

" If you please, sir," said a servant, approaching the amazed banker, " Mrs. St. Leger waits for you in her carriage."

" Will you come home and sup with us ? " said Lady Ravelgold at the same instant, joining him in the tea-room.

" I shall be only too happy, Lady Ravelgold."

The bold coachman of Mrs. St. Leger continued to " stop the way," spite of policemen and infuriated footmen, for some fifteen minutes. At the end of that time Mr. Tremlet appeared, handing down Lady Ravelgold and her daughter, who walked to their chariot, which was a few steps behind ; and very much to Mrs. St. Leger's astonishment, the handsome banker sprang past her horses' heads a minute after, jumped into his cabriolet, which stood on the opposite side of the street, and drove after the vanishing chariot as if his life depended on overtaking it. Still Mrs. St. Leger's carriage " stopped the way." But, in a few minutes after, the same footman who had summoned Tremlet in vain, returned with the Russian secretary, doomed in blessed unconsciousness to play the *pis aller* at her *tête-à-tête* supper in Spring Gardens.

CHAPTER V.

IF Lady Ravelgold showed beautiful by the uncompromising light and in the ornamented hall of Almack's, she was

radiant as she came through the mirror-door of her own
love-contrived and beauty-breathing boudoir. Tremlet had
been shown into this recess of luxury and elegance on his
arrival, and Lady Ravelgold and her daughter, who preceded
her by a minute or two, had gone to their chambers, the first
to make some slight changes in her toilet, and the latter
(entirely ignorant of her lover's presence in the house) to
be alone with a heart never before in such painful need of
self-abandonment and solitude.

Tremlet looked about him in the enchanted room in which
he found himself alone, and, spite of the prepossessed agitation of his feelings, the voluptuous beauty of every object
had the effect to divert and tranquillize him. The light was
profuse, but it came softened through the thinnest alabaster ;
and while every object in the room was distinctly and
minutely visible, the effect of moonlight was not more soft
and dreamy. The general form of the boudoir was an oval,
but within the pilasters of folded silk with their cornices of
gold, lay crypts containing copies exquisitely done in marble
of the most graceful statues of antiquity, one of which
seemed, by the curtain drawn quite aside and a small antique
lamp burning near it, to be the divinity of the place, — the
Greek Antinoüs, with his drooped head and full, smooth
limbs, the most passionate and life-like representation of
voluptuous beauty that intoxicates the slumberous air of
Italy. Opposite this, another niche contained a few books,
whose retreating shelves swung on a secret door, and as it
stood half open, the nodding head of a snowy magnolia
leaned through, as if pouring from the lips of its broad chalice the mingled odors of the unseen conservatory it betrayed.
The first sketch in crayons of a portrait of Lady Ravelgold
by young Lawrence stood against the wall, with the frame
half buried in a satin ottoman ; and, as Tremlet stood before
it, admiring the clear, classic outline of the head and bust,

and wondering in what chamber of his brain the gifted artist
had found the beautiful drapery in which he had drawn her,
the dim light glanced faintly on the left, and the broad mirror
by which he had entered swung again on its silver hinges,
and admitted the very presentment of what he gazed on.
Lady Ravelgold had removed the jewels from her hair, and
the robe of wrought lace which she had worn that night over
a bodice of white satin laced loosely below the bosom. In
the place of this she had thrown upon her shoulders a flowing
wrapper of purple velvet, made open after the Persian fashion, with a short and large sleeve, and embroidered richly
with gold upon the skirts. Her admirable figure, gracefully
defined by the satin petticoat and bodice, showed against
the gorgeous purple as it flowed back in her advancing
motion, with a relief which would have waked the very soul
of Titian; her complexion was dazzling and faultless in the
flattering light of her own rooms; and there are those who
will read this who know how the circumstances which sur-
round a woman — luxury, elegance, taste, or the opposite of
these — enhance or dim, beyond help or calculation, even the
highest order of woman's beauty.

Lady Ravelgold held a bracelet in her hand as she came
in.

"In my own house," she said, holding the glittering jewel
to Tremlet, "I have a fancy for the style antique. Tasse-
line, my maid, has gone to bed, and you must do the devoir
of a knight, or an abigail, and loop up this Tyrian sleeve.
Stay, look first at the model, — that small statue of Cytheris,
yonder! Not the shoulder, — for you are to swear mine is
prettier, — but the clasp. Fasten it like that. So! Now
take me for a Grecian nymph the rest of the evening."

"Lady Ravelgold!"

"Hermione or Aglaë, if you please! But let us ring for
supper."

As the bell sounded, a superb South American trulian darted in from the conservatory, and, spreading his gorgeous black and gold wings a moment over the alabaster shoulder of Lady Ravelgold, as if he took a pleasure in prolonging the first touch as he alighted, turned his large liquid eye fiercely on Tremlet.

"Thus it is," said Lady Ravelgold, "we forget our old favorites in our new. See how jealous he is!"

"Supper is served, miladi!" said a servant entering.

"A hand to each, then, for the present," she said, putting one into Tremlet's, and holding up the trulian with the other. "He who behaves best shall drink first with me."

"I beg your ladyship's pardon," said Tremlet, drawing back, and looking at the servant, who immediately left the room. "Let us understand each other! Does Lady Imogen sup with us to-night?"

"Lady Imogen has retired," said her mother in some surprise.

"Then, madam, will you be seated one moment, and listen to me?"

Lady Ravelgold sat down on the nearest ottoman with the air of a person too high-bred to be taken by surprise; but the color deepened to crimson in the centre of her cheek, and the bird on her hand betrayed, by one of his gurgling notes, that he was held more tightly than pleased him. With a calm and decisive tone, Tremlet went through the explanation given in the previous parts of this narration. He declared his love for Lady Imogen, his hopes (while he had doubts of his birth) that Lady Ravelgold's increasing obligations and embarrassments and his own wealth might weigh against his disadvantages; and now, his honorable descent being established, and his rank entitling him to propose for her hand, he called upon Lady Ravelgold to redeem her obligations to him by an immediate explanation to her daughter of his conduct toward herself, and by lending her whole influence to the success of his suit.

Five minutes are brief time to change a lover into a son-in-law ; and Lady Ravelgold, as we have seen in the course of this story, was no philosopher. She buried her face in her hands, and sat silent for a while after Tremlet had concluded ; but the case was a very clear one. Ruin and mortification were in one scale, mortification and prosperity in the other. She rose pale but decided, and requesting Monsieur le Conte Manteuffel to await her a few minutes, ascended to her daughter's chamber.

"If you please, sir," said a servant, entering in about half an hour, "miladi and Lady Imogen beg that you will join them in the supper-room."

CHAPTER VI.

THE spirit of beauty, if it haunt in such artificial atmospheres as Belgrave Square, might have been pleased to sit invisibly on the vacant side of Lady Ravelgold's table. Tremlet had been shown in by the servant to a small apartment, built like a belvidere over the garden, half boudoir in its character, yet intended as a supper-room ; and at the long window (opening forth upon descending terraces laden with flowers, and just now flooded with the light of a glorious moon) stood Lady Imogen, with her glossy head laid against the casement, and the palm of her left hand pressed close upon her heart. If those two lights — the moon faintly shed off from the divine curve of her temple, and the stained rose-lamp pouring its mellow tint full on the heavenly shape and whiteness of her shoulder and neck — if those two lights, I say, could have been skilfully managed, Mr. Lawrence, what a picture you might have made of Lady Imogen Ravelgold!

"Imogen, my daughter! Mr. Tremlet!" said her mother as he entered.

Without changing her position she gave him the hand she had been pressing on her heart.

"Mr. Tremlet," said Lady Ravelgold, evidently entering into her daughter's embarrassment, "trouble yourself to come to the table and give me a bit of this pheasant. Imogen, George waits to give you some champagne."

"Can you forgive me?" said the beautiful girl, before turning to betray her blushing cheek and suffused eyes to her mother.

Tremlet stooped as if to pluck a leaf from the verbena at her feet, and passed his lips over the slight fingers he held.

"Pretty trulian!" murmured Lady Ravelgold to her bird, as he stood on the edge of her champagne-glass, and curving his superb neck nearly double, contrived to drink from the sparkling brim, — "pretty trulian! you will be merry after this! What ancient Sybarite, think you, Mr. Tremlet, inhabits the body of this bright bird? — Look up, *mignon*, and tell us if you were Hylas or Alcibiades! — Is the pheasant good, Mr. Tremlet?"

"Too good to come from Hades, miladi. Is it true that you have your table supplied from Crockford's?"

"*Tout bonnement!* I make it a principle to avoid all great anxieties, and I can trust nobody but Ude. He sends my dinners quite hot, and if there is a particular dish of game, he drives round at the hour and gives it the last turn in my own kitchen. I should die to be responsible for my dinners. I don't know how people get on that have no *grand artiste.* Pray, Mr. Tremlet (I beg pardon — Monsieur le Conte, perhaps I should say?)."

"No, no, I implore you! 'Tremlet' has been spoken too

musically to be so soon forgotten. Tremlet or Charles, which you will!''

Lady Ravelgold put her hand in his, and looked from his face to her daughter's with a smile, which assured him that she had obtained a victory over herself. Shrinking immediately, however, from any thing like sentiment (with the nervous dread of pathos so peculiar to the English), she threw off her trulian, — that made a circle and alighted on the emerald bracelet of Lady Imogen, — and rang the bell for coffee.

'' I flatter myself, Mr. Tremlet,'' she said, '' that I have made a new application of the homœopathic philosophy. Hahnemann, they say, cures fevers by aggravating the disease; and, when I cannot sleep, I drink coffee. *J'en suis passablement fière!* You did not know I was a philosopher?''

'' No, indeed!''

'' Well, take some of this spiced Mocha. I got it of the Turkish ambassador, to whom I made *beaux yeux* on purpose. Stop! you shall have it in the little tinsel cups he sent me. — George, bring those filagree things. — Now, Mr. Tremlet, imagine yourself in the *serail du Bosphore*, — Imogen and I two lovely Circassians, *par exemple!* Is it not delicious? Talking of the Bosphorus, nobody was classical enough to understand the device in my *coiffure* to-night.''

'' What was it?'' asked Tremlet absently, gazing while he spoke with eyes of envy at the trulian, who was whetting his bill backward and forward on the clear, bright lips of Lady Imogen.

'' Do you think my profile Grecian?'' asked Lady Ravelgold.

'' Perfectly.''

'' And my hair is coiffed *à la Grec?*''

'' Most becomingly.''

'' But still you won't see my golden grasshopper! Do

you happen to know, sir, that to wear the golden grasshopper was the birthright of an Athenian? I saw it in a book. Well! I had to explain it to everybody. By-the-way, what did that gambler, George Heriot, mean, by telling me that its legs should be black? ' All *Greeks* have black legs,' '' said he, yawning in his stupid way. What did he mean, Mr. Tremlet? ''

" ' Greeks ' and blacklegs are convertible terms. He thought you were more *au fait* of the slang dictionary. — Will you permit me to coax my beautiful rival from your hand, Lady Imogen? ''

She smiled, and put forward her wrist, with a bend of its slender and alabaster lines which would have drawn a sigh from Praxiteles. The trulian glanced his fiery eyes from his mistress's face to Tremlet's; and, as the strange hand was put out to take him from his emerald perch, he flew with the quickness of lightning into the face of her lover, and buried the sharp beak in his lip. The blood followed copiously; and Lady Imogen, startled from her timidity, sprang from her chair, and pressed her hands one after the other upon the wound, in passionate and girlish abandonment. Lady Ravelgold hurried to her dressing-room for something to stanch the wound; and, left alone with the divine creature who hung over him, Tremlet drew her to his bosom, and pressed his cheek long and closely to hers, while to his lips, as if to keep in life, clung her own crimsoned and trembling fingers.

" Imogen! '' said Lady Ravelgold, entering, " take him to the fountain in the garden, and wash the wound; then put on this bit of goldbeater's skin. I will come to you when I have locked up the trulian. Is it painful, Mr. Tremlet? ''

Tremlet could not trust his voice to answer; but, with his arm still around Lady Imogen, he descended by the terrace of flowers to the fountain.

They sat upon the edge of the marble basin, and the moonlight striking through the jet of the fountain descended upon them like a rain of silver. Lady Imogen had recovered from her fright, and buried her face in her hands, remembering into what her feelings had betrayed her; and Tremlet, sometimes listening to the clear bell-like music of the descending water, sometimes uttering the broken sentences which are most eloquent in love, sat out the hours till the stars began to pale, undisturbed by Lady Ravelgold, who, on the upper stair of the terrace, read by a small lamp, which, in the calm of that heavenly summer night, burned unflickeringly in the open air.

It was broad daylight when Tremlet, on foot, sauntered slowly past Hyde Park corner on his way to the Albany. The lamps were still struggling with the brightening approach to sunrise, the cabmen and their horses slept on the stand by the Green Park; and with cheerful faces the laborers went to their work, and with haggard faces the night-birds of dissipation crept wearily home. The well-ground dust lay in confused heel-marks on the sidewalk, a little dampened by the night-dew; the atmosphere in the street was clear, as it never is after the stir of day commences. A dandy, stealing out from Crockford's, crossed Piccadilly, lifting up his head to draw in long breaths of the cool air, after the closeness of over-lighted rooms and excitement; and Tremlet, marking none of these things, was making his way through a line of carriages slowly drawing up to take off their wearied masters from a prolonged fête at Devonshire House, when a rude hand clapped him on the shoulder.

"Monsieur Tremlet!"

"*Ah, Baron! bien bon jour!*"

"*Bien rencontré, monsieur!* You have insulted a lady to-night, who has confided her cause to my hands. Madame

St. Leger, sir, is without a natural protector; and you have taken advantage of her position to insult her — grossly, Mr. Tremlet, grossly.''

Tremlet looked at the Russian during this extraordinary address, and saw that he was evidently highly excited with wine. He drew him aside into Berkeley Street, and in the calmest manner attempted to explain what was not very clear to himself. He had totally forgotten Mrs. St. Leger. The diplomate, though quite beyond himself with his excitement, had sufficient perception left to see the weak point of his statement, and, infuriated with the placid manner in which he attempted to excuse himself, suddenly struck his glove into his face, and turned upon his heel. They had been observed by a policeman; and at the moment that Tremlet, recovering from his astonishment, sprang forward to resent the blow, the gray-coated guardian of the place laid his hand upon his collar, and detained him till the baron had disappeared.

More than once on his way to the Albany, Tremlet surprised himself, forgetting both the baron and the insult, and feeding his heart in delicious abandonment with the dreams of his new happiness. He reached his rooms, and threw himself on the bed, forcing from his mind, with a strong effort, the presence of Lady Imogen, and trying to look calmly on the unpleasant circumstance before him. A quarrel which, the day before, he would have looked upon merely as an inconvenience, or which, under the insult of a blow, he would have eagerly sought, became now an almost insupportable evil. When he reflected on the subject of the dispute, — a contention about a woman of doubtful reputation taking place in the same hour with a first avowal from the delicate and pure Lady Imogen, — when he remembered the change in his fortunes, which he had as yet scarcely found time to realize, on the consequences to her who was so newly dear to him, and on all he might lose, now that life had become invaluable, his thoughts were almost too painful to bear. How seldom do men play with an equal stake in the game of taking life, and how strange it is that equality of weapons is the only comparison made necessary by the laws of honor!

Tremlet was not a man to be long undecided. He rose, after an hour's reflection, and wrote as follows : —

BARON, — Before taking the usual notice of the occurrence of this morning, I wish to rectify one or two points in which our position is false. I find myself, since last night, the accepted lover of Lady Imogen Ravelgold, and the master of estates and title as a count of the Russian empire. Under the *étourdissement* of such sudden changes in feelings and fortune, perhaps my forgetfulness of the lady, in whose cause you are so interested, admits of indulgence. At any rate, I am so newly in love with life that I am willing to suppose for an hour that, had you known these circumstances, you would have taken a different view of the offence in question. I shall remain at home till two, and it is in your power till then to make me the reparation necessary to my honor. Yours, etc.,   TREMLET.

There was a bridal on the following Monday at St. George's Church, and the Russian secretary stood behind the bridegroom. Lady Ravelgold had never been seen so pale, but her face was clear of all painful feeling ; and it was observed by one who knew her well, that her beauty had acquired, during the brief engagement of her daughter, a singular and undefinable elevation. As the carriages with their white favors turned into Bond Street on their way back to Belgrave Square, the cortége was checked by the press of vehicles, and the Russian, who accompanied Lady Ravelgold in her chariot, found himself opposite the open britzska of a lady who fixed her glass full upon him without recognizing a feature of his face.

"I am afraid you have affronted Mrs. St. Leger, baron," said Lady Ravelgold.

"Or I should not have been here!" said the Russian; and as they drove up Piccadilly, he had just time between Bond Street and Milton Crescent to tell her ladyship the foregone chapter of this story.

The trulian, on that day, was fed with wedding-cake; and the wound on Mr. Tremlet's lip was not cured by letting alone.

THE INLET OF PEACH-BLOSSOMS.

THE Emperor Yuentsoong, of the dynasty Chow, was the most magnificent of the long-descended succession of Chinese sovereigns. On his first accession to the throne, his character was so little understood, that a conspiracy was set on foot among the yellow-caps, or eunuchs, to put out his eyes, and place upon the throne the rebel Szema, in whose warlike hands, they asserted, the empire would more properly maintain its ancient glory. The gravity and reserve which these myrmidons of the palace had construed into stupidity and fear, soon assumed another complexion, however. The eunuchs silently disappeared; the mandarins and princes whom they had seduced from their allegiance were made loyal subjects by a generous pardon; and, in a few days after the period fixed upon for the consummation of the plot, Yuentsoong set forth in complete armor at the head of his troops to give battle to the rebel in the mountains.

In Chinese annals this first enterprise of the youthful Yuentsoong is recorded with great pomp and particularity. Szema was a Tartar prince of uncommon ability, young, like the emperor, and, during the few last imbecile years of the old sovereign, he had gathered strength in his rebellion, till now he was at the head of ninety thousand men, all soldiers of repute and tried valor. The historian has, unfortunately, dimmed the emperor's fame to European eyes by attributing his wonderful achievements in this expedition to his superiority in arts of magic. As this account of his exploits is only prefatory to our tale, we will simply give the reader an idea

of the style of the historian by translating literally a passage
or two of his description of the battle : —

" Szema now took refuge within a cleft of the mountain,
and Yuentsoong, upon his swift steed, outstripping the body-
guard in his ardor, dashed amid the paralyzed troops with
poised spear, his eyes fixed only on the rebel. There was a
silence of an instant, broken only by the rattling hoofs of
the intruder ; and then, with dishevelled hair and waving
sword, Szema uttered a fearful imprecation. In a moment
the wind rushed, the air blackened, and, with the suddenness
of a fallen rock, a large cloud enveloped the rebel, and
innumerable men and horses issued out of it. Wings flapped
against the eyes of the emperor's horse, hellish noises
screamed in his ears, and, completely beyond control, the
animal turned and and fled back through the narrow pass,
bearing his imperial master safe into the heart of his army.

" Yuentsoong, that night, commanded some of his most
expert soldiers to scale the beetling heights of the ravine,
bearing upon their backs the blood of swine, sheep, and
dogs, with other impure things, and these they were ordered
to shower upon the combatants at the sound of the imperial
clarion. On the following morning, Szema came forth again
to offer battle, with flags displayed, drums beating, and
shouts of triumph and defiance. As on the day previous,
the bold emperor divided, in his impatience, rank after rank
of his own soldiery, and, followed closely by his body-guard,
drove the rebel army once more into their fastness. Szema
sat upon his war-horse as before, intrenched amid his officers
and ranks of the tallest Tartar spearmen ; and, as the
emperor contended hand to hand with one of the opposing
rebels, the magic imprecation was again uttered, the air
again filled with cloudy horsemen and chariots, and the
mountain shaken with discordant thunder. Backing his
willing steed, the emperor blew a long sharp note upon

his silver clarion, and, in an instant, the sun broke through the darkness, and the air seemed filled with paper men, horses of straw, and phantoms dissolving into smoke. Yuentsoong and Szema now stood face to face, with only mortal aid and weapons.''

The historian goes on to record that the two armies suspended hostilities at the command of their leaders, and that, the emperor and his rebel subject having engaged in single combat, Yuentsoong was victorious, and returned to his capital with the formidable enemy, whose life he had spared, riding beside him like a brother. The conqueror's career, for several years after this, seems to have been a series of exploits of personal valor ; and the Tartar prince shared in all his dangers and pleasures, his inseparable friend. It was during this period of romantic friendship that the events occurred which have made Yuentsoong one of the idols of Chinese poetry.

By the side of a lake in a distant province of the empire, stood one of the imperial palaces of pleasure, seldom visited, and almost in ruins. Hither, in one of his moody periods of repose from war, came the conqueror Yuentsoong, for the first time in years separated from his faithful Szema. In disguise, and with only one or two attendants, he established himself in the long silent halls of his ancestor Tsinchemong, and with his boat upon the lake, and his spear in the forest, seemed to find all the amusement of which his melancholy was susceptible. On a certain day in the latter part of April, the emperor had set his sail to a fragrant south wind, and, reclining on the cushions of his bark, watched the shore as it softly and silently glided past, and, the lake being entirely encircled by the imperial forest, he felt immersed in what he believed to be the solitude of a deserted paradise. After skirting the fringed sheet of water in this manner for several hours, he suddenly observed that he had shot through a streak of peach-blossoms floating from the shore, and at the same moment he became conscious that his boat was slightly headed off by a current setting outward. Putting up his helm, he returned to the spot, and beneath the drooping branches of some luxuriant willows, thus early in leaf, he discovered the mouth of an inlet, which, but for the floating blossoms it brought to the lake, would have escaped the notice of the closest observer. The emperor now lowered his sail, unshipped the slender mast, and betook him to the oars; and, as the current was gentle, and the inlet wider within the mouth, he sped rapidly on through what appeared to be but a lovely and luxuriant vale of the forest. Still, those blushing betrayers of some flowering spot beyond extended like a rosy clew before him; and with impulse of muscles swelled and indurated in warlike exercise, the swift keel divided the besprent mirror winding temptingly onward, and, for a long hour, the royal oarsman untiringly threaded this sweet vein of the wilderness.

Resting a moment on his oars while the slender bark still kept her way, he turned his head toward what seemed to be an opening in the forest on the left, and in the same instant the boat ran head on, to the shore, the inlet at this point almost doubling on its course. Beyond, by the humming of bees and the singing of birds, there should be a spot more open than the tangled wilderness he had passed; and, disengaging his prow from the alders, he shoved the boat again into the stream, and pulled round a high rock, by which the inlet seemed to have been compelled to curve its channel. The edge of a bright green meadow now stole into the perspective, and, still widening with his approach, disclosed a slightly rising terrace clustered with shrubs, and studded here and there with vases; and farther on, upon the same side of the stream, a skirting edge of peach-trees loaded with the gay blossoms which had guided him thither.

Astonished at these signs of habitation in what was well understood to be a privileged wilderness, Yuentsoong kept his boat in mid-stream, and with his eyes vigilantly on the alert, slowly made headway against the current. A few strokes with his oars, however, traced another curve of the inlet, and brought into view a grove of ancient trees scattered over a gently ascending lawn, beyond which, hidden from the river till now by the projecting shoulder of a mound, lay a small pavilion with gilded pillars glittering like fairy work in the sun. The emperor fastened his boat to a tree leaning over the water, and with his short spear in his hand, bounded upon the shore, and took his way toward the shining structure, his heart beating with a feeling of wonder and interest altogether new. On a nearer approach, the bases of the pillars seemed decayed by time, and the gilding weather-stained and tarnished; but the trellised porticoes on the southern aspect were laden with flowering shrubs in vases of porcelain, and caged birds sang between the pointed arches, and there were manifest signs of luxurious taste, elegance, and care.

A moment with an indefinable timidity the emperor paused before stepping from the greensward upon the marble floor of the pavilion, and in that moment a curtain was withdrawn from the door, and a female, with step suddenly arrested by the sight of the stranger, stood motionless before him. Ravished with her extraordinary beauty, and awe-struck with the suddenness of the apparition and the novelty of the adventure, the emperor's tongue cleaved to his mouth, and ere he could summon resolution, even for a gesture of courtesy, the fair creature had fled within, and the curtain closed the entrance as before.

Wishing to recover his composure, so strangely troubled, and taking it for granted that some other inmate of the house would soon appear, Yuentsoong turned his steps aside to the

grove ; and with his head bowed, and his spear in the hollow
of his arm, tried to recall more vividly the features of the
vision he had seen. He had walked but a few paces when
there came toward him from the upper skirt of the grove, a
man of unusual stature and erectness, with white hair un-
braided on his shoulders, and every sign of age except in-
firmity of step and mien. The emperor's habitual dignity
had now rallied, and on his first salutation the countenance
of the old man softened, and he quickened his pace to meet
and give him welcome.

" You are noble? " he said with confident inquiry.

Yuentsoong colored slightly.

" I am," he replied, " Lew-melin, a prince of the empire."

" And by what accident here ? "

Yuentsoong explained the clew of the peach-blossoms, and
represented himself as exiled for a time to the deserted
palace upon the lakes.

" I have a daughter," said the old man abruptly, " who
has never looked on human face save mine."

" Pardon me," replied his visitor, " I have thoughtlessly
intruded on her sight, and a face more heavenly fair " —

The emperor hesitated, but the old man smiled encoura-
gingly.

" It is time," he said, " that I should provide a younger
defender for my bright Teh-leen, and Heaven has sent you
in the season of peach-blossoms with provident kindness.[1]
You have frankly revealed to me your name and rank. Before I offer you the hospitality of my roof, I must tell you
mine. I am Choo-tseen, the outlaw, once of your own rank,
and the general of the Celestial army."

The emperor started, remembering that this celebrated
rebel was the terror of his father's throne.

---

[1] The season of peach-blossoms was the only season of marriage in ancient China.

"You have heard my history," the old man continued. "I had been, before my rebellion, in charge of the imperial palace on the lake. Anticipating an evil day, I secretly prepared this retreat for my family; and when my soldiers deserted me at the battle of Ke-chow, and a price was set upon my head, hither I fled with my women and children; and the last alive is my beautiful Teh-leen. With this brief outline of my life, you are at liberty to leave me as you came, or to enter my house on the condition that you become the protector of my child."

The emperor eagerly turned toward the pavilion, and, with a step as light as his own, the erect and stately outlaw hastened to lift the curtain before him. Leaving his guest for a moment in the outer apartment, he entered to an inner chamber in search of his daughter, whom he brought, panting with fear, and blushing with surprise and delight, to her future lover and protector. A portion of an historical tale so delicate as the description of the heroine is not work for imitators, however, and we must copy strictly the portrait of the matchless Teh-leen, as drawn by Le-pih, the Anacreon of Chinese poetry and the contemporary and favorite of Yuentsoong.

"Teh-leen was born while the morning star shone upon the bosom of her mother. Her eye was like the unblemished blue lily, and its light like the white gem unfractured. The plum-blossom is most fragrant when the cold has penetrated its stem, and the mother of Teh-leen had known sorrow. The head of her child drooped in thought, like a violet over-laden with dew. Bewildering was Teh-leen. Her mouth's corners were dimpled, yet pensive. The arch of her brows was like the vein in the tulip's heart, and the lashes shaded the blushes on her cheek. With the delicacy of a pale rose, her complexion put to shame the floating light of day. Her waist, like a thread in fineness, seemed ready to break, yet was it straight and erect, and feared not the fanning breeze; and her shadowy grace was as difficult to delineate as the form of the white bird rising from the ground by moonlight. The natural gloss of her hair resembled the uncertain sheen of calm water, yet without the false aid of unguents. The native intelligence of her mind seemed to have gained strength by retirement; and he who beheld her thought not of her as human. Of rare beauty, of rarer intellect, was Teh-leen, and her heart responded to the poet's lute.''

We have not space, nor could we, without copying directly from the admired Le-pih, venture to describe the bringing of Teh-leen to court, and her surprise at finding herself the favorite of the emperor. It is a romantic circumstance, besides, which has had its parallels in other countries. But the sad sequel to the loves of poor Teh-leen is but recorded in the cold page of history; and if the poet, who wound up the climax of her perfections with her susceptibility to his lute, embalmed her sorrows in verse, he was probably too politic to bring it ever to light. Pass we to these neglected and unadorned passages of her history.

Yuentsoong's nature was passionately devoted and confiding; and, like two brothers with one favorite sister, lived together Teh-leen, Szema, and the emperor. The Tartar prince, if his heart knew a mistress before the arrival of Teh-leen at the palace, owned afterward no other than her; and, fearless of check or suspicion from the noble confidence and generous friendship of Yuentsoong, he seemed to live but for her service, and to have neither energies nor ambition except for the winning of her smiles. Szema was of great personal beauty, frank when it did not serve him to be wily, bold in his pleasures, and of manners almost femininely soft and voluptuous. He was renowned as a soldier, and, for Teh-leen, he became a poet and master of the lute; and, like all men formed for ensnaring the heart of women,

he seemed to forget himself in the absorbing devotion of
his idolatry. His friend the emperor was of another mould.
Yuentsoong's heart had three chambers, — love, friendship,
and glory. Teh-leen was but a third in his existence, yet he
loved her, — the sequel will show how well. In person, he
was less beautiful than majestic, of large stature, and with a
brow and lip naturally stern and lofty. He seldom smiled,
even upon Teh-leen, whom he would watch for hours in
pensive and absorbed delight; but his smile, when it did
awake, broke over his sad countenance like morning. All
men loved and honored Yuentsoong; and all men, except
only the emperor, looked on Szema with antipathy. To such
natures as the former, women give all honor and approbation; but, for such as the latter, they reserve their weakness!

Wrapt up in his friend and mistress, and reserved in his
intercourse with his counsellors, Yuentsoong knew not that,
throughout the imperial city, Szema was called "the *kieu,*"
or robber-bird, and his fair Teh-leen openly charged with
dishonor. Going out alone to hunt, as was his custom, and
having left his signet with Szema, to pass and repass through
the private apartments at his pleasure, his horse fell with
him unaccountably in the open field. Somewhat superstitious, and remembering that good spirits sometimes "knit
the grass" when other obstacles fail to bar our way into
danger, the emperor drew rein, and retured to his palace.
It was an hour after noon, and, having dismissed his attendants at the city gate, he entered by a postern to the imperial
garden, and bethought himself of the concealed couch in a
cool grot by a fountain (a favorite retreat, sacred to himself
and Teh-leen), where he fancied it would be refreshing to
sleep away the sultriness of the remaining hours till evening.
Sitting down by the side of the murmuring fount, he bathed
his feet, and left his slippers on the lip of the basin to be
unencumbered in his repose within, and so, with unechoing

step, entered the resounding grotto. Alas! there slumbered the faithless friend with the guilty Teh-leen upon his bosom!

Grief struck through the noble heart of the emperor like a sword in cold blood. With a word he could consign to torture and death the robber of his honor, but there was agony in his bosom deeper than revenge. He turned silently away, recalling his horse and huntsmen, and, out-stripping all, plunged on through the forest till night gathered around him.

Yuentsoong had been absent many days from his capital, and his subjects were murmuring their fears for his safety, when a messenger arrived to the counsellors informing them of the appointment of the captive Tartar prince to the government of the province of Szechuen, the second honor of the Celestial empire. A private order accompanied the announcement, commanding the immediate departure of Szema for the scene of his new authority. Inexplicable as was this riddle to the multitude, there were those who read it truly by their knowledge of the magnanimous soul of the emperor; and among these was the crafty object of his generosity. Losing no time, he set forward with great pomp for Szechuen, and in their joy to see him no more in the palace, the slighted princes of the empire forgave his unmerited advancement. Yuentsoong returned to his capital; but to the terror of his counsellors and people, his hair was blanched white as the head of an old man! He was pale as well, but he was cheerful and kind beyond his wont, and to Teh-leen untiring in pensive and humble attentions. He pleaded only impaired health and restless slumbers as an apology for nights of solitude. Once Teh-leen penetrated to his lonely chamber, but by the dim night lamp she saw that the scroll over the window[1] was changed, and instead of the stimulus to glory

---

[1] The most common decorations of rooms, halls, and temples, in China, are ornamental scrolls or labels of colored paper or wood, painted and gilded, and hung over doors or windows, and inscribed with a line or couplet conveying some allusion to

which formerly hung in golden letters before his eyes, there
was a sentence written tremblingly in black : —

"The close wing of love covers the death-throb of honor."

Six months from this period the capital was thrown into
a tumult with the intelligence that the province of Szechuen
was in rebellion, and Szema at the head of a numerous army
on his way to seize the throne of Yuentsoong. This last
sting betrayed the serpent even to the forgiving emperor, and
tearing the reptile at last from his heart, he entered with the
spirit of other times into the warlike preparations. The imperial army was in a few days on its march, and at Keo-yang
the opposing forces met and prepared for encounter.

With a dread of the popular feeling toward Teh-leen,
Yuentsoong had commanded for her a close litter, and she
was borne after the imperial standard in the centre of the
army. On the eve before the battle, ere the watch-fires were
lit, the emperor came to her tent, set apart from his own, and
with the delicate care and kind gentleness from which he
never varied, inquired how her wants were supplied, and
bade her thus early farewell for the night ; his own custom
of passing among his soldiers on the evening previous to an
engagement, promising to interfere with what was usually his
last duty before retiring to his couch. Teh-leen on this occasion seemed moved by some irrepressible emotion, and as
he rose to depart, she fell forward upon her face, and bathed
his feet with her tears. Attributing it to one of those
excesses of feeling to which all, but especially hearts ill at
ease, are liable, the noble monarch gently raised her, and with

---

the circumstances of the inhabitant, or some pious or philosophical axiom. For
instance, a poetical one recorded by Dr. Morrison : —
    "From the pine forest the azute dragon ascends to the milky way," —
typical of the prosperous man arising to wealth and honors.

repeated efforts at re-assurance, committed her to the hands of her women. His own heart beat far from tranquilly, for, in the excess of his pity for her grief he had unguardedly called her by one of the sweet names of their early days of love, — strange word now upon his lip, — and it brought back, spite of memory and truth, happiness that would not be forgotten !

It was past midnight, and the moon was riding high in heaven, when the emperor, returning between the lengthening watch-fires, sought the small lamp which, suspended like a star above his own tent, guided him back from the irregular mazes of the camp. Paled by the intense radiance of the moonlight, the small globe of alabaster at length became apparent to his weary eye, and with one glance at the peaceful beauty of the heavens, he parted the curtained door beneath it, and stood within. The Chinese historian asserts that a bird, from whose wing Teh-leen had once plucked an arrow, restoring it to liberty and life, and in grateful attachment to her destiny, removed the lamp from the imperial tent, and suspended it over hers. The emperor stood beside her couch. Startled at his inadvertent error, he turned to retire ; but the lifted curtain let in a flood of moonlight upon the sleeping features of Teh-leen, and like dewdrops the undried tears glistened in her silken lashes. A lamp burned faintly in the inner apartment of the tent, and her attendants slept soundly. His soft heart gave way. Taking up the lamp, he held it over his beautiful mistress, and once more gazed passionately and unrestrainedly on her unparalleled beauty. The past — the early past — was alone before him. He forgave her, — there, as she slept, unconscious of the throbbing of his injured but noble heart so close beside her, — he forgave her in the long silent abysses of his soul ! Unwilling to wake her from her tranquil slumber, but promising to himself, from that hour, such sweets of confiding love as had well-nigh been lost to him forever, he imprinted one kiss upon the parted lips of Teh-leen, and sought his couch for slumber.

Ere daybreak the emperor was aroused by one of his attendants with news too important for delay. Szema, the rebel, had been arrested in the imperial camp, disguised, and on his way back to his own forces; and like wildfire the information had spread among the soldiery, who, in a state of mutinous excitement, were with difficulty restrained from rushing upon the tent of Teh-leen. At the door of his tent, Yuentsoong found messengers from the alarmed princes and officers of the different commands, imploring immediate aid and the imperial presence to allay the excitement; and while the emperor prepared to mount his horse, the guard arrived with the Tartar prince, ignominiously tied, and bearing marks of rough usage from his indignant captors.

"Loose him!" cried the emperor, in a voice of thunder.

The cords were severed, and with a glance whose ferocity expressed no thanks, Szema reared himself up to his fullest height, and looked scornfully around him. Daylight had now broke, and as the group stood upon an eminence in sight of the whole army, shouts began to ascend, and the armed multitude, breaking through all restraint, rolled in toward the centre. Attracted by the commotion, Yuentsoong turned to give some orders to those near him, when Szema suddenly sprang upon an officer of the guard, wrenched his drawn sword from his grasp, and in an instant was lost to sight in the tent of Teh-leen. A sharp scream, a second of thought, and forth again rushed the desperate murderer, with his sword flinging drops of blood, and ere a foot stirred in the paralyzed group, the avenging cimeter of Yuentsoong had cleft him to the chin.

A hush, as if the whole army was struck dumb by a bolt from heaven, followed this rapid tragedy. Dropping the polluted sword from his hand, the emperor, with uncertain step, and the pallor of death upon his countenance, entered the fatal tent.

He came no more forth that day. The army was marshalled by the princes, and the rebels were routed with great slaughter ; but Yuentsoong never more wielded sword. " He pined to death,'' says the historian, " with the wane of the same moon that shone upon the forgiveness of Teh-leen.''

LETTERS FROM UNDER A BRIDGE.

LETTER I.

MY DEAR DOCTOR, — Twice in the year, they say, the farmer may sleep late in the morning, — between hoeing and haying, and between harvest and thrashing. If I have not written to you since the frost was out of the ground, my apology lies distributed over the "spring-work," in due proportions among ploughing, harrowing, sowing, plastering, and hoeing. We have finished the last; some thanks to the crows, who saved us the labor of one acre of corn by eating it in the blade. Think what times we live in, when even the crows are obliged to anticipate their income!

When I had made up my mind to write to you, I cast about for a cool place in the shade; for, besides the changes which farming works upon my *epidermis*, I find some in the inner man, one of which is a vegetable necessity for living out-of-doors. Between five in the morning and "flower-shut," I feel as if four walls and a ceiling would stop my breath. Very much to the disgust of William (who begins to think it was *infra dig.* to have followed such a hob-nail from London), I showed the first symptom of this chair-and-carpet asthma, by ordering my breakfast under a balsam-fir. Dinner and tea soon followed; and now, if I go in-doors by daylight, it is a sort of fireman's visit, — in and out with a long breath. I have worn quite a dial on the grass, working my chair around with the sun.

"If ever you observed" (a phrase with which a neighbor

297

of mine ludicrously prefaces every possible remark), a single
tree will do very well to sit, or dine, or be buried under, but
you cannot *write* in the shade of it.   Beside the sun-flecks
and the light all around you, there is a want of that privacy
which is necessary to a perfect abandonment to pen and ink.
I discovered this on getting as far as " Dear Doctor," and,
pocketing my tools, strolled away up the glen to borrow
" stool and desk " of Nature.   Half-open, like a broad-
leafed-book (green margin and silver type), the brook-hollow
of Glenmary spreads wide as it drops upon the meadow,
but above, like a book that deserves its fair margent, it
deepens as you proceed.   Not far from the road, its little
rivulet steals forth from a shadowy ravine, narrow as you
enter, then widening back to a mimic cataract ; and here, a
child would say, is a fairy parlor.   A small platform (an island
when the stream is swollen) lies at the foot of the fall, car-
peted with the fine silky grass which thrives with shade and
spray.   The two walls of the ravine are mossy, and trickling
with springs ; the trees overhead interlace, to keep out the
sun ; and down comes the brook, over a flight of precipitous
steps, like children bursting out of school, and, after a laugh
at its own tumble, it falls again into a decorous ripple, and
trips murmuring away.   The light is green, the leaves of the
overhanging trees look translucent above, and the wild blue
grape, with its emerald rings, has wove all over it a basket-
lattice so fine that you would think it were done to order,
warranted to keep out the hawk, and let in the humming-bird.
With a yellow pine at my back, a moss cushion beneath, and
a ledge of flat stone at my elbow, you will allow I had a
secretary's outfit.   I spread my paper, and mended my pen ;
and then (you will pardon me, dear Doctor) I forgot you
altogether.   The truth is, these fanciful garnishings spoil
work.   Silvio Pellico had a better place to write in.   If it
had been a room with a Chinese paper (a bird standing for-

ever on one leg, and a tree ruffled by the summer wind, and
fixed, with its leaves on edge, as if petrified with the var-
let's impudence), the eye might get accustomed to it.   But
first came a gold-robin, twittering out his surprise to find
strange company in his parlor, yet never frighted from his
twig by pen and ink.   By the time I had sucked a lesson out
of that, a squirrel tripped in without knocking, and sat nib-
bling at a last year's nut, as if nobody but he took thought
for the morrow.   Then came an enterprising ant, climbing
my knee like a discoverer; and I wondered whether Fer-
nando Cortes would have mounted so boldly, had the Peak
of Darien been as new-dropped between the Americas as
my leg by his ant-hill.   By this time a small dripping from a
moss-fringe at my elbow betrayed the lip of a spring; and,
dislodging a stone, I uncovered a brace of lizards lying snug
in the ooze.   We flatter ourselves, thought I, that we drink
first of the spring.   We do not know always whose lips were
before us.

Much as you see of insect-life, and hear of bird-music, as
you walk abroad, you should lie *perdu* in a nook, to know
how much is frighted from sight, and hushed from singing,
by your approach.   What worms creep out when they think
you gone, and what chatterers go on with their story!   So
among friends, thought I, as I fished for the moral.   We
should be wiser if we knew what our coming hides and
silences; but should we walk so undisturbed on our way?

You will see with half a glance, dear Doctor, that here was
too much company for writing.   I screwed up my inkstand
once more, and kept up the bed of the stream till it enters
the forest, remembering a still place by a pool.   The tall
pines hold up the roof high as an umbrella of Brobdignag;
and neither water brawls, nor small birds sing, in the gloom
of it.   Here, thought I, as far as they go, the circumstances
are congenial.   But, as Jean Paul says, there is a period of

life when the real gains ground upon the ideal; and to be honest, dear Doctor, I sat leaning on the shingle across my knees, counting my sky-kissing pines, and reckoning what they would bring in saw-logs, — so much standing, so much drawn to the mill. Then there would be wear and tear of bob-sled, teamster's wages, and your dead-pull springs, — the horses' knees. I had nearly settled the *per* and *contra*, when my eye lit once more on " My Dear Doctor " staring from the unfilled sheet, like the ghost of a murdered resolution. " Since when," I asked, looking myself sternly in the face, " is it so difficult to be virtuous? Shall I not write when I have a mind? Shall I reckon pelf whether I will or no? Shall butterfly imagination thrust iron-heart to the wall? No! "

I took a straight cut through my ruta-baga patch and corn-field, bent on finding some locality (out of doors it must be) with the average attractions of a sentry-box or a church-pew. I reached the high-road, making insensibly for a brush-dam, where I should sit upon a log, with my face abutted upon a wall of chopped saplings. I have not mentioned my dog, who had followed me cheerfully thus far, putting up now and then a partridge, to keep his nose in; but, on coming to the bridge over the brook, he made up his mind. " My master," he said (or looked), " will neither follow the game, nor sit in the cool. *Chacun à son gout.* I'm tired of this bobbing about for nothing in a hot sun." So, dousing his tail (which, " if you ever observed," a dog hoists, as a flag-ship does her pennant, only when the commodore is aboard), he sprung the railing, and spread himself for a snooze under the bridge. " *Ben trovato!* " said I, as I seated myself by his side. He wagged his tail half round to acknowledge the compliment, and I took to work like a hay-maker.

I have taken some pains to describe these difficulties to

you, dear Doctor, partly because I hold it to be fair, in this give-and-take world, that a man should know what it costs his fellow to fulfil obligations, but more especially to apprise you of the *metempsychose* that is taking place in myself. You will have divined, ere this, that, in my out-of-doors life, I am approaching a degree nearer to Arcadian perfectibility, and that, if I but manage to get a bark on and live by sap (spare your wit, sir), I shall be rid of much that is troublesome, not to say expensive, in the matters of drink and integument. What most surprises me in the past is, that I ever should have confined my free soul and body in the very many narrow places and usages I have known in towns. I can only assimilate myself to a squirrel brought up in a school-boy's pocket, and let out some June morning on a snake fence.

The spring has been damp for corn, but I had planted on a warm hill-side, and have done better than my neighbors. The Owaga[1] creek, which makes a bend round my meadow before it drops into the Susquehanna (a swift, bright river the Owaga, with as much water as the Arno at Florence), overflowed my cabbages and onions in the May freshet; but that touches neither me nor my horse. The winter wheat looks like " velvet of three-pile," and every thing is out of the ground — including, in my case, the buckwheat, which is not yet *put in.* This is to be an old-fashioned hot summer, and I shall sow late. The peas are podded. Did it ever strike you, by the way, that the pious Æneas, famous through all ages for carrying old Anchises a mile, should, after all, yield glory to a *bean?* Perhaps you never observed that this filial esculent *grows up* with his father on his back.

In my " new light," a farmer's life seems to me what a manufacturer's might resemble, if his factory were an indige-

---

[1] Corrupted now to Owego. Ochwaga was the Indian word, and means *swift water.*

nous plant, — machinery, girls, and all. What spindles and
fingers it would take to make an orchard, if nature found
nothing but the raw seed, and rain-water and sunshine were
brought as far as a cotton-bale! Your despised cabbage
would be a prime article, if you had to weave it. Pumpkins,
if they ripened with a hair-spring and patent lever, would
be, "by'r lady," a curious invention. Yet these, which
Aladdin nature produces if we but "rub the lamp," are
more necessary to life than clothes or watches. In planting
a tree (I write it reverently), it seems to me working immediately with the divine faculty. Here are two hundred
forest-trees set out with my own hand; yet how little is my
part in the glorious creatures they become!

This reminds me of a liberty I have lately taken with
nature, which I ventured upon with proper diffidence, though
the dame, as will happen with dames, proved less coy than
was predicted. The brook at my feet, from its birth in the
hills till it dropped into the meadow's lap, tripped down like
a mountain-maid with a song, bright and unsullied. So it
flowed by my door. At the foot of the bank its song and
sparkle ceased suddenly, and, turning under the hill, its
waters disappeared among sedge and rushes. It was more
a pity, because you looked across the meadow to the stately
Owaga, and saw that its unfulfilled destiny was to have
poured its brightness into his. The author of Ernest Mal-
travers has set the fashion of charity to such fallings away.
I made a new channel over the meadow, gravelled its bed,
and grassed its banks, and (last and best charity of all) protected its recovered course with overshadowy trees. Not
quite with so gay a sparkle, but with a placid and tranquil beauty, the lost stream glides over the meadow, and,
Maltravers-like, the Owaga takes her lovingly to his bosom.
The sedge and rushes are turned into a garden; and if you
drop a flower into the brook at my door, it scarce loses a

breath of its perfume before it is flung on the Owaga, and the Susquehanna robs him of it but with his life.

I have scribbled away the hours till near noon, and it is time to see that the oxen get their potatoes. Faith! it's a cool place under a bridge. Knock out the two ends of the Astor House, and turn the Hudson through the long passage, and you will get an idea of it. The breeze draws through here deftly, the stone wall is cool to my back, and this floor of running water, besides what the air steals from it, sounds and looks refreshingly. My letter has run on, till I am inclined to think the industry of running water "breeds i' the brain." Like the tin-pot at the cur's tail, it seems to overtake one with an admonition, if he but slack to breathe. Be not alarmed, dear doctor, for, *sans* potatoes, my oxen will *loll* in the furrow; and though the brook run till dooms-day, I must stop here. Amen.

LETTER XIV.

THIS is *return month*, dear Doctor; and, if it were only to be in fashion, you should have a *quid pro quo* for your four pages. October restores and returns; your gay friends and invalids return to the city; the birds and the planters return to the South; the seed returns to the granary; the brook at my feet is noisy again with its returned waters; the leaves are returning to the earth; and the heart that has been out-of-doors while the summer lasted comes home from its wan-derings by field and stream, and returns to feed on its harvest of new thoughts, past pleasures, and strengthened and con-firmed affections. At this time of the year, too, you expect a return (not of pasteboard) for your "visits;" but as you have made me no visit, either friendly or professional, I owe you nothing. And that is the first consolation I have found for your short-comings (or no-comings-at-all) to Glenmary.

Now, consider my arms akimbo, if you please, while I ask you what you mean by calling Glenmary " backwoods ! " Faith, I wish it were more backwoods than it is. Here be cards to be left, sir, morning calls to be made, body-coat *soirées*, and ceremony enough to keep one's most holiday manners well aired. The two miles' distance between me and Owego serves me for no exemption, for the village of Canewana, which is a mile nearer on the road, is equally within the latitude of silver forks ; and dinners are given in both, which want no one of the belongings of Belgrave Square, save port-wine and powdered footmen. I think it is in one of Miss Austen's novels that a lady claims it to be a smart neighborhood in which she " dines with four-and-twenty families." If there are not more than half as many in Owego who give dinners, there are twice as many who ask to tea, and give ice-cream and champagne. Then, for the fashions, there is as liberal a sprinkling of French bonnets in the Owego church as in any village congregation in England. And for the shops — that subject is worthy of a sentence by itself. When I say there is no need to go to New York for hat, boots, or coat, I mean that the Owego tradesmen (if you are capable of describing what you want) are capable of supplying you with the best and most modish of these articles. Call you that " backwoods ? "

All this, I am free to confess, clashes with the *beau ideal* of the

> " *Beatus ille qui procul*," etc.

I had myself imagined (and continued to imagine for some weeks after coming here), that, so near the primeval wilderness, I might lay up my best coat and my ceremony in lavender, and live in fustian and a plain way. I looked forward to the delights of a broad straw hat, large shoes, baggy habiliments, and leave to sigh or whistle without offence ; and it seemed to me that it was the conclusion of a species of apprenticeship, and the beginning of my "freedom." To be above no clean and honest employment of one's time, to drive a pair of horses or a yoke of oxen with equal alacrity, and to be commented on for neither the one nor the other, to have none but wholesome farming cares, and work with nature and honest yeomen, and be quite clear of mortifications, envies, advice, remonstrance, coldness, misapprehensions, and etiquettes, — this is what I, like most persons who "forswear the full tide of the world," looked upon as the blessed promise of retirement. But, alas ! wherever there is a butcher's shop and a post-office, an apothecary and a blacksmith, an "Arcade" and a milliner, — wherever the conveniences of life are, in short, — there has already arrived the Procrustes of opinion. Men's eyes will look on you, and bring you to judgment ; and, unless you would live on wild meat and corn-bread in the wilderness, with neither friend nor helper, you must give in to a compromise, yield half at least of your independence, and take it back in commonplace comfort. This is very every-day wisdom to those who know it ; but you are as likely as any man in the world to have sat with your feet over the fire, and fancied yourself on a wild horse in a prairie, with nothing to distinguish you from the warlike Comanche, except capital wine in the cellar of your wigwam and the last new novel and play, which should reach this same wigwam, you have not exactly determined how ! Such "pyramises are goodly things," but they are built of the smoke of your cigar.

This part of the country is not destitute of the chances of adventure, however ; and twice in the year, at least, you may, if you choose, open a valve for your spirits. One-half the population of the neighborhood is engaged in what is called *lumbering ;* and until the pine-timber of the forest can be counted like the cedars of Lebanon, this vocation will serve the uses of the mobs of England, the revolutions of France, and the plots of Italy. I may add, the music and theatres of Austria and Prussia, the sensual indulgence of the Turk, and the intrigue of the Spaniard; for there is in every people under the sun a *superflu* of spirits unconsumed by common occupation, which, if not turned adroitly or accidentally to some useful or harmless end, will expend its reckless energy in trouble and mischief.

The preparations for the adventures of which I speak, though laborious, are often conducted like a frolic. The felling of the trees in mid-winter, the cutting of shingles, and the drawing out on the snow, are employments preferred by the young men to the tamer but less arduous work of the farmyard; and in the temporary and uncomfortable *shanties*, deep in the woods, subsisting often on nothing but pork and whiskey, they find metal more attractive than village or fireside. The small streams emptying into the Susquehanna are innumerable; and eight or ten miles back from the river the arks are built, and the materials of the rafts collected, ready to launch with the first thaw. I live myself, as you know, on one of these tributaries, a quarter of a mile from its junction. The Owaga trips along at the foot of my lawn, as private and untroubled for the greater part of the year as Virginia Water at Windsor; but, as it swells in March, the noise of voices and hammering coming out from the woods above warns us of the approach of an ark; and, at the rate of eight or ten miles an hour, the rude structure shoots by, floating high on the water without its lading (which it takes in at the village below), and manned with a singing and saucy crew, who dodge the branches of the trees, and work their steering-paddles with an adroitness and nonchalance which sufficiently show the character of the class. The sudden bends which the river takes in describing my woody

Omega put their steersmanship to the test; and, when the
leaves are off the trees, it is a curious sight to see the bulky
monsters, shining with new boards, whirling around in the
swift eddies, and, when caught by the current again, gliding
off among the trees like a singing and swearing phantom of
an unfinished barn.

At the village they take wheat and pork into the arks,
load their rafts with plank and shingles, and wait for the
return of the freshet. It is a fact you may not know, that,
when a river is rising, the middle is the highest, and *vice
versa* when falling; sufficiently proved by the experience of
the raftsmen, who, if they start before the flow is at its top,
cannot keep their crafts from the shore. A pent-house,
barely sufficient for a man to stretch himself below, is raised
on the deck, with a fireplace of earth and loose stone; and
with what provision they can afford, and plenty of whiskey,
they shove out into the stream. Thenceforward it is *vogue
la galère!* They have nothing to do all day, but abandon
themselves to the current, sing and dance, and take their
turn at the steering-oars; and when the sun sets, they look
out for an eddy, and pull in to the shore. The stopping-
places are not very numerous, and are well known to all who
follow the trade; and, as the river swarms with rafts, the
getting to land, and making sure of a fastening, is a scene
always of great competition, and often of desperate fighting.
When all is settled for the night, however, and the fires are
lit on the long range of the flotilla, the raftsmen get together
over their whiskey and provender, and tell the thousand
stories of their escapes and accidents; and with the repetition
of this, night after night, the whole rafting population along
the five hundred miles of the Susquehanna becomes partially
acquainted, and forms a sympathetic *corps*, whose excitement
and *esprit* might be roused to very dangerous uses.

By daylight they are cast off and once more on the current;

and in five or seven days they arrive at tide-water, where the crew is immediately discharged, and start, usually on foot, to follow the river home again. There are several places in the navigation which are dangerous, such as rapids and dam-sluices ; and what with these, and the scenes at the eddies, and their pilgrimage through a thinly settled and wild country home again, they see enough of adventure to make them fireside heroes, and incapacitate them (while their vigor lasts, at least) for all the more quiet habits of the farmer. The consequence is easy to be seen. Agriculture is but partially followed throughout the country ; and, while these cheap facilities for transporting produce to the seaboard exist, those who are contented to stay at home, and cultivate the rich river-lands of the country, are sure of high prices and a ready reward for their labor.

MORAL. — Come to the Susquehanna, and settle on a farm. You did not know what I was driving at all this while !

The raftsmen who " follow the Delaware " (to use their own poetical expression) are said to be a much wilder class than those on the Susquehanna. In returning to Owego, by different routes, I have often fallen in with parties of both ; and certainly nothing could be more entertaining than to listen to their tales. In a couple of years, the canal route on the Susquehanna will lay open this rich vein of the picturesque and amusing ; and, as the tranquil boat glides peacefully along the river-bank, the traveller will be surprised with the strange effect of these immense flotillas, with their many fires and wild people, lying in the glassy bends of the solitary stream, the smoke stealing through the dark forest, and the confusion of a hundred excited voices breaking the silence. In my trip down the river in the spring, I saw enough that was novel in this way to fill a new portfolio for Bartlett ; and I intend he shall raft it with me to salt water the next time he comes among us.

How delicious are these October noons! They will soon chill, I am afraid, and I shall be obliged to give up my out-of-door habits ; but I shall do it unwillingly. I have changed sides under the bridge, to sit with my feet in the sun, and I trust this warm corner will last me till November, at least. The odor of the dying leaves, and the song of the strengthening brook, are still sufficient allurements, and even your rheumatism (of which the Latin should be *podagra*) might safely keep me company till dinner. Adieu, dear Doctor! write me a long account of Vestris and Matthews (how *you* like them, I mean, for I know very well how I like them myself), and thank me for turning over to you a new leaf of American romance. You are welcome to write a novel, and call it "The Raftsman of the Susquehanna."

LETTER TO THE UNKNOWN PURCHASER AND NEXT OCCUPANT OF GLENMARY.

Sir, — In selling you the dew and sunshine ordained to fall hereafter on this bright spot of earth, the waters on their way to this sparkling brook, the tints mixed for the flowers of that enamelled meadow, and the songs bidden to be sung in coming summers by the feathery builders in Glenmary, I know not whether to wonder more at the omnipotence of money, or at my own impertinent audacity toward Nature. How you can *buy* the right to exclude at will every other creature made in God's image from sitting by this brook, treading on that carpet of flowers, or lying listening to the birds in the shade of these glorious trees, — how I can *sell* it you, is a mystery not understood by the Indian, and dark, I must say, to me.

"Lord of the soil" is a title which conveys your privileges

but poorly. You are master of waters flowing at this moment, perhaps, in a river of Judæa, or floating in clouds over some spicy island of the tropics, bound hither after many changes. There are lilies and violets ordered for you in millions, acres of sunshine in daily instalments, and dew nightly in proportion. There are throats to be tuned with song, and wings to be painted with red and gold, blue and yellow ; thousands of them, and all tributaries to you. Your corn is ordered to be sheathed in silk, and lifted high to the sun. Your grain is to be duly bearded and stemmed. There is perfume distilling for your clover, and juices for your grasses and fruits. Ice will be here for your wine, shade for your refreshment at noon, breezes and showers and snowflakes ; all in their season, and all " deeded to you for forty dollars the acre ! Gods ! what a copyhold of property for a fallen world ! "

Mine has been but a short lease of this lovely and well-endowed domain (the duration of a smile of fortune, five years, scarce longer than a five-act play) ; but as in a play we sometimes live through a life, it seems to me that I have lived a life at Glenmary. Allow me this, and then you must allow me the privilege of those who, at the close of life, leave something behind them, — that of writing out my *will.* Though I depart *this* life, I would fain, like others, extend my ghostly hand into the future ; and if wings are to be borrowed or stolen where I go, you may rely on my hovering around and haunting you in visitations not restricted by cock-crowing.

Trying to look at Glenmary through your eyes, sir, I see too plainly that I have not shaped my ways as if expecting a successor in my lifetime. I did not, I am free to own. I thought to have shuffled off my mortal coil tranquilly here ; flitting at last in company with some troop of my autumn leaves, or some bevy of spring blossoms, or with snow in the

thaw; my tenants at my back, as a landlord may say. I
have counted on a life-interest in the trees, trimming them
accordingly; and in the squirrels and birds, encouraging
them to chatter and build, and fear nothing, — no guns permitted on the premises. I have had my will of this beautiful
stream. I have carved the woods into a shape of my liking.
I have propagated the despised sumach and the persecuted
hemlock and "pizen laurel." And "no end to the weeds
dug up and set out again," as one of my neighbors delivers
himself. I have built a bridge over Glenmary brook, which
the town looks to have kept up by "the place;" and we
have plied free ferry over the river, I and my man Tom, till
the neighbors, from the daily saving of the two miles round,
have got the trick of it. And betwixt the aforesaid Glenmary brook and a certain muddy and plebeian gutter formerly
permitted to join company with and pollute it, I have procured a divorce at much trouble and pains; a guardian duty
entailed, of course, on my successor.

First of all, sir, let me plead for the old trees of Glenmary.
Ah, those friendly old trees! The cottage stands belted in
with them, a thousand visible from the door, and of stems
and branches worthy of the great valley of the Susquehanna.
For how much music played without thanks am I indebted
to those leaf-organs of changing tone? for how many whis-
perings of thought breathed like oracles into my ear? for
how many new shapes of beauty moulded in the leaves by
the wind? for how much companionship, solace, and welcome? Steadfast and constant is the countenance of such
friends : God be praised for their staid welcome and sweet
fidelity! If I love them better than some things human, it
is no fault of ambitiousness in the trees. They stand where
they did. But in recoiling from mankind, one may find
them the next kindliest things, and be glad of dumb friendship. Spare those old trees, gentle sir!

In the smooth walk which encircles the meadow, betwixt that solitary Olympian sugar-maple and the margin of the river, dwells a portly and venerable toad ; who (if I may venture to bequeath you my friends) must be commended to your kindly consideration. Though a squatter, he was noticed in our first rambles along the stream, five years since, for his ready civility in yielding the way, not hurriedly, however, nor with an obsequiousness unbecoming a republican, but deliberately and just enough ; sitting quietly on the grass till our passing by gave him room again on the warm and trodden ground. Punctually after the April cleansing of the walk, this jewelled *habitué,* from his indifferent lodgings hard by, emerges to take his pleasure in the sun ; and there, at any hour when a gentleman is likely to be abroad, you may find him, patient on his *os coccygis,* or vaulting to his asylum of high grass. This year, he shows, I am grieved to remark, an ominous obesity, likely to render him obnoxious to the female eye, and with the trimness of his shape has departed much of that measured alacrity which first won our regard. He presumes a little on your allowance for old age ; and with this pardonable weakness growing upon him, it seems but right that his position and standing should be tenderly made known to any new-comer on the premises. In the cutting of the next grass, slice me not up my fat friend, sir ! nor set your cane down heedlessly in his modest domain. He is " mine ancient," and I would fain do him a good turn with you.

For my spoilt family of squirrels, sir, I crave nothing but immunity from powder and shot. They require coaxing to come on the same side of the tree with you, and though saucy to me, I observe that they commence acquaintance invariably with a safe mistrust. One or two of them have suffered, it is true, from too hasty a confidence in my greyhound Maida, but the beauty of that gay fellow was a trap against which nature had furnished them with no warning instinct. (A fact, sir, which would prettily point a moral!) The large hickory on the edge of the lawn, and the black walnut over the shoulder of the flower-garden, have been, through my dynasty, sanctuaries inviolate for squirrels. I pray you, sir, let them not be "reformed out," under your administration.

Of our feathered connections and friends, we are most bound to a pair of Phebe-birds and a merry Bob-o'-Lincoln, the first occupying the top of the young maple near the door of the cottage, and the latter executing his bravuras upon the clump of alder-bushes in the meadow; though, in common with many a gay-plumaged gallant like himself, his whereabout after dark is a dark mystery. He comes every year from his rice-plantation in Florida to pass the summer at Glenmary. Pray, keep him safe from percussion-caps, and let no urchin with a long pole poke down our trusting Phebes; annuals in that same tree for three summers. There are humming-birds, too, whom we have complimented and looked sweet upon, but they cannot be identified from morning to morning. And there is a golden oriole who sings through May on a dogwood tree by the brook-side, but he has fought shy of our crumbs and coaxing; and let him go! We are mates for his betters, with all his gold livery! With these reservations, sir, I commend the birds to your friendship and kind keeping.

And now, sir, I have nothing else to ask, save only your watchfulness over the small nook reserved from this purchase of seclusion and loveliness. In the shady depths of the small glen above you, among the wild-flowers and music, the music of the brook babbling over rocky steps, is a spot sacred to love and memory. Keep it inviolate, and as much of the happiness of Glenmary as we can leave behind, stay with you for recompense!

KATE CREDIFORD.

I FOUND myself looking with some interest at the back of a lady's head. The theatre was crowded, and I had come in late, and the object of my curiosity, whoever she might be, was listening very attentively to the play. She did not move. I had time to build a lifetime romance about her before I had seen a feature of her face. But her ears were small, and of an exquisite oval; and she had that rarest beauty of woman, — the hair arched and joined to the white neck with the same finish as on the temples. Nature often slights this part of her masterpiece.

The curtain dropped, and I stretched eagerly forward to catch a glimpse of the profile. But no! she sat next one of the slender pilasters, and, with her head leaned against it, remained immovable.

I left the box, and, with some difficulty, made my way into the crowded pit. Elbowing, apologizing, persevering, I at last gained a point where I knew I could see my incognita at the most advantage. I turned — pshaw! — how was it possible I had not recognized her?

Kate Crediford!

There was no getting out again, for a while at least, without giving offence to the crowd I had jostled so unceremoniously. I sat down vexed, and commenced a desperate study of the figure of Shakspeare on the drop-curtain.

Of course I had been a lover of Miss Crediford's, or I could not have turned with indifference from the handsomest woman in the theatre. She was very beautiful, there was

314

no disputing. But we love women a little for what we *do* know of them, and a great deal more for what we *do not*. I had love-read Kate Crediford to the last leaf. We parted as easily as a reader and a book. Flirtation is a circulating library, in which we seldom ask twice for the same volume ; and I gave up Kate to the next reader, feeling no property even in the marks I had made in her perusal. A little quarrel sufficed as an excuse for the closing of the book, and both of us studiously avoided a reconciliation.

As I sat in the pit, I remembered suddenly a mole on her left cheek, and I turned toward her with the simple curiosity to know whether it was visible at that distance. Kate looked sad. She still leaned immovable against the slight column, and her dark eyes, it struck me, were moist. Her mouth, with this peculiar expression upon her countenance, was certainly inexpressibly sweet, the turned-down corners ending in dimples, which in that particular place, I have always observed, are like wells of unfathomable melancholy. Poor Kate ! what was the matter with her?

As I turned back to my dull study of the curtain, a little pettish with myself for the interest with which I had looked at an old flame, I detected half a sigh under my white waistcoat ; but, instantly persuading myself that it was a disposition to cough, coughed, and began to hum " Suoni la tromba." The curtain rose, and the play went on.

It was odd that I never had seen Kate in that humor before. I did not think she could be sad. Kate Crediford sad ! Why, she was the most volatile, light-hearted, care-for-nothing coquette that ever held up her fingers to be kissed. I wonder, has any one really annoyed you, my poor Kate ! thought I. Could I, by chance, be of any service to you? for, after all, I owe you something ! I looked at her again.

Strange that I had ever looked at that face without emo-

tion! The vigils of an ever-wakeful, ever-passionate, yet
ever-tearful and melancholy, spirit seemed set and kept
under those heavy and motionless eyelids. And she, as I
saw her now, was the very model and semblance of the character that I had all my life been vainly seeking! This was
the creature I had sighed for when turning away from the
too mirthful tenderness of Kate Crediford! There was
something new, or something for the moment miswritten, in
that familiar countenance.

I made my way out of the pit with some difficulty, and
returned to sit near her. After a few minutes, a gentleman
in the next box rose, and left the seat vacant on the other
side of the pilaster against which she leaned. I went around
while the orchestra were playing a loud march, and, without
being observed by the thoughtful beauty, seated myself in
the vacant place.

Why did my eyes flush and moisten as I looked upon the
small white hand lying on the cushioned barrier between us?
I knew every vein of it, like the strings of my own heart.
I had held it spread out in my own, and followed its delicate
blue traceries with a rose-stem, for hours and hours, while
imploring and reproaching and reasoning over love's lights
and shadows. I knew the feel of every one of those exquisite fingers, — those rolled-up rose-leaves, with nails like
pieces cut from the lip of a shell! Oh the promises I had
kissed into oaths on that little *chef-d'œuvre* of nature's tinted
alabaster! the psalms and sermons I had sat out holding
it, in her father's pew! the moons I had tired out of the
sky, making of it a bridge for our hearts passing backward
and forward! And how could that little wretch of a hand,
that knew me better than its own other hand (for we had
been more together), lie there, so unconscious of my presence? How could she — Kate Crediford — sit next to me, as
she was doing, with only a stuffed partition between us, and

her head leaning on one side of a pilaster, and mine on the other, and never start, nor recognize, nor be at all aware of my neighborhood? She was not playing a part, it was easy to see. Oh, I knew those little relaxed fingers too well! Sadness, indolent and luxurious sadness, was expressed in her countenance, and her abstraction was unfeigned and contemplative. Could she have so utterly forgotten me — magnetically, that is to say? Could the atmosphere about her, that would once have trembled betrayingly at my approach, like the fanning of an angel's invisible wing, have lost the sense of my presence?

I tried to magnetize her hand. I fixed my eyes on that little open palm, and, with all the intensity I could summon, kissed it mentally in its rosy centre. I reproached the ungrateful little thing for its dulness and forgetfulness, and brought to bear upon it a focus of old memories of pressures and caresses, to which a stone would scarce have the heart to be insensible.

But I belie myself in writing this with a smile. I watched those unmoving fingers with a heart. I could not see the face nor read the thought of the woman who had once loved me, and who sat near me now so unconsciously; but if a memory had stirred, if a pulse had quickened its beat, those finely-strung fingers, I well know, would have trembled responsively. Had she forgotten me altogether? Is that possible? *Can* a woman close the leaves of her heart over a once-loved and deeply-written name, like the waves over a vessel's track, like the air over the division of a bird's flight?

I had intended to speak presently to Miss Crediford, but every moment the restraint became greater. I felt no more privileged to speak to her than the stranger who had left the seat I occupied. I drew back, for fear of encroaching on her room, or disturbing the folds of her shawl. I dared not

speak to her. And, while I was arguing the matter to myself, the party who were with her, apparently tired of the
play, arose and left the theatre, Kate following last, but
unspoken to, and unconscious altogether of having been near
any one whom she knew.

I went home, and wrote to her all night, for there was no
sleeping till I had given vent to this new fever at my heart.
And in the morning I took the leading thoughts from my
heap in incoherent scribblings, and embodied them more
coolly in a letter : —

"You will think, when you look at the signature, that this is to be
the old story; and you will be as much mistaken as you are in believing that I was ever your lover, till a few hours ago. I have declared
love to you, it is true. I have been happy with you, and wretched
without you; I have thought of you, dreamed of you, haunted you,
sworn to you, and devoted to you all and more than you exacted of
time and outward service and adoration; but I love you now for the
first time in my life. Shall I be so happy as to make you comprehend
this startling contradiction ?

"There are many chambers in the heart, Kate; and the spirits of
some of us dwell, most fondly and secretly, in the chamber of tears, —
avowedly, however, in the outer and ever-open chamber of mirth.
Over the sacred threshold, guarded by sadness, much that we select
and smile upon, and follow with adulation in the common walks of
life, never passes. We admire the gay. They make our melancholy
sweeter by contrast, when we retire within ourselves. We pursue
them. We take them to our hearts, — to the outer vestibules of our
hearts, — and, if they are gay only, they are content with the uncon-
secrated tribute which we pay them there. But the chamber within
is, meantime, lonely. It aches with its desolation. The echo of the
mirthful admiration without jars upon its mournful silence. It longs
for love, but love toned with its own sadness, — love that can penetrate
deeper than smiles ever came, — love that, having once entered, can
be locked in with its key of melancholy, and brooded over with the
long dream of a lifetime. But that deep-hidden and unseen chamber
of the heart may be long untenanted. And, meantime, the spirit
becomes weary of mirth, and impatiently quenches the fire even upon

its outer altar, and in the complete loneliness of a heart that has no inmate or idol, gay or tearful, lives mechanically on.

"Do you guess at my meaning, Kate ? Do you remember the merriment of our first meeting ? Do you remember in what a frolic of thoughtlessness you first permitted me to raise to my lips those restless fingers ? Do you remember the mock condescension, the merry haughtiness, the rallying and feigned incredulity, with which you first received my successive steps of vowing and love-making, — the arch look when it was begun, the laugh when it was over, the untiring follies we kept up, after vows plighted, and the future planned and sworn to ? That you were in earnest, as much as you were capable of being, I fully believe. You would not else have been so prodigal of the sweet bestowings of a maiden's tenderness. But how often have I left you with the feeling, that, in the hours I had passed with you, my spirit had been alone! How often have I wondered if there were depths in my heart which love can never reach! How often mourned that in the procession of love there was no place allotted for its sweetest and dearest followers, — tears and silence ! O Kate ! sweet as was that sun-gleam of early passion, I did not love you ! I tired of your smiles, waiting in vain for your sadness. I left you, thought of you no more.

"But now (and you will be surprised to know that I have been so near to you unperceived) I have drank an intoxication from one glance into your eyes, which throws open to you every door of my heart, subdues to your control every nerve and feeling of my existence. Last night I sat an hour tracing again the transparent and well-remembered veins upon your hand, and oh! how the language written in those branching and mystic lines had changed in meaning and power! You were sad. I saw you from a distance, and, with amazement at an expression upon your face which I had never before seen, I came and sat near you. It was the look I had longed for when I knew you, and when tired of your mirth. It was the look I had searched the world for, combined with such beauty as yours. It was a look of tender and passionate melancholy, which revealed to me an unsuspected chamber in your heart, — a chamber of tears. Ah! why were you never sad before ? Why have we lost — why have I lost — the eternity's worth of sweet hours, when you love me with that concealed treasure in your bosom ? Alas! that angels must walk the world, unrecognized till too late ! Alas ! that I have held in my arms, and pressed to my lips, and loosed again with trifling and weariness, the creature whom it was my life's errand, the thirst and passionate longing of my nature, to find and worship!

"O heaven! with what new value do I now number over your adorable graces of person! How spiritualized is every familiar feature, once so deplorably misappreciated! How compulsive of respectful adoration is that flexible waist, that step of aërial lightness, that swan-like motion, which I once dared to praise triflingly and half-mockingly, like the tints of a flower, or the chance beauty of a bird! And those bright lips! How did I ever look on them, and not know that within their rosy portal slept voiceless, for a while, the controlling spell of my destiny, — the tearful spirit followed and called in my dreams, with perpetual longing? Strange value given to features and outward loveliness by qualities within! Strange witchery of sadness in a woman! Oh, there is in mirth and folly, dear Kate, no air for love's breathing, still less of food for constancy, or of holiness to consecrate and heighten beauty of person!

"What can I say else, except implore to be permitted to approach you, — to offer my life to you, — to begin thus late, after being known so long, the worship which till death is your due? Pardon me if I have written abruptly and wildly. I shall await your answer in an agony of expectation. I do not willingly breathe till I see you, — till I weep at your feet over my blindness and forgetfulness. Adieu! but let it not be for long, I pray you!"

I despatched this letter, and it would be difficult to embody in language the agony I suffered in waiting for a reply. I walked my room that endless morning with a death-pang in every step, so fearful was I — so prophetically fearful — that I had forfeited forever the heart I had once flung from me.

It was noon when a letter arrived. It was in a handwriting new to me. But it was on the subject which possessed my existence, and it was of final import. It follows : —

DEAR SIR, — My wife wishes me to write to you, and inform you of her marriage, which took place a week or two since, and of which she presumes you are not aware. She remarked to me that you thought her looking unhappy last evening, when you chanced to see her at the play. As she seemed to regret not being able to answer your note herself, I may perhaps convey the proper apology by taking upon myself to mention to you, that, in consequence of eating an imprudent quantity of unripe fruit, she felt ill before going to the theatre, and was obliged to leave early.　To-day she seems seriously indisposed.　I trust she will be well enough to receive you in a day or two; and remain,

Yours truly,

SAMUEL SMITHERS.

But I never called on Mrs. Samuel Smithers.

THE GHOST–BALL AT CONGRESS HALL.

IT was the last week of September, and the keeper of "Congress Hall" stood on his deserted colonnade. The dusty street of Saratoga was asleep in the stillness of village afternoon. The whittlings of the stage-runners at the corners, and around the leaning-posts, were fading into dingy undistinguishableness. Stiff and dry hung the slop-cloths at the door of the livery-stable, and drearily clean was doorway and stall. "The season" was over.

"Well, Mr. B——!" said the Boniface of the great caravansary, to a gentlemanly-looking invalid, crossing over from the village tavern on his way to Congress Spring, "this looks like the end of it! A slimmish season, though, Mr. B——! 'Gad, things isn't as they used to be in *your* time! Three months we used to have of it, in them days, and the same people coming and going all summer, and folks' own horses, and all the ladies drinking champagne! And every 'hop' was as good as a ball; and a ball — when do you ever see such balls nowadays? Why, here's all my best wines in the cellar; and as to beauty — pooh! they're done coming *here*, anyhow, are the belles, such as belles *was!*"

"You may say that, mine host, you *may* say that!" replied the damaged Corydon, leaning heavily on his cane. "What! they're all gone now, eh — nobody at the 'United States'?"

"Not a soul, and here's weather like August! — capital weather for young ladies to walk out evenings, and for a drive to Barhydt's — nothing like it! It's a sin, *I* say, to
322

pass such weather in the city! Why shouldn't they come
to the Springs in the Indian summer, Mr. B——?"

Coming events seemed to have cast their shadows before.
As Boniface turned his eyes instinctively toward the sand-
hill, whose cloud of dust was the precursor of new pilgrims
to the waters, and the sign for the black boy to ring the bell
of arrival, behold, on its summit, gleaming through the neb-
ulous pyramid like a lobster through the steam of the fisher-
man's pot, one of the red coaches of "the People's Line!"

And another!

And another!

And another!

Down the sandy descent came the first, while the driver's
horn, intermittent with the crack of his whip, set to bobbing
every pine-cone of the adjacent wilderness.

"Prrr — ru — te — too — toot — pash! — crack! — snap!
— prrrr — r — rut — rut — rr*ut!!* G'lang! — Hip!"

Boniface laid his hand on the pull of the porter's bell, but
the thought flashed through his mind that he might have been
dreaming — was he awake?

And, marvel upon wonder! — a horn of arrival from the
other end of the village! And as he turned his eyes in that
direction, he saw the dingier turnouts from Lake Sacrament
— extras, wagons, every variety of rattletrap conveyance —
pouring in like an Irish funeral on the return, and making
(oh, climax more satisfactory!) straight, all, for Congress
Hall!

Events now grew precipitate.

Ladies were helped out with green veils, parasols and
baskets were handed after them, baggage was chalked and
distributed (and parasols, baskets, and baggage, be it noted,
were all of the complexion that innkeepers love, — the
indefinable look which betrays the owner's addictedness to
extras), and now there was ringing of bells; and there were

orders for the woodcocks to be dressed with pork chemises, and for the champagne to be iced, the sherry not; and through the arid corridors of Congress Hall floated a delicious toilet air of cold cream and lavender; and ladies' maids came down to press out white dresses, while the cook heated the curling-irons; and up and down the stairs flitted, with the blest confusion of other days, boots and iced sangarees, hot water, towels, and mint-juleps, — all delightful, but all incomprehensible! Was the summer encored, or had the Jews gone back to Jerusalem? To the keeper of Congress Hall, the restoration of the millennium would have been a rushlight to this second advent of fun-and-fashion-dom!

Thus far we have looked through the eyes of the person (pocket-ually speaking) most interested in the singular event we wished to describe. Let us now (tea being over, and your astonishment having had time to breathe) take the devil's place at the elbow of the invalided dandy beforementioned, and follow him over to Congress Hall. It was a mild night, and, as I said before (or meant to, if I did not), August, having been prematurely cut off by his *raining* successor, seemed up again, like Hamlet's governor, and bent on walking out his time.

Rice (you remember Rice, famous for his lemonades with a corrective), — Rice, having nearly ignited his forefinger with charging wines at dinner, was out to cool on the colonnade; and B——, not strong enough to stand about, drew a chair near the drawing-room window, and begged the rosy barkeeper to throw what light he could upon this multitudinous apparition. Rice could only feed the fire of his wonder with the fuel of additional circumstances. Coaches had been arriving from every direction till the house was full. The departed black band had been stopped at Albany, and sent back. There seemed no married people in the party — at least, judging by dress and flirtation. Here and there a belle a little on the wane, but all most juvenescent in gayety, and (Rice thought) handsomer girls than had been at Congress Hall since the days of the Albany regency (the regency of beauty), ten years ago! Indeed, it struck Rice that he had seen the faces of these lovely girls before, though they whom he thought they resembled had long since gone off the stage — grandmothers, some of them, now!

Rice had been told, also, that there was an extraordinary and overwhelming arrival of children and nurses at the Pavilion Hotel, but he thought the report smelt rather like a jealous figment of the Pavilioners. Odd, if true — that's all!

Mr. B—— had taken his seat on the colonnade, as Shakspeare expresses it, " about cock-shut time, " — twilight, — and in the darkness made visible of the rooms within, he could only distinguish the outline of some very exquisite and exquisitely plump figures gliding to and fro, winged, each one, with a pair of rather stoutish but most attentive admirers. As the curfew hour stole away, however, the ladies stole away with it to dress; and at ten o'clock the sudden outbreak of the full band in a mazurka drew Mr. B——'s attention to the dining-room frontage of the colonnade, and, moving his chair to one of the windows, the cockles of his heart warmed to see the orchestra in its glory of old, — thirteen black Orpheuses perched on a throne of dining-tables, and the black veins on their shining temples strained to the crack of mortality with their zealous execution. The waiters, meantime, were lighting the tin Briareus (that spermaceti monster so destructive to broadcloth), and the side-sconces and stand-lamps; and presently a blaze of light flooded the dusty evergreens of the façade, and nothing was wanting but some fashionable Curtius to plunge first into the void, — some adventurous Benton, "to set the ball in motion."

Wrapped carefully from the night-air in his cloak and

belcher, B—— sat, looking earnestly into the room ; and to his excited senses there seemed, about all this supplement to the summer's gayety, a weird mysteriousness, an atmosphere of magic, which was observable, he thought, even in the burning of the candles ! And as to Johnson, the sable leader of the band — " God's-my-life," as Bottom says, how like a tormented fiend writhed the Cremona betwixt his chin and white waistcoat ! Such music, from instruments so vexed, had never split the ears of the Saratoga groundlings since the rule of Saint Dominick (in whose hands even wine sparkled to song) — no, not since the golden age of the Springs, when that lord of harmony and the nabobs of lower Broadway made, of Congress Hall, a paradise for the unmarried. Was Johnson bewitched? Was Congress Hall re-possessed by the spirits of the past? If ever Mr. B——, sitting in other years on that resounding colonnade, had *felt* the magnetic atmosphere of people he knew to be up stairs, he felt it now. If ever he had been contented, knowing that certain bright creatures would presently glide into the visual radius of black Johnson, he felt contented inexplicably, from the same cause *now*, — expecting, as if such music could only be *their* herald, the entrance of the same bright creatures, no older, and as bright after years of matrimony. And now and then B—— pressed his hand to his head, for he was not quite sure that he might not be a little wandering in his mind.

But suddenly the band struck up a march. The first bar was played through, and B—— looked at the door, sighing that this sweet hallucination — this waking dream of other days — was now to be scattered by reality. He could have filliped that mercenary Ethiopian on the nose for playing such music to such falling off from the past as he now looked to see enter.

A lady crossed the threshold on a gentleman's arm.

"Ha, ha!" said B——, trying with a wild effort to laugh, and pinching his arm into a blood-blister, "come — this is *too* good! Helen K——! oh, no! Not quite crazy yet, I hope, — not so far gone yet! Yet it is! I swear it is! And not changed either! Beautiful as ever, by all that is wonderful! Pshaw! I'll not be mad! Rice! — are you there? Why, who are these coming after her? Julia L——! Anna K——, and my friend Fanny! The D——s! The M——s! Nay, I'm dreaming, silly fool that I am! I'll call for a light! Waiter!! Where the devil's the bell?"

And as poor B—— insisting on finding himself in bed, reached out his hand to find the bell-pull, one of the waiters of Congress Hall came to his summons. The gentleman wanted nothing, and the waiter thought he had cried out in his nap; and rather embarrassed to explain his wants, but still unconvinced of his freedom from dreamland, B—— drew his hat over his eyes, and his cloak around him, and screwed up his courage to look again into the enchanted ballroom.

The quadrilles were formed, and the lady at the head of the first set was spreading her skirts for the *avant-deux*. She was a tall woman, superbly handsome, and moved with the grace of a frigate at sea with a nine-knot breeze. Eyes capable of taking in lodgers (hearts, that is to say) of any and every calibre and quality, a bust for a Cornelia, a shape all love and lightness, and a smile like a temptation of Eblis, — there she was, and there were fifty like her, — not like her exactly, either, but of *her* constellation; belles, every one of them, who will be remembered by old men, and used for the disparagement of degenerated younglings; splendid women of Mr. B——'s time, and of the palmy time of Congress Hall, —

"The past — the past — the past!"

Out on your staring and unsheltered lantern of brick, —
your " United States Hotel," stiff, modern, and promiscuous !
Who ever passed a comfortable hour in its glaring cross-
lights, or breathed a gentle sentiment in its unsubdued air
and townish open-to-dustiness ?   What is it to the leafy dimness, the cool shadows, the perpetual and pensive *demi-jour*,
what to the ten thousand associations, of Congress Hall?
Who has not lost a heart (or two) on the boards of that
primitive wilderness of a colonnade ?   Whose first adora-
tions, whose sighs, hopes, strategies, and flirtations, are not
ground into that warped and slipper-polished floor, like
heart-ache and avarice into the bricks of Wall Street ?   Lord
bless you, madam ! don't desert old Congress Hall ! We
have done going to the Springs, — *we*, — and wouldn't go
there again for any thing, but a good price for a pang
(that is, except to see such a sight as we are describing) ;
but we cannot bear, in our midsummer flit through the Astor,
to see charming girls bound for Saratoga, and hear no talk of
Congress Hall !   What ! no lounge on those proposal sofas ;
no pluck at the bright green leaves of those luxuriant
creepers while listening to " the voice of the charmer ; " no
dawdle on the steps to the spring (mamma gone on before) ;
no hunting for *that* glow-worm in the shrubbery by the music-
room ; no swing, no billiards, no morning gossips with the
few privileged beaux admitted to the up-stairs entry, ladies'
wing ?

> " I'd sooner be set quick i' the earth,
> And bowled to death with turnips,"

than assist or mingle in such ungrateful forgetfulness of
pleasure-land ! But what do we with a digression in a
ghost-story ?

The ball went on.   Champagne of the " exploded " color
(pink) was freely circulated between the dances (rosy wine
suited to the bright days when all things were tinted rose),

and wit exploded, too, in these leaden times, went round
with the wine ; and as a glass of the bright vintage was
handed up to old Johnson, B—— stretched his neck over
the window-sill in an agony of expectation, confident that
the black ghost, if ghost he were, would fail to recognize the
leaders of fashion as he was wont of old, and to bow respectfully to them before drinking in their presence. Oh,
murder ! not he ! Down went his black poll to the music-
stand, and up, and down again, and at every dip the white
roller of that unctuous eye was brought to bear upon some
well-remembered star of the ascendant ! *He* saw them as
B—— did ! *He* was not playing to an unrecognized company of late comers to Saratoga, — anybodies from any
place ! He, the unimaginative African, believed, evidently,
that they were there in flesh, — Helen the glorious, and all
her fair troop of contemporaries ! — and that with them had
come back their old lovers, the gay and gallant Lotharios
of the time of Johnson's first blushing honors of renown !
The big drops of agonized horror and incredulity rolled off
the forehead of Mr. B—— !

But suddenly the waiters radiated to the side-doors, and
with the celestial felicity of star-rising and morning-breaking,
a waltz was found playing in the ears of the revellers ! Perfect, yet when it did begin ! Waltzed every brain and vein,
waltzed every swimming eye within the reach of its magic
vibrations ! Gently away floated couple after couple, and as
they circled round to his point of observation, B—— could
have called every waltzer by name ; but his heart was in his
throat, but his eyeballs were hot with the stony immovable-
ness of his long gazing.

Another change in the music ! Spirits of bedevilment !
could not *that* waltz have been spared ? Boniface stood
waltzing his head from shoulder to shoulder ; Rice twirled
the head-chambermaid in the entry ; the black and white boys

spun round on the colonnade; the wall-flowers in the ball-room crowded their chairs to the wall; the candles flared embracingly — ghosts or no ghosts, dream or hallucination, B—— could endure no more! He flung off his cloak and hat, and jumped in at the window. The divine Emily C—— had that moment risen from tying her shoe. With a nod to her partner, and a smile to herself, B—— encircled her round waist, and away he flew like Ariel, light on the toe, but his face pallid and wild, and his emaciated legs playing like sticks in his unfilled trousers. Twice he made the circuit of the room, exciting apparently less surprise than pleasure by his sudden appearance; then with a wavering halt, and his hand laid tremulously to his forehead, he flew at the hall-door at a tangent, and, rushing through servants and spectators, dashed across the portico, and disappeared in the darkness! A fortnight's brain-fever deprived him of the opportunity of repeating this remarkable flourish, and his subsequent sanity was established through some critical hazard.

There was some inquiry at supper about "old B——," but the lady who waltzed with him knew as little of his coming and going as the managers; and by one belle, who had been at some trouble in other days to quench his ardor, it was solemnly believed to be his persevering apparition.

The next day there was a drive and dinner at Barhydt's, and back in time for ball and supper; and the day after, there was a most hilarious and memorable fishing-party to Saratoga Lake, and all back again in high force for the ball and supper; and so, like a long gala-day, like a short summer carnival, all frolic, sped the week away. Boniface, by the third day, had rallied his recollections; and with many a scrape and compliment, he renewed his acquaintance with the belles and beaux of a brighter period of beauty and gallantry. And if there was any mystery remaining in the old functionary's mind as to the identity and miracle of their presence and re-union, it was on the one point of the ladies' unfaded loveliness ; for, saving a half-inch aggregation in the waist, which was rather an improvement than otherwise, and a little more fulness in the bust, which was a most embellishing difference, the ten years that had gone over them had made no mark on the lady portion of his guests ; and as to the gentleman — but that is neither here nor there.   They were " men of mark," young or old, and their wear and tear is, as Flute says, " a thing of naught."

It was revealed by the keeper of the Pavilion, after the departure of the late-come revellers of Congress Hall, that there had been constant and secret visitations by the belles of the latter sojourn, to the numerous infantine lodgers of the former.   Such a troop of babies and boys, and all so lovely, had seldom gladdened even the eyes of angels, out of the cherubic choir (let alone the Saratoga Pavilion) ; and though, in their white dresses and rosebuds, the belles afore spoken of looked like beautiful elder sisters to those motherless younglings, yet when they came in, mothers confessed, on the morning of departure, openly to superintend the preparations for travel, they had so put off the untroubled maiden look from their countenances, and so put on the indescribable growing-old-iness of married life in their dress, that, to the eye of an observer, they might well have passed for the mothers of the girls they had themselves seemed to be, the day before only.

Who devised, planned, and brought about this practical comment on the *needlessness of the American haste to be old*, we are not at liberty to mention.   The reader will have surmised, however, that it was some one who had observed the more enduring quality of beauty in other lands, and, on returning to his own, looked in vain for those who, by every law of nature, should be still embellishing the society of which he had left them the budding flower and ornament.

To get them together again, only with their contemporaries, in one of their familiar haunts of pleasure ; to suggest the exclusion of every thing but youthfulness in dress, amusement, and occupation ; to bring to meet them their old admirers, married like themselves, but entering the field once more for their smiles against their rejuvenescent husbands ; to array them as belles again, and see whether it was any falling off in beauty or the power of pleasing which had driven them from their prominent places in social life, — this was the obvious best way of doing his immediate circles of friends the service his feelings exacted of him ; the only way, indeed, of convincing these bright creatures that they had far anticipated the fading hour of bloom and youthfulness. *Pensez-y!*

EPHEMERA.

FROM SARATOGA.

TO THE JULIA OF SOME YEARS AGO.

AUGUST 2, 1843.

I HAVE not written to you in your boy's lifetime, — that fine lad, a shade taller than yourself, whom I sometimes meet at my tailor's and bootmaker's. I am not very sure, that after the first month (bitter month) of your marriage, I have thought of you for the duration of a revery — fit to be so called. I loved you — lost you — swore your ruin, and forgot you — which is love's climax when jilted. And I never expected to think of you again.

Beside the astonishment at hearing from me at all, you will be surprised at receiving a letter from me at Saratoga. Here where the stars are, that you swore by, — here, where the springs and colonnades, the wood walks and drives, the sofas and swings, are all coated over with your delicious perjuries, your " protested " protestations, your incalculable bankruptcy of sighs, tears, caresses, promises! Oh, Julia — *mais, retiens toi, ma plume!*

I assure you I had not the slightest idea of ever coming here again in the world, — not the slightest! I had a vow in heaven against it, indeed. While I hated you — before I forgot you, that is to say — I would not have come for your husband's million (your price, Julia!). I had laid Saratoga away with a great seal, to be re-opened in the next star I shall inhabit, and used as a light-house of warning. There was one banister at Congress Hall, particularly, across which

335

we parted nightly, — the next object my hand touched after
losing the warm pressure of yours ; the place I leaned over
with a heart under my waistcoat which would have scaled
Olympus to be nearer to you, yet was kept back by that
mahogany and your " no," — and I will believe that devils
may become dolls, and ghosts play around us like the smoke
of a cigar, since over that banister I have thrown my leg
and sat thinking of the past without frenzy or emotion !
And none have a better right than we to laugh now at love's
passionate eternities ! For we were lovers, Julia, — I as I
know, and you as I believe ; and in that entry, when we
parted to dream, write, contrive for the blissful morrow, —
any thing but sleep and forget, — in that entry and over that
banister were said words of tenderness and devotion, from
as deep soundings of two hearts as ever plummet of this
world could by possibility fathom. You *did* love me, monster of untruth and forgetfulness as you have since been
bought for, — *you did love me !* And that you can ride in
your husband's carriage and grow fat, and that I can come
here and make a mock of it, are two comments on love
worthy of the commonplace-book of Mephistophiles. Fie
on us !

I came to Saratoga as I would look at a coat that I had
worn twenty years before, — with a sort of vacant curiosity
to see the shell in which I had once figured. A friend said,
" Join me at Saratoga ! " and it sounded like, " Come and
see where Julia was adorable." I came in a rail-car, under
a hot sun, and wanted my dinner, and wished myself where
Julia indeed sat fat in her *fauteuil*, — wished it, for the good
wine in the cellar and the French cook in the kitchen. And
I did not go down to " Congress Hall," — the old *palais
d'amour*, — but in the modern and comfortable parlor of the
" United States," sat down by a pretty woman of these days,
and chatted about the water-lily in her bosom and the boy

she had up stairs, coldly and every-day-ishly. I had been there six hours, and you had not entered my thoughts. Please to believe that, Julia!

But in the evening there was a ball at Congress Hall. And though the old house is unfashionable now, and the lies of love are elsewhere told and listened to, there was a movement among the belles in its favor, and I appended myself to a lady's arm and went boldly. I say boldly, for it required an effort. The twilight had fallen, and with it had come a memory or two of the Springs in *our* time. I had seated myself against a pillar of the colonnade of the " United States," and looked down toward·Congress Hall; and *you* were under the old vine-clad portico, as I should have seen you from the same spot, and with the same eye of fancy, sundry years ago. So it was not quite like a passionless antiquary that I set foot again on that old-time colonnade, and to say truth, as the band struck up a waltz, I might have had in my lip a momentary quiver, and some dimness in my world-weary eye. But it passed away.

The ball was *comme ça,* and I found sweet women (as where are they not — given, candles and music?), and aired my homage as an old stager may. I danced without think-ing of you uncomfortably, though the ten years' washing of that white floor has not quite washed out the memory of your Arab instep with its embracing and envied sandal, gliding and bounding, oh, how airily! For you had feet absolute in their perfection, dear Julia! — had you not?

But I went out for fresh air on the colonnade, in an evil and forgetful moment. I strolled alone toward the spring. The lamp burned dim, as it used to burn, tended by Cupid's minions. And on the end of the portico, by the last window of the music-room, under that overhanging ivy, with stars in sight that I would have sworn to for the very same, sat a lady in a dress like yours as I saw you last, and black eyes, like jet lamps framed in velvet, turning indolently toward me. I held by the railing, for I am superstitious, and it seemed to me that I had only to ask why you were there ; for, ghostly or bodily, there I saw you ! Back came your beauty on my memory with yesterday's freshness of recollection. Back came into my heart the Julia of my long-accursed adoration ! I saw your confiding and bewildering smile, your fine-cut teeth of pearl, your over-bent brow and arch look from under, your lily shoulders, your dimpled hands. You were there, if my senses were sufficient evidence, if presence be any thing without touch, — bodily there !

Of course it was somebody else. I went in and took a julep. But I write to tell you that for a minute — a minute of enormous capacity — I have loved you once more. For one minute, while you probably were buried deep in your frilled pillow (snoring, perhaps — who knows?), — for one minute, fleeting and blissful, you have been loved again — with heart, brain, blood, all on fire with truth, tenderness, and passionate adoration — by a man who could have bought you (you know I could !) for half the money you sold for ! And I thought you would like to know this, Julia ! And now, hating you as before, in your fleshy forgetfulness,

Yours not at all.

SUMMER IN TOWN.

WE know nothing of a more restless tendency than a fine, old-fashioned June day, — one that begins with a morning damp with a fresh south wind, and gradually clears away in a thin white mist, till the sun shines through at last, genial and luxurious, but not sultry, and every thing looks clear and bright in the transparent atmosphere. We know nothing which so seduces the very eye and spirit of a man, and stirs in him that gypsy longing, which, spite of disgrace and punishment, made him a truant in his boyhood. There is an expansive rarity in the air of such a day, a something that lifts up the lungs, and plays in the nostrils with a delicious sensation of freshness and elasticity. The close room grows sadly dull under it. The half-open blind, with its tempting glimpse of the sky, and branch of idle leaves flickering in the sun, has a strange witchery. The poor pursuits of this drossy world grow passing insignificant; and the scrawled and blotted manuscripts of an editor's table — pleasant anodyne as they are when the wind is in the east — are, at these seasons, but the "Diary of an Ennuyée," the notched calendar of confinement and unrest. The commendatory sentence stands half completed; the fate of the author under review, with his two volumes, is altogether of less importance than five minutes of the life of that tame pigeon that sits on the eaves washing his white breast in the spout; and the public good-will, and the cause of literature, and our own precarious livelihood, all fade into dim shadow, and leave us listening dreamily to the creeping of the sweet south upon the vine, or the far-off rattle of the hourly, with its freight of happy bowlers and gentlemen of suburban idleness.

What is it to us, when the sun is shining, and the winds bland and balmy, and the moist roads with their fresh smell of earth tempting us away to the hills, — what is it then, to us, whether a poor-devil-author has a flaw in his style, or our own leading article a "local habitation and a name"? Are we to thrust down our heart like a reptile into its cage, and close our shutter to the cheerful light, and our ear to all sounds of out-door happiness? Are we to smother our uneasy impulses, and chain ourselves down to a poor, dry thought, that has neither light, nor music, nor any spell in it save the poor necessity of occupation? Shall we forget the turn in the green lane where we are wont to loiter in our drive, and the cool claret of our friend at the Hermitage, and the glorious golden summer sunset in which we bowl away to the city, musing and refreshed? Alas! yes; the heart *must* be closed, and the green lane and the friend that is happier than we (for he is idle) *must* be forgotten, and the dry thought *must* be dragged up like a wilful steer and yoked to its fellow, and the magnificent sunset, with all its glorious dreams and forgetful happiness, *must* be seen in the pauses of articles, and the " bleared een " of painful attention — and all this in June, prodigal June, when the very worm is all day out in the sun, and the birds scarce stop their singing from the gray light to the dewfall!

What an insufferable state of the thermometer! We knock under to Heraclitus, that fire is the first principle of all things. Fahrenheit at one hundred degrees in the shade! Our curtain in the attic unstirred! Our japonica drooping its great white flowers lower and lower! It is a fair scene, indeed! not a ripple from the pier to the castle, and the surface of the water, as Shelley says, " like a plane of glass

spread out between two heavens;" and there is a solitary
sloop, with the light and shade flickering on its loose sail,
positively hung in the air, and a gull (it is refreshing to see
him) keeping down with his white wings close to the water
as if to meet his own snowy and perfect shadow. Was ever
such intense, unmitigated sunshine? There is nothing on the
hard, opaque sky but a mere rag of a cloud, like a handker-
chief on a tablet of blue marble, and the edge of the shadow
of that tall chimney is as definite as a hair, and the young
elm that leans over the fence is copied in perfect and motionless leaves like a very painting on the broad sidewalk. How
delightful the night will be after such a deluge of light!
How beautiful the modest rays of the starlight, and the cool,
dark blue of the heavens, will seem after the dazzling clearness of this sultry noon! It reminds one of that exquisite
passage in Thalaba, where the spirit-bird comes, when his
eyes are blinded with the intense brightness of the snow,
and spreads her green wings before him!

We have been paid for letting the world know a great
many things that were of no consequence to the world whatever, and, among other nothings, a certain metropoliphobia of
our own, on which we have expended a great deal of choice
grammar and punctuation. We trust the world believes by
this, that, capable as we are of loving our entire species (one
at a time), we hate a city collectively. Having a little moan
to make, with a little moral at the close, we put this private
prejudice once more into type, trusting to your indulgence,
good reader.

This is June; and "where are you going this summer?"
though a pertinent question enough, and seasonable, and
just what anybody says to everybody he meets, has to our
ear a little offence in it. If it were asked for information,
à la bonne heure! we are willing to tell any friend where we

are going, — this side the Styx. But though the question (asked with most affectionate earnestness by your friend) is merely a preface to enlightening you as to his own "watering-place," there must still be an answer. And suppose that answer, though not a whit attended to, touches upon your secret sorrow, your deucedest bore! suppose — But you see our drift! You *understand* that we are to sweat out the summer solstice within the "bills of mortality." You *see* that we are to comfort our bucolic nostrils as we best may, with municipal grass, picking here and there a clover-top or an aggravating dandelion 'twixt post-office and city-hall. Heaven help us!

True, New York is "open at the top." We are prepared to be thankful for what comes *down* to us, — air, light, and dew. But alas! Earth is our mother, — Earth, who sends all her blessings *upward;* Earth, who, in the city, is stoned over, and hammered down, paved, flagged, suffocated, her natural breath quite cut off, or driven to escape by drain and gas-pipe, her flowers and herbs prevented, her springs shut down from gushing! This arid pavement, this hot smell of dust, this brick color and paint, — what are they to the fragrant lap of our overlaid mother, with her drapery of bright colors and tender green? Answer, O omnibus-horse! Answer, O worky-editor!

But there be alleviations! It is to these that hangs "the moral of our tale." We presume most men think themselves more worthy than "sparrows" of the attention of Providence, and of course most men believe in a special Providence for themselves. We do. We believe that we shall not "fall to the ground without" (a) "notice." (But this, let us hope, is anticipating.) We wish to speak now of the succedaneum thrown in our path for our pastoral deprivations, for the lost brook whose babbling current turned the wheel of our idleness. Sweet brook, that never robbed the pebbles of a ray of light in running over them! It became a type to us, that brook. Our thoughts ran brook-wise. Bright water, braiding its ripples as it ran, became our vehicle of fancy. We lagged, we dragged, we were "gravelled for lack of matter," without it. And now mark! Providence has supplied it (through his honor the mayor). A brook, a clear brook, not pellucid merely, but transparent, a brook with a song, tripping as musically (when the carts are not going by) as the beloved brook now sequestered to the Philistines, trips daily before us! Our daily walk is along its border for, say, a rod and a half. Meet us there, if you will, O congenial spirit! As we go to the post-office we span its fair current at the broadest, and take a fillip in our fancy for the day. Would you know its geography more definitely? Stand on the steps of the Astor, and gaze over to the sign of " P. Pussedu, wig-maker, from Italy." Drop then the divining-rod to the left, and a much-frequented pump will become apparent, perched over a projecting curbstone, around which the dancing and bright water trips with sparkling feet, and a murmur audible at least to itself. It is the outlet of the fountain in the park, and, as Wordsworth says, —

"Parching summer hath no warrant
To consume this crystal well," —

as an order is first necessary from the corporation. Oh! (if it were not for being taken to the watch-house) we could sit by this brook in the moonlight, and pour forth our melancholy moan! But the cabmen wash their wheels in it now, and the echo would be, "Want a cab, sir?" Metropolises, avaunt!

BROADWAY AND THE BATTERY.

MARCH made an expiring effort to give us a spring-day yesterday. The morning dawned mild and bright, and there was a voluptuous contralto in the cries of the milkmen and the sweeps, which satisfied me, before I was out of bed, that there was an arrival of a south wind. The Chinese proverb says, " When thou hast a day to be idle, be idle for a day ; " but for that very elusive " time when," I irresistibly substitute the day the wind sweetens after a sour north-easter. Oh the luxury (or *curse*, as the case may be) of breakfasting leisurely with an idle day before one !

I strolled up Broadway between nine and ten, and encoun-tered the *morning tide down ;* and if you never have studied the physiognomy of this great thoroughfare in its various fluxes and refluxes, the differences would amuse you. The clerks and workies have passed down an hour before the nine o'clock tide, and the sidewalk is filled at this time with bankers, brokers, and speculators bound to Wall Street ; old merchants and junior partners bound to Pearl and Water ; and lawyers, young and old, bound for Nassau and Pine. Ah, the faces of care ! The day's operations are working out in their eyes ; their hats are pitched forward at the angle of a stage-coach with all the load on the driver's seat, their shoulders are raised with the shrug of anxiety, their steps are hurried and short, and mortal face and gait could scarcely express a heavier burden of solicitude than every man seems to bear. They nod to you without a smile, and with a kind of unconscious recognition ; and, if you are unaccustomed

344

to walk out at that hour, you might fancy that, if there were not some great public calamity, your friends, at least, had done smiling on you. Walk as far as Niblo's, stop at the greenhouse there, and breathe an hour in the delicious atmosphere of flowering plants, and then return. There is no longer any particular current in Broadway. Foreigners coming out from the *cafés*, after their late breakfast, and idling up and down for fresh air; country-people shopping early; ladies going to their dressmakers in close veils and demi-toilets; errand-boys, news-boys, duns, and doctors, — make up the throng. Toward twelve o'clock there is a sprinkling of mechanics going to dinner, — a merry, short-jacketed, independent-looking troop, glancing gayly at the women as they pass, and disappearing around corners and up alleys; and an hour later Broadway begins to brighten. The omnibuses go along empty, and at a slow pace, for people would rather walk than ride. The side-streets are tributaries of silks and velvets, flowers and feathers, to the great thoroughfare; and ladies whose proper mates (judging by the dress alone) should be lords and princes, and dandies, shoppers, and loungers of every description, take crowded possession of the *pavé*. At nine o'clock you look into the troubled faces of men going to their business, and ask yourself, " To what end is all this burden of care? " and at two, you gaze on the universal prodigality of exterior, and wonder what fills the multitude of pockets that pay for it! The faces are beautiful, the shops are thronged, the sidewalks crowded for an hour; and then the full tide turns, and sets upward. The most of those who are out at three are bound to the upper part of the city to dine; and the merchants and lawyers, excited by collision and contest above the depression of care, join smiling in the throng. The physiognomy of the crowd is at its brightest. Dinner is the smile of the day to most people, and the hour approaches. Whatever has happened in stocks or politics, whoever is dead, whoever ruined since morning, Broadway is thronged with cheerful faces and good appetites at three! The world will probably dine with pleasure up to the last day — perhaps breakfast with worldly care for the future on doomsday morning! And here I must break off my daguerreotype of yesterday's idling; for the wind came round easterly and raw at three o'clock, and I was driven in-doors to try industry as an opiate.

The first day of freedom from medical embargo is equivalent, in most men's memories, to a new first impression of existence. Dame Nature, like a provident housewife, seems to take the opportunity of a sick man's absence to whitewash and freshen the world he occupies. Certainly I never saw the bay of New York look so beautiful as on Sunday noon; and you may attribute as much as you please of this impression to the "Claude Lorraine spectacles" of convalescence, and as much more as pleases you to the fact that it was an intoxicating and dissolving day of spring.

The Battery on Sunday is the Champs-Élysées of foreigners. I heard nothing spoken around me but French and German. Wrapped in my cloak and seated on a bench, I watched the children and the poodle-dogs at their gambols, and it seemed to me as if I were in some public resort over the water. They bring such happiness to a day of idleness, — these foreigners, — laughing, talking nonsense, totally unconscious of observation, and delighted as much with the passing of a row-boat or a steamer, as an American with the arrival of his own "argosy" from sea. They are not the better class of foreigners who frequent the Battery on Sunday. They are the newly arrived, the artisans, the German toy-makers, and the French boot-makers, — people who still wear the spacious-hipped trousers and scant coats, the gold rings in the ears, and the ruffled shirts, of the lands of undandified poverty. They are there by hundreds. They hang over the railing, and look off upoñ the sea. They sit and smoke on the long benches. They run hither and thither with their children, and behave as they would in their own. garden, using and enjoying it just as if it were their own. And an enviable power they have of it!

There had been a heavy fog on the water all the morning, and quite a fleet of the river-craft had drifted with the tide close on to the Battery. The soft south wind was lifting the mist in undulating sweeps, and covering and disclosing the spars and sails with a phantom effect quite melodramatic. By two o'clock the breeze was steady and the bay clear, and the horizon was completely concealed with the spread of canvas. The grass in the Battery plats seemed to be growing visibly meantime, and to this animated sea-picture gave a foreground of tender and sparkling green; the trees looked feathery with the opening buds; the children rolled on the grass, and the summer seemed come. Much as Nature loves the country, she opens her green lap first in the cities. The valleys are asleep under the snow, and will be for weeks.

A TÊTE–À–TÊTE.

SIT back in your chair, and let me babble! I like just to pull the spigot out of my discretion, and let myself run. No criticisms, if you please, and don't stare! Eyelids down, and stand ready for slip-slop.

I was sitting last night by the lady with the horn and the glass umbrella, at the Alhamra — I drinking a julep, she (my companion) eating an ice. The water dribbled, and the moon looked through the slits in the awning, and we chatted about Saratoga. My companion has a very generalizing mind, situated just in the rear of a very particularly fine pair of black velvet eyes, and her opinions usually come out by a little ivory gate with a pink portico — charming gate, charming portico, charming opinions. I must say I think more of intellect when it is well lodged.

I am literally at a dead loss to know whether she said it, or I said it, — what my mind runs on at this moment. It's all one, for if I said it, it was with the velvet approbation of her ineffable eyes, and before such eyes I absorb and give back, like the mirror that I am. These, then, are *her* reflections about Saratoga.

Why, in mamma's time, it was a different affair. There was a cabinet of fashion in those days, and the question was settled with closed doors. Giants have done being born, and so have super-beautiful women, — such women as used to lay down hearts like blocks in the wooden pavement, and walk on nothing else. There were about three in each city, — three belles of whom every baptized person in the country knew

the name, style, and probable number of victims. Their
history should have been written while they lasted; for of
course the gods loved them, and "whom the gods love die
first," and they are dead, and have left no manuscripts nor
models. Well, these belles were leagued, and kept up their
dynasty by correspondence. New York was the seat of
government, and the next strongest branch was at Albany
(where the women at one time were lovelier than at any
known place and period since the memory of woman). In
New York alone, however, were married ladies admitted to
the councils. Here and there a renowned beau was kept in
the antechamber for advice. April came, and then commenced a vigorous exchange of couriers. "The Springs,"
of course, but which? Saratoga, or Lebanon, or Ballston?
What carried it, or who decided it, was inshrined in the most
eternal mystery; but it was decided, and known to a few
beaux and the proprietors of the hotels by the middle of
May. Wine and Johnson's band were provided accordingly.
The summer was more punctual in those days, and July particularly was seldom belated. After the Fourth, the cabinet
started, and then commenced a longitudinal radiation from
north to south — after what, and to follow whom, was only a
secret to the uninitiated. And such times — for then the
people had fortunes, and the ladies drank champagne! La!
how 'ma talks about it!

But now! — *Eheu fugaces!* (Latin for "Bless my soul!")
— change has drank all the spirit of our dream. There is
so much aristocracy in New York, that there is none at all.
Beauty has been scrambled for, and everybody has picked
up a little. There must be valleys to make mountains, —
ugly people before there can be belles; but, everybody being
rather pretty, who can be divine? *Idem*, gentility! Who
knows who isn't "genteel" in New York? There are fifty
circles as like as peas, and not even an argument as to the

perihelion.   Live where you please, know whom you please,
wear what you please, and ride freely in the omnibuses, and
nobody makes a remark !   Social anarchy !

Why, what a state of things it is when it is as much trouble to find out where the prettiest people have gone to pass
the summer as it is to inquire out " good "-ness in Wall
Street !   No cherishing, either, of belle or beau descent !
The daughters of the charming tyrants of ten or twenty
years ago, the boys of the beaux of that time, walk about
unpointed at and degenerate.   The " good society " of
twenty years ago is most indifferent society now.

> " The vase in which roses have once been distilled "

goes for a crockery pipkin.

A great pity they don't have coffee at the Alhamra !   And
no curaçoa — and what is ice-cream without a drop of curaçoa !   It is a pretty place, — a very pretty place !   And there
should be nobody to wait on you here but dainty and dapper
slaves — such as the Moors had, with golden rings on their
ankles, in the veritable Alhambra.   That tall, crooked black-
amoor hurts my eye.

So there was no " Mr. Hicks," and no " legacy to Washington Irving."   More's the pity !   I wish a Mr. Hicks might
be created impromptu, on purpose.   And more Mr. Hickses
for more authors.   Birds that sing should be provided with
cages and full cups.   What could be done better with spare
moneys than to take the footworn pilgrim of genius, and send
him softly down from the temple of fame shod with velvet !
In every rich man's will there should be at least one line
illuminated with a bequest to genius.   Heaven give us a
million, that we may set the glorious example !

And now, lady, who are you that in this gossiping dream
has held converse with me ?   I have murmured to the black
cross, suspended by its braid of hair upon your throat of

ivory, without asking your name — content that you listened. But now (if spiritual visitors have arms) put your arm in mine, and come out under a better-devised ceiling ! The night is fragrant. Heaven is sifting love upon us through the sieve of the firmament — starlight, you took it for ! And as much falls in Broadway as elsewhere. And the stars are as sweet seen from this sidewalk, as they are from the Fountain of Egeria. I have sighed in both places, and know. *" Allons ! faites moi l'amour — car je suis dans mon humeur des Dimanches."*

A SUNDAY WALK.

I AM inclined to think it is not peculiar to myself to have a
sabbath taste for the water-side. There is an affinity,
felt, I think, by man and boy, between the stillness of the day
and the audible hush of boundaries to water. Premising
that it was at first with the turned-up nose of conscious
travesty, I have to confess the finding of a sabbath ramble,
to my mind, along the river-side in New York, — the first
mile toward Albany, on the bank of the Hudson. Indeed,
if quiet be the object, the nearer the water the less jostled
the walk on Sunday. You would think, to cross the city
anywhere from river to river, that there was a general hydro-
phobia, — the entire population crowding to the high ridge of
Broadway, and hardly a soul to be seen on either the East
River or the Hudson. But, with a little thoughtful frequent-
ing, those deserted river-sides become contemplative and
pleasant rambling-places ; and if some whim of fashion do
not make the bank of the Hudson, like the Marina of Smyrna,
a fashionable resort, I have my Sunday afternoons provided
for during the pigritude of city durance.

Yesterday (Sunday) it blew one of those unfolding west
winds, chartered expressly to pull the kinks out of the belated
leaves, — a breeze it was delightful to set the face to, —
strong, genial, and inspiriting, and smelling (in New York)
of the snubbed twigs of Hoboken. The Battery looked very
delightful, with the grass laying its cheek to the ground, and
the trees all astir and trinkling ; but on Sunday this lovely
resort is full of smokers of bad cigars — unpleasant gentle-

men to take the wind of. I turned the corner with a look through the fence, and was in comparative solitude the next moment.

The monarch of our deep-water streams, the gigantic "Massachusetts," lay at her wharf, washed by the waving hands of the waters taking leave of the Hudson. The river ends under the prow; or, as we might say with a poetic license, joins on at this point to Stonington, so easy is the transit from wharf to wharf in that magnificent conveyance. From this point up extends a line of ships, rubbing against the pier the fearless noses that have nudged the poles and the tropics, and been breathed on by spice-islands and icebergs, — an array of nobly-built merchantmen, that, with the association of their triumphant and richly-freighted comings and goings, grows upon my eye with a certain majesty. It is a broad street here, of made land, and the sidewalks in front of the new stores are lumbered with pitch and molasses, flour and red ochre, bales, bags, and barrels, in unsightly confusion; but the wharf-side, with its long line of carved figure-heads, and bowsprits projecting over the street, is an unobstructed walk, on Sundays at least, and more suggestive than many a gallery of marble statues. The vessels that trade to the North Sea harbor here, unloading their hemp and iron; and the superb French packet-ships, with their gilded prows; and, leaning over the gangways and taffrails, the Swedish and Norwegian sailors jabber away their Sunday's idle time; and the negro cooks lie and look into the puddles; and altogether it is a strangely mixed picture, — Power reposing, and Fret and Business gone from the six-days' whip and chain. I sat down on a short hawser-post, and conjured the spirits of ships around me. They were as communicative as would naturally be expected in a *tête-à-tête*, when quite at leisure. Things they had seen and got wind of in the Indian seas, strange fishes that had tried the metal of their copper bottoms, porpoises they had run over asleep, wrecks and skeletons they had thrown a shadow across, when under prosperous headway, — these and particulars of the fortunes they had brought home, and the passengers coming to look through one more country to find happiness, and the terrors and dangers, heartaches and dreams, that had come and gone with each bill of lading, — the talkative old bowsprits told me all. I sat and watched the sun setting between two outlandish-looking vessels, and, at twilight, turned to go home, leaving the spars and lines drawn in clear tracery on a sky as rosy and fading as a poet's prospects at seventeen.

A SPRING DAY IN WINTER.

A SPRING day sometimes bursts upon us in December. One scarcely knows whether the constant warmth of the fire, or the fresh sunny breathings from the open window, are the most welcome. At such a time the curtains swing lazily to the mild wind as it enters, and the light green leaves of the sheltered flowers stir and erect themselves with an out-of-door vigor, and the shuffled steps and continued voices of the children in the street have the loitering and summer-like sound of June. I do not know whether it is not a cockney feeling; but with all my love for the country, fixed as it is by the recollections of a life mostly spent in the " green fields " I sometimes " babble of," there is something in a summer morning in the city, which the wet, warm woods, and the solitary though lonely haunts of the country do not, after all the poetry that has been " spilt upon them " (as Neal would say), at all equal. Whether it is that we find so much sympathy in the many faces that we meet, made happy by the same sweet influences, or whatever else may be the reason, *certes*, I never take my morning walk on such a day, without a leaping in my heart, which, from all I can gather by dream or revelation, has a touch in it of Paradise. I returned once, on such a day, from an hour's ramble after breakfast. The air rushed past my temples with the grateful softness of spring, and every face that passed had the open, inhaling expression which is given by the simple joy of existence. The sky had the deep clearness of noon. The clouds were winnowed in light parallel curves, looking like white shells inlaid on the arched heavens; the smooth, glassy bay was like a transparent abyss opening to the earth's centre, and edging away underneath with a slope of hills, and spires, and leafless woods, copied minutely and perfectly from the upper landscape; and the naked elms seemed almost clothed as the teeming eye looked on them, and the brown hills took a tint of green, — so freshly did the summer fancies crowd into the brain with the summer softness of the sunshine and air. The mood is rare in which the sight of human faces does not give us pleasure. It is a curious occupation to look on them as they pass, and study their look and meaning, and wonder at the providence of God, which can provide, in this crowded world, an object and an interest for all. With what a singular harmony the great machine of society goes on! So many thousand minds, and each with its peculiar cast and its positive difference from its fellow, and yet no dangerous interference, and no discord audible above the hum of its daily revolution. I could not help feeling a religious thrill as I passed face after face, with this thought in my mind, and saw each one earnest and cheerful, each one pressing on with its own object, without waiting or caring for the equally engrossing object of the other. The man of business went on with an absorbed look, caring only to thread his way rapidly along the street. The student strided by with the step of exercise, his lips parted to admit the pleasant air to his refreshed lungs, and his eye wandering with bewildered pleasure from object to object. The schoolboy looked wistfully up and down the street, and lingered till the last stroke of the bell summoned him tardily in. The womanish schoolgirl, with her veil coquettishly drawn, still flirted with her boyish admirer, though it was " after nine ; " and the child, with its soiled satchel and shining face, loitered seriously along the sidewalk, making acquaintance with every dog, and picking up every stone on its unwilling way. The spell of the atmosphere was universal, and yet all kept on their several courses, and the busy harmony of employment went steadily and unbrokenly on. How rarely we turn upon ourselves, and remember how wonderfully we are made and governed!

EVANESCENT IMPRESSIONS.

I HAVE very often, in the fine passages of society, — such as occur sometimes in the end of an evening, or when a dinner-party has dwindled to an unbroken circle of choice and congenial spirits, or at any of those times when conversation, stripped of all reserve or check, is poured out in the glowing and unfettered enthusiasm to which convivial excitement alone gives the confidence necessary to its flow, — I have often wished, at such times, that the voice and manner of the chance and fleeting eloquence about us could be arrested and written down for others beside ourselves to see and admire. In a chance conversation at a party, in the bagatelle rattle of a dance, in a gay hour over coffee and sandwiches *en famille*, wherever you meet those whom you love or value, there will occur pieces of dialogue, *jeux d'esprit*, passages of feeling or fun, — trifles, it is true, but still such trifles as make eras in the calendar of happiness, — which you would give the world to rescue from their ephemeral destiny. They are, perhaps, the soundings of a spirit too deep for ordinary life to fathom, or the gracefulness of a fancy linked with too feminine a nature to bear the eye of the world, or the melting of a frost of reserve from the diffident genius ; they are traces of that which is fleeting, or struck out, like phosphorus from the sea, by irregular chance ; and you want something quicker and rarer than formal description to arrest it warm and natural, and detain it in its place till it can be looked upon.

358

FROST.

IT is winter — veritable winter — with *bona fide* frost, and cramping cold, and a sun as clear and powerless as moonlight. The windows glitter with the most fantastic frostwork. Cities with their spires and turrets, ranks of spears, files of horsemen, every gorgeous and brilliant array told of in romance or song, start out of that mass of silvery tracery, like the processions of a magic mirror. What a miraculous beauty there is in frost! What fine work in its radiant crystals! What mystery in its exact proportions and its maniform varieties! The feathery snowflake, the delicate rime, the transparent and sheeted ice, the magnificent iceberg moving down the sea like a mountain of light, — how beautiful are they all! and how wonderful is it, that, break and scatter them as you will, you find under every form the same faultless angles, the same crystalline and sparkling radiation. It sometimes grows suddenly cold at noon. There has been a heavy mist all the morning, and as the north wind comes sharply in, the air clears, and leaves it frozen upon every thing with the thinness of palpable air. The trees are clothed with a fine white vapor, as if a cloud had been arrested and fixed motionless in the branches. They look in the twilight like gigantic spirits, standing in broad ranks, and clothed in drapery of supernatural whiteness and texture. On close examination the crystals are as fine as needles, and standing in perfect parallelism, pointing in the direction of the wind. They are like fringes of the most minute threads, edging every twig and filament of the tree, so that the branches are thickened by them, and have a shadowy and mysterious look, as if a spirit foliage had started out from the naked limbs. It is not so brilliant as the common rime seen upon the trees after a frozen rain, but it is infinitely more delicate and spiritual, and to me seems a phenomenon of exquisite novelty and beauty.

A CONTADINA.

"PRAY, how does that face deserve framing and glazing?" asked a visitor to-day. The question had been asked before. It is a copy from a head in some old picture, one of a series of studies from the ancient masters, lithographed in France. It represents a peasant of the Campagna; and certainly, in Broadway, she would pass for a coarse woman, and not beautiful for a coarse one. I have been brought to think the head coarse and plain, however, by being often called on to defend it. I did not think so when I bought it in a print-shop in London. I do not now, unless under catechism.

To me, the whole climate of Italy is expressed in the face of that contadina. It is a large, cubical-edged, massy style of feature, which born in Scotland, would have been singularly harsh and inflexible. There is no refinement in it now, and, to be sure, little mobility or thought; but it is a face in which *there is no resistance*. That is its peculiarity. The heavy eyelid droops in indolent animal repose. The lips are drowsily sweet. The nostrils seem never to have been distended nor contracted. The muscles of the lips and cheeks have never tingled nor parched. It is a face on which a harsh wind never blew. If the woman be forty, those features have been forty years sleeping in balm, — enjoying only — resisting, enduring, never. No one could look on it, and fancy it had ever suffered or been uncomfortable, or dreaded wind or sun, summer or winter. A picture of St. Peter's, a mosaic of Pæstum, a print of Vesuvius or the Campanile, — none of the common souvenirs of travel, would be to me half so redolent of Italy.

SORROW'S RELUCTANT GATE.

THIS last-turned leaf, dear reader, seems to us always like a door shut behind us, with the world outside. We have expressed this thought before, when it was a prelude to being *gayer* than in the preceding pages. With the closed door, now, we would throw off restraint, but it is to be *sadder* than before. It is so with yourself, doubtless. You sometimes break into singing on entering your chamber, and finding yourself alone: sometimes you burst into tears.

There is nothing for which the similitudes of poetry seem to us so false and poor, as for affliction by the death of those we love. The news of such a calamity is not " a blow." It is not like " a thunderbolt," or " a piercing arrow ; " it does not " crush and overwhelm " us. We hear it at first, with a kind of mournful incredulity ; and the second feeling is, perhaps, a wonder at ourselves, that we are so little moved. The pulse beats on as tranquilly, the momentary tear dries from the eye. We go on about the errand in which we were interrupted. We eat, sleep at our usual time, and are nourished and refreshed ; and if a friend meet us, and provoke a smile, we easily and forgetfully smile. Nature does not seem to be conscious of the event, or she does not recognize it as a calamity.

But little of what is taken away by death is taken from the happiness of one hour, or one day. We live, absent from beloved relatives, without pain. Days pass without our seeing them — months — years. They would be no more absent in body if they were dead. But suddenly, in the midst of our common occupations, we hear that they are one remove farther from us, — in the grave. The mind acknowledges it true. The imagination makes a brief and painful visit to the scene of the last agony, the death-chamber, the burial, and returns weary and dispirited to repose. For that hour, perhaps, we should not have thought of the departed, if they were living, nor for the next. The routine we had relied upon to fill up those hours comes round. We give it our cheerful attention. The beloved dead are displaced from our memory; and perhaps we start suddenly, with a kind of reproachful surprise, that we can have been so forgetful, — that the world, with its wheels of minutes and trifles, can thus untroubled go round, and that dear friend gone from it.

But the day glides on, and night comes. We lie down, and unconsciously, as we turn upon our pillow, commence a recapitulation that was once a habit of prayer, — silently naming over the friends whom we should commend to God, did we pray, as those most dear to us. Suddenly the heart stops, the breath hushes, the tears spring hot to the eyelids. *We miss the dead!* From that chain of sweet thoughts a link is broken, and for the first time we feel that we are bereaved. It was in the casket of that last hour before sleeping, embalmed in the tranquillity of that hour's unnamed and unreckoned happiness, that the memory of the dead lay hid. For that friend, now, we can no longer pray! Among the living, among our blessings, among our hopes, that sweet friend is namable no more! We realize it now. The list of those who love us, whom we love, is made briefer. With face turned upon our pillow, with anguish and fears, we blot out the beloved name, and begin the slow and nightly task of unlearning the oft-told syllables from our lips.

And this is the slow-opening gate by which sorrow enters in! We wake on the morrow, and remember our tears of the past night; and as the cheerful sunshine streams in at our window, we think of the kind face and embracing arms, the soft eyes and beloved lips, lying dark and cold in a place — oh, how pitiless in its coldness and darkness! We choke with a suffused sob, we heave the heavy thought from our bosom with a painful sigh, and hasten abroad for relief in forgetfulness!

But we had not anticipated that this dear friend would die, and we have marked out years to come with hopes in which the dead was to have been a sharer. Thoughts and promises, and meetings, and gifts, and pleasures, of which hers was the brighter half, are wound like a wreath of flowers around the chain of the future; and as we come to them — to the places where these looked-for flowers lie in ashes upon the inevitable link — oh, God! with what agonizing vividness they suddenly return! — with what grief, made intenser by realizing, made more aching by prolonged absence, we call up those features beloved, and remember where they lie, uncaressed and unvisited! Years must pass, and other affections must "sweep, and garnish, and enter in" to the void chambers of the heart, and consolation and natural forgetfulness must do their slow work of erasure; and meantime, grief visits us in unexpected times and places, its paroxysms imperceptibly lessening in poignancy and tenacity, but life in its main current flowing, from the death to the forgetting of it, unchanged on.

And now, what is like to this in nature (for even the slight sympathy in dumb similitudes is sweet)? It is not like the rose's perishing, for that robs only the hour in which it dies. It were more like the removal from earth of that whole race of flowers; for we should not miss the first day's roses, hardly the first season's, and should mourn most when the impoverished spring came once more round without them. It were like stilling the music of a brook forever, or making all singing-birds dumb, or hushing the wind-murmur in the trees, or drawing out from nature any one of her threads of price-less repetition. We should not mourn for the first day's silence in the brook or in the trees, nor for the first morning's hush after the birds were made voiceless. The *recurrent* dawns, or twilights, or summer noons, robbed of their accustomed music, would bring the sense of its loss — the value of what was taken away increasing with its recurrent season. But these are weak similitudes, as they must needs be, drawn from a world in which death — the lot alike of all living creatures that inhabit it — is only a calamity to man!